FORBIDDEN HILL

SINGAPORE SAGA, VOL. 1

JOHN D. GREENWOOD

monsoon

monsoonbooks

Published in 2017
by Monsoon Books Ltd
www.monsoonbooks.co.uk

No.1 Duke of Windsor Suite, Burrough Court,
Burrough on the Hill, Leicestershire LE14 2QS, UK

ISBN (paperback): 9781912049189
ISBN (ebook): 9781912049196

Cover design by Cover Kitchen.
Cover painting by Edwin A. Porcher (1824-1878), 'The River at
Singapore, November 1851', from Edwin Augustus Porcher Collection,
1849-1861, watercolour, Yale Center for British Art, Paul Mellon
Collection.
Map on page 6 from John Crawfurd, *Journal of an Embassy to the
courts of Siam and Cochin-China* (London, 1928).

A Cataloguing-in-Publication data record is available from the British
Library.

MIX
Paper from
responsible sources
FSC
www.fsc.org   FSC® C018072

Printed in Great Britain by Clays Ltd, St Ives plc
20 19 18 17   1 2 3 4 5

For Singapore and all her people.

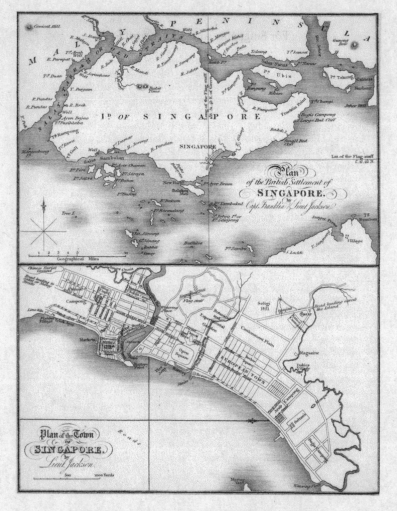

Published by Henry Colburn, London, June 1828

monsoonbooks

FORBIDDEN HILL

John D. Greenwood was born in Elgin, Scotland, and educated at the Universities of Edinburgh and Oxford. He is currently a professor at the City University of New York Graduate Center, where he specializes in the history of psychology. He is the author of six books and numerous academic papers.

He was a lecturer in the department of philosophy at the National University of Singapore from 1983-1986, when he first fell in love with Singapore, her people and her history. He returned as senior visiting scholar in 1999-2000 and as visiting professor in 2008-2009. He considers NUS to be his second academic home. He also returns regularly to Singapore to visit old friends and old haunts, and considers a trip to Pulau Ubin followed by chilli or pepper crab at in the evening at Changi Village to be a perfect day.

He lives in Richmond, Virginia, USA.

Acknowledgements

Almost twenty years ago, towards the end of my year as visiting senior fellow at the National University of Singapore, my wife and I had a couple of Scottish friends over for dinner. My friend Donald returned my copy of James Rutherfurd's *London*, which he had earlier borrowed. As he did so, he commented that someone should write a book like that about Glasgow or Edinburgh. My immediate response was that someone should write a book like that about Singapore. Once the thought was out, it became an obsession. That night I could not sleep, and rose at 2 am to write the story of Moon Ling and the pirates that forms the opening chapters of this work. So, the first person I have to thank is Donald McDermid.

Over the course of the following years I continued to write portions of the book, while amassing as much literature as I could on the history of Singapore, and returning from my regular visits to the city-state with a suitcase stuffed full of books (before the airlines became difficult about weight restrictions). Progress was slow because at the time I was serving as Executive Officer in the PhD Program in Philosophy at the City University of New York Graduate Center. At the same time, I was committed to producing two academic books on the history of psychology. Realizing I would never finish the book under these conditions, I asked my wife if she would agree to let me return to Singapore as a visiting professor so that I might complete my research and, eventually, the book. Although we knew this separation would involve considerable hardship for us both (she did not want to leave her job in order to accompany me), she told me to follow my dream. I will be eternally grateful to Shelagh for that.

When I started writing the book, my intention was to cover the first hundred years of Singapore. Half a million words later, I had only covered the first fifty years, and the narrative had extended outwards to China, Borneo and India. Two dear friends, Arne Addland and Stella Fog, both avid readers of historical fiction, volunteered to read the monster, and gave me invaluable critical comments and suggestions, including saving me from various historical, geographical and weaponry embarrassments. Beverly Swerling, the bestselling historical novelist, persuaded me that no one was going to publish a half a million-word historical novel by an unknown author, and so she helped me reshape and reduce the first third of the manuscript into the present work. I am indebted to Beverly for her enthusiastic moral support and editorial wisdom.

I also want to thank the National University of Singapore for providing me with the opportunity to spend the academic year 2008-2009 as visiting professor in the Department of Philosophy, where, in addition to my academic duties, I was able to pursue my research on the history of Singapore and draft most of the chapters of the present work. I especially want to thank the staff at the circulation desk of the NUS library who tracked down microfiche copies of the early Singapore newspapers, the *Singapore Chronicle* and the *Singapore Free Press*, and who helped me with technical difficulties I sometimes encountered with the equipment. I spent many a happy hour in the tiny blackened and air conditioned room in the heart of the library, poring over these newspaper stories of the early years of Singapore while the tropical sun beat down outside. Some of these stories provided the germ of plotlines that later made their way into this work.

Of the many books I read about the history of Singapore and the surrounding region, two deserve special mention. The first is Charles Burton Buckley's *An Anecdotal History of Old Times in Singapore* (Fraser and Neave, 1902). While it covers the same material as the newspaper accounts in the *Singapore Chronicle* and *Singapore Free Press*, it provided an invaluable double check on my narrative timeline. The second is Owen Rutter's *The Pirate Wind: Tales of the Sea-Robbers of Malaya*, (Oxford University Press, 1986), which provided excellent source material on the Illanun pirates who play such a large role in the novel, as well as inspiring some of the characters and plot-lines. Where the other stories came from I do not know, but I hope they ring true, and do due credit to the early pioneers of Singapore.

I have done my best to maintain historical accuracy with respect to the real characters and episodes, to the best of my knowledge and reasonable belief, with only one exception. I have exercised artistic license by having the main protagonist Ronnie Simpson join Raffles and Farquhar in the longboat from the Indiana when they travelled to meet the Temenggong of Singapore on Monday, January 18, 1819. Ronnie is a fictional character and was not in the longboat, although I suspect that if he had been aboard the *Indiana*, Raffles and Farquhar might well have welcomed him to come along.

John D Greenwood

PROLOGUE

1812

Moon Ling sat huddled on the deck of the junk, her hands clasped over her ears, trying desperately to block out the sound of the rising storm and the raging sea. She was cold and frightened. She tried to force her mind to focus on happier times. She remembered sitting by the river in the late afternoon sunshine, watching her mother cooking noodles over an open fire. In the distance, further downriver, Moon Ling could see her father mooring his boat, and dividing the day's catch with his neighbour. Her younger sister sat by her mother's side, singing an old song about a magic bird. She remembered the sunshine warm against her cheek, the cooking smells, and the sound of the gently rolling river in the background.

A wave crashed over the bow of the junk, drenching her body as she sat on the exposed deck. Then the painful memory returned. She no longer had a mother, or a father, or a sister. They had all perished in the worst winter that anyone could remember in Fukien province. Her aunt Xue Zheng had dragged Moon Ling from their frozen bodies and had looked after her for a few months. But Xue Zheng was an elderly woman with a large family of her own, and she had been forced to sell Moon Ling to the owner of a travelling street opera. Moon Ling had a natural talent for singing and acting, and had quickly established herself as one of the leading players in the company. This year they were travelling by junk on the Northeast monsoon to the port city of Malacca on the Malayan Peninsula, which had become a major trading centre since it was founded by Iskander Shah centuries before. Although it no longer dominated the maritime trade as it had in the days of the Great Malaccan Sultanate, it remained a regional centre of commerce and was home to a thriving Chinese merchant community.

Another wave crashed over the bow of the junk, this time with such force that it rolled Moon Ling onto her back on the crowded deck. The night sky was black as pitch. Suddenly a fork of lightning struck the mast of the junk, sending a violent shudder down the length of the deck. The mast and rigging collapsed and toppled over the side into the dark raging sea, narrowly missing Moon Ling, but carrying away some families and sailors who became entangled in the rigging. A howling gale ripped the night air, and huge waves spun the junk around, like a twig cast upon the great Yangtze River where it roars through Qutang Gorge. Moon Ling grasped her only baggage close to her chest—a sturdy lacquered wooden box that contained her face paints and powders, wrapped in an oilcloth to protect it from the rain and salt water. The next moment a gigantic wave lifted the junk clear out of the water and pitched its passengers into the black depths.

As the darkness and cold engulfed her, Moon Ling clung desperately to her lacquered box and prayed. She prayed to her ancestors, and to Ma Cho Po, Queen of Heaven and protector of travellers and mariners. As she spun around in the water, gasping for air, she lost all track of time. She could not tell whether it was night or day. She could not tell how many seconds, minutes or hours passed before she began to notice the increasing warmth of the water, and the sand and stones under her body. The rolling surf drove her onto the shore of the island. Gulping in the air that she had fought for so desperately and so long, she almost passed out in relief at having survived. But she dragged herself forward, as the returning surf threatened to pull her lacquered box from her grasp. Clutching her only worldly possession to her breast, she made her way up the long stretch of beach, stumbling over the coconut shards that lined the shore, and collapsed behind a large rock at the edge of the jungle, where she fell into a deep and exhausted sleep.

When she woke, the sun was already high in a clear blue sky, and its heat felt like a comforting warm blanket. Moon Ling had no idea where she was, and wondered if any other members of the opera troupe had survived. What would she do if they had not? How would she survive? The thirst and hunger that suddenly gripped her quickly crowded out these thoughts. She made her way cautiously through the dense foliage of the jungle, trying to overcome her fear of snakes and wild animals, and could scarcely contain her delight when she came upon a small stream and a rambutan tree heavily laden with fruit. She drank from the stream and gorged herself upon the rambutans, which fortified her spirit, and she came to appreciate that at least she was alive, wherever she might be.

Then in the distance she heard shouting voices coming from the direction of the beach. Perhaps the mariners had managed to right the junk and save the company, and had come searching for her, she thought. She scrambled to her feet and made her way back quickly to the edge of the jungle, where she recognized the great rock in whose shadow she had recently slept, and grew excited at the prospect of her rescue. She was about to run down the beach to the water's edge, when a grizzly sight stopped her dead in her tracks.

She saw that the scattered coconut husks upon which she had stumbled the night before were not coconut husks at all, but the severed heads of men and women, some with their hair and skin still clinging to their skulls. Others had been picked clean by birds and animals, and bleached by the sun and sea. Her legs turned to jelly and she dropped to her knees beside the rock. She peered out at the party of fierce-looking men dragging their longboats ashore. Though she did not know where she was, she knew who these men were. They belonged to one of the many bands of pirates that brought death, slavery and terror to those who braved the voyage from China to the Nanyang.[i] She had thought the stories of their cruelty and depravity hard to believe when she had first heard them in Fukien, and again when the sailors on the junk had repeated them in all their gory detail. But now, as she kneeled at the edge of the silver white beach carpeted with human skulls and bones, she found them only too believable.

She crouched behind the rock, terrified that she might have been seen. Yet she felt compelled to peer out at the pirates, as they drove forward a party of bound prisoners, jabbing them fiercely with their krisses[ii] and spears. She watched in horror and disbelief as the pirates made sport with them, while gorging themselves on food and drink served to them by slave boys and girls. The pirates tied some prisoners to bamboo stakes that they had driven into the ground, and used them for archery practice. They roared in laughter as their arrows struck the unfortunate men, women and—the sight of it made her retch—children, in the head, chest, arms, legs and groin. The pirates buried others in the sand, and covered their heads with molasses. Then they watched in cruel glee as the ants devoured their eyes, their lips and their screams. Two young girls were raped repeatedly, and then had their living bodies torn apart in a bloody tug of war.

Moon Ling watched this grisly display for hour upon hour, crouched upon her haunches behind the rock. She wanted to run as fast as her legs could carry her, but she dared not risk discovery by running along the beach or into the jungle. So she remained behind the rock most of the day, until she saw one of the pirates leave the company and make his way up the beach directly towards her. He was a tall Illanun pirate from the island of Mindanao in the Sulu Archipelago (although Moon Ling knew nothing of this). He was

---

i Southern Ocean (Southeast Asia).
ii Daggers with distinctive wavy blades favoured by Malays.

dressed in a short tunic and skirt, with dark swirling tattoos over his broad chest and his strong arms and legs. As he strode up the beach, he swung an ugly and bloody club by his side. Moon Ling made to raise herself and creep back into the jungle, but the muscles of her legs were so cramped in frozen terror that she fell over helpless on the sand beside the rock. As she lay there, dreading the pirate's approach, she tried to pray, but her thoughts were crowded out by dreadful images of the young girls who had been abused by the pirates. She wished that she had a knife or some other weapon to end her life if she was caught. She wondered if she could suffocate herself by holding her breath—she had heard that this could be done, but did not know if she could do it.

But hold her breath she did, as the pirate came closer and closer. He trampled crab shells and coconut shards and human remains underfoot. He was now so close that Moon Ling could hear his grotesque song, in some unfamiliar tongue. Just as she was sure that she was about to be discovered, the pirate suddenly stopped at the other side of the rock, where he proceeded to relieve himself with great noise and gratification, belching in chorus to his loud excretions.

The smell was overpowering. Moon Ling clamped her hands over her mouth and nose, desperately trying to block it out and the sound of her own retching. An eternity seemed to pass as she lay trembling on the ground, but finally the pirate rose and made his way back down the beach. As he did so, Moon Ling let out a long slow breath, and almost fainted when she breathed in again and the oxygen rushed to her brain. As she lay flat on the sand, she watched as the pirates suspended their last living prisoner from the branch of a banyan tree that sat on an elevated grassy slope close to the shore, and began to prepare a fire beneath him. They were going to burn him alive, and, she imagined in her horror, eat him afterwards. She turned her eyes away, as the sun began to sink behind the dark green depths of the jungle. As she did so, her eyes fell on her lacquered box, lying about a foot in front of her, and which would have been in plain view of the pirate had he happened to turn his attention away from the antics on the beach. She leaned forward very slowly and carefully, and grasping the box with both hands, dragged it back behind the cover of the rock.

* * *

Badang bin Aman cursed his luck. The rope cut deep into his wrists, and threatened to wrench his arms from their sockets. He hung suspended over the fire they were preparing below him. He had no quarrel with these Illanun pirates, and if his memory served him well, he had traded with them in the past. He had been aboard a Bugis proa[iii] when they had attacked. He had been selling the Bugis sailors part of his catch, but the pirates had assumed he was one of their crew. His protests had been futile because the Illanun did not tolerate any, and he would have been dead by now if he had tried to protest further—he had seen men killed and mutilated for much less. Yet he was surprised by the slaughter on the beach. Although they were fierce fighters, the Illanun usually kept their prisoners alive to sell as slaves, particularly the women and children. Something must have angered them, he supposed, or perhaps they already had enough prisoners for the slave markets and were simply disposing of the remainder through their cruel sport. Badang tried to pull himself up on the rope in an effort to loosen the knots that bound him, but soon realized that it was hopeless. His attempts to raise himself only tightened the knots. He also knew that even if by some miracle he could free himself, he had no chance of escaping the pirate horde that cavorted around him, piling brushwood and flotsam below him, and occasionally prodding him with their spears

---

iii A multi-hulled sailing vessel.

and krisses. He would be cut down the moment he reached the ground, or felled by poisoned arrows and spears before he could make it to the sea or jungle.

He resolved to pray to God and wait for death. He looked out beyond the pirates and the pirate fleet to the crescent moon that hung low in the eastern sky. All men die, and die when their time is come, he thought. If it is my time, it is the will of God, and I will face my death with faith and without fear. A strange calm descended upon him, and his attention wandered from the wild scene below him, as the pirates worked themselves into a frenzy and prepared to put a torch to the firewood.

Badang bin Aman looked out over the dark sea, flecked with white breakers that sparkled in the moonlight, the sea that he had fished for most of his life. He remembered when as a child his father had taken him out for days at a time, and taught him to spear the fish and preserve them by rubbing their flesh with salt and wrapping them in palm leaves. He remembered the lonely nights after his father had died from the bite of the dreaded banded sea krait, the most venomous sea snake, but also how he had come to love the solitude of nights alone on his fishing boat, with only the moon and stars for company. He thought of the kind grey eyes of his aged mother and of her holy power of healing—she was surely a blessed woman.

He remembered the stories his parents had told him about his ancestors, such as the great warrior Badang. He had captured a jinn,[iv] who had been stealing from his fishing baskets, and the jinn had promised him great strength if Badang would eat his vomit, which Badang had done. He had become the champion of Paduka Sri Pikrama Wira, one the rajahs of the old city of Singapura. When the leader of a Majapahit[v] invading force had threatened the rajah's

iv Genie.
v Javanese.

life in battle, Badang had killed the man by flinging a great stone that struck the Majapahit leader in the head, and together they had managed to drive the invaders back into the sea. Legend had it that Paduka Sri Pikrama Wira had raised a stone monument to his champion when Badang had died, upon which accounts of his great deeds were inscribed.

He wondered if the stories were true. Although he had never seen the stone monument himself, he had been able to trace the remains of the old city walls on the island. Badang bin Aman's thoughts drifted back to an imagined past, and he suddenly felt a momentary sadness at having to leave this world without knowing the love of a wife and children, and without being able to relate to them his father's stories. He heard the crackling of the fire, as the Illanun chief put a lighted torch to the dry timbers and brushwood. He closed his eyes and prayed for a speedy death as the burning wood hissed beneath him like a pit of vipers.

But now another sound disturbed his consciousness, more violent and vivid. A blood-chilling scream rent the air, so shrill and piercing that it seemed to penetrate the farthest reaches of his soul. He heard the shouts and cries of the pirates as they gesticulated wildly towards the edge of the jungle, and stumbled over themselves as they ran towards their ships, abandoning him to the flames. He looked to where the pirates were pointing, and felt the same cold chill of unholy dread that had overcome the hard-bitten and hard-hearted Illanun pirates. The piercing scream came from the lips of a female jinn, a spirit demon that had suddenly emerged from the shadows of the jungle. As she drifted down towards the shore, Badang made out her dreadful aspect in clearer detail. Her naked skeletal frame was pale white and tinged with blue, the colour of the daylong dead before burial. Her jet-black hair streaked stiff and high behind her, flecked with silver in the shadow of the moon. Dark red blood flowed from her eyes, her lips and her sharp pointed fingernails. Badang easily imagined, as the pirates imagined, that she had fed on the recently dead, but had not yet quenched her ghastly appetite. And all the while the dreadful scream continued unabated, with such piercing strength that it could only have issued from a demon's fiery lips. The sound seemed to have weight and mass, and threatened to suffocate his very soul. Badang bin Aman watched with mounting horror as the hellish apparition glided past him in pursuit of the pirates. The flames crackled under his feet, and the smoke began to scorch his nostrils.

By this time the pirates had scrambled into their longboats and headed out to their prahus, and some had already raised their anchors and begun to row out to sea. The jinn glided down to the edge of the seashore, her scream turning into a dreadful howl, like a hellish gale pursuing them across the water and the waves, as she waded out into the surf towards them. Through the smoke and heat Badang prayed that the jinn had not noticed him, and that he would die before she returned. Yet as he prayed, and as the flames licked higher and the smoke choked his lungs, he saw the jinn turn from the sea and the pirates, and make her way directly towards him. He grew faint with fear. He who had recently embraced the prospect of death with dignity now hung in mortal terror of the supernatural powers of the jinn. She would suck his soul from his body and he would be bound to her evil will for all eternity. Now she was almost upon him, and she reached down to seize a bloodied sword that one of the pirates had abandoned. The jinn raised the sword to strike him, her face a grotesque white mask of pale and bloody death.

He heard a thudding cut upon the rope and crashed down into the fire, landing on a loose log that sent him spinning onto the sand and free of the flames. Turning in surprise and terror, he saw the jinn standing before him. Yet she had changed dramatically. The naked form, once deathlike in its blue paleness, now revealed large expanses of pink living flesh, and the surf had washed the bloody streaks away. Her soul-piercing scream turned first into a hysterical laugh, and then into uncontrollable sobbing. The jinn grasped a scarlet cloak that had been left by one of the fleeing pirates, and tried to cover her nakedness. Then he realized that she was no demon, but a young Chinese girl, as frightened and helpless as he was. Badang bin Aman gave thanks to God and raised himself from the ground. He tried to rub life back into his hands and arms as he removed the ropes that bound them. He had a minor burn on his shoulder, but otherwise had suffered nothing more than a few cuts and bruises, and a dry stinging sensation in his mouth and lungs. Looking back out to sea, he tried to indicate with a sweeping motion of his hand that the pirates might return at any time, and that they should escape into the darkness further along the beach. Moon Ling understood what he meant and nodded her agreement.

Her heart was pounding with such ferocity that she thought her chest might burst. Her impersonation of the jinn had been the most desperate and dangerous performance of her life, but it had worked better than she had hoped. It had saved her life and that of the young man who now ran along the beach beside her. Her legs still trembled beneath her, and she was overcome with shame by the nakedness she had displayed before him, but she followed the young Malay along the beach and into the darkness. In her stunned relief to be alive, she left her paints and powders and the lacquered box that she had carried from Fukien, which now lay scattered in the sand at the edge of the dark jungle, close by the rock where she had hidden for most of the day.

They followed the line of the beach, stumbling through the darkness, clambering over the rocky promontories, and groping their way through patches of jungle and mangrove that reached down to the edge of the ocean. After they had put some distance between themselves and the place where the pirates had landed, they rested against the body of a fallen coconut tree. They felt safe in the darkness. Heavy grey clouds rolled across the sky and obliterated the light of the moon and the stars, as if to protect them. Within a few moments they both fell into an exhausted and dreamless sleep.

Moon Ling woke shortly after dawn, as the sun crept up in a clear blue sky dotted with powder puff clouds. She went down to the sea and washed the remaining paint and powder from her face and body. She arranged the pirate cloak into a makeshift sarong, and made her way back up the beach. She had a sudden moment of panic when she realized that the young man was gone from the place where she had left him sleeping, but her panic turned to relief when she saw him emerge smiling from the jungle with a bunch of bananas in his hand. In the clear light of morning, she saw that he was a tall Malay, with a strong muscled body and long brown hair. As he drew closer, she noticed that his face was strangely angular, as if it had been carved from hard teak wood, with a long aquiline nose and sharp chin, but with soft and friendly brown eyes, which seemed to sparkle as he smiled.

They ate the bananas and drank the fresh water he had brought in an empty coconut husk. Then they set off again along the beach, hand in hand, a secret bond now formed between them after their narrow escape from death. They made their way around the end of what she now saw to be a small island, about two miles long. On the way they came across many grisly reminders of the fate they had escaped. Human skulls and bones were littered across areas of the beach, and they picked their way between them in grim gratitude for their salvation.

When they reached the far side of the island, Moon Ling could see a larger landmass a few miles distant, with a long strip of silver beach shimmering in the early morning sunlight. Then the young man let out a great yell, and pulled her along beside him as he ran towards a figure in the distance, who stood smoking a pipe beside his fishing boat.

'Baya Kay!' he yelled out, recognizing the man. The pipe smoking fisherman called back to him in return, 'Badang bin Aman!'

Moon Ling recognized that this was the young man's name, and pointed to herself and announced her own. Badang nodded his head in recognition and smiled at her. For the first time since they had met, he held her gaze for a few moments. She was strangely beautiful, he thought to himself. She had long jet-black hair and an oval face, with soft brown eyes and full red lips. She had a slim but full figure, with small hands and feet. Badang motioned her into the boat, and Baya Kay guided the craft across the water. They passed sandy beaches and mangrove swamps, until they landed a few miles to the east at the mouth of a river. There were a few small huts scattered along the beach, and stilted cottages and boats moored inside the mouth of the river.

Moon Ling went to live in the cottage of the Malay fisherman called Badang bin Aman. In due course she learnt his language, and helped him tend his nets and vegetable garden. She learned that the small community at the mouth of the river dwelt on the site of what had once been the ancient city of Singapura, which had been destroyed centuries before by the Majapahit, during the reign of Sri Sultan Iskander Shah, the last great rajah. One day Badang had shown her the remains of the walls of the old city, but although she begged him many times, he would not venture up the hill overlooking the mouth of the river, which was called Bukit Larangan,[vi] because he said that the ghosts of the dead warriors of Singapura still walked upon it. He claimed that on some nights the sounds of a great battle could be heard, when the battle cries of men and the lamentation of women were carried on the night breeze. She also learned the name of the island where she had saved them both from the pirates. It was known as Pulau Belakang Mati.[vii]

---

vi Forbidden Hill.
vii The Back and Beyond of Death. Present day Sentosa Island.

A number of Malay families lived in attap[viii] cottages along the seashore east of the river. A few hundred orang laut, or sea gypsies, dwelt just inside the mouth of the river. Some lived on stilted houses along the eastern bank, but many lived on their boats and only rarely came ashore. They were small and dark-skinned, with tight wooly hair, and dressed in flimsy skirts. They slept and cooked under attap shelters erected over their dugout boats, although they often ate their fish raw, and tossed the entrails into the bottom of the boat. This caused a disgusting smell, but protected them against the attention of sharks and crocodiles. They were a simple people who kept themselves to themselves and seemed to have no interest in the world beyond their boats and fishing grounds. They had no written laws but followed a strict moral code, and crime and warfare were strangers to them. Further up the river there was a larger compound of Malays. They served the Temenggong Abdul Rahman, who ruled the island in the name of the Sultan of Johor, Riau and Lingga. The temenggong's bamboo and attap lodge was set back from the river, with a commanding view of the strait and the islands beyond.

There were a few Chinese living near the temenggong's compound, under their Capitan China.[ix] Further inland, there were also Chinese gambier and pepper farmers. From them Moon Ling learned that a Chinese trading junk came down once a year on the Northeast monsoon and bought their produce, and later returned to China with the Southwest monsoon. There were also occasional Bugis or Malay trading vessels that put in on their way to Malacca and Penang, where there were thriving Chinese communities. She did not know what she would do. Her family was dead, and her opera troupe likely drowned, but she supposed that she could persuade a captain to take her on board the first junk bound for China or the Malayan Peninsula.

---

viii Thatch made from the leaves of the attap palm.
ix Leader of the Chinese community.

Yet when a junk bound for Amoy arrived six months later, she did not leave on it. By that time the secret bond that had developed between the Malay fisherman and the young Chinese opera performer had blossomed into a deep and lasting love. Shortly after Moon Ling bade farewell to the captain of the Amoy junk, they became man and wife. Ten months later their first child was born, in the holy month of Ramadan, a boy of unusual strength and beauty. Moon Ling set up a small joss-house near the fresh water stream that ran behind Bukit Larangan and debouched into the sea beside their cottage, and dedicated it to Ma Cho Po, the Queen of Heaven and protector of mariners and fishermen.

* * *

1819
The boy sat alone on the beach, playing carelessly with some seashells. His mother, sitting with her younger daughter, watched him lovingly from the shade of the cottage doorway. Yet all the while she kept her eyes on the square-rigged ships anchored in the bay. Presently she watched three men descend into a longboat, which made its way towards the mouth of the river. Moon Ling had learned from the Capitan China that they were not pirates, but barbarians come to meet with the temenggong. But she was not taking any chances. She snatched up the boy and carried him back inside the cottage, as she watched the longboat enter the mouth of the river. There was an axe hanging on the wall by the back door, and she took it down for protection.

PART ONE

THE SETTLEMENT

1819

PART ONE

THE SETTLEMENT

1819

1

To the east lay miles and miles of sandy beach, sparkling sheer white against the dark green of the jungle, and to the west lay mangrove swamps. The *Indiana* headed for a point in between, where James Pearl, the captain, had been told there was a river hidden behind a jutting strip of headland. The longboat was lowered and Raffles climbed down into it.

He was thirty-eight years old, still fresh-faced despite his past troubles and recurrent ill-health, a short but upright man whose bright eyes shone with a fierce intensity of purpose. He was dressed formally in clerical black, as if he were about to visit the offices of the East India Company[1] in Leadenhall Street.

Sir Thomas Stamford Bingley Raffles,[2] a servant of the East India Company, was Lieutenant-Governor of Bencoolen and former Lieutenant-Governor of Java. The man he had come to see was Temenggong Abdul Rahman, the hereditary prime minister of the Johor-Riau-Lingga Sultanate, who lived on the island with his followers.

Both men spoke for absent masters, and beneath the long shadow of the powerful Dutch merchants and their soldiers and ships that dominated most of the Eastern Archipelago. But Raffles and the temenggong were about to make history.

Lord Hastings, the Governor-General of India, had authorized Raffles to explore the possibility of establishing an East India Company base near the southern tip of the Malayan peninsula. This was to prevent the Dutch from gaining monopoly control of the Strait of Malacca, now that Malacca and other ports administered by the Company had been returned to the Dutch at the end of the Napoleonic wars. The British needed a southern port to service their ships trading between India and China—the recently established British settlement in Penang was too far north to serve that purpose. Raffles had come down from Penang with a small fleet of ships— both armed cruisers and survey vessels—with a view to establishing a Company factory[i] on the Carimon islands. However, Captain Ross, who commanded the survey ship *Discovery*, had declared that the Carimon islands were unsuitable, given the lack of a deep-water harbour. Raffles had then ordered the fleet to Johor, which he had intended to explore if the Dutch had not already occupied it.

At four o'clock in the afternoon of the following day, the ships anchored off Pulau Sakijang Bendera,[ii] a few miles south of the island of Singapore. When some local Malays came out that evening in their prahus to sell them fish and turtles, Raffles learned that Temenggong Abdul Rahman was resident on the island. He had resolved to visit him the next day.

From the verandah of his lodge, Temenggong Abdul Rahman watched the small fleet drop anchor off Pulau Sakijang Bendera. He'd been greatly relieved to recognize the distinctive black and yellow square-riggers of the East India Company. He had feared that they were Dutch ships come to drive him from the island. Temenggong Abdul Rahman ruled Singapore and Johor in the name of the sultan, but was less sure than Raffles who his master was.

When the old Sultan Mahmud Shah had died in 1812, Abdul Rahman had supported the claim of Mahmud Shah's oldest son, his own son-in-law Tengku Long, whom Mahmud Shah had designated as his rightful heir. But the Dutch had moved in with their residents and soldiers and supported the claim of his younger son Tengku

i Commercial settlement. The agents for companies who set up such settlements in Southeast Asia were known as factors.
ii Barking Deer Island, present day Saint John's Island.

30

Abdul Rahman, a delicate boy who spent most of his time in religious devotion. In return the Dutch had been awarded exclusive rights to set up factories throughout the islands of the Johor-Riau-Lingga Sultanate, including the island of Singapore.[3] Temenggong Abdul Rahman had been forced to quit the royal court at Lingga, and remove himself and his followers to Singapore. There he had lived a peaceful existence for the past few years, spending his days in study and prayer, and adjudicating the minor disputes between his followers.

The temenggong derived a modest income from leasing out large acreages in the jungle to the Chinese gambier[iii] and pepper farmers, but had known that it would all come to an end if the Dutch came to take over the island.

Major William Farquhar,[4] the former Resident of Malacca, had been preparing to return to his native Scotland on leave when Raffles had met with him in Penang and asked Farquhar to join him in his search for a site suitable for a southern factory. Farquhar had agreed when Raffles had told him that the Governor-General of India had authorized him to appoint Farquhar as resident for any new factory that they established. At the moment, Farquhar's role was to introduce Raffles to Temenggong Abdul Rahman the following day.

Farquhar was forty-eight years old when he stepped down into the longboat to join Raffles. He was tall and erect in his military bearing, with a bald pate and thick flowing white hair and side-whiskers. That day he wore his dress uniform as major in the Madras Engineers: a bright red tunic with golden braid and epaulettes.

Raffles and Farquhar had known each other for many years. They had much in common. Both spoke fluent Malay and had a deep interest in the language, history and culture of the region.

---

iii A vine whose astringent resinous extract is used in tanning and dying. Also chewed by local Malays with betel-nut.

Like Raffles, Farquhar was an avid naturalist, who made a number of significant discoveries of new species, and corresponded with botanists and zoologists in Europe. He had kept a veritable menagerie in Malacca, which included monkeys and birds, and a tame leopard and tiger. And like Raffles, Farquhar was concerned to promote British interests in the region. In other ways the two men were quite different. Raffles was an Englishman full of enlightenment zeal, who dreamed of bringing the blessings of civilization and free trade to the Malay peoples. Farquhar was a more pragmatic Scot.

That morning they were joined in the longboat by another pragmatic Scot, Ronnie Simpson, the captain of the merchant ship the *Highland Lassie*. Ronnie had served in the Royal Navy, but had left after the War of 1812, and joined the merchant marine of the East India Company as captain of his own ship. With his savings and navy prize money, he had put down a substantial deposit on his own vessel, and he and his father planned to begin trading between Calcutta and Penang, hoping to be able to pay off the *Highland Lassie* with the profits from their first year.

Ronnie was tough and lean, with a muscular frame and angular features. He had curly brown hair, which he tried to keep under control beneath his old-fashioned tricorn hat, with long pointed sideburns and sharp blue eyes. Ronnie had a modicum of ambition—to own his own vessel, to make a success of his trading business with his father, and to find himself a wife and live in the Far East. He had wanted to spend his life in the Far East since as long as he could remember, or at least since his mother had read him stories from a book about the Spice Islands. He wanted to live among the palm trees and frangipani, and to say goodbye forever to the frigid winters—and summers—of Ardersier, the village on the Moray Firth where when he had been born. He was proud of his Scottish heritage, but having spent part of his naval service liberating French possessions in the Caribbean and the Maldives, he could never understand why any man with the opportunity to live where the sun shone bright and warm all year long would chose to live in any place where it did not. He did recognize that his desire to live in the Far East conflicted with his desire to find himself a wife, for he knew that women, or at least white women, were very thin on the ground, even in a British settlement such as Penang. He supposed he would be content with some dark-haired Malay, or perhaps an exotic Chinese, although he had recently learned that they were also thin on the ground, at least in Penang. Still, what's for me won't go by me, he thought to himself, remembering his mother's old saying.

He had had very little education in the one-room village school in Ardersier, but sufficient for him to read and write. He also had a good head for figures, which was useful for his business, and possessed a natural gift for languages. He had picked up the old Gaelic language from a fisherwoman in Ardersier as a child, and the languages of the French and Spanish prisoners taken after successful naval engagements. Since arriving in Penang some weeks before, he had already mastered the rudiments of Malay, the lingua franca of the British settlement.

Ronnie had been in Penang trying to rent some space in a merchant godown,[iv] before returning to Calcutta to pick up his father, who was on his way out from Scotland. Before returning to his ship one evening, he had dropped by a hostelry on the waterfront, where he had met and shared a few drinks with another trader, Captain James Pearl of the *Indiana*. When Ronnie began asking him questions about Penang, Captain Pearl told him there might be better prospects further south, and that he was taking Sir Stamford Raffles out the following evening to meet up with Colonel Farquhar and a small fleet of armed cruisers and survey vessels. He was sure that Sir Stamford would not mind him coming along, since he was just the sort of merchant adventurer that Raffles wanted to

---

iv Warehouse or other storage space, usually on a dockside.

attract to his new settlement.

Ronnie had followed the ships out of Penang the following evening. When they rendezvoused at the Carimon islands, Ronnie had been introduced to Raffles, who welcomed him to their company. He had followed the ships down to Johor, where they anchored off Pulau Sakijang Bendera. When he visited Captain Pearl aboard the *Indiana* that evening, Raffles invited Ronnie to join him and Colonel Farquhar when they visited Temenggong Abdul Rahman on the island of Singapore the following day. Ronnie was twenty-seven years old when he joined Raffles and Farquhar in the longboat. He wore an old-fashioned black frockcoat and his tricorn hat, but thought he looked no more absurd than Raffles in his clerical black. He looked out across the bay to the shimmering silver sands of the island of Singapore, and licked his lips in anticipation. Ronnie Simpson knew he had made the right decision when he joined this expedition. He could feel it in his bones. He could almost taste it in the sweet salty breeze blowing from the island.

It was the twenty-ninth of January 1819.

2

A single sepoy armed with a musket manned the longboat, and rowed them toward the river mouth. As the boat cut quickly through the water, Raffles mopped his brow with his handkerchief. He peered out at the silver shoreline at the mouth of the river and his excitement mounted. He felt sure that this was an ideal spot, although the motley collection of huts and boats clustered at the mouth of the river might have appeared unpromising to a less visionary observer. The blazing headache that had clouded his thoughts and denied him sleep on the journey down from Penang seemed to dissipate in the faint breeze that came off the water.

Raffles clapped his hand on Farquhar's shoulder. 'A first-rate prospect, Major, if I say so myself,' he exclaimed with enthusiasm.

'As may be, y'r honour, but I think we should tak' a closer look before getting carried away,' Farquhar replied. 'But I'll grant ye it looks like a grand location. The wonder is that the Dutchy hasna taken it over already.'

Turning to Ronnie, Raffles asked, 'What do you think of it, Captain Simpson?'

Ronnie looked out over the silver sands and dense green tropical foliage beyond, and felt a sudden sense of deja vu, as if he was coming home after a long voyage. But he knew that he had never been there before, save in his dreams.

'Looks a lot more promising than the Carimons, Sir Stamford,' Ronnie replied, 'and a much better situation. The river looks like a natural shelter for boats.'

'I agree, Captain Simpson, I do most heartily agree,' Raffles replied, his face beaming.

The boat pulled into the river, carefully avoiding the rocks at the river mouth. Once they passed the narrow channel at the entrance, the river opened out into a wide basin. The left bank of the river was a mass of low mangrove swamps and tidal creeks; the right bank rose a few feet above the river and opened out onto a wide plain. Along the right bank were a number of huts built on bamboo stilts, with gangways linking them to the riverbank.

'These are the homes o' the orang laut, the aboriginal people of Johor,' Farquhar informed them. 'Maist o' them spend a' of their lives in their boats, or in huts like these built out over a river or seashore.' As they approached, many fled upriver, while the braver souls watched from their boats or the verandahs of their huts.

The three men disembarked, leaving the sepoy in the long boat, and climbed up the bank until they emerged onto the plain, which was covered with myrtle, rhododendron and lalang grass.[v] They paused a moment under the shade of a Eugenia tree, and looked upriver. Beyond the huts and boats of the orang laut they saw a compound of more substantial palm and attap houses that faced the sea, the largest of which they assumed to be that of the temenggong. A party of Malays armed with spears emerged from the compound, and made their way towards them.

The Malays were led by Encik Salleh, the temenggong's chief councillor, who introduced himself and invited them to the temenggong's lodge. The three men exchanged greetings, and followed Encik Salleh and his party along the edge of the river to the temenggong's compound. On the way they passed Malay houses raised on stilts, with scrawny hens pecking around between them. A few cautious orang laut and Malay fishermen followed behind at a safe distance.

---

v Long tall grass native to Southeast Asia.

They entered the compound through the main gate of the stockade, which was fringed by palm trees, and halted before the largest house, a bamboo and attap structure with a wide verandah. At the head of the steps stood Temenggong Sri Maharajah Abdul Rahman, flanked by his followers, who were armed with spears, swords and krisses. Abdul Rahman was a short, dark-skinned Malay with wiry black hair and a narrow chin, whose black eyes sparkled as he smiled down upon them. He was dressed in a blue and yellow sarong and baju, with a jewelled headpiece. Two attendants stood behind him, bearing the yellow umbrella of royalty.

The temenggong came down to greet them, and Farquhar introduced him to Sir Stamford Raffles and Captain Simpson. The temenggong in turn introduced them to his brother, Abang Johor, before inviting them to sit with him on the verandah, on high and elabourately carved chairs that had been set out. They were served rambutans and other fruits, while the Malay fishermen and orang laut gathered in a semi-circle in front of the house. After they had exchanged pleasantries, Major Farquhar asked if he and Captain Simpson might be excused, so that they could look around the island while Raffles conducted the negotiations. As Farquhar explained to Ronnie afterwards, it was best to leave the negotiations to Raffles, for only he had the authority to make any agreement on behalf of the Company.

'Of course, my good friend,' said the temenggong, with a knowing smile, indicating to Raffles that they should go inside to talk.

Once inside the lodge, Raffles got straight to the point.

'Maharajah,' he said, 'I have come on the authority of the Governor-General of India and the Directors of the East India Company to ask your permission to found a settlement here at Singapore. We believe this would be an excellent location for a factory, to serve both the local and the China trade, and that such an arrangement would be of great benefit to your people. You would have British protection and we would pay you a generous allowance for the lease of the property.'

The temenggong was an astute man. He knew very well the opportunities that the establishment of such a commercial port would bring—not only a government allowance, but also the promise of customary gifts from the captains of trading ships, and the prospect of additional revenue from the lease of land to merchants and their suppliers. But he was also a cautious man, and careful to cover his own position.

'I would dearly like to oblige you, Sir Stamford,' he said politely, 'but I am nothing. I have no authority to grant you permission to found such a settlement. This island of Singapore, and the islands surrounding, belong to the Sultan of Johor, who is the only person who can approve such an arrangement.'

* * *

While Raffles and the temenggong were talking, Farquhar and Ronnie walked back along the riverbank toward the beach. As Ronnie looked around him, he could immediately see the advantages of the place as a company factory. As he remarked to Farquhar:

'There seems to be plenty o' wood, fresh water, and sand that could serve as ballast for ships. All the basics for setting up a factory.'

'Aye Ronnie, there certainly is. And from my point of view, it's a reasonably defensible position, given a sufficient garrison and munitions—in case Dutchy decides to dispute any arrangement that Raffles makes.'

When they arrived back on the plain, they walked eastwards along the beach. They crossed a freshwater stream and continued on until they arrived at a second river mouth. When they returned, they rested in the shade of the Eugenia tree. Farquhar took out his handkerchief and wiped his brow, and Ronnie took off his perfectly useless tricorn. Some of the Malays and orang laut gathered around, and began to question Farquhar about the ships and their purpose on the island. He explained that Sir Stamford Raffles was hoping to establish a settlement, the beginnings of a commercial port like Malacca and Penang.

'Will you be in charge, Tuan Farquhar?' they asked, knowing Farquhar's reputation for fair treatment among the Malaccan Malays. 'Will you be our Rajah Singapura?'

Farquhar's reputation had preceded him. During his years in Malacca, Farquhar had become known affectionately as Tuan Farquhar and Rajah Malacca. He had an almost infinite capacity for patience and tolerance, and was scrupulously fair in his dealings with both rich merchants and poor labourers and farmers. In many ways he had acted like a regular Malay rajah, and even dressed in native sarong and baju when not engaged in official ceremonial duties. He was frequently to be seen and hailed by natives and merchants as he strode around Malacca with his walking stick and favourite dogs, smiling genially to all as he passed them by.

'I hope so,' Farquhar responded, 'I certainly hope so, even if it's only for a wee while, although that will depend upon your temenggong. We'd best be getting back to him, to see what he has worked out with Sir Stamford.' The two men rose and the Malays and orang laut followed them back to the compound.

On their way they met Captain Ross, who had just returned from surveying the bay and the river.

'There's an excellent anchorage close to the shore, Major, deep enough for most ships and safe from rocks and reefs,' Ross informed Farquhar. 'The river could take dozens of cargo boats if we can clear the sand and rocks from the entrance. And we could easily build a settlement and fortifications on the plain.'

'Excellent work,' Farquhar replied. 'I entirely agree with your judgment, Daniel. Seems we've found the right place at last, and thankfully no sign of Dutchy—I don't think they've ever explored the island. See if you can get some of the temenggong's men to help you set up a temporary camp. We're going back to see how Sir Stamford is getting on.'

* * *

When they returned, Raffles and the temenggong were discussing the succession. The temenggong had explained to Raffles that his personal allegiance was to Tengku Long, the eldest son, and the true and lawful sultan. He was, however, obliged by force of circumstance to acknowledge Tengku Abdul Rahman as his master, given that Tengku Abdul Rahman was backed by the Dutch, with their fleets of ships and soldiers.

'You need not worry about that,' Raffles assured him. 'As Major Farquhar has already promised you, we will guarantee you British protection and acknowledge Tengku Long as the true and lawful sultan, if you will bring him to Singapore.'

'I can arrange for that,' the temenggong replied, 'although it will have to be done in secret. If we are found out we will have Dutch ships in the bay long before we see Tengku Long on this island. But I will do as you say. I would like to make an agreement with Tuan Farquhar and yourself, especially one that will bring official recognition of Sultan Hussein by the British government.'

Raffles and Farquhar were not so sure that recognition by the British government could be brought about so quickly. They were not even sure that the Court of Directors would back them. But they bit their tongues and offered the temenggong their assurances that they would.

'Then let us send for him immediately,' Raffles replied with enthusiasm, 'so that we can seek his approval and acknowledge him as Sultan Hussein. In the meantime, let us draw up a provisional agreement for both of us to sign.'

'There is no need to sign any agreement,' replied the temenggong, frowning. 'The word of a Maharajah is enough.'

'As it is for me,' replied Raffles. 'An Englishman's word is also his bond. However, my masters are merchants and lawyers, and they have pressed me for a written agreement in case our agreement is challenged by the Dutch.'

The temenggong was doubtful, but grudgingly agreed to sign an agreement the following day, once they had decided the amount of the allowance he was to be paid. He also granted Raffles permission to land some men and stores that afternoon. As he reasoned to himself, he was in no position to resist. There were seven Company ships anchored off the island, some of which were armed, and others that contained troops and marines. If this Englishman's factory caused a problem with the Dutch, they could remove him and his soldiers themselves.

As they prepared to leave, Ronnie asked the temenggong about the dark and mysterious hill that rose behind his compound.

'It is known as Bukit Larangan,' the temenggong replied. 'On this hill the ancient rajahs of Singapura had their palaces, and men were forbidden to climb the hill without the rajah's permission. Behind the hill runs a fresh water stream, where the rajah and his consorts used to bathe, and where none other was allowed to approach.'

As they walked back down to the beach, Raffles looked back over his shoulder to Bukit Larangan.

'Nice spot for a bungalow, Farquhar,' he remarked as he strode ahead, not waiting for a response.

When they came back on board the *Indiana*, Raffles gave orders to bring up the rest of the ships. Later that afternoon, eighty sepoys of the 20th Bengal Native Infantry landed on the beach and began to erect tents, as the sailors cut down the shrub and grasses on the plain, and dug a well under the Eugenia tree, as the temenggong had advised them to do. As the three men looked out from the *Indiana* that night, they could see their campfires flickering red against the darkness of the jungle. They had arrived.

3

In the early morning, about an hour before dawn, Batin Sapi, the headman of the orang laut, stepped into a waiting prahu, which carried him to the temenggong's dock. The temenggong's brother, Abang Johor, and one of his advisors, Encik Wan Abdullah, stepped into the boat. In the darkness, the sleek black prahu slipped out of the river and past the ships anchored in the bay. It presented a ghostly sight in the early morning mist, but none of the ships' lookouts saw it. The oars dipped and rose in the water as they set a course for Pulau Bulang, where they hoped to persuade Tengku Long to return with them to Singapore and give his approval for a British settlement.

Later that morning Raffles visited the temenggong again, and they signed a provisional agreement. This granted the East India Company the right to establish a factory at Singapore, in return for which the Company guaranteed the protection of the temenggong and his people, and agreed to pay him an allowance of three thousand Spanish dollars[vi] per year. Meanwhile more troops and supplies were landed on the plain. Lieutenant Henry Ralfe of the Bengal Artillery supervised the unloading of twelve ten-pounder guns, which were winched from the ships' holds into waiting boats, and then rowed ashore. The lascars hauled the guns up the beach while the European and Indian gunners built bastions of earth and stones, with the guns pointing out to sea. When Ronnie came ashore with some of his crew, he looked over the gun emplacements. They had done a good job, he thought to himself, although he knew these

---

vi The primary currency in the region at the time.

light field pieces would cause little damage to the heavy timbers of a Dutch man of war. Once they had completed the bastions, the lascars set to work clearing the plain, using parangs and cutlasses, piling felled trees and cut bushes and grasses into huge bonfires along the beach. They stripped off their dark blue coats, and worked bare-chested in the hot sun. A few of the temenggong's followers came down to the plain and volunteered to work with them.

A red-faced Major Farquhar strode over to where Ronnie stood, cursing aloud.

'Those damned Bengal Infantry,' he fumed. 'They won't lift a finger to help us, on account of their being soldiers not labourers, they say. Just look at the Bengal Artillery, working their backs off in the hot sun, with no complaint!'

'We could lend a hand if you want,' said Ronnie, indicating the men he had brought ashore.

'Be very grateful if you did, Ronnie,' Farquhar replied. 'And while you're here, why don't you go down and ask the orang laut if they can help. Your Malay is better than mine already.'

Ronnie said he would be happy to, and he and his men strode off towards the houseboats of the orang laut on the Singapore River. But as they approached the orang laut, many fled their boats in panic and swam out toward the mouth of the river.

'Wait up, wait up, we come in peace!' Ronnie called out to them. 'You've nothing to fear from us!'

But most of the orang laut ignored him, and continued to swim desperately towards the river mouth.

As Ronnie reached the river's edge, he noticed the headman had not fled. A wizened and wiry old man, he stood with his head aloof and arms crossed.

'Why do they flee?' Ronnie exclaimed. 'They have nothing to fear from us!'

'They heard a rumour they were about to be taken as slaves,' replied the headman in a firm voice.

'But that is nonsense! We've no intention of taking them as slaves, we merely wanted to ask for their help in clearing the plain.'

'It is not nonsense,' said the headman. 'Many came before with that intention, and took our people away.'

'But believe me, we don't, we only want your help. Please call them to come back.'

The headman looked hard at Ronnie with his dark eyes. 'I believe you, young man. I will bring them back.' He called out to his people, and sent his remaining followers to run along the riverbank to direct those furthest away to return.

The orang laut returned to their boats as quickly as they had fled, to Ronnie's great relief. He was about to offer the headman payment if they would agree to help clear the plain, when he suddenly noticed a small boy in difficulty at the mouth of the river. Ronnie called out the alarm and pulled off his shirt and boots, then dived into the river and swam as fast as he could towards the boy. He was quickly followed by some of his crew and a number of orang laut.

Ronnie swam until his lungs were bursting, but he watched in despair as the boy was dragged down by the strong current and swept out to sea. After a few moments of hopeless diving in search of the child, the party returned to the riverbank.

'I am so sorry,' Ronnie said to the headman, when he had gathered himself together. 'It was my fault. I should have come alone and spoken to you in the first place. What was the boy's name? I would like to compensate his family for the loss of their son, although I know it will bring them meager comfort.'

'The name of the boy's body was Wa Hakin, but no man knows the name of the boy's soul,' replied the headman. 'I thank you for your offer, young man, but only the sea can compensate the boy's father, for it was the sea that took his son.'

Ronnie found this no consolation for his own guilt, but he acknowledged the headman's position with a slow nod of his head, and returned with his men to the plain. He reported the incident to Farquhar, who in turn reported it to the temenggong. The temenggong instructed the orang laut to provide the settlers with fresh fish and fruit, for which they received money and tobacco in return. But they would not join in the work of clearing the plain.

A few days later some Chinese labourers from the gambier and pepper plantations came to help, having heard that the British were paying for the work. Plank and attap huts were erected to serve as a temporary commissariat for the Company. Ronnie continued to bring some of his crew ashore to join in the work, and late one afternoon he went for a long walk along the east bank of the river until it disappeared into the thick jungle. He then set off along the east beach, by the edge of the jungle rather than the shoreline, intending to go as far as the second river [vii] that he and Farquhar had discovered on their first day on the island.

But just before he crossed the freshwater stream, a vision stopped him in his tracks and took his breath away. For standing before him was a beautiful young woman, with jet-black hair, soft brown eyes and full red lips. And she was Chinese! Ronnie had heard there were Chinese gambier and pepper farmers in the interior of the island, but nobody had told him about Chinese women! She bent down in supplication before a small joss-house set up on the beach, and then went to sit at the door of an attap hut, where she attended to her two children, a boy and a girl. Remembering the unfortunate incident with the orang laut, he approached her cautiously and introduced himself in Malay.

But she was not afraid, and understood what he was saying, despite the Scottish lilt of Ronnie's Malay. She introduced herself,

---

vii Later known as the Rochor River.

and told him that she lived on the beach with her husband, who was a fisherman, and her two children. When Ronnie asked her how she came to live in Singapore, Moon Ling told him her family had perished in Fukien province during the great famine, so she had been forced to join a Chinese opera troupe. They had been shipwrecked in a terrible storm on their way to Malacca. She explained how she had been washed up on Pulau Belakang Mati, where she and her husband Badang bin Aman had managed to escape from the pirates who had landed on the beach. She had scared the superstitious men away by disguising herself as a pale-faced and blood–streaked jinn, using her theatrical paints that she had preserved from the shipwreck.

While they were talking her husband arrived, carrying a catch of fish upon his spear. Moon Ling introduced Ronnie to him, and he smiled when Ronnie told him how much he had enjoyed his wife's story of their escape from the pirates. He was a giant of a man, but he had a gentle nature. Ronnie had known his sort before, burly highlanders who were murderous in battle, but had the softest hearts for women and children.

Ronnie started talking to the fisherman, and asked him if he knew anything about the early inhabitants of the island. On his walks he thought he had been able to make out the ruined lines of an ancient city.

'Oh, you have come to the right man to ask about that!' Moon Ling laughed, grinning towards her husband. 'He's a great storyteller, and knows all the legends of the early rajahs of Singapore. He entertains the young children with his stories, and some of the older folk as well.'

'Why don't you come back tomorrow evening,' Badang bin Aman said, 'when I will tell my son the stories of our ancestors, as I promised him I would.'

Ronnie replied that had business to attend to the following

morning, but that he should be able to come ashore again in the late afternoon.

'Then you must share our food as well as our stories,' Badang bin Aman said with a smile, and Ronnie agreed that he would join them for their evening meal.

As he walked back to the longboat that was waiting to take him back to the *Highland Lassie*, Ronnie wondered idly to himself if Moon Ling had any sisters. Then he remembered what had happened to her sister during the great famine in Fukien province.

* * *

Ronnie returned the following evening, bringing along some fresh fruit as his contribution to the evening meal. He was surprised by the number of Malay children—and a good number of adults—who had come to listen to Badang bin Aman's stories about the early rajahs.

Badang bin Aman related how the ancient city of Singapura[viii] had been founded many centuries ago by Sri Tri Buana, the former ruler of Palembang, who mistakenly thought he had seen a lion when he first landed on the island at Temasek.[ix] He told how his ancestor Badang had saved the life of Sri Tri Buana's son Paduka Sri Pikrama Wira, by hurling a giant stone at a warrior who was about to strike the rajah with a battle axe, and helped him drive the invading forces of the Majapahit back into the sea. It was said that Badang became the Rajah's champion, and that his great strength was the gift of a jinn, whom he had caught raiding his fishing nets. The jinn had said he would grant Badang any wish if he would only set him free. Badang agreed, and wished for strength. The jinn made Badang drink his vomit from a banana leaf, and when he vanished, Badang attained the strength of ten men.

---

viii Lion City.
ix Seatown.

48

He also told the tale of Rajah Paduka Sri Maharaja, who saved the city from an attack of giant swordfish, by following the advice of a young boy who suggested that he build a barricade of stakes, on which the swordfish impaled themselves. The local Malays called the place where the swordfish were destroyed Tanjong Pagar.[x] Fearing that the boy was a sorcerer in disguise, the ungrateful rajah ordered the murder of the boy. The following night, three men from the rajah's bodyguard made their way to the poor hut where the boy lived with his grandmother, on the crest of a small hill west of the city wall. Grey clouds hid their shame from the face of the moon, but not the screams of the boy and his grandmother when the rajah's men put them to death. But when the people came to investigate, they found no sign of the boy or his grandmother, or of the guards who had killed them. All they found was an empty hut, whose walls and floor were stained with dark red blood that flowed down the hill like a great river, seeping into the earth until the whole hill had turned red. And so it has remained since that dreadful night, and the people call the place Bukit Merah. [xi]

Finally Badang told the tale of Iskander Shah, the last Rajah of Singapura. He was the most powerful Rajah in the history of Singapura, who commanded a great pirate fleet and possessed a large harem. He had taken as one of his many wives, Zuraidah, the daughter of his chief treasurer, Sang Ranjuna Tapa, but he had ordered the princess strangled when he suspected her of taking a lover. That night a heartbroken Sang Ranjuna Tapa knelt in silent prayer before his daughter's lifeless body, as the silver moonlight swept like an angry ghost across the room. In the morning he plotted his revenge. He invited the forces of the Majapahit to attack the city, with the promise that he would open the city gates to them. Sang Ranjuna Tapa was the first to die as the Majapahit stormed

x Cape of Stakes.
xi Red Hill.

through the gates. Then they put the city to fire and sword, and tore down the walls.

A hush fell over the listeners, as they imagined the dreadful night when the ancient city of Singapura had been destroyed. Ronnie was about to ask what happened to Iskander Shah, but one of the children beat him to it.

'Iskander Shah managed to make his escape,' Badang bin Aman replied, 'and travelled up the west coast of the peninsula, where he established the city of Malacca and converted to Islam. Although,' he added, 'others say his body was returned to Singapura and laid to rest in a keramat[xii] on the hill above us, which is known as Bukit Larangan.'

This time Ronnie could not contain his curiosity. 'Have you seen the keramat on the hill?' he asked.

'Oh no,' Badang replied. 'I have never been up that hill. It is forbidden.'

When Ronnie returned to his ship that evening, his dreams were filled with strange visions of an ancient city, of murderous swordfish and a strangled Malay princess. When he woke the following morning, he was surer than ever that he had come to the right place.

---

xii Malay shrine.

4

On the first of February a large war-prahu, bearing the yellow flag of royalty, entered the bay. The heavily ornamented craft was about seventy feet long and fifteen feet wide, and carried two long brass cannon on her bow. Although it had taken much persuasion and cajoling, Tengku Long had agreed to come to Singapore to meet with Raffles.

The temenggong, who had been advised of his approach, went out to meet him, and directed the war-prahu towards the *Indiana*, where Raffles and his entourage waited to greet him.

Raffles welcomed the royal party on board, and seated them on chairs arranged on deck. Ronnie, who had been invited to the ceremony, thought that Tengku Long was perhaps the ugliest man he had ever seen. He had skinny legs that threatened to collapse under the weight of his immense body. He had a sallow complexion, and a very wide mouth, which almost filled his face when he smiled. He sweated profusely, and his hand was wet and clammy when Ronnie shook it. He spoke in a hoarse and rasping voice, which sounded as if he was always trying to catch his breath.

But Raffles seemed unfazed by his appearance, and was all charm. He explained to Tengku Long that they sought his permission, as Sultan of Johor, to establish a factory at Singapore. Tengku Long smiled graciously in return, and fixed Raffles with his beady brown eyes.

'Highness, we will acknowledge you as the rightful heir to the Johor-Riau-Lingga Sultanate, in the name of the Governor-General of India and the Honorable East India Company,' Raffles continued, 'if you will sign a treaty granting us permission to build a factory on Singapore island. We offer you the protection of the British flag, and an annual allowance of five thousand Spanish dollars.'

Like the temenggong, Tengku Long recognized the opportunities for great wealth that such a factory offered. And like the temenggong, he understood very clearly the deal he was being offered. After making a show of considering the matter very carefully, and warning Raffles that the Dutch would protest the agreement, he consented to sign the treaty in a few days' time, after he had consulted with the temenggong, with whom he was planning to stay. Once he had committed to signing the treaty, Tengku Long expressed great enthusiasm for the idea of a factory, and his gratitude for the Company's support as rightful heir to the sultanate. In fact he was so grateful, he assured Raffles, that he offered to massacre all the Dutch on the Riau islands. Raffles thanked him, but said that was quite unnecessary. He led Tengku Long back to his war-prahu, and ordered that a royal salute be fired in the sultan's honour.

Ronnie was no politician, but he could see the sense of acknowledging Tengku Long as sultan. By recognizing his rightful claim and accepting the Singapore concession in his name, Raffles and Farquhar could reasonably maintain that they were serving the interests of the Sultan of Johor as well as those of the East India Company. Yet he also knew that they had exceeded their authority in doing so. Raffles had told him that Hastings had explicitly warned against interference in the politics of the Johor-Riau-Lingga succession, to avoid antagonizing the Dutch authorities. Well, they were well and truly in it now. They could only hope that Lord Hastings would support them once he recognized the great benefit that Singapore would bring to the Eastern trade. Otherwise they would all be hung out to dry.

Whatever doubts Ronnie might have had, Raffles was supremely confident that they had done the right thing. That evening he stood with Ronnie and James Pearl and watched the sun set over the mouth of the river from the deck of the *Indiana*. 'One could hardly conceive a more commanding and promising station,' Raffles said. 'Here we have planted the British flag among the ruins of the ancient capital of Singapura, the City of the Lion! Here we will advance the interests of the East India Company and raise the Malay people to their former glory. Not to mention the interests of our merchant friends like yourselves,' Raffles added, clapping the two men on the shoulder.

'I'm grateful to have played my small part in it, Sir Stamford,' Pearl replied, 'and with your permission I plan to establish my own base in Singapore. I hope to make my fortune trading in the archipelago, and to build myself a fine house here someday.'

'That's the spirit!' Raffles replied. 'And of course you have my permission, although you will need to talk to Major Farquhar about the allocation of land once we have signed the treaty.'

'And how about your good self, Captain Simpson?' Raffles said, turning to Ronnie. 'Do you intend to stay? Our new settlement could do with some canny Scots.'

Ronnie paused as he looked out over the gold-flecked waters, but not because he was wrestling with his decision. He was merely admiring the brilliant sunset.

'I surely do, Sir Stamford,' he eventually replied. 'I canna think of a better place for my father and me to establish ourselves. I just hope you and Major Farquhar can keep the Dutchman away, for we've had our fill o' fighting.'

'You can count of us,' Raffles assured him, although Raffles knew he could not. Everything would depend upon Colonel Bannerman, the Marquis of Hastings, and the Court of Directors.

5

The next few days saw a flurry of activity on the plain, as the soldiers and sailors prepared the ground for the treaty signing. A Chinese carpenter from the *Indiana* erected a flagstaff on the beach, and a pavilion was built facing the temenggong's compound, with its back to the sea. On the evening of Friday, the fifth of February, Lieutenant Crossly sent out a message announcing that the treaty would be signed at one o'clock the next day.

The following morning a red cloth carpet was laid out between the temenggong's house and the pavilion, which was hung with flags and bunting, as were the refreshment tent and all the ships at sea. Lieutenant Ralfe stood before his shore batteries, while his gunners formed a parade line behind them. They were dressed in their dark blue coats and pants, with high black boots, and dress swords hanging from their belts. The men of the Bombay Marine Regiment, commanded by Captain Maxfield of the *Nearchus*, formed a ceremonial line from the temenggong's house to the pavilion. They wore blue-faced and gold-embroidered jackets, with white shirts, belts and cross straps. Their silver buttons flashed in the morning sun, which bore down from an almost cloudless blue sky.

Just before one o' clock Tengku Long emerged from the temenggong's lodge dressed in a yellow silk robe. His Malay honour guard, carrying spears hung with red and white pennants and feathers, formed behind him. As his standard bearer opened the yellow umbrella of royalty above his head, three small cannon were fired to announce the approach of the sultan. As the royal party proceeded, a light drizzle began to fall, sending thin rainbows of light dancing among the British officers, who were assembled in full dress uniform at the edges of the pavilion. Tengku Long and the temenggong shared a knowing smile—the rain was an excellent omen.

Raffles came out to greet the two men and seated them behind a long trestle table draped with a British flag. Outside the pavilion a crowd of soldiers and sailors from the ships were assembled; they were soon joined by the followers of the temenggong and the sultan, the orang laut, the Malay fishermen and the Chinese gambier and pepper farmers. The terms of the treaty, which recognized Tengku Long as his Highness Sultan Hussein Mohammed Shah of Johor, Riau and Lingga, were read out in English and Malay. They reiterated the terms of the provisional agreement that Raffles and the temenggong had signed a few days earlier, which granted the East India Company the right to establish and maintain a factory on the island of Singapore. In return, the Company offered the protection of the British flag to the sultan, the temenggong, and their followers, and authorized the previously agreed annual allowances. The treaty prescribed that British authority would regulate the port of Singapore, but that justice would be administered in accord with the laws and customs of the native peoples residing therein. The sultan and temenggong bound their heirs and successors to the terms of the treaty.

The assembled sepoy guard fired three volleys, after which Raffles, the sultan and the temenggong affixed their seals to the two documents. Lieutenant Crossly announced the appointment of Major Farquhar as resident and commander of the troops at Singapore, under the authority of Sir Stamford Raffles, the Lieutenant-Governor of Bencoolen. Raffles presented the sultan with gifts of opium, silk, and arms, then led the pavilion party to the flagstaff, where the British flag was raised for the first time over the new settlement. A loud cheer went up from the assembled soldiers and sailors. The sepoys fired another three volleys, followed by salutes from the shore batteries and the ships out in the harbour.

The party then adjourned to the refreshment tent, where the ships' cooks had laid out cold dishes, with barrels of beer and bottles of wine. Champagne was served in crystal glasses, and toasts were drunk to the King of England, the Governor-General of India, the Court of Directors of the East India Company, his Highness the Sultan, the temenggong, and Sir Stamford Raffles, Lieutenant-Governor of Bencoolen.

After the toasts were completed, Captain Pearl and Ronnie stood talking with Lieutenant Ralfe and Francis Bernard, Farquhar's son-in-law, who told them he had just been appointed acting harbour master.

'What exactly does a harbour master do?' Ralfe asked Bernard.

'Oh, I'll be recording the arrivals and departures of vessels, and their passengers and cargoes. Making arrangements for wooding, watering, and ballasting ships, and determining the charges for such services. I'll also function as registrar for imports and exports, and as postmaster for overseas mail.'

'But no import or export duties, right Francis!' said Captain Pearl, who was enthusing over the champagne and the prospects for the new settlement.

'Right you are, Captain Pearl, no duties on imports or exports,' Bernard assured him.

'Mark my words, gentlemen,' Captain Pearl continued. 'This place will be a gold mine. You should get your hands on as much land as you can when Major Farquhar makes his allocations. Be worth a fortune in a few years when this place takes off.'

'That's if the Dutch don't shut us down first,' Ralfe replied. 'We don't have much to defend ourselves with if they determine to drive us out. Half a dozen men of war and they could blast us off the island in less than an hour.'

'Not to mention pirates,' said Francis Bernard. 'Have you looked further along this beach and the surrounding islands. Skulls all over the place, and some of them not that old, I can tell you. I'll need to get these cleared away before we can attract merchant ships to this port.'

'You're right about them not being that old,' Ronnie replied. 'The fisherman and his Chinese wife who live beside the freshwater stream have a rare tale to tell about how they escaped from Illanun pirates only a few years ago.'

'Well I doubt pirates would risk a landing with our guns on the beach,' Ralfe responded, 'although I would not want to depend on the 20th Bengal Infantry. They're close enough to mutiny as it is. Due to return home before Raffles had them sent down here, although that's no excuse.'

'I expect he's already arranging for more troops and guns,' said Bernard hopefully.

Turning to Captain Pearl, he continued, 'I see you're already ahead of the game.' He pointed to the shipment of bricks that Pearl had carried down from Penang and unloaded at the eastern mouth of the Singapore River.

'Indeed I am, Mr Bernard,' Pearl replied. 'I expect there will be a lot of building soon, and I expect to make a healthy profit! I'm going to bring back another load as soon as I can, and one day I intend to build myself a house on one of these hills close to the river.'

'Well let's drink to our future success,' Bernard said, and the three men raised their glasses.

Ronnie thought he ought to see about getting hold of some bricks, not to mention timber, tools and utensils, and the multitude of other items that the new settlement would need. It was a risk of course—they all recognized that—but a risk worth taking, for the potential profits boggled the mind. But first of all he would have to go back to Calcutta to pick up his father, although he intended to stay a few days more before he left. He needed to talk to Major Farquhar about securing a choice piece of land along the riverbank—the natural place to locate a godown.

* * *

The festivities ended around four o'clock, when Raffles led Sultan Hussein and the temenggong back to the temenggong's lodge. Sultan Hussein was in high spirits, and once again offered to massacre the Dutch on the Riau islands. Once again Raffles replied that it was not necessary, and not politic either. Sultan Hussein then announced that he wanted to build a royal istana out on the eastern shore, to accommodate his family and followers, who would soon be joining him. The temenggong promised to begin work on it as soon as possible, and that it would be a palace fit for a sultan.

Raffles thanked both men, and returned to the plain, where the soldiers and sailors were clearing away the tables and dismantling the marquees. He walked down the beach to join Major Farquhar, who was standing looking out to sea, under the great banyan tree at the edge of the freshwater stream that separated the plain from the rest of the eastern beach.

'The spell is broken, Major! The spell is broken! Here we will build a great commercial emporium that will break the Dutch monopoly and restore British influence through trade. We must make a success of this place; it is our best chance, my good friend. Here we can give the Dutchman a run for his money.'

Raffles deeply regretted the fact that he had to leave for Penang the following day. Hastings had instructed him to depart on a mission to Achin, to discuss the disputed succession there with the Malay princes who were resisting Dutch intrusion. He had only just secured his dream, and now he had to immediately abandon his 'child' to the care of Major Farquhar. Although he had chosen Farquhar for the job, he chaffed at having to hand over control.

'As you know, I have been instructed by Lord Hastings to communicate our interests to the Malay princes in Achin, so I will have to leave tomorrow. As soon as I get to Penang, I will instruct Colonel Bannerman to send down more troops and money as soon as he can. I have already arranged for about four hundred sepoys from Bencoolen to join you in a few weeks time. I just hope they arrive in time, and will be enough to deter the Dutch.'

'We'll do our best wi' what we have,' Farquhar replied. 'I'm nae worried about Dutchy.'

'Well, you should be, Major Farquhar,' said Raffles, with a smile. 'I know you and your men will acquit yourselves well, whatever the outcome, but let's hope diplomacy will win the day without any fighting.'

'I will stop off again for a short while after I return from Achin, but then I must return to Bencoolen, where my duty lies. But you must keep me up to date with the progress of the settlement. Regular reports, Major Farquhar, regular reports.'

'As you wish, Sir Stamford,' Farquhar replied. 'Regular and I trust positive!'

'Good man,' said Raffles. 'But now I have to get back on board the *Indiana*. Look after our child while I am gone. We did a great thing today.'

He extended his hand, which Farquhar shook.

'Aye, a grand thing it was,' Farquhar reflected.

Raffles looked back over the new settlement at the mouth of the river, the small city of tents and huts with the Union Jack fluttering above, and declared:

'Well, if this last effort fails, I'll quit politics and become a philosopher.'

Then he marched off down the beach to the waiting boat.

6

Raffles left the next day and arrived in Penang on the fifteenth of February, to be greeted with the news that his wife, Lady Sophia, was expecting their second child. He had met his wife when he had returned to England in 1816, on his first home leave after ten years serving the Company in the Eastern Archipelago, first as assistant to the Governor of Penang, and then as Lieutenant-Governor of Java. He had returned in disgrace after being relieved of his position as Lieutenant-Governor of Java, after the Company suffered heavy financial losses, and deeply depressed over the loss of his first wife Olivia, who had died suddenly of a fever. Raffles suffered from crippling headaches, and had thought that his life was over.

He travelled to Cheltenham, having been advised by his doctors that the waters there might restore his health. They had done little for his health, but had done much for his heart, for one day in the Pump Room[xiii] he met Sophia Hull, the daughter of an Irish factor who had served with the Company in Bombay. Raffles thought her smile a greater tonic than any mineral waters. Their meeting quickly blossomed into romance, and they were married in February the following year. In contrast to his first wife's dark beauty, Sophia was rather plain and pale-skinned, but she had the most beautiful blue eyes that he had ever seen.

And almost immediately his fortunes had turned around. When Raffles published his *History of Java* the following year, it was widely read and admired. He became something of a celebrity in London society, and was knighted by the Prince Regent at a levee

---

xiii Spa building in Cheltenham where mineral waters were dispensed.

held at Carleton House in May. Suddenly his future seemed bright again, and he had accepted the Company's offer of the Bencoolen residency in Sumatra, at the rank of Lieutenant-Governor. On their journey out, Sophia had given birth to their first child, a baby daughter Charlotte. And now their second child was due—he hoped he would be able to return in turn for the birth.

* * *

As he prepared to sail for Achin, Raffles wrote a letter to the Marquis of Hastings reporting the establishment of a British factory in Singapore, and his official recognition of Tengku Long as Sultan Hussein. He knew he had overstepped his mark, but hoped that Hastings would support him when the governor-general recognized the wisdom of his action.

Raffles also sent a copy of his letter to Hastings to Colonel Bannerman, the Governor of Penang, with a request to immediately dispatch two hundred soldiers and money to help defend Singapore against the Dutch. When Bannerman received the letter and Raffles' request he exploded in anger.

'I'll do no such thing,' he complained to his secretary, 'the man's an irresponsible fool. I had two captains in from Malacca yesterday telling me that the Dutchman is furious. He's going to attack Singapore and drag Farquhar back to Batavia in chains. Next damn thing we'll be at war again!'

The Dutchman to whom Bannerman referred was Baron Godert van der Capellen, the Dutch Governor-General of Java, who had been outraged when he heard of Raffles' establishment of a British factory on Singapore, and had vowed that it would not stand. Capellen was at that moment arranging to send troops to the Riau islands in preparation for an invasion of Singapore.

Bannerman sent a note to Raffles denying his request. He also wrote a letter to the Marquis of Hastings, criticizing Raffles' action in founding the settlement, and rejecting Hussein's claim to the Johor-Riau-Lingga Sultanate. He informed Hastings that he had declined Raffles' request for troops and money to support the new settlement, since he considered it an unnecessary risk and waste of money. He urged the Marquis to recall Raffles immediately.

A few days later, Colonel Bannerman received the official Dutch protest from Baron van der Capellen, which he forwarded to the Marquis of Hastings. Bannerman immediately wrote to Capellen in response, criticizing Raffles in the strongest possible terms. He assured Baron van der Capellen that Raffles had acted without Company authority, and that his action would be quickly repudiated and countermanded by the governor-general in Calcutta. Bannerman also wrote to Farquhar demanding that he evacuate Singapore before it was too late.

Meanwhile, the temenggong and Sultan Hussein were dispatching grovelling letters to the Bugis prince Muda Rajah Ja'afar, the power behind the Riau regency, in full knowledge that they would be forwarded to his Dutch masters. [5]

* * *

Farquhar ignored Bannerman's demand that he evacuate Singapore, although as a matter of form he wrote to Raffles in Bencoolen referring the matter to him—knowing full well that Raffles was in Achin. He also knew that Raffles wanted him to stay, and in any case he was far too busy trying to establish the settlement to quit it now. He had cleared the rest of the plain to the edge of the freshwater stream, and back to the foot of Bukit Larangan, where he had set up the sepoy cantonment,[xiv] just east of the temenggong's compound. He prepared palisades and entrenchments for his guns,

---

xiv Military encampment.

and distributed them in a manner better suited for defense than ceremony. He had the *Ganges* winched into the river to avoid the rocks at the entrance, where it served as a temporary commissariat until he could have storehouses on the eastern mouth of the river.

Meanwhile, Farquhar had sent out messengers from Singapore soliciting settlers and supplies from Malacca and the neighbouring islands. He promised a free port, open to ships and vessels of every nation, and free of import and export duties that were the rule at Dutch ports. Farquhar's good reputation as the former Rajah of Malacca did much to encourage merchants and traders from other islands and ports in the archipelago to come to Singapore. He was respected as a fair and honest man, who understood the local Malay and Chinese merchant populations. Chinese traders arrived from the neighbouring Lingga and Riau islands within the first few weeks. Shortly after, Farquhar was happy to welcome a contingent of Malacca merchants who set up businesses supplying meat, fruit and vegetables, lumber, tools and other necessities. Their prices were inflated, but the ready supply of vegetables and other food staples helped to avert malnutrition and sickness. As he walked through the small bazaar of huts and tents that had sprung up on the plain, Farquhar had reason to be pleased with his modest success. He looked out over the harbour at the dozens of small Javanese craft dotting the water: a Siamese[xv] junk was approaching from the distance, an American clipper that had stopped to explore the port and take on water was anchored off Pulau Sakijang Bendera.

Farquhar was annoyed by Bannerman's refusal to send troops, but was grateful when the contingent of four hundred sepoys that Raffles had promised arrived from Bencoolen at the end of March, under the command of Captain Manley. Unfortunately, like the troops that had been sent down from Penang with the original expedition, they were so desperately unhappy that they were close

---

xv From Siam, present day Thailand.

to mutiny, because they had also been scheduled to return to India at the end of their tour. They would put up a decent fight if it came to it, of that Farquhar had no doubt, but he also had no illusions about his military prospects. If the Dutch did attack it would all be over very quickly, and he would be a major embarrassment to Raffles and the Company–if he lived. But he soldiered on, as soldiers must.

* * *

Ronnie took his leave of Major Farquhar a few days later.

'I'm sorry tae leave you to it, Major,' he said, 'but I need tae get back to Calcutta to pick up my father. I'm losing money as it is, coming down wi' a load of betel nuts and tin that nobody here can use. But I'll be back as soon I can wi bricks and a' the necessities of a new factory.'

'I fully understand, Ronnie,' Farquhar replied, 'and I'm glad you've agreed to set up in business here. We should have everything in order before you return.'

Ronnie gave him a bemused look, but Farquhar just grinned from ear to ear.

'We'll do as much as we can before his lordship comes back.'

'I'd like you to save us a good piece of land, if you could, Major. We'll be wanting tae build ourselves a godown when we get back.'

'I'll do what I can Ronnie, but I'll need to wait for further advice from Raffles when he returns from Achin. He's got some strange ideas about where to locate you merchants.'

'Surely along this side of the river,' Ronnie replied, 'unless he has an idea to move us all across to the anchorage that Captain Ross discovered further west.'

'So you would think,' Farquhar replied, 'so you would think. But don't worry about it, Ronnie, I'll make sure you'll be well settled. You run off and fetch your father back as soon as ye can.'

Farquhar offered his hand and Ronnie took it.

'You take care of yourself, Major,' he said, as he shook Farquhar's hand. 'And if you see any more Chinese lassies on the beach, keep them safe for me!'

Then he went down and climbed aboard the longboat that was waiting to take him back to the *Highland Lassie*.

When the Marquis of Hastings received Raffles' letter announcing the establishment of a factory at Singapore, and the treaty with Sultan Hussein, he was furious that Raffles had overreached his instructions. He was on the point of recalling him, when his secretary drew attention to an editorial in the *Calcutta Journal*, which praised Sir Stamford Raffles' establishment of the free port of Singapore and celebrated the future prospects for trade with China. It also reported on the favourable response of the merchant community in Calcutta, and praised the Governor-General's own actions in helping to end the Dutch commercial monopoly in the Malay Archipelago. This quickly changed his mind about Raffles' action, to what he now came to think of as his vision in sending Raffles to explore the prospects of a southern factory. He was certainly not reluctant to take his share of the credit when he met with a group of representatives from the Calcutta merchant community the following day.

He was consequently in no mood to receive Colonel Bannerman's letter a few days later, condemning Raffles' establishment of a factory in Singapore and his recognition of Sultan Hussein. Hastings wrote a scathing response, reminding Bannerman that his duty was to support Sir Stamford Raffles, who acted as agent for the Governor-General. He ordered Bannerman to immediately send reinforcements, money and supplies to Singapore, and warned him that he would be held personally responsible if as a result of his actions the Dutch were encouraged to attack an undefended Singapore.

He then wrote to Raffles praising his foundation of a factory in Singapore, while regretting his conflict with the Dutch. But he gave Raffles his provisional approval of the settlement, subject to confirmation by the Court of Directors.

* * *

Major Farquhar was out on his early evening stroll. He walked along the edge of the Rochor River, where it bordered Kampong Glam,[xvi] about two miles east of the Singapore River. He wore an old linen jacket, a dusty red sarong, and a pair of sandals. His Cairn terrier Paddie trotted along beside him. This was a walk he regularly took. It helped him relax as he thought over the affairs of the day, and his plans for the morrow. There had been a thunderstorm, and the ground and jungle steamed around him. But as the sun began to set against a dark blue sky streaked with red and gold, a light breeze cooled the sweat on his brow. It had been a busy—not to say expensive—few weeks.

First there had been the business of the rats. Hundreds of them, flocking out of the jungle as if some Pied Piper was calling them. They had attacked Lieutenant Ralfe's cat—three of the buggers!—and his own poor dogs. The damned things had run all over his tent at night, making sleep impossible. You never knew when one of them would jump up on your bed and attack you! But he had put paid to them all right. He had declared a bounty of a wang[xvii] a rat. The Malays and Chinese brought them in by the dozen, and he had ordered a giant pit dug to dump them into. He had needed to up the bounty to two wangs the second week, when enthusiasm

---

xvi Village area occupied by Sultan Hussein and his followers, named after the Glam tree, whose resin was used for caulking ships, and whose leaves were used for medicinal oil.
xvii Early Malay coin.

waned while the rats still ran about, but that had finished them well and good. Or at least for a time. Then he had had to do the same thing with giant centipedes the next week—hellish biting things that dropped off the roof onto your head. But he'd fixed them too, this time for only a wang—they were big centipedes but not as big as rats.

A pretty penny it had cost him all in all, drawn from the pittance that Raffles had allocated him to operate what he claimed would soon become the 'greatest emporium in the East!' Full of grand ideas was Raffles–and if truth be told he had to admit that some of them were grand–but he had no sense when it came to money. All well and good establishing a free port, but how was he going to pay for it? Raffles had told him not to incur any unnecessary expenses, as he was sure Hastings must have told Raffles, but where was he going to get the money for government buildings and roads? He would have to think of something.

But what a business! Talk about the seven plagues of Egypt. What next? A few minutes later he got his answer.

The terrier slipped into the water to cool itself, and paddled along the edge of the river, keeping pace with its master. Then in a sudden roaring rush of water, a huge crocodile rose from the river and snatched up the poor animal, whose panicked yelps quickly turned to plaintive whimpers, as Farquhar watched in dazed disbelief. He could hear the bones crunch between the powerful jaws, and his beloved terrier fell silent. The crocodile slipped back into the river and disappeared from view.

Farquhar was apoplectic with rage. Nobody had told him there were crocodiles in the river. The air was blue with his curses as he ran back along the path and the beach road. When he got back to his quarters, he called for the captain of the guard, and ordered him to organize a work party to dam the river and kill the crocodile. When he returned the next morning, he was glad to see that the men had cornered the beast and speared it to death. But his rage returned when he thought of his beloved terrier in its great jaws.

'String the monster up,' he cried to the assembled party. 'Hang it up on yon great banyan tree aside the fresh water stream.'

The officer in charge of the work party looked at him quizzingly. Farquhar returned his look.

'Ye can just forget about any wangs for thae big bastards,' he said, and stormed off.

8

Major Farquhar built a residency close to the edge of the east beach, a few hundred yards from the river. It was a humble affair with a bamboo frame, an attap roof and matting sides, although it was raised upon high pillars of brick, and contained an office, a bedroom, and a strong room with a military guard. Farquhar's residency stood at the bottom of High Street, the road of beaten earth and sand that Lieutenant Ralfe had laid out between the shore and the foot of Bukit Larangan, on the eastern[6] side of the river.

As chief engineer, Ralfe continued to work like a man possessed. He remained in charge of the gun emplacements, the guards and the sentries, but he also supervised the laying out of the streets and the building of warehouses and temporary government offices. He constructed a masonry reservoir at the western end of Hill Street, which he had laid to make a T-junction with High Street, where it met the river at the foot of Bukit Larangan. A pipe ran out from the reservoir into the river, so that boats from the ships in the harbour could fill their empty barrels with fresh water. The reservoir was served by an aqueduct that Ralfe had built around the back of Bukit Larangan, which was fed by the stream that ran down from its summit, where the wives and concubines of the ancient rajahs of Singapura had bathed.

* * *

Mr Samuel Garland, the acting first assistant, had his work cut out for him. He was in charge of the commissariat, which provided the rations for the troops, and the Company's warehouse, where its trading goods were stored. When the flotilla had first arrived, he had been forced to have most of the supplies from the *Ganges* unloaded on the beach, so that the ship could be winched into the shelter of the river, where it served as temporary commissariat and Company warehouse. But the flour had spoiled in the sun and rain, the rice and dahl had to be stored in a temporary shed, and most of the barrels had spilt their contents onto the beach. Even when everything was loaded back on board the *Ganges*, confusion reigned. The sergeant responsible for collecting and distributing the supplies to the soldiers could not read, and Garland had no weights or measures to record his inventory or estimate his disbursements, even though he was supposed to account to Bencoolen for every item. Soldiers who went directly to draw their stores from the deep holds of the ship created havoc as they spilt vinegar, oil and tamarind, which ran into the sugar, biscuits and tobacco.

Things began to improve when the stores were finally transported from the *Ganges* to the commissariat storehouse and general warehouse that had been built next to the residency, and finally, one day in late March, the Company's goods were put on display for the merchants who had come to Singapore from Malacca, Penang and the neighbouring islands. The trade goods had been rushed down from Penang with the flotilla, and they were a sorry sight: a load of old and rusted iron, leaking barrels of pitch and paint, bails of cotton goods half-eaten by cockroaches and damp and moldy piles of sail canvas. Not the most auspicious start to the greatest emporium of the east, thought Garland to himself.

The merchants and the market traders from the bazaar on the plain wandered through the warehouse all morning. Most wandered right out again, some shaking their heads in disbelief. But around one o'clock Mr Garland had an offer. He was not very happy about it, however, and went off to ask Major Farquhar his advice, leaving the writer in charge of the store. He was not concerned about possible theft. 'Who is going to steal this stuff?' he thought to himself.

'Major Farquhar, sir, I've got a Chinaman named Keat says he wants to buy two hundred and fifty hundredweight of that old iron. I'll be glad to be rid of it, but he's asking for three months credit.'

'I dinna think that's such a good idea, do you, Mr Garland? Remembering as how ye'll hae to answer to Raffles' secretary when he comes back to take on your job.'

'I know,' Garland replied, 'but there's an older Chinese merchant who looks very respectable and says he'll stand surety for Keat, name of Tan Che Sang.'

'Tan Che Sang, you say,' Farquhar exclaimed, 'well that's a different matter altogether! I kent the auld fella back in Malacca, and hoped he would come down. Ye can trust him all right; he'll be good for the loan and a lot more. I'll come back with ye and say hullo.'

As they entered the warehouse, a Chinese merchant in a long black gown shuffled towards them, his hands folded into his sleeves. His black hair was flecked with grey, and drawn back tightly into his queue, which stretched down the length of his back. He was in his late fifties, and his body was bent, but he held his head high and proud, and his dark eyes flashed with warm recognition. He bowed to Major Farquhar, who greeted him warmly, and the two men discussed the prospects for the new settlement. Tan Che Sang joked that Raffles would need to do a lot better than these leftovers from Penang to start a commercial trading centre to rival Malacca and Batavia. Farquhar replied that many Chinese merchants had already come down from Malacca and were beginning to fill their own temporary godowns, and that he was expecting private European merchants and agents for some of the British and Indian companies soon. Tan Che Sang told Farquhar that he was setting up his own and was planning to act as a consignment agent for the junks that would come down from China in the new year on the northeast monsoon. Both men were pleased at what they heard.

* * *

Tan Che Sang was born in Canton,[xviii] the capital of the southern Chinese province of Guangdong, in 1763. He left home at the age of fifteen, and made his fortune trading in Riau, Penang, and then Malacca, during the period that Farquhar was resident there. When he heard that Farquhar had been appointed resident of the new British factory at Singapore, he had sold his godown in Malacca, and arranged for most of his goods to be shipped down to Singapore. When he set sail from Singapore, he shared a berth with Lim Guan Chye, another Malacca merchant who had sold up and shipped his goods south.

Lim Guan Chye was a wealthy Hokkien merchant who had taken a Malay bride. He was a Peranakan or Straits Chinese, a member of the Chinese community that had been in Malaya since the fifteenth century, and which was well integrated with Malay society. [7] The Peranakans maintained the dress and beliefs of traditional Chinese, but absorbed many aspects of Malay culture. They spoke a distinctive Peranakan patois, which was a mixture of Hokkien, Malay, and a smattering of English words drawn from business and commerce. They also developed a distinctive cuisine, which combined Chinese ingredients such as rice, noodles, and stir-fried dishes with Malay staples such as coconut milk, green chillies, lime and lemon grass. Given their established links with the Malay community and the good relations they had developed with the British in Malacca and Penang, they were ideally situated to mediate commercial relations between the Chinese, British and

---

xviii Guangzhou.

Malay communities in Singapore, and many seized the opportunity to reestablish themselves in the new free port governed by the former Rajah of Malacca, whose generosity and fairness were legendary. Many other Peranakans followed Tan Che Sang down from Malacca to Singapore, dodging the gunboat that the Dutch authorities had stationed in the Malacca Strait to discourage immigration.

On the same boat on which Tan Che Sang and Lim Guan Chye travelled was Tan Hong Chuan, another Hokkien born in Malacca. Hong Chuan's parents had emigrated from China at the beginning of the century, but both had died of smallpox when the boy was only eight years old. A local Chinese merchant had let him work in his shop-house, and allowed him to sleep in the storehouse at the back of the shop. With the little money he had saved, he had set himself up at age fifteen as a hawker of poultry, fruit and vegetables; now at age twenty, he had his own roadside stall, which was doing good business. From an early age he had recognized Malaya as a land of great opportunity, where a clever and hard-working man like himself might make a lot of money. Having heard the stories about the thriving new settlement at Singapore, he had decided that this was the place he ought to be. He sold off his remaining stock, packed up his street-hawking pole and baskets, and bought himself passage to Singapore.

The boat on which the three men had travelled managed to elude the Dutch gunboat, and they reached Singapore in safety. Others were not so lucky. A party of forty Malaccan Malays in a prahu transporting supplies to Singapore managed to avoid the gunboat, but they were surrounded by pirates in the strait, and slaughtered to the last man. The women and children were taken away and sold in the slave market at Bultmgan in north Borneo.

* * *

It was time, Farquhar decided, to explore Bukit Larangan. He organized a party of Malay men who had come down with him from Malacca, and whom he could trust to do his bidding. He sent a message to the temenggong asking him if he could send some of his followers to clear the trees and undergrowth, and to help his men drag one of the ten-pound guns up the hill. The temenggong politely replied that he regretted that he could not, because his men were afraid of the ghosts that walked upon the hill and beat upon their drums.

When Farquhar heard this, he roared with laughter. 'I wid like tae see these ghosts! I'm no afraid of bogey-men!'

He tried to enlist the orang laut and the local Malay fishermen, including the quiet giant of a man who lived with his Chinese wife in a cottage close by the sepoy cantonment. They all refused. They all feared the ghosts, and the sounds of war and lamentation they said could be heard at night, and sometimes even during the day. Shaking his head, Farquhar ordered his Malacca men to cut through the undergrowth and drag the ten-pounder up the hill. They did not refuse him, but obeyed with great reluctance. About halfway up the hill the advance party came upon an abandoned keramat, and immediately downed their parangs and axes. When Farquhar came up to investigate the delay, they told him they had disturbed a royal tomb. Some said it was the tomb of Iskander Shah, the last rajah of ancient Singapura, and founder of Malacca. This surely proved that ordinary men were forbidden to walk upon the hill, and that an evil fate would befall them if they continued to offend the ghosts of the dead.

Farquhar was patient but persuasive. He promised them that the tomb would be respected and not disturbed, but insisted that they keep clearing the hill. He had them cut a path all the way from the plain to the summit of the hill, where he planned to build a small fort. When the work was completed, he had the gun hauled to the summit, and a flagpole erected. When Lieutenant Ralfe arrived with a party of gunners, he gave orders for the Union Jack to be raised, and the cannon fired twelve times.

'That should scare off any ghosts!' Farquhar declared, satisfied with his day's work. He then instructed Ralfe to begin laying a road from the cantonment to the summit of Bukit Larangan.

The cannon fire seemed to have the desired effect, at least for the moment. The fear of Bukit Larangan was dispelled, and even the orang laut and the local Malay fishermen were sometimes seen to walk upon it. Some brought flowers to the keramat, and decorated it with yellow ribbons, the colour of Malay royalty. But others still maintained that they could sometimes hear the din of ghostly battles, and stayed away.

9

there was!

In late April, Raffles returned to Penang from his mission in
Achin. He was overjoyed to learn that his wife Lady Sophia had
given birth to their second child during his absence, a healthy boy
named Leopold. Raffles received a frosty reception from Colonel
Bannerman, which changed to grovelling accommodation when
Bannerman received Hasting's letter of rebuke a few days later.
Bannerman immediately dispatched two hundred men and sixty
thousand rupees to Singapore, and wrote an abject letter of apology
to the Governor-General. He offered to help Raffles with his venture
in any way possible, to the very best of his ability, given his great
admiration and deep respect for Sir Stamford.

In late May, Raffles set off for Singapore en route to Bencoolen,
with Lady Sophia, baby Leopold, and a party of Chinese, Malay
and Indian immigrants from Penang. He also carried supplies of
timber, bricks, tiles, and building implements. He was eager to see
how his enterprise had progressed, and planned to file a report with
the Governor-General before he departed for Bencoolen.

When they entered the Singapore roads, Raffles looked out
from the foredeck of the *Indiana* and was amazed by the sight
that greeted his eyes. It was beyond even his most optimistic
expectations. The bay with filled with boats—Malay tambang and
Bugis proa, Cochin[xix] topes and Chinese sampans, and square rigged
ships displaying the flags of Britain, France, Germany and the
United States. There was a flurry of activity at the river mouth, and
the Union Jack fluttered over the sepoy cantonment on the plain

---

xix Cochin China, present day Vietnam.

and on top of the hill the temenggong had called Forbidden Hill. How much had changed in three short months! What a great future there was!

Major Farquhar met Raffles and Lady Sophia at the jetty on the east beach. As they walked up between the lines of scarlet-clad sepoys, the Bengal artillery fired a seventeen-gun salute, which was answered by a cannonade from the ships in the harbour.

'Thanks for sending the sepoys,' Farquhar said to Raffles, 'but Dutchy never came, thank God.' [8]

'Dutchy never came, and Lord Hastings has provisionally approved our settlement,' Raffles replied with a smile.'

'Well that's grand news,' said Farquhar.

'So far so good,' Raffles agreed, 'now we wait on the Court of Directors.'

As Farquhar led Raffles and Lady Sophia to his Residence and the soldiers dispersed, the other passengers disembarked on the beach and the eastern shore of the river. A short stout Indian with a brilliant white dhoti wrapped around his waist jumped out of one of the boats and strode through the shallow surf and up the beach. His white teeth sparkled as his lips parted in a huge smile. Naraina Pillai was excited by the great future that lay before him in Singapore, about which Sir Stamford Raffles had assured him repeatedly. He was so enthusiastic that he had persuaded many of his Tamil friends to follow him down from Penang.

Dr William Montgomerie also disembarked that day. A native of Edinburgh, Scotland, he had recently joined the service of the East India Company as a surgeon. He was one of the few persons in Singapore who did not see the extensive jungle as an obstacle or hindrance. As a dedicated horticulturalist and botanist, he saw it as a source of rare specimens and plants for medicines. Raffles had appointed him as medical officer to the new settlement, but had also encouraged his naturalist pursuits.

Impressed as he was, Raffles became quickly convinced that with the rapid expansion of Singapore, more careful planning was required. Over the next few days he had detailed discussions with Farquhar about the future development of the settlement, from the general town plan to the administration of justice. Raffles decreed that except for the temenggong's compound, all the land on the east side of the river up to the fresh water stream, or the Bras Basah[xx] stream as it was now called, was to be reserved for government buildings. He ordered that the native bazaar, which had sprung up on the plain around the mouth of the river close to the resident's compound, was to be removed immediately and situated on the west bank of the river. The Chinese and Malay townships were also to be relocated on the west bank, save for the land at the river-mouth, which was to be reserved for a military fortification. The Chinese were to occupy the west bank of the river south of a point opposite Bukit Larangan; the Malays were to occupy the west bank north of that point. The European town was to be laid out along the edge of the beach east of the Bras Basah stream, with twelve separate allotments to be reserved for the first 'respectable European applicants.' Raffles further instructed Farquhar to build a wooden bridge at the foot of Bukit Larangan to link the Chinese and Malay kampongs[xxi] with the Government quarter and the European town, with a circular road cut in each direction, and to build a bungalow on Bukit Larangan to serve as the new residency. What he did not do was to tell Farquhar how he was to pay for all this, although he did as usual admonish him to keep his expenses to an absolute minimum.

Raffles and Farquhar signed a new agreement with the

---

xx Meaning wet rice, because native traders used to unload their cargoes of wet rice on its banks to dry.
xxi Villages.

temenggong and Sultan Hussein, which specified that the Company's authority would extend from Tanjong Malang in the west to Tanjong Katong in the east, and inland the range of a cannon shot, except for the lodge and istana of the temenggong and Sultan Hussein. Major Farquhar would conduct a bechara court[xxii] at ten o'clock on Monday mornings, with the temenggong and the sultan (or their deputies) in attendance, to hear the reports and complaints of the captains or headmen of the various native populations, and the appeals of their subjects against any perceived injustice.

His business concluded, Raffles left for Bencoolen in June. More than three years would elapse before he returned again.

* * *

Naraina Pillai was less enthused by the success of Singapore. He explored the new 'emporium of the East', but found that it amounted to little more than a collection of bamboo and plank houses and tents scattered haphazardly across the plain, interspersed with gun emplacements, and surrounded by dense jungle. He was hoping to get some support and advice from Sir Stamford, who had persuaded him to come to Singapore, but Raffles had already left. A good many of his Tamil friends had already decided to return to Penang, but Naraina decided to stick it out for a while. He found himself a temporary job as a shroff[xxiii] in the Treasury, checking for counterfeit coins, and asked his departing friends to send down carpenters, cloth merchants and bricklayers. He planned to set up a shop in the bazaar, but it also occurred to him that what they needed most in Singapore was bricks. If the settlement really was

xxii Bechara court or consultation sessions were known as 'rooma bechara' (an early Malay spelling of 'rumah bicara', literally a house or meeting hall for talks or discussions).
xxiii Chief clerk.

going to be a great success, they would need bricks—they would need a great many bricks! If he could build his own kiln on the island, he could produce them at a fraction of what it would cost to transport them from India or Penang—perhaps he might yet make his fortune in Singapore!

Shortly before Raffles had departed he had welcomed two distinguished Arab merchants, Syed Omar Bin Ali Al-Junied and his uncle Syed Mohammed bin Harun Al-Junied, who had taken up residence in Singapore, linking the new port with their extensive commercial networks in Sumatra and Java. Syed Omar was a wealthy merchant from Yemen who had established a successful business at Palembang in Sumatra, where he traded in spices. He was fed up with the heavy duties imposed by the Dutch authorities and their constant interference in his business, so when he heard favourable reports about the free trading conditions at Singapore, he and his uncle had decided to move their operations there. But Syed Omar was more than a successful businessman, he was an acknowledged descendent of the prophet Mohammed. The Malays honoured him with the princely title Pangeran Sherif, whose mission was to spread the Muslim faith in the East.

Major Farquhar leased him a prime piece of land between High Street and the river, where Syed Omar built a substantial wooden house. At the entrance he erected a balei,[xxiv] on a raised platform with a shaded attap roof. There Syed Omar, dressed in flowing white robes and a green turban, would meet with fellow Arabs and advise them in accord with the teachings of the Prophet. Syed Omar also paid for the construction of a mosque in Kampong Malacca, on the opposite side of the Singapore River, the first Muslim place of worship in Singapore, known as Masjid Omar Kampong Melaka.

About a month later, Mr Dunn, a European gardener who had been recommended by Raffles, also arrived in Singapore. He planted

xxiv Meeting place.

clove and nutmeg gardens around the foot of Bukit Larangan, close by High Street and the Christian cemetery, which already had its first sorry inhabitants, who had been taken by dysentery and fever. Along the eastern shore near the mouth of the river, Rajah Hadjee planted angsana trees, which he had brought down from Tanjong Kling in Malacca. When they grew to their full height, their leaves provided a rich golden shade for townspeople taking an evening stroll along the shorefront.

10

Raffles arrived back in Bencoolen in July. He and Sophia were overjoyed when they were reunited with their daughter Charlotte, now eighteen months old. They were also pleased to discover that the shrubs and trees that Raffles had planted around Government House were now in full bloom—tall casuarinas waved in the sea breeze above the nutmeg, clove, cocoa and cassia plants that surrounded the building.

Bencoolen, however, was a disappointment after the excitement of Singapore. Raffles was chaffing for news of the Company's response to his founding of the settlement, but he knew it might take months or even years before they reached their final decision. Life improved for Raffles and Sophia when they built a bungalow at Pematang Balam, a hillside retreat about thirty miles north of Government House. It offered refuge from the sickness and disease that seemed to plague the populated areas around Government House and Fort Marlborough, and gave them some quiet time for family life. A wide, covered verandah ran all the way round the bungalow, and captured the early evening breezes. Raffles built an aviary, and continued to add to his collection of plant specimens and local animals. Within a short period of time the house was home to a veritable menagerie, including two tame tiger cubs, which the children loved. They called the bungalow the 'Hill of Mists', after the name of the hill on which it was built. They were to have many days and nights of happiness there, but also days of darkness and despair.

* * *

Later that month Raffles and Sophia set off on an expedition into the Pasemah highlands, accompanied by the botanist Dr Joseph Arnold and a party of local Malays and Chinese coolies. The jungle was teeming with life. They saw mouse deer and wild boar, and signs of elephant and tiger. They heard monkeys screeching by day and owls hooting by night, while lizards and butterflies vied to display the most exotic varieties of colour. One day, as they forced their way though high ferns and stepped into a clearing, they came across what they all thought was the most beautiful flower they had seen in their lives, and certainly one of the largest. Raffles, Sophia and Dr Arnold stood in hushed awe before the spectacular cabbage-like blossom, with its bright red, yellow and purple petals. It was almost three feet across, a giant parasite attached to the lower stem and roots of a cissus vine.

'A magnificent specimen,' Dr Arnold cried out, 'a new species. This will make you famous, Raffles! I'll make you famous–I'm going to call it *Rafflesia*!'

They all laughed, but Raffles noticed the dark looks of the Malays, who would not go near the flower. He asked one of them what was the matter, and the man replied that the flower was an evil thing that brought sickness and death. When they stepped forward to get a closer look, they understood why. They almost gagged on the sickly putrid smell that assaulted their nostrils. The beautiful plant smelt like carrion, and its sack was thick with blue bottle flies.

'What do you call that plant?' Raffles asked the man, but he would not reply.

Raffles snapped at him, demanding an answer.

In a whisper, the Malay reluctantly replied, 'The devil's betel-box.'

Raffles shivered involuntarily, and Sophia noticed.

'What wrong, Stamford?'

'Years ago, when I was leaving London for Penang, my mother warned me to be careful, and to remember what the black Jamaican midwife who birthed me aboard the *Anna* had said to her. She said that slaves would bless me, but that I must beware of the devil's flower.'

'But it's just superstitious nonsense,' he said dismissively. 'Let's move on.'

A few days later he had cause to eat his words. As they exited the jungle one morning and came upon the coast, they stopped and picnicked on the beach for lunch. The sun shone hot and strong in a cloudless blue sky. Later in the afternoon Dr Arnold collapsed from sunstroke, and became delirious. They carried him on a litter back to Bencoolen, but as they came within sight of Fort Marlborough, Dr Arnold breathed his last. [9]

* * *

Badang bin Aman lay awake beside Moon Ling. He could not sleep. He had not slept for the past few days. He was uneasy in his soul.

He had no special reason to be concerned. Moon Ling had recently given birth to a second baby boy, who lay beside them on the bed. He had a ready market for as much fish as he could catch, and his carved birds and animals seemed to be popular with some of the merchants, who bought them for their wives, mistresses and concubines. He was a little uneasy about the speed with which the new settlement had grown, and how the sprawl of tents and huts drew closer and closer to his own once isolated cottage. But that was the way of the world and the will of God he supposed.

But still he could not sleep. He raised himself from the bed and walked out into the dark night, illuminated only by the thin moonlight that bled through the low grey clouds. Then he heard the singing. It was very faint at first, as if it came from far off in the dark depths of the jungle, but now seeming closer and closer and increasing in sweet and mysterious intensity. It sounded like children singing, but a song so sad and mournful that it seemed to penetrate the very depths of his soul. Enchanted by the melancholic beauty of the singing, he found himself drawn to it as he walked slowly up the beach, and arrived at the foot of the Bukit Larangan.

He stopped dead in his tracks. He could not go on. It was forbidden. He had never ventured up the hill, for he had heard the ghostly sounds of battle on stormy nights when the black wind roared through the palm trees. But now he could not stop himself. The mournful singing drew him on and on, as he made his way up the rough path that the Malacca men had cut. The path was steep in places, but he felt as if he was walking on air—as if he was walking in a dream.

He came upon the keramat, the royal tomb. He had never visited the place, but knew what it was. The tomb was decked with yellow flowers and ribbons that Muslim women had placed upon it. Beyond the tomb he could dimly see the dark entrance to a massive cave cut into the sheer rock. The singing had suddenly stopped, and an eerie silence descended like a gloom upon the place. Badang stood in the darkness, frozen in terror.

And then he saw them emerge from the trees and thickets. A long procession of men, women and children walked across the clearing, past the keramat and into the black depths of the cave. Badang stepped back into the darkness, afraid that they might see him, but none of them looked his way. They stared straight ahead, their eyes as empty as the eyes of the dead. Most of the women and children wore everyday clothes, baju kurung and sarongs, but the men were dressed for war. They wore body armour and carried swords and spears and bows and arrows, and all displayed their cherished krisses upon their persons. Many had dreadful wounds on their heads and bodies, blood red against their pale white skin. Some even carried their heads in their arms, a ghastly sight that made his blood run cold. The procession passed in silence before him, seemingly oblivious to his presence. Then, at the very last minute, a giant of a man, with a massive chest and bearing a great war-sword, turned and looked directly at him. The warrior raised his arm in a gesture of farewell, and then disappeared with the others into the cave.

Badang emerged from his place of hiding and followed them to the entrance of the cave. He could not help himself—he had to discover who they were and where they were going. But as he approached, he found there was no cave, only a mass of solid black rock. He reached out and traced every inch of the rock with his trembling hands, but there was no opening, no crack, not even the smallest fissure. He stood there amazed, and his head began to spin. Bright lights and strange images flashed and danced before his eyes, and he fell to the ground in a swoon.

* * *

When Badang awoke, it was pitch black. He raised himself from the ground, and peered into the darkness, but saw nothing. He stumbled across the clearing, feeling his way around the keramat, and made his way back down the path, supporting himself on the small trees and shrubs that lined the way.

Then he realized to his great surprise that the sun was shining strong on his face, and he heard Moon Ling calling his name.

'Where have you been?' she cried. 'We have been searching all morning.'

Then Badang bin Aman realized he was blind. 'I was lost,' he replied, 'but now I am found.'

Badang bin Aman fished no more. No longer did his hands

carve boats and birds out of the wood of the trees. One day when his son was sick with fever, when the Indian doctor said that death was near, he sat before the boy and placed his hands on his fevered brow. In a few hours the boy's fever broke, and he recovered fully some days later. Word of this miracle spread quickly, and many came to have Badang bin Aman lay his healing hands upon them. Mainly the Malay fishing families, but also some of the Chinese, and even the occasional soldier or sailor afflicted with beriberi or snakebite. He did not manage to save them all, but many came to believe in his healing powers, although they were also afraid of him. For Badang bin Aman had troubled visions, which he would share with all those who would listen to him. He talked of a great white city of stone, with massive towers reaching up to the heavens, and giant silver birds that soared across the sky. They thought he was a little mad, although no one told him so.

One day he rose early, and despite his blindness, managed to find his old fishing boat and pushed it out to sea. He was never seen again, and no trace was ever found of his craft. When Moon Ling awoke that morning, she knew that he was gone for good. She took her children down to the joss house she had set up in honour of Ma Cho Po, protector of travellers and mariners. She placed an offering in memory of her husband, of their life together, and of the day they had escaped death on Pulau Belakang Mati.

PART TWO

THE MEETING

1820-1823

1

1820

One early morning in February, Major Farquhar heard shouting outside and looked up from his papers. Lieutenant Ralfe came running up the residency steps and stopped in the doorway.

'Better come quick, Major!' he exclaimed. 'Looks like trouble. There's near a hundred prahu just entered the bay, and they're heavily armed. Pirates, if I'm not mistaken.'

The major responded immediately. 'Call out the guard, Lieutenant Ralfe, and have your men man their guns. Sergeant Dow, get the civilians off the plain and behind the sepoy lines–we don't want them between the pirates and our guns.' Farquhar strapped on his sword, and then snatched up his telescope and pistol. He followed Lieutenant Ralfe out of the residency and down to the jetty on the beach.

'I've already called the men out, sir,' said Lieutenant Ralfe, 'and they're ready to fire on your orders.'

'Good man,' said Farquhar, looking through his telescope at the approaching prahus. He could see that the lead boats sported long brass cannon on their prows. The men on board were dressed in bright costumes and armour and were armed to the teeth, with spears, swords, bows and muskets. He took a deep breath. He had expected the Dutch might turn up one day, but had not thought that pirates would have dared a direct attack on the settlement. He would teach them a lesson they would never forget, but he would lose good men in doing so. You left at the right time, Sir Stamford, he thought to himself, as he issued orders for the disposition of the troops.

'Load with shot while they're still far out and try and sink them before they get close, then grape and canister when they come into the shallows. They winna get past the sandbar, so we'll gie it to them as they wade in through the surf. On my command!'

Then he noticed that one of the prahus had separated itself from the rest and was making its way toward the jetty. The boat was ornately decorated, with bright flags fluttering in the light morning breeze. One of the flags was the yellow flag of royalty, and the other a white flag of truce.

'Tell the men to hold their fire and wait for my command,' Farquhar ordered, 'but be ready for anything. This could be a trick!'

The royal prahu anchored a few hundred yards from the landing site, and a man and two women took their places in a tambang,[xxv] which the crew rowed to the shore. A tall, bronzed warrior-chief stepped out and onto the jetty, and raised his arm in salute to Major Farquhar.

'I am Arong Bilawa, a Bugis prince of the Riau islands,' he said in Malay. 'We have been fighting the Dutch. They have killed my brother, and they tried to kill me, because we spoke against Tengku Abdul Rahman, who then accused us of treason. We come in peace to you with our families. We wish to make this island our home and place of trade, under your protection, if it is your will.' He then brought his wife and daughter out of the tambang and introduced them to Major Farquhar. They flashed their white teeth and dark eyes as they acknowledged him.

'You are most welcome,' Farquhar replied, greatly relieved. 'Singapore is an open port, and you are welcome to trade here as long as you wish. You will receive the protection of His Majesty's

---

xxv Small wooden craft with a pitched roof and benched seats.

Government, and you need have nothing to fear from the Dutch.'

Brave words, thought Farquhar to himself, but the right ones. The Bugis dominated much of the trade in the Eastern Archipelago, so to have them settle in Singapore would do wonders for the local commerce. And one in the eye for the Dutch, without even a whiff of 'interference'! Farquhar ordered the soldiers to stand down, and instructed the Bugis chief to settle his followers at the end of Kampong Glam, just beyond the point where Sultan Hussein was building his istana, on the bank of the Rochor River. He walked back to the residency with a spring in his step. What had threatened to be a disaster had turned into a godsend. The Bugis trade! Wait till he told Raffles!

* * *

And still they came: Malays from Malacca, Riau, and Sumatra, and Bugis, Indians, Arabs, Jews, Europeans and Eurasians. February also saw the arrival of Aristarchus Moses, an Armenian merchant from Brunei, the first of the small but prosperous Armenian community that came to establish itself in Singapore. But most of all the Chinese—the Peranakans from Malacca and Penang, the merchants and coolies[xxvi] from the archipelago and mainland China, all seeking their fortune. And whatever deity or deities they professed to worship as Muslim, Christian, or Buddhist, they all laboured in the service of Mammon. Money! You could almost smell it in the humid air, thought Farquhar.

The reasons for the success of the settlement were simple enough. The established traders in the region immediately recognized the advantages of Singapore as a place of business. It was ideally situated for both the local trade of the archipelago and the shipping routes to India and China. It offered freedom of trade and law and

xxvi Labourers.

order, backed by the Company and the British Crown. Singapore quickly captured much of the trade of the Riau islands, the previous centre of operations for Bugis and Sumatra merchants, and soon surpassed both Malacca and Penang in terms of the tonnage that passed through her harbour.

Singapore was especially attractive to the Nanyang[xxvii] Chinese, those traders, farmers, miners and labourers who had left their native land—despite the official Chinese ban on emigration and overseas trade—and settled in the 'southern ocean' of Southeast Asia, seeking escape from poverty, famine and political upheaval in their homeland. They congregated in various ports and cities in the archipelago, but found that none were ideal, and most were subject to Dutch interference, arbitrary fees and often blatant discrimination. When they heard that Singapore was established as a free port, and governed by Tuan Farquhar, whose reputation for honesty and fair dealing was well known throughout the region, they simply packed up their businesses and moved.

And yet, Farquhar recalled, as he reflected on the dramatic success of the settlement, he had just received a letter from the Governor-General of India, warning him to keep expenses to a bare minimum, and cautioning him to discourage immigration to what might prove to be nothing more than a temporary military post. Too late for that, Farquhar thought. He had recently authorized a major program of public construction, as per Raffles' instructions, to include a courthouse, jailhouse, hospital, and government offices, a network of solid roads, and a bridge linking the west and east banks of the river. Farquhar knew he had to do this in order to assure the merchants and traders that the Company was committed to a permanent settlement (even if Farquhar was not so sure that it was). Yet Raffles had not provided any additional financial support, so he would have to find the money himself, by the only way he

---

xxvii Meaning 'southern ocean' (Southeast Asia).

knew. He would raise revenue by the sale of tax-farms[xxviii] for opium, gambling and arrack,[xxix] as he had done with great success in Malacca. He knew Raffles would not like this one little bit; oh no, not one little bit! Raffles would consider it immoral and exploitive. Which it was, Farquhar granted, but it would bring in much-needed revenue.

If only those rich wigs in Leadenhall Street could see the wisdom of even a wee investment, Farquhar thought to himself. They'll take all the profit if we make a success of it, and none of the blame if we don't. But the thing was going too well to fail now, and he would do his level best to see it through.

The temenggong and Sultan Hussein were rather less optimistic, and one day in January both had come to see Farquhar, accompanied by the Capitan China who represented the owners of the pepper and gambier plantations in the interior of the island. They had heard rumours that the Company was going to recall Sir Stamford Raffles and abandon the settlement to placate the Dutch authorities. Farquhar did his best to dispel these rumours, and they cautiously accepted his reassurances. But what convinced them most was the arrival of the first junks from China in February, on the tail end of the northeast monsoon. Soon they were unloading their commercial and human cargoes: tea, silk, spices, porcelain, a few rich merchants, and dozens of indentured servants and coolies seeking their fortune. The temenggong and Sultan Hussein took this as a sure sign of a secure commercial future, from which they would surely profit handsomely.

On board one of the junks were Lee Yip Lee and Ho Chew

---

xxviii Monopoly licenses for the sale of opium and arrack, and for running gambling houses, which were sold at public auction, mainly to the Chinese.

xxix A distilled drink that could be sold to Muslim Malays, since it technically did not violate the prohibition against alcohol, being distilled from coconut flowers rather than grain or fruit.

Teck, two Hokkien peasants from the coastal region of Fukien province in southern China, who had become destitute when they could no longer pay the rent on their small farms. Standing on the deck with the others, Lee looked out over the bay, to the collection of huts, houses and godowns scattered around the river mouth. It did not look like much. Would life in the Nanyang be as glorious as the broker had promised?

Like many of the other coolies who had set out from the southern port of Amoy, Lee had been too poor to pay for his passage, and had travelled on a 'credit ticket', for which he owed a year's labour to the broker. A few had managed to pay their own way and were not indentured, and some who had not believed the broker's stories of the fortunes to be made had been kidnapped by gangsters, and were locked up in the holds of the junk. All the travellers on deck were men, who hoped to save up enough money to be able to return to their home provinces and arrange a good marriage. They looked forward to having sons who would be filial while they lived and mourn them when they died. In the holds were a few young women, none of whom had come willingly. They would all be sold as virtual slaves to the brothels, opium dens, and arrack houses that were developing to cater to the needs of the rapidly growing population of the new port.

The junk dropped anchor, and sat in the bay for hours, amidst the native prahus and square-rigged merchant ships. A dark rumour began to circulate among the men. Some said that those on 'credit' tickets would not be given work in Singapore, but would be shipped out to the tin mines on the Malayan mainland or to the tapioca plantations in Sumatra. Lee, Ho and some other coolies from Fukien made a pact to resist the brokers if the rumour turned out to be true: they would jump overboard and swim to shore. They hoped they would be able to find work on their own, and they hoped there were no sharks in the bay! They sat waiting on deck for most of the day, as the hot sun blazed down upon them, and pondered their fate. In the early evening two Chinese men boarded the junk from an Indian lighter, and talked with the captain, but then returned to shore without any passengers or cargo.

And nothing happened the following day. They waited on deck with only a small ration of rice and water to sustain them. One man who had died during the night was dumped overboard without ceremony, as had the dozen or so others who had died on the passage from Amoy. At night they slept on deck under the stars, dreaming of the fortunes they would make, or the drudgery and death that might await them in the tin mines–visions of earthly joy and terror that for many were conjured up by the opium that had been distributed with their rice and water.

On the third day the local Chinese agent came on board and the men disembarked to a number of waiting lighters. Lee and Ho were directed to a tongkang, a lighter craft manned by an Indian helmsman. Waiting on board was another Hokkien, the headman of a gambier plantation in the interior of the island, about a mile from the shore. He explained that they would be employed for one year, and would be provided with food, shelter, and clothing. During that time their labour would pay off the price of their ticket. After that they would be free to follow their own fortunes.

As the tongkang made its way up the Singapore River, Lee's heart leapt at the sight of the thriving bazaar and the construction along the riverbank. This was surely the beginning of a great thing, and a new beginning for him. He would work hard and stay out of trouble, and try to save a little money to start his own business, even if it was only hawking or farming. There was obviously going to be plenty of work available for years to come, and whatever work he got was vastly better than seeking out an existence by beggary or worse in his home province of Fukien.

Their craft carried them past a sizeable hill to their right, and followed the river as it snaked through the jungle and mangrove swamps. Eventually they waded ashore at the point where the river mouth disappeared into the jungle, and followed the headman through a jungle path that led to the plantation.

2

Mehmood bin Nadir guided his tongkang back down the river to pick up more coolies from the waiting junks.

Business was good, and would only get better as the settlement expanded. Tuan Farquhar had been right about that, and Mehmood was glad he had stayed on with his wife and son after his service as a lascar with the Company had ended. He had borrowed money to buy his boat from a Tamil Chettiar^{xxx} who had come down from Penang, and would be able to pay it off in no time if business continued as good as it had been these past few months. What great opportunities there were! He would write to his brother and cousins back in India, who eked out their livings as boatmen along the southern Coromandel Coast, as Tuan Farquhar had urged him to do.

* * *

A few days after the junks arrived, Major Farquhar received an envoy from the Dutch authorities on Riau, demanding the surrender of Arong Bilawa, the Bugis prince. Farquhar advised the Dutch envoy that he had granted asylum to Bilawa and his followers, under the protection of the British flag. A year later the Dutch authorities granted Bilawa amnesty, and invited him and his followers to return to the Riau islands, but they were content to remain in Singapore.

Farquhar came to realize why the temenggong and Sultan Hussein were so concerned about the abandonment of Singapore.

---

xxx South Indian trader and moneylender.

They were worried about their loss of revenue from the gifts they received from the ships' captains, an informal levy expected by most of the rajahs in the archipelago, and which they had managed to extract from the captains of the Chinese junks. Farquhar did not ban these gifts, but he was concerned about the reputation of Singapore as a free port, so he instructed his son-in-law, Francis Bernard, the harbour master, to inform the captains that such gifts were entirely voluntary and not required.

Later that week Captain George Ramsey came into the office of the harbour master, accompanied by his young son Adam. Ramsey was the captain of the armed Company schooner the *Fair Maid of London,* whose commission was to bring British trade goods to the merchants of Achin, in the hope of securing their support for British interests in Northern Sumatra. He was a widower from Cornwall whose wife and daughter had died of smallpox the previous year. He had taken his twelve-year-old son Adam—his only surviving child—to sea to teach him the basics of shipcraft, and hoped to be able to save enough money to send the boy to naval college in a few years' time. The boy was bright-eyed and eager to learn, with a top of hair as red as his father's.

'Good morning, Mr Bernard,' said Captain Ramsey. 'I'd like you to meet my son Master Adam Ramsey. We'll be off first thing tomorrow morning.'

'Very pleased to meet you, Master Adam.' Bernard shook the boy's hand. 'And how do you like the life at sea.'

'Wonderful, sir,' Adam replied. 'I'm going to be the captain of my own ship one day, just like father. That's if I don't die first eating ships' biscuits with weevils,' he added with a grimace. 'Horrid things!'

'Well, you have to learn to take the rough with the smooth, as any sailor will tell you,' Bernard replied.

At that moment Major Farquhar entered.

'Ah, Captain Ramsey,' he said, 'I thought it was you, and I'm glad I caught you. We seem to be in need of your services. We have a consignment of silver bullion sent down from Penang and due to be shipped to Bencoolen to pay the troops and the local rajahs. The *Marie Clare* was supposed to be taking it, but she's no come in yet, and I need tae get it out right away.'

'Not a problem,' said Captain Ramsey. 'I'll come back this afternoon and arrange for it to be taken aboard the *Fair Maid of London*–so long as I have your written authority for the diversion.'

After Farquhar promised him he would have it right away, Captain Ramsey introduced Adam.

While the three men talked and joked with the boy, the Malay messenger who had brought requests for petitions to be heard at the next bechara court slipped out of the room. His bare feet made no sound and he left as quietly as he had come in. Nobody paid him any attention as he made his way out of the residency and walked along the beach to where another Malay sat waiting under the great banyan tree by the Bras Basah stream. After a brief conversation, the man got up and the messenger followed him along the beach to the sultan's compound in Kampong Glam. They both knew they would be well paid for this information by the sultan, who would in turn be well paid by one of the pirate captains who plagued the waters of the Malay Archipelago.

As Major Farquhar was leaving the harbour master's office, his aide-de-camp met him at the top of the stairs.

'*Marie Claire* been sighted in the roads, sir,' he informed Major Farquhar.

'No need to bother about the Bencoolen silver then,' Farquhar said, turning back to Captain Ramsey and Francis Bernard. 'Enjoy your voyage, Master Adam!'

When he returned to the residency, Farquhar found a familiar figure waiting in his office. It was Captain James Pearl of the

Indiana, the ship that had borne him and Raffles to Singapore just over a year before.

'Good morning, Captain Pearl,' he said, and the two men shook hands. 'What brings you back to Singapore?'

'Oh, business as usual,' Pearl replied, 'I've brought a cargo of rice and tin, and I'm taking a load of sugar and sapang wood to Bencoolen. My, but this place is booming! I've been taking a look around, and I'm thinking of settling down here myself after I've made a bit more money trading.'

'I suppose you'll be looking for a piece of land on the eastern bank of the river, like a' body else?' said Farquhar.

'Well no, actually,' said Captain Pearl. 'I'm been thinking of going into the plantation business. Always fancied myself as a farmer, although I never fancied I'd do it out here. As I said, I've been looking around, and I'd like to build a house on the hill opposite Bukit Larangan on the other side of the river.'

'But there's already some Chinese on that hill, gambier and pepper farmers,' Farquhar replied. 'Raffles wants to keep the Chinese there, and the Europeans on the east beach. Although God knows none of them want to build their godowns there.'

'I'm sure he won't mind, Major, Stamford and I are good friends. I'll have to buy out the Chinese of course, which is why I'll need to keep trading for a year or two. But when I'm finally settled I'll call it Raffles Hill, which I'm sure will gratify him.'

'Aye, I'm sure it will,' Farquhar replied, 'but you should probably write and tell him what you plan to do, just in case. You'll also need to ask permission from the temenggong, for the hill you speak of is just beyond the boundary that we agreed with him.'

'But man it's good to see you, James,' said Farquhar, dropping the formality. 'Will you join me for tiffin?'[xxxi]

'I'll write to Stamford, William, and I'd be happy to join you

---

xxxi Indian name for lunch or any light meal.

for tiffin. I'll bring along a little something I brought from Calcutta. It will help to wash it down.'

* * *

In March, Raffles and Sophia welcomed to Bencoolen his sister Mary Anne, whom he had brought out with her new husband, Captain William Flint, and their baby, Charles. The Flints did not stay long, because Raffles had decided to appoint William as harbour master at Singapore. They left at the end of March, much to Sophia's disappointment. They were accompanied by Captain Thomas Otho Travers, Raffles' long-time friend and aide-de-camp, whom Raffles had instructed to take over from Major Farquhar as resident at Singapore.

3

One morning in early April, Cathcart Methven, a captain in the Company's service, entered Farquhar's office and introduced himself. Captain Methven was thirty-two years old, the son of a magistrate from St. Andrews in Scotland, who had joined the Company's service as a cadet at the age of sixteen. Major Farquhar asked him jokingly if he fancied a game of golf on their very sandy links, to which Captain Methven replied that he preferred horse racing. Pity the poor horse, thought Farquhar, taking in the size and girth of the man, as he strutted about in his scarlet uniform, looking to all the world like a giant turkey-cock.

Methven informed Farquhar that he had accumulated some money during his time in India, and planned to use it to establish himself as a merchant. He had written to his commanding officer in India requesting a discharge, which he was sure would be accepted given his exemplary service, something he declined to expand upon.

'I'd be obliged if you could deed me a piece of land so I can set myself up,' he informed Farquhar.

'I can set you up with a piece of land,' Farquhar replied. 'But you must understand it will be subject to the approval of Sir Stamford Raffles, the Lieutenant-Governor of Bencoolen, and ultimately the Court of Directors of the Company.

'That's a risk I'm prepared to take—I'm sure this place will make us all rich!'

'I hope you're right' Farquhar replied. He then led Methven down the steps of the residency to the eastern entrance of the river, where the two men marked out a plot near Ferry Point.

Soon afterwards Captain Methven began the construction of his house and godown. He ferried stones downriver, and brought in boatloads of sand and brick. Carpenters, bricklayers, stonemasons, smiths and an army of labourers worked on it from dawn to dusk. When it was completed six months later, it was larger than any other building in the settlement, including the residency. Methven's massive structure stood like a Martello tower at the mouth of the river, with walls so thick it looked more like a military fortification than a dwelling house and warehouse. The walls were painted white and sparkled in the morning sunshine, and the green verandah and Venetian shutters gave it a distinctly Italianate appearance. With its own pier built out over the river, where lighters and sampans could unload their goods from the ships in the roads, it looked not unlike a Venetian Palazzo. Captain Methven was swelled with pride, and fancied he would make a great merchant. While he was building his great house and godown he received word from his commanding officer in India that his request for a discharge had been denied, but it did not bother him. He simply carried on as usual, and wrote a letter of appeal.

Shortly after Captain Methven's arrival Farquhar had the doubtful pleasure of greeting another Scot, John Morgan, who marched into Farquhar's office one day and demanded a good plot of land near the river.[10] Farquhar knew this man was going to be a troublemaker—he could feel it in his bones. But he assigned Morgan a plot of land between High Street and the river, about halfway between the residency and Hill Street, where he built a wooden bungalow.

Morgan would prove to be a troublemaker, but he was no fool, and he had a good head for business. While most of the other European merchants used Chinese—and especially those Peranakans who spoke a patois of Hokkien and Malay—as compradors[xxxii] in their relations with local traders from the archipelago, Morgan thought he might improve his commercial position by taking lessons in Malay, and accordingly contracted with Abdullah bin Abdul Kadir [11], known locally as 'Munshi,'[xxxiii] to teach him the language. He progressed well, having, Abdullah said, a natural gift for languages.

---

xxxii   Native intermediaries or agents.
xxxiii   Malay for 'teacher of language'.

4

Later that month, Farquhar received two new visitors at the residency, who followed each other in quick succession. Both had come from Bencoolen. One was Captain Robert Otho Travers, who had the audacity to inform Farquhar that he could now take his well-deserved leave and return to Scotland, since Sir Stamford Raffles had sent him to take over his duties as Resident of Singapore. Major Farquhar told Travers he would do no such thing. He had just received news that the Marquis of Hastings had appointed him to the rank of colonel for his service as resident and military commandant of Singapore, and he had no intention in resigning his position until he had seen the settlement properly established. Although Travers carried a letter of authorization from Raffles, he did not make an issue of it, and took ship for India shortly after.

The other visitor was not so easy to deal with, nor so easily to be rid of. This was Captain William Flint,[12] who bore a letter from Raffles confirming his official appointment as Harbour Master of Singapore. Farquhar had met Flint nine years before, during Lord Hasting's campaign that liberated Java from the Dutch. He did not like the man. Flint was tall and fat, with a round baby face and a small, very thin mouth, which gave the impression that he was continually sulking—as he probably was, thought Farquhar. Flint had long sideburns that were carefully curled down the sides of his face, which made him look like he had just left his barber. He was dressed in full naval uniform, although he had resigned his commission in the navy. Another pompous fool, thought Farquhar.

But he was also Raffles' brother-in-law. Flint had married

Raffles' favourite sister, Mary Anne, and she and their son, Charles, had come to join him in Singapore, so Farquhar could not ignore this appointment. His own son-in-law, Francis Bernard, was presently acting harbour master, but Raffles had made it clear the previous year that his appointment was only temporary. Ah well, thought Farquhar, I'll just have to find something else for Francis to do.

Captain Flint demanded he be given the piece of land just behind the battery at South Point on the western bank of the river, between the river and the sea, where he planned to build a house and office from which to direct harbour operations. Aye, thought Farquhar, Raffles has picked you the best piece of land on the western bank of the river, in one of the few areas that were not flooded at high tide; the Chinese had of course taken the rest. One of these days he was going to tell these stuck-up captains what to do with their demands, but he held his tongue, and consoled himself with the thought that Methven would be driven to distraction by Flint's house on the other side of the river, which was sure to be at least as grand as his own.

* * *

Lee Yip Lee lay exhausted on the packed earth floor of the bamboo and attap hut that he shared with the other plantation workers. They had been working since the day they had landed, and all for three dollars a month to pay their passage fee. Picking and beating the gambier was backbreaking work, and Lee Yip's muscles were aching. He was constantly hungry. They were only given enough to keep them alive and fit enough to work; porridge in the morning and some rice at night, with a few vegetables or bits of fish if they were lucky. So much for the rich life in Singapore!

Lee was tempted to accept the opium that the headman of his plantation offered them on credit, which he said would help to ease the physical pain of their labours. But Lee declined, because he knew that if he did that he would be enslaved to the plantation and the opium until the day he died. He was determined to stick it out, but few of his fellow workers were so resolute.

One evening after work the headman came to visit Lee, and spoke to him in Hokkien.

'Good evening, Lee Yip Lee. I have some good news for you. In a few days' time, I will take you to a meeting of the Ghee Hin kongsi.' xxxiv 13

'Where will this meeting take place, and who else will be going?' Lee replied cautiously. He knew of the Ghee Hin, which had branches in his native province of Fukien, and wondered how they had organized so quickly in Singapore.

'It will take place in a secret place in the jungle, and your fellow Hokkiens will join us. Also some Cantonese and Teochow. Our branch was formed by members who journeyed down from Penang when they heard of the foundation of the new settlement.'

'But what about the initiation fee?' Lee replied. He knew the Ghee Hin always charged a fee.

'Don't worry about that,' the headman responded. 'Your fee will be paid by your employer, Tan Chee Soon, who is one of the leaders of the society.'

On credit, of course, Lee thought to himself, but said nothing. He was not sure that he wanted to pledge himself to the Ghee Hin, but he also knew that one day he might need their protection and support, so he agreed to come to the meeting.

'You must not breathe a word of this until you are a member of the Ghee Hin,' the headman warned him sternly. 'Swear it!'

'I swear it,' Lee responded immediately.

The headman then left him and made his approach to other workers, all of who indicated their agreement. Except for Ho Chew Teck, who cursed the society at the first mention of its name.

---

xxxiv Secret Society.

'Phah!' he exclaimed, and spat on the red earth. 'They'll take your money but you'll see nothing for it, like those cheating whores they bring to us. I'm keeping my money. I'm not going to give it to a bunch of gangsters who call themselves the "rise of righteousness". More like the descent of devils, I say!'

He stormed off and went into his hut to smoke an opium pipe. He did not mention that his brother had been a member of the Ghee Hin in Fukien, who had been executed by the authorities after being betrayed by a fellow society member. He saw no need to mention it. He did not care what they thought.

5

George and Adam Ramsey stood on the foredeck of the *Fair Maid of London*. George was showing his son how to calculate longitude using the recently invented marine chronometer.

The voyage had passed uneventfully so far, and they had made good speed until the third day, when the wind had dropped suddenly to a light breeze. They were making slow progress over the glassy sea, as the sun beat down like a great golden furnace in the sky. In the early afternoon a large flotilla appeared off starboard and the lookout shouted down in alarm:

'Ships ahoy! Ships ahoy! Looks like a pirate fleet, Captain!'

Captain Ramsey gave orders to his first officer, Lieutenant Yates, to man the decks and run out the guns, and told the boson, Mr Oates, to let out as much sail as possible, in the hope that the wind would pick up. But it did not. As he looked through his telescope, Captain Ramsey could see the long prahus approaching, driven through the water by banks of oars that rose and fell like the dark wings of so many black birds.

'Papa, papa! Are we going to fight the pirates!' Adam exclaimed beside him. The boy was very excited and trying his best to appear brave, although the slight trembling in his voice betrayed his fear.

'Unless we can get out of here fast, it looks like we are,' his father replied calmly. 'But if it comes to fighting, Adam, I want you go down below and hide in the short cupboard behind my cabin door.'

Adam said nothing in reply.

'Do you understand!' Ramsey exclaimed, in a sharper tone.

'But father,' Adam protested, 'I'm a seaman now, and I can fight.'

'That you are, my dear boy, but this is no fight for you. Your blessed mother would never forgive me if I exposed you to danger. For her sake, Adam, please.'

The mention of his mother moved the boy, and he nodded his agreement. But he could not hide his disappointment at missing the fight, despite his fear.

'Hopefully we can avoid an engagement,' said his father, adopting a lighter tone, when he noticed that one of the boats had pulled out ahead of the main fleet under a white flag of truce.

He called over Mr Oates, who was fluent in Malay, and asked him to determine their business.

'Says they want to sell you a load of pepper and cloves,' Oates reported, after he had exchanged words with the Malay at the head of the boat. 'But don't trust 'em, Captain. They're pirates sure as anything. You can see the bastards peeping out behind the rattan matting, and I can tell by their looks they're not trading men.'

'I agree,' said Captain Ramsey. 'Tell them that we do not wish to have any business with them, and that if they sail away in peace they will come to no harm. But tell them if they come in any closer we will blast them out of the water.'

He then turned to Lieutenant Yates and ordered the gun crews ready to fire at his command. The marines and the sailors who had been issued muskets were ordered to hold their fire until the pirates were in range.

Oates communicated the captain's message to the Malay, and reported back his response.

'They're pirates all right, and they're no pretendin' any more. He says if we hand over the silver bullion they will spare us, otherwise they will add many studs to their blades today.'

'He means the studs they add to their blades for each man they kill,' Oates explained. 'They're Illanun trash, for sure—the worse kind o' pirate.'

'Tell him we have no silver bullion, and that they must retire or we will fire upon them!' shouted Captain Ramsey. 'Men, prepare your stations!'

The moment Oates had communicated this response, the Malay flung away the flag of truce. The other pirates leapt out from their hiding places beneath the rattan, discharging their muskets at the ship. They also managed to get off a shot from the bronze canon that was mounted on their prow, which struck the *Fair Maid of London*, although with insufficient force to do any damage. The pirates manning the gun were immediately cut down by musket fire from the marines and blue jackets,[xxxv] as were most of their comrades in the prahu, which soon ran red with the blood of dead and dying men.

The first victory was theirs, but they knew it was a small thing. The pirate fleet was bearing down upon them rapidly, and the wind was still no more than a light breeze on their hot faces.

From the deck, and without need of his telescope, Captain Ramsey could see the pirate chief on the lead ship urging his men forward with a great two-handed Tampilan sword, which he waved high above his head. He and the other pirates were decked in scarlet robes and chain mail, with bright-feathered headdresses. They were armed with swords, spears, muskets, and bows and arrows, and as Ramsey well knew, each man carried his own kris, which he valued as much as his own life. He suddenly remembered the conversation he had had with Major Farquhar back in Singapore about the silver bound for Bencoolen. But there was no point wondering about that now, with the fight at hand.

---

xxxv Sailors.

'Now, Adam, below!' he snapped to his son, placing his hands on the boy's shoulders and turning him in the direction of the cabin. But before he let him go he held the boy close to his chest, and uttered a silent prayer.

'Prepare to fire!' he ordered, looking back out at the Illanun fleet, which was now closing upon them.

The first volley of shot destroyed two war-prahus, and the second volley of grape blasted life and limbs from the decks of the pirate ships. But then the pirates were in close and under the range of the ship's guns, and returned fire from their prow-mounted cannons. They poured musket fire and shot arrows up to the ship's decks, as they swarmed around the *Fair Maid of London,* and trapped her between their black hulls. The marines and blue jackets kept up a steady fire, killed and wounding many, but already some of the pirates were clambering up the ship's sides.

An arrow struck Lieutenant Yates on the shoulder.

'It's nothing, sir,' he said, snapping off the arrow at the head. But a few minutes later he collapsed on deck from the poison carried on the tip of the arrow, and died of asphyxiation not long afterwards. Although Captain Ramsey and his men fought fiercely, the Illanun pirates were soon scrambling over the ship's sides and swarming over the deck, cutting and hacking their way through the marines and blue jackets. Ramsey engaged one of them, an ugly brute of a man with whirling black tattoos who wielded a curved beheading sword, but a blow from a heavy war-club struck him from behind and sent him sprawling to the deck. By the time two pirates dragged him to his feet it was all over. They had captured his ship, and killed most of the marines and crew. They had spared the native Malay sailors, who they no doubt intended to use or sell as slaves, and Mr Oates, who they may have thought would be useful as an interpreter and informant. They had also spared three of his officers, who were held bound in a small group on the starboard deck. Ramsey struggled helplessly as they tied him to the mizzenmast, binding his neck, chest and legs, but leaving his arms free.

Two of the pirates stood directly before him, looking at him with the scorn of the victor over the easily vanquished. One of them, a tall and tightly muscled figure in a scarlet tunic and headdress decked out with silver and gold, called out orders to the men assembled on deck, which were instantly obeyed. He stood leaning on his two handed Tampilan sword. He was Si Apip Rahman, chief of the sixty-galley squadron of Illanun pirates. He had a cruel face, with a long aquiline nose and sunken cheeks, and he fixed his cold black eyes upon Captain Ramsey. The man next to him was dressed in a similar fashion, although he carried a two-headed axe rather than a sword, which he had taken from the Irish mate of a merchant vessel six months before. He was Sri Hussein, the younger half-brother of Si Apip Rahman. Ramsey thought he had a strangely beautiful face, with deep brown eyes and long flowing brown hair, which tumbled down over his shoulders. His smile was as sweet as that of a young girl, but as deadly as a sea snake. Ramsey guessed that the older pirate was in his early twenties, and the younger in his late teens. He knew he would get no mercy from these men, and prayed that they had not discovered his son below. He did not bother his Maker with a prayer for his own speedy end, for he could tell from their eyes that he would not receive one.

Si Rahman shouted to one of his captains, who brought Oates forward. He had an ugly cut on his right cheek, but otherwise appeared unharmed. Si Rahman questioned him in Malay, and the two men got into a heated argument, which Ramsey feared would have fatal consequences for his first mate. But then they stopped arguing, and Oates came over to him and said:

'He wants to know where the silver is, Captain. I told 'im we ain't carrying any silver, that we only have iron and bricks on board, but he won't listen, sir. Tells me you must know where it's hidden, and you have to tell him quick or he will make you pay for your trickery.'

'Tell him there has been some mistake. We never took on any silver, and we are not hiding any.'

Then, remembering the exchange with Major Farquhar before he left Singapore, he added:

'Tell him we were supposed to take some silver to Bencoolen, but the request was cancelled at the last minute.'

Yet as he said it he realized how implausible it would sound, and how it would only confirm the pirate's suspicions that there was silver on board.

When Oates reported this Si Rahman grew angry, and on his orders the three surviving officers were brought forward, and made to kneel before Captain Ramsey.

'He means to kill them, sir, and slowly, unless you tell 'em where the silver is hidden.'

'Oh God,' Ramsey moaned, shaking his head in denial. 'Tell him for the love of God these men are innocent and there is no silver. Have mercy on them!'

He raised his arms in supplication to the pirate, but his plea was met with a cold black stare from Si Rahman, who seemed to grow angrier by the moment. He nodded curtly to one of his men, who carried a long sword with a curved head—a beheading sword.

But the pirate did not behead the hapless officers. With some help from his companions, he cut off their hands and then their arms. One of the officers, a battle-hardened veteran who had served with Collingwood, maintained an attitude of cold contempt throughout the ordeal, but the two younger men screamed and moaned and begged for mercy.

While the pirates held the bleeding men upright by their heads and shoulders, Oates was made to ask the captain once again where the silver was hidden. But Ramsey said nothing. He knew it was too late to save his men and no use trying to persuade the pirates that they were mistaken about the silver.

6

While the slaughter took place on deck, Adam sat cramped in the cupboard in his father's cabin, holding the door closed by its slatted vents, since the locking mechanism was on the outside. He could hardly breathe in the hot and dusty enclosure, he was dripping with sweat, and he was trying desperately not to sneeze. He had heard the muffled sound of fighting up on deck, and when it subsided he feared that the pirates had overrun the ship. If he had any doubts about that, they were soon dispelled as he heard the clatter of feet on the stairs and the pirates crashing through the door and into the cabin, which they then proceeded to loot—laughing and yelling and smashing whatever they decided was not worth stealing. Adam wanted to leap out of the cupboard and run up on deck to see what had happened to his father, but he was frozen with fear where he sat; they would surely cut him down as soon as he revealed himself. He heard them opening and closing drawers, ransacking his father's trunk. And then one of the pirates flung open the cupboard door and Adam tumbled out. He closed his eyes and waited for death. He prayed that he would meet his mother and father and sister in Heaven.

* * *

The pirate with the beheading sword continued his grisly work. He cut off the officers' feet, and then their legs below the knee. As the three men lay bleeding to death on the deck, the pirate stood astride their mutilated bodies, and with three great blows from his sword he split their sculls and spilled their brains upon the blood slicked boards.

'Please tell 'em something, Captain, or we'll be next,' begged Oates. But Captain Ramsey was already resigned to being next, and said nothing.

Si Rahman then ordered another pirate forward, who drew his kris and began to saw through Ramsey's right forefinger at the first joint. The pain was excruciating, and he almost fainted from it. The pirate then proceeded to saw through all his other fingers at the joints, first on his right hand, and then on his left. Ramsey did not scream, but now and again he let out an involuntary groan of pain, shaking his head vigorously in denial, forestalling the inevitable questions about the silver.

By this point Si Rahman was in a violent rage, pacing up and down the deck in frustration. He signalled the pirate with the kris to continue with the second joints, and Ramsey braced for the pain. But then the younger brother with the beautiful face and soft brown eyes stepped forward and held the man's arm, indicating that he was to discontinue the torture.

What was happening? Ramsey thought. Did this young man have a dram of mercy?

Though the haze of his pain, he saw the younger brother talking to the elder. As he did so, Si Rahman's expression turned from rage to a cruel smile, as Sri Hussein pointed towards the stern of the ship. Si Rahman was nodding to his brother, and Ramsey turned his head to see what had caught their attention. The haze of his pain cleared in an instant, as if caught by a sharp and sudden breeze, when he saw with horror that Adam was being led on deck by a group of pirates. He was discovered!

The boy blanched white when he saw the mutilated bodies of the officers, and his father's amputated fingers.

'I'll be brave, father,' he stammered. 'You can count on me.'

'Don't worry, Adam,' his father responded, his own voice trembling with emotion. 'They won't harm you, they know you'll fetch a good price as a slave. Be brave, and know I love you.'

The pirates dragged the boy to the edge of the deck, where they bound his feet with rope. Then they tied the end of the rope to one of the ship's anchors, which they had cut from its hawsers. Father and son stared in horror when they realized what the pirates intended to do. Adam clenched his teeth in fear and determination, as a yellow trickle of urine ran down his white pantaloons.

'No! No! No!' Ramsey screamed. 'For the love of God, tell him Oates, tell him not the boy. Tell him I'll bring him as much silver as he wants, so long as he spares the boy!'

'He says this is your last chance, Captain. If you don't tell 'im where the silver is, he'll drown the boy!'

'Tell him I swear to God there is no silver. Tell him, man, tell him!'

When Oates translated his response, Si Rahman gave the order and the pirates threw the heavy anchor over the side of the ship. Adam's body was whipped overboard in an instant. A few minutes later he lay drowned at the bottom of the ocean.

Captain Ramsey strained on his ropes like a wild animal, all his senses screaming back to life in his hatred of Si Rahman. His whole universe was reduced to one thing only, his burning desire to kill the man, to rip out his throat with his bare hands. He foamed at the mouth and his eyes bulged red in their sockets, as the blood pumped from his severed fingers onto the deck.

Si Rahman looked him up and down with a cold eye, and then spoke to Oates.

'He says he believes you, Captain,' Oates said, before he was dragged off with the other prisoners. 'God bless you, sir, and poor Adam.'

The pirates were now removing everything worth stealing from the ship, and forcing the prisoners down to their war prahus.

'I'll see you in hell, you bastards,' Captain Ramsey screamed, as the two brothers prepared to climb overboard. But his scream only came out a hoarse whisper, so parched was his throat and mouth. He felt himself slipping into unconsciousness, as hopelessness and misery descended upon him. He grieved for his son and the cruel death he had suffered. The last thing he remembered was the acrid smell of burning timbers, as the pirates torched his ship before they abandoned it.

7

Raffles was overjoyed in May when Sophia gave birth to Stamford Marsden, their second son. He called the child Marco Polo, because he joked that Stamford Marsden would follow in the footsteps of the great explorer. He was disappointed but relieved to hear from Hastings in June that the although the Court of Directors had expressed their displeasure at Raffles for having exceeded his instructions, they were not at this point in time prepared to disavow his actions in Singapore and recall him. However, his spirits were lifted when he received a letter from Farquhar advising him the volume of trade in Singapore already exceeded that of Batavia, and that the Dutch were furious about that!

Then one evening some months later, as he sat on the verandah at the Hill of Mists, he read a dispatch that he had just received from the Chairman of the East India Company, which read:

> I consider the possession of Singapore, and the occupancy of the place, to be very important to the British interests; and I heartily wish that it may be found consistent with the rights of the two nations that Great Britain may keep possession of it. I think it is remarkably well situated to become a commercial emporium of the seas. I have no doubt that it will very soon rise to great magnitude and importance; and if I may be permitted to allude to the conduct of any individual on this subject, I must say that I think the whole of the proceedings of Sir T. S. Raffles must have been marked with great intelligence and great zeal for the interests of his county.

Raffles leapt up and shouted out for joy. When Sophia ran to see what was happening, he lifted her up and danced her though the air, kissing her repeatedly as he gasped out his good news.

'I'm vindicated at last! The Company has approved Singapore! A commercial emporium of the seas, they say!'

'Well done, my love,' Sophia said when he eventually set her down. 'I know how much this means to you. I really do.'

'Let's have a celebration!' Raffles exclaimed. 'Friends, family, animals and guests!'

Sophia's brother, William Hull, and her brother-in-law, Harry Auber, joined them for dinner, along with the children and their nurse, Mrs Grimes. Raffles had recently been presented with an orang utan by one of the local Malay chiefs, and the children delighted in dressing him up. He came to the table dressed in a dinner jacket that Raffles had outgrown, with a top hat perched upon his head. He sat at the end of the table and ate his rice like any Christian gentleman, as William put it.

'The Malays call him a wild man[xxxvi],' said Raffles, 'but I've seen many less civilized gentlemen in my travels. Let's drink a toast to our success.'

Champagne was served to the ladies, gentlemen, the orang utan and the bear cub that the children had raised. The little brown cub, which was seated between Leopold and Charlotte, put down the mango he had been eating and accepted a bowl of champagne with a huge grin.

'Why can't we have some too?' chorused the children, looking on in envy.

'You're too young for human animals,' Sophia responded with a smile.

As they raised their glasses for a toast, their blue mountain

---

xxxvi The word 'orangutan' comes from the Malay words 'orang' (man) and '(h)utan' (forest), literally 'man of the forest'.

parrot croaked out a shrill 'hip, hip, hurray!' and everyone laughed. The two tame tiger cubs padded around the table, trying to see what was going on, then rolled over and wrestled with each other on the floor.

Raffles looked up at the silver stars scattered like hard diamonds against the black velvet sky. He savoured the light evening breeze on his face, as the whirring of the crickets roared in his ears like primeval applause.

'These are magical nights,' he said to Sophia. 'I can't imagine I'd be happier if I were a gentleman at court. We are so lucky. We have three beautiful and healthy children, and family and friends that would be the envy of anyone. We must be the happiest couple in whole wide world.'

Raffles closed his eyes and smiled in contentment, but then his happiness evaporated. He felt suddenly chilled, as if—suddenly remembering the old saying—someone had walked over his grave.

'We should not be so complacent,' he said, suddenly serious. 'Remember what the old Greek said. Call no man happy 'till he's dead.'

'Don't be such a stuffed shirt, Stamford,' Sophia replied. 'In any case, he said call no *man* happy 'till he's dead. He didn't say anything about women!'

Raffles laughed, and his laughter seemed to lift the chill from his heart.

When the food was cleared away and the children sent to bed, Raffles invited William and Harry to join him for brandy and cigars, to discuss the latest developments in Singapore.

The orang utan, which had followed the children to wave them goodnight, sloped back to the table, and took a seat beside them. He reached over and grasped the bottle of brandy, from which he took a hearty swig.

'Well I'll be damned,' said William, handing the hairy gentleman a lit cigar.

The hairy gentleman took the cigar and puffed on it contentedly, as he leaned back in his chair in imitation of his fellows.

Raffles also leaned back in his chair, and reflected once again on his own contentment. Sophia had been right.

Eight months later she gave birth to their second daughter, Ella Sophia. Two boys, two girls, and an orang utan!

8

It was late at night when the plantation headman came for Lee Yip Lee and the others. He led them into the jungle along a roughly cut path, and stopped at a place where two trees had fallen across the track. There he distributed red packets containing their initiation fees and gave them their instructions. Lee looked carefully at his red packet. It reminded him of the red packets that parents gave their children at Chinese New Year, and at birthdays and weddings, to bring them good luck. The packet he held had a more sinister significance, but he still hoped it would bring him luck. They waited for about ten minutes until the other initiates arrived, then the headman handed them over to the brother from the Ghee Hin secret society who emerged suddenly from the gloom of the jungle.

The brother led them the rest of the way along the winding path. The moonlight that had flooded the plantation scarcely penetrated the jungle, but their way was lit by Ghee Hin members who stood with candles at the edges of the path. Lee had the impression of walking though a dark tunnel or cave, the way he imagined the passageways between the ten courts of Hell.[xxxvii] He gave an involuntary shiver, despite the humid heat that rose from the jungle floor, but dismissed the feeling. Something to fear when he was dead, he reflected, but tonight he was very much alive. His senses were alert, having again refused the opium that had been

xxxvii According to Chinese folk religion—and Taoism and Buddhism—the spirits of the dead must make their way through the ten courts of Hell, where they suffer gruesome punishments for their sins on Earth, before receiving final judgment about their form of reincarnation from His Infernal Majesty Lord Zhuan Lun.

offered, and he suddenly noticed that Ho Chew Teck was not with them. His loss, he thought to himself.

Their journey ended in a wide clearing, illuminated by the moon and the light from the candles held high by the society men. At one end of the clearing stood a high wooden altar arrayed with the flags and emblems of the Ghee Hin. Three wooden structures had recently been assembled before the altar. Lee knew they were laid out to represent a walled city, with three gates signifying the Hung Gate, the Hall of Loyalty and Righteousness, and the Hall of the City of Willows. Amid the flickering candlelight, the initiates waited in silence, as the society men placed more flags and emblems around the wooden compound. As the chants of the society men beckoned the spirits of their ancestors to witness the initiation, the master of ceremony sanctified the area in preparation for the rites.

After a long theatrical introduction, during which society members played the parts of the original founders of the first Tiandihui[xxxviii] in Gaoxi, Lee and the other initiates were handed burning joss sticks and led to the Hung Gate. They knelt down with their right arms and shoulders bared and their left trouser bottoms rolled up, symbolizing the union of Heaven, Earth and Man. Like the others, Lee unbraided his queue and let his hair fall loose over his shoulders. He felt a sudden sense of freedom. The braided queue was a mark of submission demanded by the hated Manchu Emperors of China, who had usurped the Middle Kingdom from the Ming dynasty nearly two hundred years before. Lee felt he was now his own man, free to join his brothers in the Ghee Hin.

Then Lee and the other initiates were led before the master of ceremony, an imposing figure in red and golden robes, who asked them some questions in verses, to which they replied in verses they had been taught by the plantation headman. The master of ceremony then proceeded to administer the first of twelve oaths,

---

xxxviii Heaven and Earth Society.

which he intoned in a strong and deep voice:

'The first duty of a brother is to honour his parents. It is forbidden to abuse his brothers and parents, and if he be so dishonourable as to break the law, may he, within a month, be drowned in the ocean, his flesh float upon the surface of the waters, and his bones be buried on the ocean bed.'

Lee and his comrades repeated these oaths. Lee found this easy to do, since the virtue of filial piety had been instilled in him since early childhood. He still revered his father and mother, although they had died some years ago, and remembered his brother and sister back in Fukien. He hoped to be able to send money back to them one day, so they could honour their parents with proper funeral tablets, and one day to save enough money to return home himself. He hoped that the Ghee Hin would provide him with the means and opportunity to do so.

When they had completed their oaths, Lee and the others extinguished their joss sticks in a bowl of water, then vowed on pain of death never to reveal the secrets of the Ghee Hin kongsi. The master of ceremony next introduced them to the society hierarchy: the headman; the deputy and assistant chiefs, who represented the society in its relations with other kongsis and the civil administration; the Red Rod, who was in charge of society discipline; and the White Fan, who was in charge of the Black and White Tiger Generals, who enforced society discipline with their Tiger soldiers. Lee wondered if he would become a tiger soldier—he knew this was one of the surest means of working his way up the society hierarchy. He also knew that this would involve killing and torturing other men, and he was not sure he had the stomach for it. He had been in fights before, and had always come out best, but he had never killed a man, in hot or cold blood. There was only one way to find out.

Lee did not falter as they were led though the Hung Gate into the Hall of Loyalty and Righteousness. As they passed through, the society men patted them on their backs with knives. The master of ceremony then administered another twelve oaths, which began:

'If a brother enters the house of another brother, tea and rice must be served to him. If any brother fails to do so, may he die by losing his blood along the street.

'A brother must not steal another brother's property. If anyone should do so, may he die under millions of knives or be eaten by a tiger as he walks abroad, or bitten by a snake in the water.'

As Lee intoned these oaths, he felt a deep sense of brotherhood with the other initiates and established members of the society—a sense of something greater than themselves that bound them all together.

When the oaths were completed, they passed through to the Hall of the City of Willows, which represented the Heavenly City, where they incanted the last twelve oaths, which began:

'If a brother cheats another brother, the matter must be reported to the Society and left for it to judge. If a brother fails to conform to this rule, may he be blasted by lightning.

'A brother must not defame another brother, slander him, or cause the brethren to quarrel among themselves. Whoever infringes the law, may he die under a million knives, and be deprived of descendants forever.'

Lee repeated these oaths with enthusiasm and rising excitement, as he imagined himself enforcing the strict rules of the society. He could tell by the bright eyes of the other initiates that they were imagining the same thing, even if the brightness was opium induced.

When these oaths were completed, the master of ceremony committed them to the final blood oath of the Ghee Hin:

'Tonight before Heaven, and in the presence of the brethren assembled for this religious ceremony, you must prove yourself sincere, faithful and righteous, and must imitate the chastity of our Ancestors, so far as concerns widows and orphans. Having passed through the Hung Gate and become a brother, you must, before you confirm your action by severing the cock's head and mingling your blood with ours, bear in mind these 36 oaths, established by the Five Ancestors. They have been faithfully handed down to us, and every brother here has pledged himself by the same oaths and has agreed to obey them. If therefore, anyone be so brazen as to break any of these laws, may he die by losing his blood from the seven apertures, or be drowned in the great ocean and his body lost forever. May the spirits of his ancestors be cursed and damned, and may his progeny exist in the deepest misery and want for a thousand generations.'

Then Lee and the other initiates were led from the City of Willows to the Red Flower Pavilion, which contained the ancestral tablets of the five founders of the Tiandihui. Set apart from the rest of the compound, the Red Pavilion represented life after death and the place of their rebirth as society members. As a Ghee Hin official stood beside him with an umbrella over his right shoulder, Lee knelt before the Altar of the Five Ancestors, decked out with flags and emblems of the Ghee Hin, in the centre of which stood a picture of Guan Di, the god of war. Another official decapitated a cockerel, and mixed its blood with wine and sugar in a porcelain bowl. While the headless fowl lay twitching on the ground, Lee cut his finger with a ceremonial knife, which he then passed to the others, who repeated his action. They mingled their blood with that of the cockerel, which they drank from the porcelain bowl, before they swore their final blood oath to the Ghee Hin.

Lee found the taste of the blood invigorating, and it seemed to course though his veins, giving him strength and determined purpose. As he licked the last droplets from his lips, he thought to himself—maybe I could kill a man.

Then the initiates took turns laying the knife over the dead body of the cockerel, as they repeated their earlier vow of secrecy. They were now members of the society, and their names were added to the membership scroll. They handed over their initiation fees, and were presented with membership certificates and documents describing the rules, regulations and punishments of the Ghee Hin. Like many with him there that day, Lee felt a strong sense of comradeship with his Ghee Hin brothers. He would do anything for them, as he knew they would do anything for him, so long as he remained true to the oaths he had sworn that day.

There was to be a final feast of celebration, which Lee looked forward to with eager anticipation. He knew they would get their first meat since coming to Singapore. There would be pork for sure, and perhaps some choice pieces of chicken or beef. But the feast was delayed while some men who had not taken part in the initiation were led into the clearing, tied together with ropes. These were men who had refused to join the society, and Lee suddenly recognized Ho Chew Teck, who had cursed the society when first approached by them. The headman managed to persuade a few of the young men to join, while others had to be beaten before they agreed to do so. Two men steadfastly refused, and were led back into the jungle. One of them was Ho Chew Teck. Lee wondered what would happen to them, although in his heart he knew. They would not be allowed to betray the secrets of the Ghee Hin.

The next day Ho's body was found floating in the Singapore River, his throat cut from ear to ear. Dr Montgomerie reported his demise as death by murder, by person or persons unknown.

9

In June, Farquhar used some of the tax-farm revenues from opium,
gambling and arrack to create a small police force, which had
become a necessity. With the accumulation of merchant goods and
silver bullion to pay for them, there was an increasing danger of
gang robberies, especially from the Chinese kongsis, which he knew
were forming in the town and the country.

He broke the good news to his son-in-law Francis Bernard over
breakfast at the residency one morning.

'I'm sorry you lost your position as harbour master, Francis.
I had hoped Raffles would keep you on, but he was clearly set on
saving it for his own brother-in-law.'

'No matter,' said Bernard. 'I always knew it was only an acting
appointment, although I did enjoy working with the Kling[xxxix]
crews. But I'm sure I'll find something else.'

'I've already found you something else,' Farquhar replied.
'Congratulations, Francis. You are now our new chief of police!'

'I'm honoured, sir,' Bernard replied. He was not actually sure
this was such a good idea, but he could not turn down an offer
from his commandant and father-in-law. 'But I didn't know we had
a police force.'

'We do now!' Farquhar enthused. 'We have a Malay clerk named
Radin Mohammed, a jailer, an Indian jemadar[xl], and seven Malay
and Indian peons.[xli] We don't have enough money for uniforms or

---

xxxix Indian.
xl Junior officer.
xli Constables.

arms for them yet, although they will be issued bamboo canes for protection.'

'Not much protection against a Chinese axe or Malay kris, although I'll do my best with what we have,' Bernard replied, in a confident voice that masked his own misgivings.

He was not reassured when Farquhar told him that the peons were to be paid five Spanish dollars a month. That was less than most coolies earned, and made them ripe for bribery and corruption, especially by the kongsis.

* * *

In July, another Scottish merchant came to Singapore. Alexander Laurie Johnston[14] was a tall, thin man, mild-mannered, sociable and easy-going. Colonel Farquhar took to him immediately. Johnston bought Lieutenant Ralfe's former bungalow at the foot of Bukit Larangan, with its fine view of the town and the bay, and rented space for his goods in one of Captain Methven's outbuildings, at what he considered to be a usurious rate.

Later in the month he founded Johnston and Co, the first European company to be established in Singapore, and began to build his own brick godown. Although he conducted many business transactions over the next twenty-one years, probably few had greater significance and poignancy than the one he made on the day he established his company.

As he was wandering back through the bazaar after a visit to Major Farquhar at the residency, he was astounded to see a Bugis trader offering a fourteen-year-old Caucasian girl for sale as a slave. At first, Johnson was outraged, but he kept a cool head, for he quickly realized the more interest he showed in the girl the more it would cost him to free her. So he began an elaborate series of offers and counter offers with the trader, as was the custom among the

Bugis. Eventually they agreed upon a price, and Johnson led the young girl away by the hand.

When they were some distance from the bazaar, Johnston stopped and knelt beside her. 'Don't you worry, young lady,' he said softly. 'My name is Alexander Johnson, a merchant in this town. You will be safe with me, you can be assured of that. What is your name child?'

'Elizabeth Walker, if you please, sir. But everyone calls me Lizzie, including the man you bought me from. And I am no longer a child.'

'All right then,' Johnson responded. 'I will call you Lizzie if you will call me Alex.'

Lizzie happily agreed and followed Johnson back to his bungalow, where he charged his servant Mr Burns to look after her. Mr Burns brought some lemonade and sandwiches, which Lizzie quickly devoured.

'You must have been famished, Lizzie. Did he not feed you, child?'

'Oh no, Mr Alex, he fed me well enough. It's just that I never like to waste good food. Waste not, want not, my mother always told me.'

Johnston looked carefully at the girl. In truth she did not appear undernourished.

'What happened to you, Lizzie?' Johnson said gently. 'How did you come to be a Bugis slave? But if it hurts you to talk about these things, we can save it for another day.'

'It used to,' Lizzie replied, 'but now it seems so long ago, tho' I still get nightmares sometimes. We were passengers on the Dutch cruiser De Vrede five years ago, on our way to Batavia, when pirates attacked us. They boarded the ship and murdered my parents.'

Lizzie paused a moment, took a deep breath, and then continued.

'But cruel as they were—and I still hate them for what they

did—they did me no harm, and gave me to the Rajah of Lampong as a present. He was very kind to me, but eventually got bored with my company, he said, and sent me to the slave market at Pulau Nias in Western Sumatra. Daeng Kemboja bought me there.'

'Daeng Kemboja was the Bugis in the bazaar?' Johnson asked.

'Yes, Mr Alex,' Lizzie replied. 'He too was kind to me. He promised he would sell me to a good man, and as you can see he kept his word.'

That night Alexander Johnson made his first entry in his Singapore account book:

'*A. L. Johnston: Paid subscription for release of female English slave, answering to the name of Lizzie Walker: $10*'

10

Colonel Farquhar rose, as usual, with the five o' clock gun, which he had ordered fired from the ten-pounder gun emplacement at the summit of Bukit Larangan every morning except Sundays. By half past six, he was washed, dressed, and had finished his breakfast, which he took with his wife and children. The sepoy guard entered and announced that he had a visitor, a Mr John Simpson.

Farquhar rose and went out on the verandah to greet his guest, dressed in a white linen shirt and faded red sarong.

'Colonel Farquhar, at your service,' he said, reaching out his hand.

'John Simpson,' replied the other. 'I'd like to talk to ye about getting a piece of land for trading.'

'You must be Ronnie's father,' Farquhar said. 'A fine young man, and glad to see you made it back safely. But where is your son.'

'He's makin' arrangements to unload our cargo, and he'll be along presently. But he said he trusted you to fix us up wi a guid place.'

Farquhar noticed that John Simpson was giving him a strange look.

'Och, the dress,' he laughed. 'You try walkin around this town in a dress uniform 'a day. Nae thank ye. This pits a bit of wind in your sails, and it's the closest thing tae a kilt!'

'I take your point,' said Simpson, 'and I winna ask the obvious question.'

Farquhar picked up his walking stick and whistled for his dogs.

'Well let's gang and see what we can do for you,' he said, leading Simpson down the front steps of his bungalow and heading out towards the east beach.

As they walked, Farquhar noticed that Simpson was limping, although the man kept his back erect as a soldier as he followed along beside him.

'Were you wounded, Mr Simpson?' he asked. 'Were you in the army?'

'That I was, Colonel. Twenty years as quartermaster of the Seaforth Highlanders. But this is nae wound. My feet were bitten raw by cockroaches on the way out on my laddie's ship. I woke up every morning wi' the dirty beasties nipping at my toes.'

'Best to put some mustard or chillies on yer feet,' replied Farquhar, 'then they'll leave you alone.'

'I'll remember that the next time … I just wish my laddie had!'

'Were you at Waterloo,' asked Farquhar, remembering the distinguished record of the Highland regiments during the famous battle.

'No, I was in the Peninsula with Wellington, but left the service after Leipzig and Fontainebleau. My laddie Ronnie was wi' Nelson at Trafalgar as a junior lieutenant.'

'I know,' replied Farquhar. 'He told me about his service, although very modest he was on the subject. But you didna get to serve wi' Nelson unless ye showed what you were made of.'

By this time they had arrived at the great banyan tree at the edge of the Bras Basah stream that marked the outward eastern boundary of the plain, and stood for a few minutes in its shade.

Farquhar pointed with his stick to a number of wooden huts that were scattered on the far side of the stream. 'I can set you up just beyond yon huts,' he said.

John Simpson looked out to where Farquhar was pointing. He watched the white surf roll over the silver sands. For a moment he said nothing, and then he shook his head.

'We canna go there,' he said. 'I'm nae daft. How do you expect us to load anything on that beach? Ye canna get in close. See for yersel, there's a great sandbar right out there, and the water is so shallow ye'd have to carry a' the stuff in by foot. We're no staying if that's the best ye can offer! We'll take our chances in Penang.'

Farquhar sighed. 'I didna take ye for a daftie, Simpson. That's just what Mackenzie and Johnston said. But at least I tried. Sir Stamford instructed me to put the European merchants along the beach, but as you can see it's quite impractical.'

Farquhar continued, turning around, 'Let's go back, and I'll show where the others are.'

John Simpson was none too happy to have been offered a piece of land that Farquhar knew was totally unsuitable, but he bit his tongue and hoped that the colonel had known he would refuse it.

When they arrived back at the residency, they looked out to Ferry Point, where Captain Methven had his house and godown.

'That's mair like it,' said John Simpson. 'Looks very substantial.'

'Looks mair like a bloody castle,' Farquhar huffed. 'Ye could garrison the troops in there.'

They walked past the Company store and through the double rows of shops and stalls that formed the already bustling bazaar. Farquhar pointed out the largest shop, which sold cotton goods. It belonged to Naraina Pillai, who had come down from Penang with Raffles on his second visit.

'Smart one, that,' said Farquhar. 'He runs a building company and brick factory as well.'

They walked up the hard packed earth of High Street toward Bukit Larangan, past the houses and godowns of Claude Queiros, Tan Che Sang, Graham Mackenzie, Syed Omar, and Lim Guan Chye. They passed by the wooden footbridge that Lieutenant Ralfe had built across the river close to the mid-point of High Street, and skirted the temenggong's compound until they arrived at the foot of Bukit Larangan. Farquhar pointed out the spice gardens and Christian cemetery to their right, and then pointed left towards the river.

'John Hay has got his place down by the river there. I can give you a space just beyond him. The ground starts to get a bit soft here, so you may need to do some filling, but you'll have no trouble unloading if ye build a wee pier; still plenty deep enough for lighters and sampans.'

'Fine with me, Colonel Farquhar, how much?' Simpson replied, getting straight to the point.

'Och, I'm afraid I canna sell ye the land, leastways not yet, although I can give ye a temporary permit like everybody else. Sir Stamford Raffles, the Governor-General of Bencoolen with overall authority for Singapore, wants all this side of the river reserved for government buildings and offices. He wants the European merchants on the east beach—you saw what a bad idea that was—and the Chinese on the other side of the river—ye can see for yoursel whit a bad idea that is.'

John Simpson looked across the river to the swampland beyond, which was presently flooded because it was high tide. There were only a few wooden structures built upon stilts, with sampans tied up alongside.

'Most of the Chinese—and ye canna blame them—have insisted on having their godowns this side of the river, except for those canny enough to set up shop at the mouth of the river, where the ground is dry. Though I expect Raffles' brother-in-law Captain Flint, the new harbour master, will chase them out pretty quick.'

Simpson looked thoughtfully across the river, rubbing his chin.

'Surely the answer is obvious, Major. You'll just need tae fill in the swamp at the other side, as ye just suggested I do wi my soft ground'.'

'Och, dinna think I haven't thought of that myself, John

Simpson. It's aye very well, but where do ye think I'm going tae get the money to fill it in? I've nae enough money to run the settlement as is, and if I tried to introduce any new taxes to pay for such a "lavish expenditure" I'd be out on my ear. I've asked the merchants if they'd be willing to chip in, but they're not interested. They're perfectly happy where they are, and I canna blame them. East river is the best place for unloading, at least as things stand.'

'I've written tae Raffles trying to explain the impracticalities of his original plan, and how the others threatened to leave if they didn't get to put their places up here. I'm sure he'll acknowledge this when he understands the full situation, but I've heard nothing back these last six months. Of course it sometimes takes that long tae get a letter there and back from Bencoolen, so it's nae that surprising. But for the moment, if ye built anything here it would hae to be at your own risk. Raffles might just overrule a' the land allocations I've made so far—he can be a bit of a stickler aboot these things.'

'Weel, I suppose I'll just hae to take a chance wi the others,' Simpson replied. 'After a', that's why we're here, isn't it'? he said with a wink. 'Now where can I get some good men to put up a quick shed till we get settled?'

'Try Pillai,' Farquhar suggested. 'You'll probably find him back at the bazaar this afternoon. Meanwhile, let's get back and do the paperwork.'

They walked back down High Street. The sun was rising white-hot in the morning sky, and Simpson stopped to wipe his brow with his handkerchief.

'Man, it's hot,' he said. 'How dae ye keep cool in this place?'

'Try a sarong,' Farquhar suggested.

'One thing has struck me,' Simpson said, as they continued walking. 'Most o' these merchants—aside frae the Chinese and Arabs—are Scots, aren't they?'

'Aye they are,' Farquhar replied, 'a right little home frae home we have here!'

When they got back to Farquhar's residency, they found Ronnie waiting for them.

'Well, did the major find us a guid place, father,' he said. 'He promised me he would.'

'Welcome back, Ronnie,' Farquhar replied in his stead, stretching out his hand to welcome him. 'Of course I did—John and I have just been up to see the place.' The two men were now on first name terms.

As Ronnie shook Farquhar's hand, John Simpson chipped in:

'Of course he tried to fob us off wi' a place along the beach that was nae use to anybody, but I wasn't having any o' that, so he's got us fixed up on the riverbank, near the foot of the hill.'

'But why did ye do that, Major?' Ronnie responded, giving Farquhar a hard look. 'I though you said you would keep us a place.'

'And I did Ronnie, I surely did. In fact I had a prime piece set aside for ye, until Raffles came along and assigned it to Syed Omar. I just had to go through that bit of nonsense on the beach so that I could report to Raffles that you turned it down, as I knew you would. His idea not mine.'

'But I've got you a grand spot just beyond Syed Omar, close by the bridge and the fresh water outlet. You'll do fine there, if Raffles let's ye all stay.'

Ronnie's look softened when he heard this, and turned into a smile.

'Thank you, Major, but why would Raffles not want us to stay? It's obviously the best place to do business.'

'To everyone but Sir Stamford. But let's hear what he says when I tell him you all refused the east beach.'

'Thank you, Major,' said Ronnie. 'I don't suppose you found any ...'

'No more dark-eyed beauties, I'm afraid,' Farquhar replied.

11

Mehmood bin Nadir was not happy.

He had been making good money ferrying passengers and goods to and from the ships in the roads, and transporting firewood and water out to them. But now Captain Flint had built his own lighters, and forced all the nakodahs[xlii] to use them, whether they be masters of small native prahus or captains of black-hulled junks or yellow-striped East Indiamen. Flint hired Chulia crews from the Coriander coast, so Mehmood's cousin and his friends had found themselves jobs, but Flint paid much less than they could have earned with their own hired craft. Captain Flint behaved like a petty dictator, and especially liked to demonstrate his superiority and power by keeping everyone waiting, but especially the native captains.

All applications for cargo boats and water had to be made through his office, which also handled all ship repairs. Flint also introduced a variety of new fees, and eventually established monopoly control over lighterage services, including the hire of lighters to the government. Colonel Farquhar found this intolerable, but there was little he could do about it. Raffles' letter of appointment had stipulated that Flint was to submit his reports and statistics directly to Raffles in Bencoolen, and was answerable only to him. Nevertheless, Farquhar wrote to Raffles registering his strong objections to the arrangement, appealing to his sense of fair play—surely Raffles would recognize that his brother-in-law was violating Raffles' cherished principles of free trade and competition. Meanwhile Captain Flint built himself a fine two-storey brick house

---

xlii Malay term for ship's captain.

at South Point, where he also relocated the harbour master's office.

Mehmood bin Nadir went to Colonel Farquhar to complain about Captain Flint. 'Why do you allow him to keep all the business to himself?' he asked Farquhar. 'Is this not a free port, and its commerce open to competition among all persons? Why do you let this man dictate to everyone—he is not even a real officer like yourself!'

Colonel Farquhar was sympathetic, but told Mehmood that there was nothing he could do at the moment, and advised him to work for Captain Flint until he managed to pay off the loan on his own lighter. Mehmood was too proud to do such a thing, but knew he would probably have to swallow his pride if he wanted to keep his boat and feed his family. Happily, Mr Bernard, who had arrived at the residency to visit his father-in-law, offered a possible solution.

'Fact is, Mehmood,' he said, 'I'm desperately in need of another peon for my police force. I know it's not what you want, but if you worked for me, even for a short while, you ought be able to pay off the loan on your lighter while you wait until the situation improves, as it surely must.'

'As it surely must,' echoed Colonel Farquhar. 'I trust that Sir Stamford Raffles will intervene to ensure fair competition once he learns about the unfortunate situation.'

Mehmood was not sure that he wanted to be a police peon, even a temporary one, but it least it was better than working for Captain Flint, and his five-year-old son Adil was very proud to have a father who would be a policeman.

'Will you arrest people and put them in prison?' he asked when Mehmood told his family the news. 'Will you hang the criminals?'

'I certainly hope not,' Mehmood replied with a grin, but also with a sudden moment of nameless fear.

* * *

Ebenezer Oates rowed hard. His life depended upon it.

After the pirates torched the *Fair Maid of London*, they had bound their prisoners hand and foot, and carried them into to the waiting prahus. There they had been joined in pairs by rattan halters fixed to a pole in the centre of the boat, and beaten on their elbows, knees and the muscles of their arms and legs. Then they had been forced to man the oars. One Malay seaman had resisted the rattan halter—he had been krissed to death on the spot and thrown overboard. Another, a Welsh sailor, had dived into the sea and attempted to swim to safety, but the pirates had dragged him back with a three-hooked pole, and krissed him in the water. There was no chance of escape from the prahu. The pirates kept them awake during the long days and nights by rubbing pepper in their eyes and into the wounds they had inflicted on their bodies. Anyone who slackened or sickened was krissed and thrown overboard. So Ebenezer Oates rowed hard because his life depended upon it.

The pirate prahu was about ninety foot long, and he estimated its weight at around sixty tons. It had a double tier of oars, manned by about a hundred slaves and prisoners like himself, who sat cross-legged in pairs in the galleys. The prahu was also fitted with a sheer, which enabled its huge matting sail to be raised when the wind was fair. A heavily timbered cabin in the bow of the ship enclosed a twelve-pound cannon, whose long brass barrel protruded through a forward aperture; another cannon was mounted on the captain's cabin in the stern of the vessel. Swivel guns were mounted on both sides, and on her upper works. In the middle of the prahu was a large cabin made of bamboo and attap, in which the women and children lived. When they were not fighting, the captain sat in his cabin chewing betel nut and smoking opium. The pirates sat on a wooden platform above the main cabin, where they stood when attacking other vessels, as they had done five times since the destruction of the *Fair Maid of London*. They had mainly picked upon helpless native craft, but they had also attacked a rival pirate squadron.

I'm happy to let them kill each other, Oates thought, as he rowed on. He prayed to his God, and prayed that he had not forsaken him. But he kept his eye on the position of the sun and moon and stars, and on the outline of the shoreline when it came in view. He would remember the good captain and his brave young son, but most of all he would remember the way back if he ever got the chance to escape.

* * *

Tan Che Sang was doing very well and making a lot of money. He had built a godown between High Street and the residency and already had two shops in the bazaar. He had made arrangements with the captains of the junks from China and Cochin China to act as their agent, and also served as a comprador for some of the European merchants, such as A. L. Johnston & Co and G. Mackenzie & Co. He was making a small fortune buying and selling cargoes for India and China, and he liked to let everyone know it.

He was fifty-six years old, but still going strong. He was a familiar figure in the bazaar, as he shuffled between the stalls, his hands folded within the black sleeves of his long silk gown. His carefully coiffured queue hung long behind his back, bound up with bright red ribbons.

Although Tan Che Sang made lots of money, he did not spend it lavishly, but kept most of it in gold and silver bullion, locked away in gunmetal chests in his bedroom. He liked to see it and touch it, and would take some out each morning and evening, before safely locking it away again. While it brought him great pleasure, it also brought him great anxiety, not only because of his fear of robbery, but also because of his love of gambling. Sometimes he would lose more money in a single night than most men accumulated in a lifetime, and it brought him great anguish.

One morning after a night of heavy losses he decided to punish himself severely, in the hope that it would deter him from gambling in the future. He instructed his servant to bring him a knife, a block of wood and some bandages. Then he proceeded to methodically sever the first joint of the little finger of his right hand. It caused him so much pain that he almost fainted. But it did not stop him gambling.

Tan Hong Chuan was also doing well, if not in the same league as Tan Che Sang. He had made enough from hawking poultry and fruit and vegetables to set up a stall in the bazaar. Coming from Malacca he knew Malay, so he found it easy to trade with the local fisherman and farmers, and was able to sell their produce—always at a sizeable profit—to the merchants and ships' captains. He had needed to borrow money from the Ghee Hin to get started, but had now managed to pay most of it back, and had no problem advancing their protection fee, which was included in his payments.

12

Raffles was visiting Government House to deal with the official correspondence and local petitions when Sophia burst into his office.

'Oh, Raffles!' she exclaimed. 'William is desperately ill. He's got a dreadful fever, and he's been vomiting all day.'

Raffles immediately got up and comforted his wife. 'Let's get him here right away,' he said. 'Let's take your carriage and bring him from the fort—I'll send one of the boys for Dr Jack.'

Two hours later they returned to Government House with Sophia's brother, who was shivering violently despite the blazing heat of the day. He was too weak to walk, so Raffles carried him into one of the guest rooms, where they put him to bed. Sophia held a glass of water to his mouth and tried to get him to drink as much as possible, but he continued to vomit and was racked with diarrhoea.

Dr Jack examined him and spoke kind words of comfort and hope. But when he rose and turned to Raffles his face was grim.

'Captain Hull has a severe case of dysentery,' he said. 'If the fever breaks tomorrow, we might be able to save him, but he has lost a lot of fluid.'

Yet the fever did not break the following day, even though Sophia sat with him all night, while the Malay servants slipped in and out bringing fresh water and towels to bathe him.

As William lay doubled over with stomach cramps and moaning in pain, Sophia begged Dr Jack: 'Is there nothing we can do for him?'

'You can pray,' replied Dr Jack.

William died early the next morning, and was buried in the European ceremony.

When Raffles returned from the funeral to Government House, he found a letter from Farquhar, who had recently been promoted to colonel, notifying him that he intended to stay on as resident in Singapore. He found another letter from his friend Captain Otho Travers, complaining that Farquhar had refused to give up his position, and advising Raffles that he was returning to India. Raffles threw the letters down on his desk in frustration, and held his head between his hands. He felt a powerful headache coming on. He pushed the letters aside—he would deal with them later. As he prepared to leave Government House for the Hill of Mists, he received a message from Fort Marlborough that two other soldiers had died of dysentery. Their deaths proved to be the first of many, with funerals almost a daily occurrence. He just prayed that Sophia and his children were safe at the Hill of Mists.

* * *

Lee Yip Lee and his two companions crept up the beach at the mouth of the river. They had come out of the jungle and made their way down the Rochor River and into the bay in a small skiff, which now lay anchored about a quarter of a mile out to sea. They had come this long way round to avoid being seen. And they could return along the east beach without being seen, for few were around this time of night because the road to Kampong Glam was notorious for robberies and murder.

They were making their way towards Captain Methven's godown, as ordered by the Ghee Hin. They were going to relieve him of a shipment of opium they knew he had recently received, and anything else they could get their hands on. Yet this was no random robbery. The leaders of the Ghee Hin had been furious to learn that Methven had been processing opium and distributing it among the Chinese coolies and stevedores, employing coolies who were indebted to him for loans.

The Ghee Hin owned the opium farms in Singapore, for which they paid Rajah Farquhar a fair price, and controlled most of the coolie loans in Singapore. So they resented Methven on both counts, and planned to teach him a lesson.

They knew the godown would be guarded, but they also knew it would be guarded by only a single Sikh. He would be armed, but there were three of them, and if they crept up quietly they should be able to overpower him before he could raise the alarm. The other tiger soldiers waited further down the beach. They would run up to carry back the opium chests once they had been given the all-clear signal. Lee Yip Lee and his two companions crept around the edge of the godown. In the dim light they could see the Sikh guard standing in the doorway. They crept up as close as they could, and then rushed out of the darkness at him. Lee Yip Lee and Wang Aik Mong were armed with clubs; Pek Sin Choon carried a kris that he had taken off one of the sultan's entourage.

The Sikh guard was a giant of a man, over six foot tall and heavily bearded, but very fast moving. He raised his rifle in an instant and aimed it directly at Yip Lee's head. Yip Lee saw him squeeze the trigger and prepared for death. But the rifle misfired with a dull click, and his heart leapt in his breast. The guard swung the rifle like a club at Wang's head, and knocked him unconscious to the ground; then he quickly drew his short sword and drove it into Pek's chest. As the Sikh struggled to remove it, Yip Lee flung himself upon him, and the three men fell to the ground. The blade snapped off at the hilt, and the guard threw away the handle in disgust.

Yip Lee fought hard, punching and scratching, gouging and biting, but the guard was too strong. He tried to push out the man's eyeballs, but the Sikh brushed his hands away, like a man swatting flies, then straddled his chest and seized his neck in a powerful stranglehold. The Sikh pressed hard with his thumbs on Yip Lee's throat, and Yip Lee began to panic as he fought for breath, and saw the gleam of triumph in the other man's eyes. He kicked his legs in the air, and flailed his arms in the sand, but it was no use—his life force was fading fast. Then his right hand found something metallic, the blade of Pek's kris, which he had dropped when the Sikh had stabbed him to death. Yip Lee fumbled for the handle, which he clenched tight in his right fist. He brought the black wavy blade up and drove it into the guard's stomach and under his rib cage. The blood gushed out over his hand and arm, and splashed onto his face and chest. The Sikh's eyes widened in fear and pain, but his grip around Yip Lee's neck tightened, as he strove desperately to drive the last breath from his opponent's body. Yip Lee pressed upwards with the blade, harder and harder until he found the man's heart. Then the vice-like grip around his neck slackened, and he felt the life go out of the man's body as he saw the soul go out of his eyes.

The Sikh fell forward over Yip Lee, who quickly scrambled out from under him. He tried to stand up, but fell down on his knees and emptied the contents of his stomach on the sand, his body trembling like a man with a chill fever. He had killed a man, a man he had never known and to whom he bore no grudge. His spirit felt sick and dirty.

He recovered enough to signal to the tiger soldiers on the beach, and tried to rouse Wang. But Wang was already dead, his skull crushed by the rifle blow. They took the keys from the dead Sikh and made their way into the godown. It was not long before they had the chests of opium back in the boat, along with the bodies of their comrades. They made their way along the eastern coast to the mouth of the Rochor River. As the boat slipped upriver under the blanket of night, Yip Lee looked back over the gloomy darkness of the river and the black sea beyond, flecked with the sudden whiteness of the surf.

He no longer trembled, and a deep feeling of calm suffused his body. His spirit was no longer troubled, but excited and exhilarated. He had killed a man. He had driven his soul from his eyes and out of this world. He longed to have that power again, and was amazed by the strength of his own cold-blooded desire.

13

1821

Colonel Farquhar had had enough. He had been listening to Captain Methven's complaints for the past half-hour.

'All right, Captain Methven,' he said as he interrupted Methven's tirade about incompetence and cowardice. 'I'm very sorry about your loss, and especially the death of your guard, but we're very short of peons, and I can't place an army guard on your godown. They're here to protect the settlement, not the merchandise of individual merchants. Just give me a list of what you had stolen, and I'll ask Mr Bernard to get his men to keep a look out.'

'Oh, I'm sure I've seen the last of it,' replied Methven, who had no intention of reporting the loss of his cases of opium to the colonel, since distributing opium to the local Chinese was illegal without a farming license. 'Probably hidden deep in the jungle by now. I just want you to find the men who did it and hang them from the nearest tree.'

'I'm afraid there's not much chance of that,' Farquhar replied, 'without a list and without witnesses. Not that they'd be much damn use if it was the work o' the Ghee Hin, which I suspect it was. I hope you've no given them any cause to mak you their enemy.' Farquhar had heard rumours about Methven's dealings, but had been unable to confirm them.

'Whose side are you on?' Methven exploded. 'You're the law around here, and it is your duty to see that it is enforced. I'm going to complain to the lieutenant-governor about your recalcitrance, sir!' he exclaimed as he stormed out of the residency.

You just do that, Farquhar thought to himself. Sir Stamford's welcome to you.

A few minutes later he received word of the loss of the *Fair Maid of London*, which was rumoured to have been taken and burned by pirates. He was deeply saddened, and would never forget the eager expression on young Adam's face.

In January, Farquhar welcomed yet another Scot to the settlement. Alexander Guthrie[15] arrived with a large stock of British goods—building hardware, clocks, ships' rope and canvas, stationary, salted beef and pork, cheeses, wine, sherry and brandy, and woolen and cotton goods for sale to the European and Chinese merchants. He founded Guthrie & Co as a branch of Thomas Talbot Harrington & Co of Cape Town, who had put up much of the original capital for the enterprise.

Like Johnston and Simpson, Guthrie flatly refused to accept a piece of land on the east beach, and told Colonel Farquhar frankly that he would quit Singapore if he did not get a place on the east riverbank, which was obviously the best place to do business. Farquhar once again explained that he could only give him a temporary lease, subject to the approval of the Governor-General of Bencoolen and the Court of Directors. Guthrie said he would take his chances, but prudently rented a brick house and godown for twelve months until a proper ruling on land had been made. The godown had been built by Syed Mohammed on the east bank of the river just above Hill Street.

* * *

Guthrie had only been in Singapore just over a week when he found himself invited to attend a reception and dinner at the residency in cerebration of the second anniversary of the founding of the settlement. The other guests included Sultan Hussein, the temenggong, John and Ronnie Simpson, Alexander Johnston, Captain Methven and John Morgan, Captain and Mary Anne Flint, Dr Montgomerie, Tan Che Sang, Lim Guan Chye, Syed Omar Al-Junied, Aristarchus Moses, Naraina Pillai, Captain John Campbell of HMS *Dauntless*, whose ship was in port taking on water and wood, the Reverend Thomas Moore from the London Missionary Society, and Miss Sarah Hemmings, who was staying with him. Miss Hemmings was living with her sister in Penang, who had married a writer in the Company's service. She had come on a visit to Singapore because she had been intrigued by the stories she had heard about it, and not because, as Mr Morgan had offensively put it, she was looking for a husband.

A great variety of foods had been laid out for the guests. There were joints of Bengal mutton and Yorkshire hams with Java potatoes, traditional Chinese rice and noodle dishes, with chicken, beef and fish, and bird's nest soup; Peranakan dishes flavored with coconut milk, green chillies, lime and lemongrass; various curries and breads; Malay standards such as beef rendang, nasi goreng, and nasi padang; and a separate table on which the cook had laid out halal dishes for the devout Muslims such as Syed Omar Al-Junied. There were tropical fruits in profusion—mangosteens, mangoes, langsats, rose apples, papayas and pineapples. There was beer and wine, both European and Chinese, champagne, arrack, opium and betel nut.

Toasts were drunk to the foundation of the settlement, the King of England, the Lieutenant-Governor of Bencoolen, the Marquis of Hastings, Sultan Hussein and the temenggong. After the meal was completed, Colonel Farquhar asked Miss Hemmings if she had enjoyed her trip down from Penang, and what she thought of Singapore.

'Very pleasant, Colonel, but also very uneventful,' she said. 'We saw absolutely no sign of pirates. But I think Singapore is the most exciting city in the world. You can almost hear the place breathing as you walk about, and you can almost smell the activity.'

'That's probably a' the money you're smelling,' said Farquhar with a grin. 'That's whit they're a' trying to sniff out!'

'Or the raw sewage in the river,' said Dr Montgomerie.

'I can smell that too,' she replied, 'and much more—but you get used to it very quickly.'

'I'll never get used to it,' said Captain Methven, with a snarl. 'Or the heat. Don't you find it horribly oppressive.'

'Not really,' she said, 'After nearly twenty summers of wet and cold in Kendal—in the Lake District, where I come from—and long frozen winters, I'm in no rush to return. I'd much rather live out here where the sun shines every day.'

'I know the feeling,' said John Simpson, 'and it grows stronger the older I get.'

'Well, I'll be goin' back to Scotland once I'm finished here,' said Farquhar. 'Weather or no weather—I still miss the place.'

'Och I do too,' Simpson replied, 'and I'll probably do the same in the end. I just wish I could tak' the weather wi me!'

'But you shouldn't joke about pirates, Miss Hemmings,' Farquhar continued. 'They're a serious problem around here. They attack the native vessels a' the time, and sometimes within sight of the town. And they're no afraid to take on a Chinese junk or armed East Indiaman at times—sometimes they go out in hundreds of war-prahus, all heavily armed. I'm afraid we may have lost one of our own to them recently—Captain Ramsey and his wee son Adam. I spoke to them only a few months ago; poor little fellow wanted so badly to be a ship's captain like his father. Only twelve years old, a great tragedy.'

Sarah blanched at this, but then regained her composure. 'I did not mean to belittle the danger, Colonel,' she said, 'and I am very sorry about Captain Ramsey and his son. I'm sure these pirates are as cruel and cold-blooded as those of the Caribbean, and I don't really want to meet any of them. But the very danger just adds to my fascination with his place.'

Colonel Farquhar thought to himself that she had already met some of them. The temenggong, who was being his usual charming self, was almost certainly one of them, or at least provided the pirates with shipping intelligence. No doubt his Highness the Sultan was involved as well. But Farquhar said nothing, for he could do nothing about it, at least not in present circumstances.

'They used to use St. John's Island as a base,' said Mr Bernard. 'When I first sent men out there to set up a hailing station, the beach was covered with skulls, and worse. All cleared away now though.' Bernard had renamed Pulau Sakijang Bendera as St. John's Island.

'They won't dare come close anymore,' interjected Captain Flint, who was now in charge of St. John's. 'And if they do, I'll blast them into the sea!'

'Now, now,' said Mary Anne, Flint's wife, 'stop trying to scare Miss Hemmings. Let's talk about something else, such as the news from Calcutta and England.' Then, looking around at Colonel Farquhar, Messrs Guthrie, Johnston, McKenzie, Methven, Montgomerie, Morgan, Simpson, and her own husband, she added 'Oh, and Scotland too, of course!'

'I think you're very brave...' exclaimed Ronnie Simpson, who had said very little for most of the evening. He could scarcely take his eyes off Sarah Hemmings. She was the most beautiful woman he thought he had even seen, even in pictures, although there were precious few European women to be seen in Singapore. She was of medium height, with a slim figure and small bosom, dressed in a long green silk dress, buttoned tight at the neck and cut in the Chinese style; she had had it made up by a Chinese tailor from some silk she had admired. The dress matched her eyes, which were the most amazing green he had ever seen. Looking into her eyes was like looking into an enchanted sea, in which he would gladly drown. Her dark brown hair tumbled over her shoulders and shone brightly in the candlelight.

'At least for a ...' His father kicked him very hard under the table, and he winced in pain.

'You mean for a woman,' Sarah finished for him, giving him a cold look. The soft green of the enchanted sea had turned into the hard green of emerald, and it crushed his heart.

'You need the opportunity to be brave,' she continued. 'It just so happens that men get the opportunity far more often than women in our society, although oftentimes they fail as badly as any woman might. We may have weaker bodies but we have steel in our backbones and more common sense than most men. And I'll wager I'm a better shot than most of the men in this room—my uncle taught me from an early age, even though he was a man of the cloth.'

'Bravo!' said Mr Johnston, clapping his hand on his knee, and raising his glass.

'A toast to Miss Hemmings, our crack pistol shot! We may have need of her services one day! Mr Bernard, did ye no not tell me you were short of constables?' he said with a grin.

'Aye, indeed we are,' Bernard laughed, 'but we have no need of any female constables at present.'

'Please,' said Reverend Moore to Sarah, in a hushed voice, 'you shouldn't talk that way. It's not proper for a lady.'

She nodded her submission, but thought to herself that Singapore was not a proper place, which was why she liked it so much.

'I only meant...' Ronnie began, his face flushed red.

'I know exactly what you meant,' she snapped back at him.

John Simpson felt for his son—he was only making a bad situation worse. But then Ronnie blurted out what turned out to be the right thing to say.

'I'd be happy to take up your wager—I think I'm a pretty good shot myself. My father was a grand teacher too.'

This time his father did not kick him. And Sarah Hemmings gave him just the suggestion of a smile as she looked at him more carefully.

He was a strange combination, this Ronnie Simpson. He was about five foot ten in height, very lean and strong. She had seen his muscles rippling beneath his badly fitting and very old-fashioned frockcoat, which looked like it had been purchased from a pawnshop (which it had in point of fact). His features were so sharp and angular that his face looked liked it had been chipped out of a block of flint, an impression accentuated by his long and pointed side-whiskers, which looked like the sharp ends of an ancient war helmet. He was otherwise clean-shaven, with a narrow, almost cruel mouth, except when he smiled, as he was trying his best to do now. He had piercing blue eyes that also seemed to have a trace of flint, and a mop of curly brown hair. He had a white scar about three inches long just above his right temple.

Sarah thought he looked like a hard man, a man who would use all his strength and guile against anyone who tried to cross or better him, but he did not seem a rude and arrogant man like Morgan. His bumbling gaucheness in her presence even had a certain charm, his insult to her sex notwithstanding.

'I would love to,' she replied, quite formally, but Ronnie did not care—he was so pleased that she was not casting him one of her withering looks. 'Please call on me early Monday morning. Bring your pistols and I'll show you what I'm worth. I'll be staying with Reverend Moore for the next two weeks, and then I must return to Penang. You don't mind, Reverend Moore, do you?'

'Of course I mind,' the reverend replied, 'and well you know it, my girl. But I suppose there's no real harm in it, and I could be your chaperone. Used to be quite a good shot myself,' he added, helping himself to some mangosteens.

The conversation then turned back for a while to news from Calcutta and England (and Scotland), the situation in Penang and Malacca, and the protests of the Dutch against the settlement, which Farquhar assured them would come to nothing (he just wished he could believe it as strongly as he assured them of it). But eventually it returned to the dangers of life in the Eastern Archipelago. Over the whisky and cigars, Captain John Campbell of HMS *Dauntless*, who had just returned from the Philippines, reported that in late December the native population had rioted in Manila. They had slaughtered as many white people as they could find, including English, French, Spaniards, Danes and a few Americans. In all, about twenty-six persons had been killed, including women and children.

'I hope there's no chance of that happening here, Colonel Farquhar,' he said. 'I suppose you are a lot safer with the sepoy regiment at hand.'

'There is no need to worry about that,' said the temenggong, leaning forward to answer the captain's question before Farquhar had a chance.

'As you English say, why should we bite the hand that feeds us? We are well compensated, and the Chinese and everyone else are here to make money. As you also say, why should we rock the boat? With Tuan Farquhar in charge, nobody has any cause to complain of hardship or unfair treatment. We live in harmony, God be praised!'

'Thank you for these kind words, sir,' Farquhar replied, as he brought the evening to an end. But as he prepared for bed, he thought to himself, Tuan Farquhar be damned! The temenggong will only keep the peace among the Malays so long as we pay him his allowance, and he takes his own cut from the pirates. The Chinese societies will only keep the peace so long as it pays them to do so. With the number of immigrants increasing every day, God help us if they ever did rise up against us. He shook his head with a worried frown, but as always slept like a baby as soon as his head touched the pillow.

Ronnie Simpson could not sleep at all. He lay on his cot, thinking only of her lips and eyes, and what he could possibly say to her the next time they met. The moonlight crept with a fierce intensity over the floor of the godown, where he and his father slept under their mosquito nets, as he imagined himself standing with her in the moonlight, locked in a passionate embrace. But what would he say to her? He, who as a young man without a care had led the bloody repulse of a French boarding party from Nelson's flagship at the Battle of Trafalgar, felt his stomach churn at the thought. His father had been no use at all. 'Just be yourself, laddie,' he had said. What else? But what would he say to her? Maybe he should have read more books, but he only had a Bible, the collected works of Robert Burns, and a Shakespeare anthology that he had picked up at a bazaar in Cochin China of all places. He never was very good with words, and they didn't teach you any of this in school or church!

Sarah Hemmings could not sleep either.

14

With February came the first junks from China, carried by the northeast monsoon. The crew of a Malay tambang signalled the arrival of the junks, while they were still a few miles out in the roads. A multitude of small boats went out to meet them, like bees swarming round honey pots. Few could board the junks, since their decks were crowded with sinkeh,[xliii] but the Chinese merchants shouted up to the nakodahs for news of China, and offered to make arrangements for the sale of their goods. Indian lightermen offered their services to transport their goods to the merchants' godowns along the river, and to replenish their supplies of food and water. The sinkeh were rowed ashore, their anxious faces scanning the shoreline, some to be met by family or friends, but most by agents holding their work-tickets. Meanwhile the crews erected makeshift rattan roofs over the junks to protect the goods that would be displayed for sale on the deck.

Sultan Hussein had one of the nakodahs arrested and placed in stocks on the beach for his failure to provide the customary present. Farquhar had the man released immediately, but the incident caused no end of trouble. First there was Captain Flint, who demanded that the sultan—and the temenggong—be flung in jail and heavily fined.

'You're the martial authority here, Farquhar!' he barked. 'You ought to uphold the law!'

'Oh yes,' Farquhar replied, 'now pray tell me, Captain Flint,

---

xliii Chinese immigrants.

what law gives me the authority to arrest or fine His Highness Sultan Hussein Mohammed Shah of Johor, Riau and Lingga, which includes Singapore and a' the islands and waters surrounding it. Technically he probably has every right to tribute, but I've persuaded him to be satisfied wi' the allowance I pay him from the farm revenues, which I have agreed to increase, in return for his promise to make no further demands upon the nakodahs. But I'd thank you not to interfere, Captain Flint, and stick to your own business.'

'Bah, you're too easy on these people!' Flint responded with contempt, thinking that Farquhar really was like one of them, waddling around in his old sarong, with his Malay wife and half-breed children. 'Sir Stamford will hear of this,' he said, storming out of the residency.

'I dinna think even Sir Stamford would want me to imprison the sultan. Not the way to promote the emporium of the east. Not at a'!' he said to no one in particular, since Flint had already left.

Damn the man, thought Farquhar to himself, and what a hypocrite. If anyone should be accused of fleecing the nakodahs, it was Captain Flint, with his anchorage and port clearing fees and monopoly control over lighterage and ship repairs. Flint just loved to keep the Chinese nakodahs waiting——it gratified his inflated sense of his own authority and superiority. Farquhar thought he really ought to protest to Raffles about it, but knew it was a waste of time. Raffles was sure to take the side of his brother-in-law. The man could be as blind as a bat sometimes, despite his noble talk of free trade and commerce.

Farquhar also had a deal of sympathy for the rights of Sultan Hussein, who after all did own the land and had legal authority over the surrounding waters. For generations, the Malacca and the Johor, Riau and Lingga sultans who had made treaties with Portuguese, Dutch and British trading companies had profited through their lease of land and dues or presents paid to them in tribute, by both native and foreign craft. And it was more than a mere matter of economics—it was a matter of pride. Without some form of demonstrated respect for their rights over their own lands, they were nothing more than paid minions.

Yet it was hard to have much sympathy for the sultan himself, who was the epitome of idleness and debauchery. He had brought his family and his large harem from Riau, along with over two hundred retainers and followers, who lived in the outbuildings around the istana that he had built at Kampong Glam. He was already deep in debt to Tamil Chettiars, despite the Company's allowance and the fees that Farquhar paid him. He had grown so fat that his body was a shapeless mass, almost as wide as it was tall. He had a small, square head that sank into his shoulders in layers of fat, which gave the disconcerting impression that he had no neck. The sultan had a huge potbelly that hung over his spindly legs in folds, which made walking very difficult for him; he usually had to be supported by one or more of his retainers. His skin was a sickly yellow, and he had a wide mouth that seemed to stretch the length of his face when he smiled; and when he smiled he revealed two rows of teeth stained dark red with betel-juice. He looked, thought Farquhar, like one of the monsters from the *Arabian Nights*. The sultan spoke with a low raspy voice, like stone being dragged over stone, which only accentuated the impression.

The temenggong was a different kettle of fish. He was lean and wiry, with sparkling black eyes, and always spoke with humour and intelligence. Farquhar liked him a lot, and had known the man for years. But he was a wily one, was Abdul Rahman, and he wouldn't trust the man with a ha'penny. He could smile at you sweetly and then sell your course to the pirates.

A few minutes after Flint had left, Farquhar received a delegation from Messrs. Johnson, Guthrie, Queiros, Methven, Morgan and John and Ronnie Simpson, who presented him with a copy of a letter they had just delivered to Sultan Hussein, demanding an apology and his promise that such an incident would never occur again.

'This is almost as bad as regular port charges, Colonel, and it undermines our reputation as a free port,' Alexander Johnston, the leader of the delegation, remonstrated. 'It may even stifle the China trade—a trade we will need to depend on in the long run.'

Farquhar liked Johnston, and considered him a friend, but could not abide any more interference.

'I've already taken care of it, Mr Johnston,' he replied. 'But I must remind you that as resident I am solely in charge of relations with the sultan and the temenggong. You merchants should stick to your own business and leave me to mine. I consider this letter of yours improper, premature and quite unnecessary interference. I have already sorted out the situation with the sultan and the temenggong, and have their assurance that we will have no repetition of this unfortunate incident. But I'll thank ye a' to stay out of matters that dinna concern you in the future,' he said, politely showing them the door.

The delegation left, but the merchants, including the Chinese and Arab merchants, continued to protest the sultan's action. Farquhar wrote to Raffles asking him to rule on the question of whether the sultan and temenggong could levy fees on the profits made by Chinese merchants returning to their homeland, and asking him to approve his temporary expediency of paying them an extra allowance from the tax-farm revenues. He also advised Raffles once again about the severe impracticality of his original town plan. The European merchants simply refused to build on the east beach, and most of the Chinese refused to build on the west bank of the river. He could not blame them, as he pointed out to Ronnie one afternoon as they were out walking together. Farquhar pointed across the river with his stick.

'Just how does he expect anybody to build on that,' he said.

It was high tide, and the west bank of the river, which was about nine feet lower than the east bank, marked the edge of a huge inland lake that stretched back about half a mile to the hills beyond, and which both men knew became a marshy bog at low tide. There were only a few raft houses occupied by native traders and the few remaining orang laut; most were now dispersed to the other rivers and inlets around the island.

'You'd need to fill all that in and build up a wharf,' he complained, 'but I canna do that.' He though he might try to appeal to Ronnie, as he had tried to appeal to him before, in the hope that the other merchants would follow his lead if he agreed. 'Do ye think you and the other merchants might club together and raise the money to do that?'

'I doubt it,' Ronnie replied, 'and I dinna see why we should. Everybody's happy where they are. The east bank is grand—a wide tidal basin, wi' a firm sheltered bank for easy loading and unloading, and guid access to fresh water and timber. And it would be easy enough to put the government buildings further back, since—as we both know—nobody's building godowns on the beach.'

Yet Farquhar was not so sure; Raffles could be very stubborn at times. Farquhar had only issued the merchants with temporary land grants, since the treaty with the sultan and temenggong did not give the Company the right to grant permanent title, but most had already built substantial brick godowns to protect their goods from fire. The merchant godowns, the bazaar, and the residency compound, which included the police station and the Company warehouse and commissariat, now occupied most of the east bank of the river between Bukit Larangan and Ferry Point.

The Company warehouse was a disaster. None of the merchant houses or free traders were interested in buying the rubbish that was sent down from Penang, and it was a waste of time and money. He would have to close the place down soon.

* * *

The merchants were not interested in contributing to the reclamation of the west bank, but after the robbery and murder at Methven's godown, they did agree to contribute fifty-four dollars per month for the establishment of a night watch fund to augment the police force. The night watch was dedicated to the patrol and protection of the godowns, and comprised one jemadar[xliv] and nine peons. On the recommendation of the police committee chaired by Mr Johnston, Colonel Farquhar suggested to the capitans of the Chinese, Malay, Indian and Bugis communities that they should institute a subscription for their own night watches.

---

xliv Sergeant

15

Ronnie had sent Sarah a note inviting her to join him in a morning ride out by Bukit Selegie, and she had agreed to meet him at eight o'clock on Monday morning. She had also persuaded Reverend Moore that a chaperone was quite unnecessary, which was not difficult since the reverend hated horses. Ronnie arrived at the appointed time with two horses that he had hired from the Indian stable behind the sepoy cantonment.

Sarah was dressed in a pair of men's britches and a white cotton shirt, with her hair tied up beneath a straw hat. He thought she looked more beautiful in these clothes than she had in her formal dinner wear, and managed to tell her so. She said she liked to dress appropriate to the occasion. She mounted the horse with ease and without assistance, and they rode off up High Street and turned east on Hill Street. They rode by the Bras Basah stream as it skirted Bukit Larangan, and then rode east past the sepoy cantonment and out toward Bukit Selegie and the open country—there was an ancient path that had been cut between the bamboo groves and towering Seraya and Merawan trees. The sun was rising against a dusky blue sky, with a few cotton wool clouds scattered here and there.

'I brought the pistols,' he said, pointing to a dark wooden box strapped to his saddle. 'A pair of dueling pistols I relieved from a French lieutenant at the Battle of Lissa.'[xlv]

'My God, I hope you're not going to challenge me to a duel! I'd hate to have to dispatch you to your Maker on our first meeting!'

xlv British naval defeat of a French invasion force off the island of Lissa in the Adriatic Sea in March 1811.

she laughed. Ronnie laughed too, and the jest seemed to break the ice between them.

When they reached the foot of Bukit Selegie, Ronnie asked if she wanted to stop there, or ride on further.

'The road leads on to the plantations. Could be a bit risky, since there are supposed to be gangs of Chinese robbers in the jungle.' Then, not wishing to offend again, 'But I'm sure that's not going to bother you.'

'Why should it?' she responded with grin. 'We're armed, are we not? I'm sure we crack shots can hold off a bunch of robbers.' She turned her horse down the path leading into the jungle. The canopy of trees provided shade from the sun, but not much relief from the heat and humidity, which seemed to rise up from the ground beneath them. He could see the beads of sweat that had formed at the base of her lovely neck, and he was embarrassed to notice his own arousal was showing beneath his britches. He tried to concentrate his mind on not making a fool of himself again.

They rode on at an easy pace for half an hour. Eventually the path opened up into a wide clearing. They dismounted and tethered their horses to a fallen tree. Ronnie produced a canteen of water and two cups, and they drank each other's health in mock ceremony.

'I've brought some bread and cheese, and some mangosteens,' he said. 'I thought we could have a picnic later.'

'Sounds a good idea,' Sarah replied, 'once I've shown you how to shoot!'

As she returned her cup of water, her hand brushed his, and her eyes met his for an instant, before she turned away. He felt as if some powerful force had passed from her body to his. He suddenly recalled a pamphlet he had read about some French doctor who claimed that our minds and bodies are governed by magnetic forces, which could attract or repel the forces of others like physical magnets. He hoped that their forces would attract if this were true.

He took out some targets that he had drawn the day before using his ship's compasses, and nailed one to a tree about twenty feet away. He took out the pistols, then primed and loaded them.

'Choose your pistol,' he said, and she did.

'Before you say anything, you go first,' she said, nodding towards the target. Ronnie stood by the line he had marked in the earth and took careful aim. He still felt a little nervous in her company—although whether it was really nervousness or arousal he could not tell—but he felt confident of his own eye and steady hand. The pistol cracked, and the smoke from the discharge floated upwards in the windless air. Birds and animals crashed upwards and outwards in the trees and thick brush and ferns. He hit the target without difficulty, just within the second ring.

It was Sarah's turn. She stood her position, her right sleeve rolled up to the elbow, her arm steady as a steel rail. Her face bore a look of extreme concentration and determination—the pink tip of her tongue stuck out from between her white teeth. Then she fired, and he saw the ball slap into the target. They walked forward to take a look, but his seaman's eye had already seen that she had pierced the first ring!

'First win to me,' she exclaimed with obvious pleasure. 'Did you doubt me?'

'Not I,' Ronnie replied, 'but the game is just begun.'

They each fired three more times, but each time Sarah was closer to the bullseye.

He was surprised to be losing, but although he was competitive by nature, he found that he did not really care. He just enjoyed being in her company, and she was being very gracious about her obvious superiority with a pistol.

'One last shot,' Ronnie said, 'Winner takes all!'

'Done,' she replied, 'but we have not yet agreed on the terms of our wager.'

'A kiss,' he blurted out, and then apologized. 'I'm sorry—I just got carried away.'

'Don't be sorry,' she said, 'nothing ventured, nothing gained.'

'So it's agreed,' she continued, reaching out her hand so they could shake on it. 'But what can you do for me if I win? I know—you can take me up Bukit Larangan. The Reverend told me about it last night; it's supposed to be haunted by ghosts.'

'I don't know if you'd see many during the day, but I'd be happy to take you, win or lose. I've a fancy to see it myself, if only for the view, which the colonel says is quite spectacular.'

'Oh, but the Malays say that there are day as well as night ghosts,' she said in a soft whisper, 'spirits of the dead that can swallow your soul.'

You've already swallowed my soul, he thought to himself as he prepared to fire one last time. Now she had offered him a prize he just had to win; it is what he had dreamt of since they had first met. He took his position and willed himself to win, and prayed to the Lord to grant him this one selfish favour. He wiped the sweat from his eye, and lined up his pistol carefully towards the target. His arm was steady, and he felt suddenly sure of himself. Go true, he whispered as he squeezed the trigger. The pistol cracked, and he walked calmly toward the target, knowing he had shot well.

'A bullseye!' he cried, 'Damn near dead centre! Let's see you beat that, Miss Hemmings!'

'If you insist,' she responded with an easy smile, and took up her own position. She aimed her pistol slowly and carefully, and once again the pink tip of her tongue appeared through her white teeth. It drove him crazy with desire! He closed his eyes and waited for the shot, which came quickly. As he followed her toward the target his heart rose. He could see no other mark on the target. Had she missed intentionally? Would she have done that? Why would she have done that? But as he approached she turned with a look of triumph, and handed him the target. It took a sharp eye, but he saw that her ball had struck at the edge of his own—dead centre in the target!

'Don't look so dejected,' she laughed at him. Then she stepped forward and kissed him hard. 'My pleasure,' she whispered, 'but now it's your turn to take me up Bukit Larangan.'

'Come on,' she said, as he stood dumbstruck with the target in his hand. 'Let's pack up your pistols and go. The ghosts are calling.'

* * *

They rode back though the bamboo and high trees, this time together and at a slower pace, not wishing to make the horses suffer too much in the rising heat of the day. Ronnie was surprised to find that he was becoming more and more relaxed in her company, despite the shock—albeit the pleasant shock—that her kiss had wrought to his system. Sarah sneaked a look at him out of the corner of her eye.

He was not much of a charmer or talker, she thought, but he had a presence, a kind of animal magnetism that made him so fascinating. She suspected it might have something to do with his rugged looks, his muscular body and hawk-like face, with the jagged scar that spoke of danger and adventure. She certainly felt safe in his company, although she was not looking to be safe. Yet she found herself attracted to what it was that made her feel safe in his company— his quiet strength and power that so enticed her, and so aroused her.

When they reached the foot of Bukit Larangan, they returned their horses to the Indian stable. Ronnie unloaded the saddlebags containing the pistols and their lunch, before they walked up through the clove and nutmeg plantation at the foot of the hill, a bright sunlit profusion of white and yellow blossoms. They breathed the smell of the East, so different from that of the forests and cities back home.

'Everything even smells different here,' she said to him, 'it's like a different world.'

'That's true, but there are some universal verities of the senses,' he said, impressing himself with his unusually eloquent turn of phrase, despite its disparaging conclusion. 'Just try taking a walk one night by the river when they're emptying the night soil buckets—same the world over, I'd say.'

'Are you inviting me out again?' she replied with a wicked smile, 'because I'd be inclined to give that invitation a miss.'

'I'd love to,' he said, 'and I can think of much better places. St. John's Island, which the natives call Pulau Sakijang Bendera—where Mr Bernard found all the human skulls—or Pulau Belakang Mati, which means the Back and Beyond of Death. Must be a good story there.'

'Yes, that sounds much more fun,' she said, as she strode up the footpath that had been cut by the Malacca Malays and laid out by Lieutenant Ralfe.

About halfway up the hill they came across the keramat, the royal tomb. It was made of black marble, and decked out with yellow flowers and ribbons and flags. A Malay woman, her face shadowed by her tudung,[xlvi] was arranging some flowers at the grave.

'They say this is where the last rajah of Singapore is buried,' she said, slipping her arm into his. 'But Reverend Moore says it's probably the grave of one of the earlier rajahs. Iskander Shah, the last rajah, is supposed to have escaped the sack of the city by the Javanese and gone on to found Malacca.'

'I heard that story too,' he said, 'from the Malay fisherman who used to live with the Chinese woman on the beach. But he also said it might be Iskander Shah.'

---

xlvi A scarf worn by Muslim women that conceals the hair but not the face.

'Was the kingdom Mohammedan then?' he asked, assuming that was why the rajah was honoured by a keramat.

'I don't think so,' she replied, 'Reverend Moore says it was probably Hindu or Buddhist. Iskander Shah is supposed to have converted when he founded Malacca. We'd better not get too close, though, since we're infidels.' She tried not to giggle but could not stop herself, although she managed to keep it between them. Ronnie pulled her away with a look of mock severity, and they continued climbing until they reached the top of the hill.

Major Farquhar had been right. The view was spectacular. They looked out over the harbour and the roads beyond, dotted with European square-riggers and Chinese and Cochin-Chinese junks, Malay prahus, Bugis padewakangs and Arab dhows, the water turning from lime green to aquamarine to deep blue as they looked out over the scattered islands toward the distant horizon, while the sand of the east beach shimmered in the sunlight like a length of pure white silk. They could see the godowns and houses of the merchants lined along the east bank of the river, which was crammed with lighters loading and unloading their cargoes, with Captain Methven's old house and Captain Flint's new two-storey dwelling vying for prominence at the mouth of the river.

They made a picnic of the bread and cheese and mangosteens he had brought, as they sat upon a sandstone block, and wondered if it might have been part of the ancient city. Ronnie produced two bottles of pale ale, which he had procured from Mr Johnston, and two fine Bengal cigars.

'I brought two just in case,' he said, 'for you never know with Miss Hemmings.' He smiled at her. She smiled back and took the cigar and the light he offered. She crossed her legs and stretched out her arms. Then she yawned in contentment, like a cat that had just devoured a bowl of milk.

'I think I'd like to stay here,' she mused. 'It's such a beautiful and fascinating place, and the people are so interesting. They come from all around and have their different customs and languages, but they are all seeking the same thing. And it's not just money, but a new way of life...even if they don't all know it themselves.'

'That sounds very profound,' he said. 'But do you really want to stay, Sarah?' It was the first time he had called her by her Christian name. 'Don't you want to go back to your sister in Penang, or return to England and get married?'

'Oh I can be profound at times,' she replied, 'when the occasion demands it. But there is something about this place that gets into your bones ... into your very spirit. I don't want to go back to boring old Penang, where my sister would probably try to marry me off to some government clerk with a "decent" position, and I want to go back to England even less. I don't want to be dependent on any man. My father was a good man in his way, he fought for his country and died at Salamanca,[xlvii] but he left my mother with nothing but gambling debts and two daughters, and we were out on the street within the year. Fortunately my sister Rosemarie found a good husband, and my Uncle Harry took me in. He taught me independence...and how to shoot! But mother found it too hard to bear, and she died of a broken heart; she just gave up the will to live and wasted away. I swear that will never happen to me.'

'I'm sorry to hear that,' he said. 'I also lost my mother at an early age—she died of consumption. A cold and dreary place is where I came from, which is why I love this place so much.'

They both sat in silence for a moment, looking out over the sea.

Then he knew what he had to say. He did not know if it was the right thing to say, or how she would react, or whether it would ruin the day for them both. But he did not think of these things, and found that he was as sure as any man could be when he said it. He

---

xlvii Battle fought during the Peninsular War, in which the Duke of Wellington's forces defeated the French on July 22, 1812.

got up and stood before her, and looked into her eyes as she looked up into his.

'Sarah, I love you,' he said. 'I know I will never meet anyone like you, and I want to spend the rest of my days with you, until the day I die. Sarah, will you marry me?'

Her cheeks flushed, but she said nothing in response, although she still held his eyes in hers. Then she rose suddenly and turned away, and walked past him to look out over the ocean. She stood deep in thought for a few minutes. To Ronnie it seemed like an eternity, but the thing was said and done and there was no going back. She would answer him one way or the other.

But she did not. She turned again suddenly and walked briskly back and stood before him, the pink tip of her tongue flickering over her teeth once more.

'Well you are a man of surprises, Ronnie Simpson! What am I to say to you?'

'Say yes, of course,' he responded immediately, 'Father and I have a good business, and it's growing every day. I'd be able to look after you very well.'

'I don't want to be looked after,' she said haughtily.

He did not react to her haughtiness. 'I think I know you well enough to know that by now, Sarah,' he said. 'All I meant is that we won't want for money. I love you the way you are and never want you to change.'

Then he remembered some lines from the one love song he did know:

'As fair thou art, my bonnie lass
So deep in luve am I
And I will love thee still, my dear
Till a' the seas gang dry.'

'That's beautiful' she said. 'Nobody has ever called me a bonnie lass before!'

But still she did not answer him. She stood with her arms folded and eyebrows crossed, as if she was about to deliver some rebuke. Ronnie thought he had lost her.

'Well, Ronnie Simpson,' she said at last, 'if I ever were to consider marrying you, I would want to have lots of adventures first. I would want to see your Back and Beyond of Death for a start. I would want you to take me to all the exotic places you travel to in your ship—to Sumatra, Borneo, and Canton! And if I ever did decide to marry you, I'd want to be your partner as well as your wife. I've always fancied being a merchant too, and I have an excellent head for figures. My Uncle Harry taught me that as well.'

'Does that mean yes?' Ronnie said, his heart thumping in his chest. Surely it was close to it!

'I said I would consider it,' she said with a warm smile, but no more than that. Then she broke off the discussion. 'We'd better get back. Reverend Moore will be getting anxious about us being up here alone among the ghosts. But I've not seen or heard any, have you?'

'Not a spook nor specter, my bonnie lass!'

They packed up the remains of the food, and she slipped her arm back in his as they made their way back down Bukit Larangan, along pathways where the wives of the rajahs had walked four hundred years before. As they talked easily together, both thought they heard a gentle whispering around them, as if the wind was carrying their hopes and dreams—although neither mentioned this to the other until some months later. He took her hand in his and she did not draw it away, but grasped it tightly. She gave him one last hard kiss before she left him on Hill Street and made her way back to the mission house, where she and Reverend Moore were staying.

She had already decided, but she did not tell him. Ronnie did not care. He was in love wi' a bonnie lassie, and she had not said no!

16

Sarah stayed on a few more weeks, which turned into a few more months. Ronnie took her out to St. John's Island, to the Island of the Back and Beyond of Death, so-called he said because two pirates had died in a duel after stabbing each other in the back with their krisses; and to Pulau Ubin,[xlviii] a beautiful island off the east coast of Singapore, which was inhabited by only a few woodcutters and their families.

They went to fancy dinner parties at Captain Flint's house and bought fried pork belly and rice from Chinese roadside hawkers. Ronnie took Sarah to the Lombong waterfalls at Kota Tinggi on the Malayan Peninsula, about twenty-five miles north east of Singapore, where a native guide led them through the jungle. He took her to the Mulu caves in Sarawak, and on the journey back to Singapore Sarah had her first taste of real pirates, when their course was suddenly blocked by a Balanini war-fleet. They were the worst of the lot, Ronnie told her afterwards, for they did not take any prisoners, not even women or children, who would fetch a good price in the slave markets. But luckily they turned around and rowed away when two American men-of-war bound for Manila came into view.

Back in Singapore, they rode out one early morning to Bukit Timah,[xlix] the highest hill on the interior of the island. Pausing to rest their horses, they enjoyed the cool shade of a bamboo grove set

xlviii Granite Island. The rocks on the island were used by Malays to make floor tiles.
xlix Tin Hill.

off from the dirt road, and they lay down on the dark leaves and made love on the jungle floor, as if it was the most natural thing to do—as in their hearts they knew it was.

They announced their engagement in October at a party Colonel Farquhar threw for them at the residency, and were married in Singapore at the Mission Church on New Year's Day by the Christian calendar. The wedding reception was held in the home of Chua Chong Long, the Peranakan merchant who had come down from Malacca, who wanted to show off the new house and godown that he had built between High Street and the river.

* * *

Captain Pearl marched up the hill to where Chia Lin Sien lived in a small house of bamboo and attap. He carried a bag of silver over his shoulder. Chia was walking back from his gambier plantation, and beckoned the captain into his home. There was a table and set of chairs in the front; his bed was in the back. Chia hailed a boy who brought them a pot of tea and some English biscuits, to which Mr Chia was partial. The two men haggled for nearly an hour over the price of Mr Chia's gambier plantation. In the end Pearl had to throw in a case of brandy along with the silver to clinch the deal, but with Mr Chia's agreement, he was now the proud owner of four of the gambier plantations on the hill.

But these Chinese were hard bargainers, and he knew that the few who remained would probably drive an even harder bargain than Mr Chia. They had him over a barrel, even though their own days on the hill were numbered—for the gambier plants quickly exhausted the soil, and they would eventually have to move further inland to plant new vines. But it did not matter, for they knew that Captain Pearl was desperate to have his hill, and would pay good money for it as soon as he earned it.

One day in July, while young Leopold was playing ball with his sister Charlotte in the garden at the Hill of Mists, he suddenly vomited all over her dress. When Sophia ran to him she found him curled up and clutching his stomach in pain. He had diarrhoea and a high fever. He cried for hours while she tried to comfort him, as the servants stood hushed outside his bedroom. Leopold died the following morning, in the grey ghostly hour before the dawn. They supposed that he had died of cholera, but Dr Jack said that he had died of enteritis, which was just as deadly.

Sophia screamed and screamed and screamed. 'Not my baby! No, no, no, God! Please no, not my baby!' She clasped little Leopold to her breast, and it was only with great difficulty that Mrs Grimes and two Malay servant girls managed to persuade her to part with the limp little body for burial.

'It is too hard, my love,' said Raffles later, as he tried hopelessly to comfort her, wounded by his own tearing grief.

'You were right, Stamford,' she replied in a leaden voice. 'We were too happy.'

Yet her tragedy was not over. Three days later her brother-in-law Harry Auber died of cholera.

Sophia became hysterical. She retreated to her room, with the shutters drawn, and refused to eat or drink. She sobbed uncontrollably for days, and Raffles and Dr Jack feared for her sanity. She refused to see either of them, or any of her other children. When Mrs Grimes came and offered comfort Sophia chased her out exclaiming 'Let me die rather than my babies!' Raffles felt helpless. His own heart was broken, and his brain was pounding with a skull-splitting headache that drove him to distraction.

Early on the morning of the fifth day an old Malay woman, a poor widow who was employed as a house sweeper, entered

Sophia's room, as the morning light crept through the shutters and picked out the shadow of the figure who lay on the couch by the far wall.

'Go away, I don't need you!' Sophia sobbed, as she turned to face the intruder. But the old woman stood her ground, and gave Sophia such a searching look that she was hushed like a small child.

'I have come,' the woman began, in her quietly lilting voice, and speaking in Malay, 'because you have been here many days shut up in a dark room and no one dares come near you.'

She paused for a moment to brush her grey hair away from her face, while she kept her eyes sharply focused on Sophia.

'Are you not ashamed to grieve in this manner,' she remonstrated, 'when you ought to be thanking God for having given you the most beautiful child that was ever seen? Were you not the envy of everybody? Did anyone ever see him, or speak of him, without admiring him?'

Sophia did not reply, for they both knew the answer.

'Instead of letting this child continue in the world till he should be worn out with trouble and sorrow, has not God taken him to heaven in all his beauty? For shame, mother, leave off your weeping and let me open a window.'

With that the old Malay sweeper walked over and raised Sophia from the couch. She opened the shutters to let in the early morning sunlight, and then quietly padded out of the room on her bare feet without another word.

'I am ashamed,' Sophia whispered to herself. 'I was blessed to have him and now he is blessed to be with the Lord.' Then she left her room to rejoin her family once again.

But she and Raffles needed all their strength. Three months later all three of their remaining children fell sick, first Marsden, then Ellen, and then Charlotte.

'How much suffering must we bear,' she asked Raffles, as they held each other in desperate closeness the night after Charlotte succumbed to the fever. 'Is it to be death heaped upon death?'

Mercifully, Marsden and Ellen soon recovered. Charlotte lay gravely ill for three weeks, but then she also recovered. By this time Raffles was suffering almost daily headaches, which forced him to lie down for hours on end in a darkened room, and Sophia was a nervous wreck in fear for their children.

Yet they all survived, and were grateful for the cheerful if subdued Christmas they spent together as a family. On New Year's Eve Raffles offered a toast to his friends and family, remembering William, Harry and dear Leopold, and thanking God for preserving their remaining children.

17

1822

Three days into the New Year, at four o'clock in the afternoon,
Raffles was sitting at his desk in his office at the Hill of Mists. He
was contemplating a letter he had recently received from Farquhar,
which had brought both good news and bad. Farquhar reported
that the trade of the settlement continued to expand rapidly, but
that most of the Europeans and Chinese had already built their
houses and godowns along the east bank of the river, because they
considered the east beach and the west bank of the river unsuitable.

'Damn him!' Raffles said to himself aloud. 'I told him I wanted
that area reserved for government buildings!'

He heard someone enter the open door behind him, although
they did not speak. He turned around to see Sophia standing red-
eyed in the doorway, holding baby Marsden in her arms. With his
head slung back as if in sleep and his brown curls hanging down,
he looked like a sleeping angel. But he was no sleeping angel, only
another dead child. Marsden, his beloved boy, his Marco Polo, gone
forever! Raffles went to Sophia and tried to speak, but he could not.
His heart felt like it was bursting and his throat was so tight that he
could scarcely breathe. They knelt down on the bare wooden floor
and held each other and their child between them. The hours passed
and the light faded and the evening gloom descended, but they
did not move and no one disturbed them. One by one the Malay
servants slipped in and sat praying in a silent circle around them.

Eventually Dr Jack came and gently persuaded them to give up
the poor dead boy, so he could be prepared for burial.

When they returned from Marsden's funeral they were forced to call in Dr Jack again, when Charlotte succumbed to an attack of enteritis. She lingered on for twelve more days, then slipped away one early morning as Raffles and Sophia sat by her bedside.

Sophia was devastated. 'We must leave,' she informed Raffles, in a tone that would brook no argument, 'or we shall all die in this charnel house.'

Raffles had a strong sense of duty, and knew how much remained to be done in Bencoolen. But he did not contradict her, so empty was his soul of meaning and purpose. When they returned heart-broken from Charlotte's funeral, he wrote to the Court of Directors advising them of his intention to resign his position due to family tragedy and ill health. He informed them that he planned to visit Singapore in September and remain there until June the following year, after which he would return to Bencoolen and prepare for his departure the following January. He arranged for their remaining daughter, Ella, to return to England with her nurse Mrs Grimes on the first available ship.

'My heart is sick and broken,' he told Sophia, 'but we must save Ella and ourselves.'

He was not able to say goodbye to Ella. Two days before she left in late February, Raffles became dangerously ill with a high fever. Dr Jack confined him to his room for three weeks, and bled him frequently with leeches. Raffles was stricken with violent headaches that burned to the very core of his brain, and which drove him to suicidal despair and the darkest depression he had ever known. He had always suffered from headaches, especially at times of great stress, but these were the worst he had ever known. Dr Jack warned him that he might have a brain tumour, and that he should return to England with Sophia immediately. Raffles considered his advice carefully, but then told him he wanted to see Singapore, his 'other child', one last time before he died.

Before they left for Singapore in September, Raffles and Sophia visited the European graveyard where their children were buried. Raffles was a broken man, and little more than a skeleton. He had grown dangerously thin and his skin was yellow. He walked like an old man, supported by Sophia, who seemed to have grown in strength to support her husband in their desperate hour of need.

'We shall never forget them,' he said in a near whisper. 'We must thank God for having them, for even so short a time. Who ever had such wonderful children?'

'Try not to dwell on it, dear heart,' she said, as she led him away from the graves. 'It is too hard.'

They said goodbye to Dr Jack as they boarded the ship for Singapore, and thanked him for the loving care that he had given to their poor children. Dr Jack said that he only wished he could have saved them, and wished them safe passage. One month later Dr Jack woke with searing stomach cramps, and died later in the day from cholera.

18

Chief of Police Francis Bernard walked through the bazaar to the edge of the river, where a large hut constructed of planks and attap had been raised. It was rectangular in shape, and about the size of a small barn. Above the open door hung a sign made from a length of black teak, whose neat white painted letters inscribed the legend 'Captain Kelly's Bar, Restaurant and Games Room'.

'My goodness,' said Bernard, chuckling to himself, 'and a purveyor of fine wines, spirits and Belhaven's Best Bitter, no doubt.' He knew that Colonel Farquhar had given Captain Kelly permission to locate his premises there, at least on a provisional basis, but he thought that as chief of police he ought to check it out.

He stepped through the doorway and looked around. To his right a long bar made out of rough planks stretched the length of the wall, behind which stood a stout middle-aged man with curly black hair and a thick black moustache. He wore a grey flannel shirt, rolled up at the sleeves, and tipped his battered straw hat to Mr Bernard as he entered. There were a number of tables and chairs spread across the packed dirt floor, and at the back of the room stood a magnificent mahogany billiard table, the green felt shimmering in the sunlight that filtered in through the attap roof and open windows. Two artillery officers were playing a quiet game, no doubt for a wager, thought Bernard, wondering idly whether Sir Stamford Raffles' objections to gambling extended to these harmless flutters. He recognized John Morgan sitting at a table at the far left of the room. Morgan had his back to him, but had turned when Bernard had entered. Bernard touched his head in acknowledgement, and

Morgan returned the greeting with a slight wave of his hand.

Across the table from Morgan sat one of the strangest figures Bernard had ever seen. He was a slim built young man, no more than twenty-five years of age, to judge by the smoothness of his clean-shaven face, but with long thin hair that hung over his shoulders, and which was as grey as that of a man three score years or more. He wore a smart black frockcoat with a clean white collarless shirt, and a magenta waistcoat, from which hung an ornate silver watch and chain. He held a glass of red wine in his left hand while his right hand rested upon his silver walking cane. Behind him sat a large Negro, dressed in blue cotton overalls, who stared at him with bloodshot eyes. The young man continued his conversation with John Morgan with scarcely a glance at Bernard, but the Negro did not take his bloodshot eyes off him.

'Good afternoon,' Bernard said to the proprietor, whom he presumed to be Captain Kelly, as he approached the bar. 'I'm Mr Bernard, the chief of police in this fair city of Singapore'

'And to you, y'r honour. My name is Captain Kelly, who was the skipper of the *Aurora*, and now owner of this 'ere hostelry. I hope we done nothing wrong—I got all the proper papers from the colonel, and I can show ye them right now.'

'No, no,' Bernard assured him, 'no need for that. I was just dropping by for a friendly visit, to see how you were getting along.'

'Well in that case, what's your fancy, Mr Bernard? Would you like a Belhaven's or a Guinness? Something stronger, perchance? All a bit warm, I'm afraid, since we have no ice. But we do our best—we keep them in the river, with a big Kling watching over them with a big stick.'

'I'll be damned,' said Bernard, pleasantly surprised to hear that they had his favourite beer. 'I'll have a Belhaven's then! It's thirsty work walking around keeping the peace in the hot sun!'

The captain signalled to a Malay boy who stood waiting at the end of the bar, who quickly disappeared outside. A few minutes later he returned with the bottle of beer, which the captain poured into a pewter tanker.

'Your health, Captain Kelly, and may your business prosper,' said Bernard, raising his drink.

'And yours, Mr Bernard,' replied the captain. 'Now how about something to eat? I've got a Chinaman back o' the house can rustle ye up some fresh chicken and rice, quick as you like and as hot as you want.'

Bernard declined, and also declined to inquire what other services Captain Kelly might provide. There were no women on the premises, but he knew well enough that there was already a lively trade in prostitution in the settlement, given the terribly low ratio of women to men for all races, except among the Malays.

'Chief of police, you are then. Well, we certainly need some law and order around here. I saw a Malay cut down dead in broad daylight the other day, and nobody paid a bit of attention.'

'Very likely the sultan's men fighting the Malaccans,' Bernard replied. 'They seem to hate each other with a vengeance. We don't get much trouble from the Chinese or the Klings; the Bugis look a fearsome bunch, but they keep to themselves. Glad of it, since you and I have more fingers on our two hands than I have peons.'

'Maybe things will get better as the place grows, as it surely will,' the captain suggested.

'Well, I'm sure of that, Captain Kelly, but it will probably be faster than John Company's payroll,' Bernard responded, finishing his drink. 'How much do I owe you?'

'On the house, Chief,' said the captain, 'and we hope to see you back again soon.'

Before he left, Bernard walked across to where John Morgan

was sitting.

'Good afternoon, Mr Morgan,' he said. 'How goes your trade with Siam?' Bernard knew that Morgan had made a great success of a trading mission to Siam that Colonel Farquhar had sent him on, with his ship loaded with cotton goods and ironware, and bearing gifts from Farquhar for the King of Siam as a token of their good will. Morgan had contracted with a local Siamese merchant to act as a comprador, and had made a great deal of money on his subsequent voyages.

'Excellent, Bernard, truly excellent,' Morgan replied, beaming with pride. 'I'm planning a return trip, just as soon as I can organize new cargoes.'

'While you're here, Bernard, I'd like you to meet Mr Harry Purser, a gentleman from the American south, from Savannah in Georgia. He's thinking of starting up a plantation here, gambier or perhaps nutmegs.'

Mr Purser rose and learned across the table to shake Bernard's hand. The man was thin as a rake, but nearly six foot tall, and the grip of his pale white hand was like an iron vice.

'Pleased to meet you, sir,' he said in a slow Southern drawl. 'I understand you are our new chief of police, whose duty it is to protect from danger the citizens of this wonderful new eastern emporium. But I assure you we have all been behaving ourselves, so you need have no concern on behalf of our good selves,' he continued with a thin smile. His eyes were blue, not the deep blue of the sky, or the warm blue of the lagoon, but the thin cold blue of the assassin's knife. They were mesmerizing, like a cat's eyes, and sent a cold chill down Bernard's spine. This was not a man with an interest in gambier or nutmegs, he thought.

He wished them both well, and left Captain Kelly's establishment. He had planned to continue to walk up High Street to visit Mr Johnson, but returned to his office. He told Constable

Ramaswamy to position himself near one of the shops at the end of the bazaar, and to keep an eye on Captain Kelly's bar. When a young man in a black frockcoat and long grey hair came out, likely accompanied by a large Negro man, he was to follow him discreetly, and then report back to the office. Since Bernard's peons wore no official uniform, there was little likelihood of him being detected. Bernard then left to visit Mr Johnson.

The following day Constable Ramaswamy reported that the man had left the bar in the early evening, and travelled with the Negro to the sultan's compound in Kampong Glam. He had stayed about an hour, and then returned to town, where he had taken an Indian lighter out to a Malay prahu in the harbour.

'Damn him to hell,' said Mr Bernard, although Constable Ramaswamy did not know which gentleman he was wishing to send to that place.

* * *

Captain Pearl returned to Singapore in the *Indiana*. After he had seen to the unloading of his cargoes, he rode out to his new house on the hill overlooking the western shore. He had completed his final sale with the last of the Chinese gambier farmers on his previous voyage. It has cost him a pretty penny, but now he owned the whole hill, which his coolie labourers had planted with the nutmeg and coffee vines that he had brought from Sumatra.

Pearl leaned back in his chair on the verandah of his newly completed house at the summit of the hill, and surveyed the scene below him with satisfaction. He could see the bustle of the town and the river, the merchantmen and native craft in the bay and roads, including his own *Indiana*. He sighed with satisfaction, and lit a fine cigar that he had been saving for the occasion. He was now a plantation owner as well as a ship's captain. He wondered whether he should sell the *Indiana*, or keep on trading a little longer. After all, he thought to himself, business had never been so good.

To celebrate the occasion, he invited Ronnie and Sarah Simpson to dinner. Pearl admired Ronnie's new wife Sarah, and wished he could find himself a woman to match her. But women, especially European women, were as scarce as cold mornings in the settlement. Perhaps he should import a Chinese concubine, like the rich Peranakan merchants, he joked to the couple.

'Or a Malay princess,' suggested Sarah, 'I'm sure the sultan has plenty to spare.'

Captain Pearl told them of his plans to name the hill Mount Stamford, in honour of his good friend Sir Stamford Raffles, whom he had heard would soon be returning to Singapore for a final visit. He would host a grand party then to celebrate the occasion. Ronnie told Captain Pearl about the brick house he was having built by Naraina Pillai next to his godown.

19

Raffles and Sophia arrived in Singapore on the tenth of October. When Raffles saw the shipping in the roads and the extent of the development in the town, his heart leapt. The headache that had plagued him all the way from Bencoolen lifted, and his spirits rose for the first time since the death of his children. He may have failed to achieve what he had striven for in Java and Sumatra, but he at least had done some real good here, and would now work to make this 'other child' his lasting legacy.

Colonel Farquhar met them on the dockside, accompanied by Captain Flint and Mary Anne. The sepoy honour guard presented arms and the Bengal Native Artillery fired a seventeen-gun salute. At the residency, Farquhar told Raffles that he had just received figures indicating that the total trade for the past two and half years was eight million dollars, with nearly three thousand vessels passing through the port; he estimated that by the end of the year the trading volume would surpass that of Penang and Malacca combined. The population of the settlement had recently been estimated at around ten thousand, with a small but solid nucleus of well-established European, Chinese and Arab merchants. The Malays still represented the largest percentage of the population, with the Chinese the second largest. But these numbers were already out of date and changing fast, as more and more Chinese immigrants arrived with the junks on the northeast monsoon, and it was only a matter of time, Farquhar thought, before they would form the largest ethnic group.

Raffles was very glad to hear this news, but declined Farquhar's offer of accommodation at the residency, and his invitation to dine with some of the leading merchants. He told Farquhar they were going to stay with his sister Mary Anne and her husband Captain Flint, and asked him to pay Captain Flint their monthly rent, which would be one hundred and fifty dollars. He also asked Farquhar to apologize to the merchants. He and Lady Sophia were tired from their journey, and had not properly recovered from their recent ill health—he would meet with them all in due course.

Yet when they arrived at the Flints' house Raffles was all energy and enthusiasm, and Sophia was amazed by the change that had come over him in the space of a few short hours. All the tragedy and disappointment that had shadowed his life seemed to have been blown away by the soft sea breezes of Singapore. She herself felt refreshed and rejuvenated, and was overjoyed to see Mary Anne and her son Charles again.

The next morning, after what Raffles described as an excellent night's sleep, he told them over breakfast that he felt like a new man, and was ready to get down to work as soon as possible.

While he was delighted with the progress of the settlement, Raffles strongly disapproved of many aspects of Colonel Farquhar's administration. He thought his taxation of legalized gambling highly objectionable, and found him altogether too lackadaisical in his dealings with the sultan, the temenggong, and the merchant community. Even his dress was offensive—most of the time the man wore a native sarong, and sometimes even on official occasions, such as the meetings of the bechara court. How could he expect the native populations to respect the authority of the Company and the British Government if he dressed like that! And day after day Captain Flint fed him complaints about the profligacy and inefficiency of Farquhar's administration, his nepotism, such as his appointment of his own son-in-law as chief of police, and the many defects of his character.

However, most of all Raffles objected to Farquhar's provisional lease of land to both European and Chinese merchants along the east bank of the river, which he had specifically instructed him to reserve for government buildings. Something he had recently reminded Farquhar of when the man complained about the unsuitability of both the east beach and west bank of the river for merchant godowns. Yet now, despite Raffles' specific instructions, there was a string of plank and brick houses and godowns stretching from the foot of Bukit Larangan to the residency at the mouth of the river. The bazaar he'd ordered Farquhar to remove still stood, and was about four or five times its former size—a bustling, thriving community, to be sure, but with no order or direction to it.

He would soon put an end to all that.

However, a few days later, after he had talked with Alexander Guthrie and Ronnie Simpson and they had shown him the sand bar that prohibited the loading and unloading of goods on the east beach, he had to grudgingly admit it was quite unsuitable as a location for European merchant godowns. And now, as he stood outside the police station and jail house with Colonel Farquhar and Lieutenant Jackson, the new chief engineer, looking across to the west bank of the river at high tide, he saw that it was quite unsuitable for the location of Chinese merchant godowns.

'Of course the obvious solution to our problems would be to fill in the marsh and build it to the height o' this bank,' Farquhar said. 'But we had no money for it. I tried to get the merchants to contribute to the cost, but they wouldna have any o' it.'

Raffles stood silent and thoughtful for a few moments. 'But that would clearly be the best thing to do,' he eventually said. 'Then we could relocate the European and Chinese merchant godowns on the west bank, and redistribute the other races.'

Raffles then asked Lieutenant Jackson how difficult it would be to fill in the swamp and build up the west bank.

'The best thing to do would be to break up the hill at South Point, and use the earth and stones to fill in the swamp and the small streams. But as Colonel Farquhar says, Sir Stamford, it would cost you a pretty penny in labour.'

'We'll just have to deal with that,' said Raffles. 'We can charge the merchants for their use of the land on the east river, and use that to finance the costs of reclamation. And if that's not enough, I can draw money from Calcutta on my authority as lieutenant-governor.'

Aye, so ye can, thought Farquhar to himself. So much for keeping expenses to a bare minimum! But he held his tongue.

* * *

Raffles consulted with George Drumgoole Coleman, the Irish architect and surveyor who had come out to Singapore in June, and whom Raffles had commissioned to draw up plans for a bungalow on Bukit Larangan, about the feasibility of reclaiming the land on the west bank of the river. Coleman saw no special problems, so Raffles made his decision without further delay. He formed a Land Allotment Committee on 17th October, comprising three persons whom he described as 'disinterested': Dr Wallich, of the Botanical Gardens in Calcutta, whom Raffles had appointed to supervise the creation of a new botanical garden on Bukit Larangan, Dr Lunsdaine, Dr Wallich's assistant, and Captain Salmon, the harbour master at Bencoolen. He charged them to consider his scheme for relocating the merchant godowns on the west bank of the river.

A week later the Land Allotment Committee approved the reclamation of the west bank of the river, which was to be raised to the height of the east bank, and formed into an embankment to confine the river and drain the adjacent ground. They also recommended that the embankment be formed into a wharf extending about six or seven hundred yards in a crescent shape from the road opposite

Ferry Point to the point that Lieutenant Jackson had marked out for the new wooden bridge across the river. They allowed sixty feet for the front of the godowns, with a space of twelve feet between, and a depth of one hundred feet, with an additional fifty feet for a rear yard and back entrance. This would allow for about twenty to thirty godowns or other commercial buildings along the wharf. They also approved a tax on existing godowns and houses on the east bank and plain, and on future properties on the west bank, to partly offset the cost of land reclamation.

20

'Colonel Farquhar!' Raffles screamed as he stormed into the residency. 'Colonel Farquhar!'

Farquhar almost fell off the chair on which he had been dozing. He rubbed his eyes and looked up to see Raffles standing before him, red in his rage. Farquhar worried about him—the man seemed about to have an apoplectic fit.

'Calm yourself, Sir Stamford, and tell me what troubles ye.'

Raffles looked with disdain upon the colonel, who was dressed in a loose shirt and sarong.

'I'll tell you what troubles me, sir. Your crass neglect of the law, which by Act of Parliament forbids the trading of slaves. But yet you sit here sleeping, ignoring a slave market taking place right under your eyes. The Bugis are selling slaves in the bazaar—about fifty in all—and had the audacity to send me two young women as a present! God's blood man—it is a public disgrace!'

'I know about it, Sir Stamford,' Farquhar calmly replied. 'I was presented with two myself, but sent them back. I trust you did the same.'

Raffles' cold look told them that he had.

'What do you want me to do about it, Sir Stamford?'

'Do about it, Colonel Farquhar? I demand that you put an end to it, this very instant. As I told you, trading in slaves is illegal through out all British possessions.'

Farquhar rose from his chair and stood facing Raffles at full height, with his arms clasped behind him. As he was the taller of the two men, this meant that he looked down upon Raffles, which

Farquhar knew annoyed him intensely. But at this moment he did not care, for he was fed up with Raffles' sanctimonious claptrap.

'Well, I could move them back to the Bugis village, if it suits you, but there's not much else I can do. And it has one unfortunate consequence ...'

'Which is?' snapped Raffles, interrupting him.

'Which is,' Farquhar replied, 'that we are likely to miss any bonnie wee white laddies and lassies that they put up for sale. We've saved a goodly number that way already. As Alex Johnston will tell you, Lizzie Walker was his first purchase in Singapore. Where would she be now if he had not? In some hell hole in Borneo or Sulu, no doubt.'

'But you must put a stop to it!' Raffles responded.

'And exactly how do you propose that I do that, Sir Stamford? May I remind you that you did not think a police force was necessary? And God forbid that I should send our poor force against the Bugis, who number hundreds of fighting men. And if ye send the troops against them, ye'll have a bloodbath that wid drive a' the other traders away like a shot—a' the Malacca men wid tak themselves right back tae Malacca.'

'You should never have allowed this,' Raffles responded.

'Och aye, and what do you think I should have done? Should I have denied Arong Bilawa and his followers sanctuary when they fled from the Dutch? They were a godsend, Raffles—they brought most of the archipelago trade with them. Do you really want to lose them now?'

Raffles was about to respond, but Farquhar beat him to it.

'And another thing. You were very happy to welcome Syed Omar and his uncle here just afore ye left the last time. You told me to reserve them a good piece of land, to ensure that they would stay and secure for us the benefit of their established Arab trading networks. A grand idea, which has already borne fruit. But do you really want me to go into their houses and inspect their servants, whom I know for a fact were a' bought at the slave markets. Or whit aboot our friends the temenggong and Sultan Hussein— their compounds are full o' slaves. And whit about the hundreds of Chinese enslaved through indentured service, which is almost impossible for them to git out of, with their arrack and opium charged to their accounts. Do ye want me to send them back tae China, then? Man, the whole settlement would collapse if ye did that!'

Raffles stood still for few moments, livid with anger, before he responded.

'You seem not to have heard me, Colonel Farquhar,' he said with cold but now calm formality, 'or mean to willfully ignore me. May I remind you again that trading in slaves is illegal through out all British possessions.'

'That may be so, and I dinna approve of the trade myself, but may I remind you that Singapore is no a British possession—we were only granted authority to establish a factory on this part of the island. But if it bothers you so much I'll get the Bugis to move themselves out to the sultan's compound.' So saying, Colonel Farquhar picked up his walking stick and prepared to go out.

'You disappoint me greatly, Colonel Farquhar, in this and many other respects. I will put a stop to this!' Raffles replied, turning on his heel and storming out of the residency.

Farquhar was not sure in which other respects he had disappointed Raffles, or what Raffles intended to put a stop to. But he had no regrets, other than not being able to prevent Captain Flint taking over as harbour master. He had brought the Peranakan merchants and Malays down from Malacca, he had welcomed Arong Bilawa and the Bugis, and he had kept the merchants happy on the east bank, which had enabled the settlement to grow at its remarkable pace, with little disruption and discord between the races, the sultan and the temenggong's men excluded. And all on a shoestring, with no thanks frae His Lordship.

He whistled for his dogs, and went out to have a quiet word with the Bugis in the bazaar.

* * *

After he received the Land Allotment Committee approval, Raffles moved quickly. On October 29 he issued a proclamation in the name of the (yet to be formed) Town Committee, which was circulated among the merchants, with copies posted in prominent places.

Whereas several European merchants and others having occupied and constructed buildings of Masonry on portions of ground on the East Bank of the Singapore River and elsewhere, within the space intended to have been reserved exclusively for public purposes, viz., between the old lines and Singapore River from the sea inland to the back of the hill:

Under the present circumstances of the Settlement it is not the desire of Government to insist on the immediate removal of such buildings as may have been constructed of Masonry by Europeans and completed before the 10th April last, unless the same may become indispensable for the public service, but the parties interested are warned of what is intended, and the construction by individuals of all further buildings whatever, as well as the outlay of all further sums of money on those already constructed within the limits aforesaid, after this date, is most strictly prohibited.

The merchants were taken aback by this sudden and unexpected proclamation, and deeply concerned about the future of their enterprises. Many, such as Claude Quieros and John Morgan, expressed their anger, and Alexander Guthrie was particularly incensed. He had thought he had been canny renting a godown from an Arab merchant, but when the fellow had sold the building to an Armenian, he had gone ahead with the building of his own brick godown on the land that Farquhar had offered. Given the buildings that had sprung up all around, he had thought it was a safe bet. Surely Raffles would not destroy all the merchant buildings on the east bank? Others questioned each other about what they knew of Raffles' intention. Did he intend to move them back to the east beach? Many said they would leave if Raffles did that. Tan Che Sang and Lim Guan Chye said they would return to Malacca, and they were sure others would follow. The merchants sent a deputation to Colonel Farquhar to see what they could glean from him, but Farquhar told them the matter was out of his hands. He informed them that it was his understanding that the Land Allotment Committee had approved a plan to reclaim the west bank of the river and relocate the merchant godowns there, a piece of news that was even less well received.

'Why can't we just stay where we are?' said Alexander Johnston, 'We're a' doing just grand as it is.'

'I agree,' said Ronnie, 'but we are in no position to argue if Raffles sticks to his guns. As you all ken, Colonel Farquhar warned us that our leases were only temporary and provisional, and that the Lieutenant-Governor might refuse to honour them. I suggest we send one of our party to meet wi' Raffles and ask him to clarify the situation, so that we will be in a better position to make our own judgments—including whether we will want to remain under the new arrangements.'

'I nominate Ronnie Simpson,' said Graham Mackenzie. 'There

is no merchant more respected, and Ronnie and Raffles go way back ... to the day the settlement was founded. We know that he will represent our interests well.' The nomination was quickly seconded, and approved by all, including the Chinese and Arab merchants.

'So be it then,' Ronnie said, and thanked them for their support. 'I will try to arrange a meeting tomorrow with Sir Stamford. Today being a Thursday, I hope to be able to report back to you gentlemen by the weekend—I ken we are all anxious about these matters.'

But Ronnie did not need to arrange a special meeting with Raffles. When he returned to his home he received a note from the Governor–General, which had been delivered by Nilson Hull, Raffles' acting secretary and brother-in-law:

> My dear Sir
>
> I am sorry to observe that you are going on with a Brick Building in a very objectionable part of your Compound and that I am compelled to stop your progress in it.
>
> If you and Captain Thompson would favour us with your company to dinner on Friday, I shall explain more fully.
>
> Yours sincerely,
> T. S. Raffles

At dinner the following evening with Raffles and the Flints, Ronnie listened patiently while Raffles outlined his grand schemes for the settlement: for the new layout of the town; for the resettlement of the merchants and the various races; for the new system of justice he planned to introduce; and for the creation of an educational institution of higher learning for the sons of Malay royalty and princes, so that this once great civilization could receive the intellectual and technological benefits of the European enlightenment and the scientific and industrial revolutions.

'Most interesting, Sir Stamford,' Ronnie said when Raffles had completed his vision, 'but let me get right tae the point that concerns the merchant community—who, by the way, yesterday afternoon appointed me to be their representative in this matter, and to report back tae them on your intentions. We have heard that you plan to move a' the merchant godowns across the river, once the west bank has been filled and contained. But would it nae be better—and cheaper—to leave them where they are, which suits us a' just fine, and locate the government buildings further back.'

'But then we would have to move the European town further east, closer to the sultan's compound,' Raffles replied. 'And then all the races would be mixed up, save for the Chinese already established along the western shore at Telok Ayer. If all the races are settled on the plain, there can be no ordered planning of the development of the settlement, and it may be generations before the west bank is developed for commence; for the more established the merchants become on the east bank and the plain, the less will they be inclined to move their businesses. No, Captain Simpson, the thing has to be done now if it is to be done at all. Colonel Farquhar should have done it long ago, of course, but I fully intend to make up for his negligence over these past few years.'

Ronnie thought this remark was appallingly unfair to Farquhar, whose financial resources for the administration of Singapore had been desperately constrained by Raffles himself, who had even begrudged his small police force. He knew that Farquhar had been forced to hire clerks for the resident's office from his own pocket when Raffles had authorized funding for only one, while at the same time authorizing three clerks and a peon for his brother-in-law Captain Flint. But this was neither the time nor the place to defend Colonel Farquhar.

'But how are ye going tae pay for this move, Sir Stamford? Are we going to be assessed on our properties tae pay for the reclamation, as some o' us have heard? What about those of us who have already gone to the expense of erecting substantial brick godowns, and did so to seize the opportunities that the new free port opened up. We couldna build on the beach or the west bank, and we couldna just sit and twiddle our thumbs either.'

Raffles acknowledged Ronnie's point with a smile.

'I grant that you were in a difficult position, and it is unfortunate that my original plan proved to be unsuitable. But in the end it is no excuse, and the godowns will have to be removed. But to answer your first question, you will be assessed on your present properties, as you will be assessed on the new land leases I hope you will accept when they are put up for auction in the New Year. These assessments will, it is true, be used in part to pay for the reclamation, but these assessments would have been made in any case, and you must all have expected that. The port is free, but that does not mean everything in the port is free! We need to assess every property owner and lessee to raise revenue for administration and essential services. But don't worry about your present buildings, just so long as you don't add anything more to them. You will be properly compensated for your loss according to the assessments of their value that I have asked Colonel Farquhar to draw up. Half will be paid in advance; half upon the removal of merchants to their new locations. I may have to draw on money from Calcutta to pay for it, but I consider it an investment worth making.'

'Well, that certainly puts a better complexion on things,' Ronnie responded, rubbing his chin as he reflected on it. 'I think most o' the merchants could be persuaded to move under these circumstances. I'll report this back to them as soon as possible.'

'Oh, I want you to do more than that, Captain Simpson,' Raffles replied. 'I want you to help me persuade them! I would like you to serve on my new Town Committee to represent the merchants. There will be two other Europeans, Captain Charles Davis of the

23rd Bengal Native Infantry, and George Bonham, whom I have brought from Nattal to serve as deputy resident—an excellent fellow and a good administrator. There will also be representatives from the Chinese, Malay, Arab, Bugis, Indian and Javanese communities, and we will consider everyone's special needs and interests when it comes to the redistribution of land and resettlement of the different races. We will gather all relevant information, with power to summon any person who may assist us in our deliberations, before we make our final determinations. I hope you will honour me by agreeing to serve on this consultative committee.'

'I wid be honoured to, Sir Stamford,' Ronnie replied, 'and you can count on my full cooperation.'

Ronnie had no desire to serve on any such committee, but he immediately recognized how important it was for him to have a voice on it, to represent his own interests as well as those of his fellow merchants. He felt a little uncomfortable doing so, however, for he recognized the slight to Colonel Farquhar in Raffles' selection of the new assistant resident George Bonham as a member of the Town Committee but not the resident himself, and did not want to be associated with it.

Raffles seemed to have read his mind. 'I'm very grateful to you Captain Simpson, and thank you in advance for your time and trouble. In case you are wondering why Colonel Farquhar is not included, it is because he will be busy enough supervising the reclamation work and preparing assessments for the buildings presently occupying the east bank.'

And so it was agreed.

21

In November, Lieutenant Jackson completed a new wooden drawbridge across the river to replace the old wooden footbridge that had fallen into disrepair. The new bridge was called Presentment Bridge, but also became known as Monkey Bridge, because of the dexterity required of pedestrians trying to cross the narrow thoroughfare during the busiest hours of the day.

* * *

Raffles set up his Town Committee, with Captain Davis as chair, which met with representatives from the various communities and races, and summoned individuals to give evidence and information before the committee. While they deliberated, Lieutenant Jackson set about the task of reclaiming the land on the west bank of the river. He employed a force of close to three hundred Chinese, Malay, Indian and Javanese labourers to excavate the hill at South Point and deposit the earth into the marsh, and to built up the embankment using crushed stones and cut timbers, until they had raised the ground and formed a quay that ran in a crescent shape seven hundred yards along the river's edge.

Each morning Raffles, Farquhar, Lieutenant Jackson and George Coleman, now employed in an advisory capacity, were out directing the coolies as they laboured with pickaxes and shovels in the hot sun. Long lines of men, balancing buckets of earth on poles carried over their shoulders, snaked their way down from the hill to the edge of the river, where they deposited their loads into the marsh, and then returned for more. At the end of each day a party of soldiers arrived with a bag of money to pay the labourers.

* * *

At the end of December, Raffles and Sophia moved into the bungalow that George Coleman had built for them on Bukit Larangan. It was a modest affair with plank walls, Venetian windows, and an attap roof, but the sea breezes provided some relief from the oppressive heat of the town. It was about one hundred feet long and fifty feet wide, and consisted of two parallel halls with front and back verandahs. Two square wings at the back contained the sleeping apartments. Despite his new vigor and enthusiasm, Raffles still suffered from crippling headaches, which laid him out for days on end. He confessed to Sophia that he thought he had not long to live, and that if he were to die in this place, it would give great comfort to his soul if his bones could be buried among the rajahs of the ancient city of Singapura. Sophia told him not to be morbid, that he had years of happy retirement to look forward to, and to the final recognition, she was sure, of his great achievements in the East.

Raffles and Dr Wallich laid out a new Botanical and Experimental Garden at the back of Bukit Larangan, close by the Bras Basah stream, extending nearly fifty acres beyond the original clove and nutmeg plantations that had been laid out by Mr Dunn in the first year of the settlement. Raffles also arranged for the Christian cemetery at the foot of the hill to be relocated to the far side of the hill.

But as the weeks passed his headaches worsened. After an especially severe attack, Dr Montgomerie advised him to depart for England immediately. Raffles declined to do so, insisting that he had important work to complete before he left. But he did write to the governor-general in Calcutta formally requesting to be relieved of his position, and stating that he intended to return to England for the sake of his health, after he had made his final arrangements in Singapore and Bencoolen. In the same letter he described in detail what he considered to be the demonstrated inefficiency and general inadequacy of Colonel Farquhar's administration of the settlement over the past three years. Colonel Farquhar had not followed his instructions with respect to the location of merchant godowns and government buildings, and had proved himself incompetent in many other matters. Raffles advised the governor-general that he considered Colonel Farquhar totally unequal to the task of administering the rapidly developing commercial asset that Singapore had become.

He also complained that the colonel had been far too indulgent in his relations with the sultan and the temenggong, to the point that he had almost turned native himself. Recalling that Farquhar had a Malay wife, Raffles suggested that the closeness of his relations might create problems for the future development of the settlement:

'The Malay connection might create an opening for such a combination of peculiar interests as not only to impede the progress of order and regularity but may lay the foundation of future inconvenience which may be hereafter difficult to overcome.'

Raffles asked the governor-general to appoint a replacement for Farquhar as soon as was convenient, and before any further damage was done. He also recommended that the new residency be placed under the direct control of the governor-general, rather than the new Lieutenant-Governor of Bencoolen. In the meantime he would stay on in Singapore until a new resident was appointed, and then return to Bencoolen to settle up his affairs before returning home.

22

1823

In January, Raffles held a dinner in honour of Sultan Hussein and the temenggong at his new bungalow. He had commuted their claims to revenue from a variety of different sources—from presents from ship's captains, from the lease of land and levies on the profits of Chinese merchants returning to their homeland—into a fixed monthly payment. But he felt a little guilty about treating them as little more than paid servants of the Company, despite the fact that he despised Sultan Hussein and did not trust the temenggong. So he thought he would reward the two men with a public display of British munificence. First he offered to educate their sons in Calcutta at the Company's expense, but they both politely declined. Then he advised them that he was willing to set them up in business, now that the settlement had proved itself to be such a commercial success. He was arranging to have a consignment of cotton goods shipped out from Calcutta for them to sell on commission.

'We cannot do that,' Sultan Hussein replied haughtily. 'A sultan and the descendant of a sultan trading, whoever heard of such a thing? Who do you think we are?'

Raffles was astonished by this response, and said in jest, 'Do you mean it is better to be a pirate than a trader, then?' He suspected both of involvement with the piracy that plagued the waters around Singapore.

'Of course,' replied Sultan Hussein, and not in jest. 'We have always been pirates. We inherited this noble way of life from our ancestors, and there is no disgrace in it. But trade...?' He rolled his eyes, and turned his pouting lips into a sneering expression of contempt. Raffles was flabbergasted, and turned bright red with embarrassment. He fumed within, and wished he could throw the pair in jail and ship their followers back to Riau and Johor.

Ronnie and Sarah held their sharp gaze across the table, and only by sheer force of mutual will managed to prevent each other from bursting into laughter.

* * *

Nathaniel Wallich, the superintendent of the new Botanic and Experimental Gardens, returned to Calcutta in late January. Dr Montgomerie, who was a keen naturalist himself, was appointed to the vacant position. Montgomerie cleared the land that Raffles and Wallich had marked out, and planted more spice trees on the terraces along the hillside. The evergreen nutmeg trees produced a riot of colour along the base of the hill, with their peach blossoms and crimson and cream fruits. The clove trees were planted between the nutmegs, their crimson flowers sparkling bright against their dark green leaves in the midday sun. Montgomerie had a brick wall with ornamental pillars and woodwork erected to front the gardens, with a hedge of bright green Chinese bamboo running along the edge of the hillside.

He suggested to Raffles that the government should employ coolies to clear more land to cultivate these spices, and arrange for plots of land to be assigned to Chinese market gardeners, who were bound to make a success of them. He confidently advised Raffles that the cultivation of these spices could eventually satisfy most of the considerable European demand for them, and would serve as a stable source of profit for the settlement during times of economic depression.

Dr Montgomerie was so pleased with the progress of the gardens that he started his own plantation—which he called Woodsville—about two miles north east of the gardens, along the track leading past Bukit Selegie. He planted nutmeg, sugar cane, and a variety of experimental crops, such as coffee, tobacco and cotton—none of which flourished. He also built a mill driven by a waterwheel to process his sugar cane.

One day, while walking along the edge of his plantation, he came across a Malay woodcutter sitting in the shade of a tree, paring a log of wood with his parang. The day was exceptionally hot, and the sun beat down fiercely from a cloudless sky. Montgomerie stopped beside the woodcutter to remove his hat and wipe his brow with his handkerchief. The woodcutter laid down his parang, and wiped his own sweating face with a piece of cloth, smiling in acknowledgement of the doctor.

Montgomerie looked down at the parang, and back at the woodcutter. The man was clearly sweating as much as he was, but the blade had never once slipped in his grasp. He asked the man if he could look at his blade; the woodcutter was surprised by his request, but readily agreed. When he picked up the tool, Montgomerie was surprised by the firmness of its grip. He swung it vigorously in the air, but it never once slipped from his sweating hand. He looked closer at the handle of the blade. It was not made of wood, as he had originally supposed, but of a hard substance that had been fitted to the shaft and shaped into the woodcutter's grip.

He asked the man what the handle was made of, and the woodcutter replied that it was formed from gutta-percha, the sap of a tree that grew in the jungle. He told him that when the sap was collected, it hardened, but would grow soft again when placed in hot water. There it could be formed into any shape, and would set firm into that shape when it was removed from the water. At Montgomerie's request, the woodcutter took him into the jungle and identified one of the gutta-percha trees. It stood straight and tall, about three feet at the base, with dense ascending branches. The ends of the buds of the tree were white with gutta sap. Montgomerie took out his notebook and sketched the tree, while the woodcutter cut a notch in the tree and collected a sample for him in a hollowed piece of bark. Montgomerie thanked the man, and returned to his office, where he sat thinking about the possible uses for the sap. One immediately sprung to mind. A surgeon working in tropical conditions, or a nervous surgeon working under any conditions, had difficulty maintaining a firm grip on scalpels and clamps. But instruments with handles set in this versatile substance might solve the problem. He resolved to write to his colleagues in the Medical Society of Calcutta about it.

* * *

It took them over three months, but by the end of February, the reclamation work was completed, and only a giant rock, about the size of a bull elephant, remained. When Tan Che Sang heard about this, he offered to have the rock removed for free. He sent along his servants to break it up, and later sold the rubble to a builder. Lieutenant Jackson discovered a far more interesting rock close to the mouth of the river, which had previously been hidden by some brushwood. It was about ten feet high, about the same in length, and about five feet wide. Some fifty lines of script were engraved upon its smooth surface, although much of it was illegible, having been worn away by rain and salt breezes. Raffles, Farquhar, Coleman, Jackson and others pondered over it, but none could decipher the script. Raffles, who poured powerful acids over the rock in an attempt to highlight the characters, declared that the writing was Hindu, but others thought that it was more likely to be Chinese.

Munshi Abdullah, who was working for Raffles as a scribe, maintained that the writing was Arabic, and offered an explanation of the purpose of the inscribed rock. He reminded them of the passages in the *Malay Annals* that told of the legendary feats of the giant Badang, who had supposedly flung a great rock across the mouth of the river. That would have been truly miraculous, Abdullah said, and he thought it more likely that the rock was a monument erected in his honour by the son of Sri Tri Buana, to celebrate the great deeds that Badang had performed for the rajah.

Raffles ordered that the Singapore Stone, as it came to be known, be protected against future damage, but unfortunately neglected to assign any official to that charge. [16]

23

a mile west of the Chinese Town. Land was reserved for the Arabs

On 28th February, just over two weeks after the fourth anniversary
of the founding of the settlement, the Town Committee completed
their work, and the new town plan was published and distributed,
posted in every prominent place, and declared upon the beating of
the gong in every quarter in all the languages of the settlement.

The ground east of the Singapore River to the Bras Basah stream,
extending from the beach to the rear of Bukit Larangan, was to be
reserved exclusively for the government. All other buildings would
be destroyed or appropriated for government purposes as required;
those who had been issued temporary permits by the resident would
be compensated for their losses. The European and the 'respectable'
Chinese merchants were to be relocated to the reclaimed land on
the west bank of the river, where they would be allowed to bid for
allotted spaces on the newly raised quay.

The European town was to be located east of the Bras Basah
stream, extending out towards the sultan's istana at Kampong
Glam, and inland as far as the Rochor River and foothills. The bulk
of the Chinese community was to be resettled in the area west of
the river, beyond the commercial quarter, extending through Telok
Ayer and beyond. Different areas of the Chinese town were to be
reserved for the different dialect groups—such as the Hokkien,
Teochew, Cantonese, Hakka and Hainanese—in order to avoid
disputes between them. The Chuliahs, the south Indian Muslims
from the Coromandel coast, most of whom made their living as
lightermen, were situated on the upper region of the west bank of
the river. The temenggong and his dependents and followers were

to be resettled on a large plot of land at Telok Blangah, a quarter of a mile west of the Chinese Town. Land was reserved for the Arabs in the vicinity of Sultan Hussein's istana, and the Bugis were moved further east to the mouth of the Rochor River.

The committee also directed that the streets and highways of the town and kampongs be laid out at right angles, and of uniform breadth, according to their status as primary, secondary or tertiary roads. Each street was to be assigned a name, and all houses, commercial properties and government buildings were to be numbered. The principal commercial and government buildings were to be constructed of masonry with tiled roofs, to avoid the danger of fire. As a special accommodation to the public, each house was to have 'a verandah of a certain depth, open at all times as a continued and covered passage on each side of the street'. Coleman later determined that the covered passageways should have a depth of five feet, and they became known as the 'five-foot ways'. Ground rent was to be assessed on all buildings, which would become due on the first day of January every year.

Provision was also made for Chinese and Muslim burial grounds, and the fish market was to be moved to Telok Ayer, with the pork, poultry and vegetable markets redistributed as appropriate. The bazaar on the plain was to be dismantled and the buildings destroyed, with the shops and stalls relocated to the respective communities of their owners.

Raffles then disbanded the Town Committee and appointed another committee to enact and enforce these allocations and regulations, which comprised George Bonham, the assistant resident, who was now also the registrar in charge of land allocation, Lieutenant Jackson, and Francis Bernard, the chief of police. The merchants grumbled, but most saw that the writing was on the wall. They accepted the compensation offered, and bid for the new lots when Bonham put them up for public auction in March, and declared all previous permits and leases null and void.

Two of the first to move were Alexander Johnston and Tan Che Sang. Johnston had been quick off the mark and had purchased the plot closest to the mouth of the river, where he built his godown and offices. His godown extended all the way back to the area of land set aside for the new Commercial Square, and he had his own private dock built out over the river. Johnston's godown came to be known as Tanjong Tangkap[1], because he was able to 'capture' the first tongkangs and sampans that entered the river mouth.

Tan Che Sang built his godown further up river, also backing onto Commercial Square. He had little need to capture business, since he acted as agent for the Chinese and Cochin-Chinese junks, and as comprador for many of the European houses. When he heard that the fish market was to be moved to Telok Ayer, he offered to build it at his own expense, so long as he was allowed to maintain it free of tax for a number of years. His offer was readily accepted.

The other merchants quickly followed, and soon Alexander Guthrie, John Hay, John and Ronnie Simpson, Graham Mackenzie, Lim Guan Chye and Tan Hong Chuan were established along the west bank of the river, which was named Boat Quay. The Chinese, Malay and Indian merchants in the bazaar were more reluctant to move, but a fire that had raged though their wooden shops and stalls in late December had preempted their protests. One of those who suffered most from the fire was Naraina Pillai, who had the largest shop in the bazaar. He appealed to Raffles, who assigned him a plot of land near Commercial Square. Naraina complained that he could not afford to pay for the new plot, since he had only paid for a small portion of the cotton piece goods that had been destroyed in the fire. Raffles told him not to worry, for the high prices of lots in the new commercial area quoted at auction were a mere formality, designed to ensure that only respectable traders

---

1 Meaning 'arrest' in Malay.

could secure them; they were not expected to pay the auction price, only the ground rent. For this Naraina was very grateful.

He was also grateful that most of the European and Chinese merchants who had sold him goods on credit had given him a year to repay his debts; he still operated his brick kilns and construction company, which were doing a roaring business, so they saw him as a good investment. The exception was John Morgan, who demanded immediate payment. Naraina managed to repay him the thousand dollars he owed within three months.

Not everyone relocated peacefully. Claude Quieros, the agent for Palmer & Co of Calcutta, bitterly protested the removal of the wharf he had built out over the river in front of his godown on the east bank. He refused to let Lieutenant Jackson tear it down, but backed down when Mr Bernard arrived with a group of peons. Captain Methven refused to quit his property, rejecting the generous offer made by Raffles, who wanted to convert it into a courthouse. Methven demanded more money—a lot more money—and gave Raffles a piece of his mind about his abuse of authority. In response Raffles requisitioned the property in the name of the East India Company and ordered Methven to quit the settlement.[17]

One other man refused to move, and curiously neither Raffles nor Bernard did anything about it. John Morgan remained in his large property on the east bank of the river, with his schooner docked at his private wharf. Some speculated that it was because Raffles did not wish to jeopardize the fledgling trade with Siam that Morgan had initiated. Others believed that Morgan, who had trained as a lawyer, had threatened the lieutenant-governor with legal action, which might cause the Court of Governors to overrule Raffles' treatment of the merchants, and threaten his new town plan.

Whatever the reason, most of the merchants were happy not to have Morgan as their neighbour on Boat Quay, although they remained annoyed at his behaviour, including his irritating habit of firing off his own gun in response to the official five o'clock morning gun fired from Bukit Larangan.

* * *

The peons came to the cottage where Moon Ling lived with her sons and daughter, and told her that she had to move to the west side of the river, where the Chinese community were to be resettled. They told her they would have to dismantle her cottage and joss house to Ma Cho Po, and advised her to remove any contents she wished to take with her. With the help of a Chinese family who lived nearby, Moon Ling and her children moved to a small plank and attap hut on the beach at Telok Ayer, where she set up a new joss house to Ma Cho Po. This became very popular with the hundreds of sinkeh who disembarked in Telok Ayer Bay, and who gave thanks to the goddess for their safe passage to Singapore.

One day when Moon Ling was preparing her offerings, her daughter asked her how Ma Cho Po had become a goddess.

'Well, pretty one,' Moon Ling began, 'the story goes like this. During the time of the Northern Song Dynasty, a baby was born on Meizhou Island in Fukien Province to a family called Lin. They had six children, only one of whom was a daughter. The mother prayed to Kuan Yin, the goddess of mercy, for another daughter. Kuan Yin came to the mother in a dream, and gave her a flower blossom to eat, which made her pregnant.

When the baby girl came into the world, the birthing room was filled with brilliant light and the soft fragrance of blossoms. Although she was bright-eyed and healthy, the baby girl never cried, so they called her Muonjiang, which means 'keeping silent'. Lin Muonjiang grew up by the sea–shore, and watched the fishing boats and trading junks set out in all weathers.

One day when she and her friends were gazing at their reflections in a rock pool, a monster appeared with a bronze talisman in its claws. The other girls fled, but Muonjiang was very brave and stood her ground, and reached out and took the talisman from the monster. From that day forth she developed strange powers of healing and prophecy. She could predict the coming weather, and warned sailors when it was too dangerous to set out on a voyage. She was a powerful swimmer, and would often rescue sailors when their ships sank in a storm.

One afternoon, while she was weaving a blanket for her sister, Muonjiang fell into a deep sleep. In her dream, she saw her father and brother washed overboard from their fishing boat in a great storm, and dived into the sea to rescue them. She grasped her brother in her arms, and held her father's sleeve in her teeth as she swam towards the shore.

Her mother came into the room, and seeing her daughter asleep, went to wake her. She touched Muonjiang gently on the shoulder, and asked her if she was unwell. Still half asleep, Muonjiang tried to answer, but as she opened her mouth in her dream she let go of her father's sleeve, and he was swept away by the angry sea. Muonjiang woke with a start and exclaimed 'Father and brother are in great danger!' Soon afterwards a fisherman came running to their house, and told them that there had been an accident at sea. The young master had been saved but the old man had drowned.

Muonjiang ran down to the beach and pushed her boat out to sea. She searched for three days and three nights, until she found her father's body washed up upon a promontory. She carried his body home and prepared the funeral rites. After the mourning period was complete, Muonjiang announced to her family that it was time for her to leave them.

She climbed up the mountain in the middle of the island. When she reached the top, she was engulfed by thick clouds, and carried up to heaven on a golden shaft of light. Beautiful music drifted down from the mountaintop, and when she disappeared from sight a giant rainbow appeared in the sky, uniting Heaven and Earth.

Muonjiang became an Empress of Heaven and protector of sea travellers. When sailors are in great danger, they know that if they call out her name, she will come and rescue them. Even in the darkest storm, she will appear in the sky carrying a red lantern, to guide the sailors to safety. And so she is known as the goddess of the sea, or Ma Cho Po.'

Her daughter sat silent for a few moments. Then she asked Moon Ling, 'Mother, did the goddess rescue father?'

'No,' Moon Ling replied, 'but I believe he followed her red lantern all the way to Heaven.'

24

Captain Pearl saw Colonel Farquhar coming up the hill. He rose from his chair on his verandah and went out to greet his old friend.

'Good morning, Colonel,' he said, 'to what do I owe the pleasure of this visit?'

Colonel Farquhar looked grim. 'I'm afraid I'm here on business, Captain Pearl. Sir Stamford is furious that you never asked his permission to build upon this hill. I have come with Mr Bernard and his peons to take possession of your property, and to bring you back to town.'

Captain Pearl saw Mr Bernard and the peons coming up behind the colonel, and shook his fist at them.

'You have no right!' he shouted at them. 'I received permission from the temenggong, and paid fair and square for every foot of this hill. I'll not give it up!'

'Calm down man,' said the colonel. 'I understand your position, and I'll do my best to square things with Raffles. Hopefully he'll change his mind when he thinks about it a bit more. But ye'll no advance your case by pittin' up a fight now.'

So Captain Pearl returned to the town with Colonel Farquhar, while the peons took charge of his property. He went round all day complaining about Raffles' behaviour to his merchant friends, and spent the night with the Simpsons, who listened patiently to his complaints about his property being taken by force of arms. It was not fair. He had lost everything and would have to start over once again.

But early next morning he received a letter from Raffles

summoning him to a meeting at the residency with Colonel Farquhar. Ronnie went with him to serve as a witness and lend moral support. When they arrived at the residency, Farquhar greeted them warmly.

'He's changed his mind,' Farquhar said. 'I talked to him yesterday, but I dinna think he paid me any mind—said it was a' my fault for letting you go ahead. But most of the other merchants supported your case, including Ronnie here and Mr Johnston, so he has decided to accept the status quo. I have ordered the peons to quit your property.'

Captain Pearl thanked him, and returned to his house upon his hill. He directed his manservant to send out invitations for the party he had been planning to hold to celebrate the completion of his house and plantations. He did not name his hill after Sir Stamford Raffles, and did not invite Sir Stamford to his celebration of Pearl's Hill.

* * *

Farquhar accepted the changes recommended by Raffles and the Town Committee stoically, although he bridled at Raffles' constant references to his unfortunate deviations from Raffles' original town plan. After three years of frugality enforced by the Governor-General of India and the Lieutenant-Governor of Bencoolen, it galled him to see Raffles spending money like water, including money drawn on account from Calcutta. But like the merchants, he too saw the writing on the wall. He went along with most of the changes, although he and Raffles quarreled over other matters, such as Captain Flint's monopoly control over lighterage, and his arbitrary treatment of the ships' captains, particularly those from China and Cochin China. Raffles always took his brother-in-law's side against Farquhar, and increased his powers, appointing Captain Flint as magistrate in charge of all disputes relating to shipping.

There was one aspect of the new town plan that Farquhar did vigorously protest, which was the assignment of all the land between the east bank of the river and the Bras Basah stream for government buildings. Farquhar wanted an area of eight hundred yards running along the edge of the beach reserved for public use, and demanded that the matter be referred to the governor-general in Calcutta. Raffles did not so refer it, but agreed to reserve the land, which came to be known as the Esplanade, and later as the Padang. [li]

* * *

Ebenezer Oates, former first mate of the *Fair Maid of London*, recalled once again with heavy sadness the fate of Captain Ramsey and his poor son Adam. Oates gazed out from the hut in which he was quartered with the other prisoners, who were mostly Malay. He had hoped that when the pirates returned to their base he might get a chance to escape, but he was carefully watched and the camp was heavily guarded.

They had arrived a few days earlier, at a stockade about half a mile inside of the mouth of a river. They had completed unloading the plunder, and were waiting to see what their fate might be. Yet it seemed their lives were to be spared, and all things considered he had to admit they had not been badly treated; they had been given ample food and drink since they had returned, and had not been beaten or tortured. Unlike the unfortunate captains and officers the pirates had captured. They had been buried up to their shoulders in the red earth, and a withered old man with a long white beard and toothless smile had danced around them. He had then proceeded to slice off their ears, noses, and lips, before splitting their sculls like coconuts with his club. Oates later learned that the old man had once been a great pirate chief, and was exercising his traditional rights.

---

li Meaning 'field' in Malay.

His gorge still rose when he thought about their cruelty, and their violation of European standards of treatment of captured enemy officers. So he was surprised to see a tall thin European gentleman leaving the central compound, bidding farewell to Si Rahman, and walking with his brother to the main gate. The man was dressed in a black frockcoat and maroon waistcoat, with a silver watch and chain, and long grey hair that fell over his shoulders. Ebenezer Oates crept out into the bright sunshine to get a closer look, knowing that the man must pass his way.

As he approached the hut, the stranger noticed Oates and spoke first.

'I'll wager you're the mate of the *Fair Maid of London*,' he said. 'A most unfortunate incident.'

'That it was,' Oates replied. 'Begging your pardon, sir,' he continued, 'you seem to know these fellows, and you don't look short of a shilling. Please buy me from them and take me with you——I'll pay you back double or triple the amount they ask as soon as I get myself a new ship. Whatever you ask. The good Lord would surely remember you for it.'

But when he looked into the stranger's cold blue eyes, he knew it was not to be.

'I dare say he would,' Purser replied, smiling sweetly. 'But I think I'll pass,' he said, and walked off towards the main gate of the compound.

Oates cursed the stranger under his breath, and hoped that this coldhearted man would perish along with pirates when their day of reckoning finally came.

25

Raffles appointed the first town magistrates, [18] two of whom were now required to sit with the resident on the weekly bechara court, which dealt with civil and criminal cases, with two others serving in rotation on the magistrates court, which met bi-weekly, and dealt with minor disputes.

In early March, the bechara court met for its weekly session. The first case before the court was that of Syed Yassin, who traded between Pahang and Singapore. Syed Yassin had received goods from Syed Omar, but had not paid for them, and Syed Omar was suing him for the price of the goods. Colonel Farquhar, after consulting with Messrs Johnston and Guthrie, informed Syed Yassin that it was the court's opinion that he owed Syed Omar fourteen hundred dollars.

At first Syed Yassin denied that he owed the money, but when witnesses were brought forward to prove the debt, he acknowledged it but pleaded poverty. 'But Tuan Farquhar, I have no money to pay this huge sum,' Syed Yassin protested. 'I have barely enough money to feed my family.'

'He has the money, but he will not pay,' Syed Omar interjected. 'He is not an honest man. He is a disgrace to the followers of the Prophet.'

'Syed Yassin, you must pay Syed Omar the amount assessed,' said Colonel Farquhar, 'or provide some security. Otherwise you will go to jail.'

Syed Yassin looked at him sullenly, but did not respond, so Farquhar ordered that he be taken to the jail. 'Next case,' he continued, as he motioned the officers to remove Syed Yassin from the court.

Syed Yassin was taken to the jail, a ramshackle wooden structure next to the resident's compound. It was just after two in the afternoon, and the cell in which he was placed was unbearably hot. It was also alive with flies and cockroaches, which ran over his feet as he sat on the plank bench and cursed Colonel Farquhar and Syed Omar. They had insulted him, Syed Yassin, who was a descendant of the Prophet. For hours he simmered and plotted his revenge, fingering the blade of the kris that he carried concealed within his robe.

Late in the afternoon he asked the jailer to summon Mr Barnard, the chief of police. The jailer was not inclined to grant his request, but Syed Yassin gave him such a cold and evil look that he thought the better of it, and decided there could be no harm. When Mr Bernard arrived, Syed Yassin asked if he could meet with Syed Omar, so that he could humbly beg his forgiveness, and plead for some more time to repay the money he owed to him in installments. He had learned his lesson, God be praised, and did not wish to spend any more time in this filthy cell.

Mr Barnard was glad to hear that Syed Yassin was being more reasonable about his debt to Syed Omar, and thought it best to let the two men try to work things out amicably between them. He was sure that Colonel Farquhar and the other magistrates would approve. After all, Syed Omar was unlikely to get his money while Syed Yassin languished in jail. So he released Syed Yassin into the custody of Constable Mehmood bin Nadir, who had just come on duty. Barnard instructed him to take Syed Yassin to the house of Syed Omar to let him make his apology and plead his case for more time to repay his debt. After the two men had spoken, he was to return with Syed Yassin to the police station and report what had been agreed. Then he would make a decision about whether Syed

Yassin should stay in jail or be released.

It was growing dark as Mehmood bin Nadir and Syed Yassin left the jailhouse, with Syed Yassin walking ahead. The sun was setting, casting its golden rays like streamers across the dark waters of the river. Mehmood watched the lightermen guiding their tongkangs up and down the river, like black animals crawling through the shadows of the night. He wished he was with his brothers on the river, but he had vowed that he would never work for that scoundrel Captain Flint. He did not mind the police work, which enabled him to support his family and pay off the loan on his boat, but he longed for the day when he could return to his true vocation as a lighterman.

When they reached the house of Syed Omar, Mehmood waited by the outer gate, and told Syed Yassin to go ahead and conduct his business, after which he was to return with him to the police station to report to Mr Bernard. When Syed Yassin approached the house, Syed Omar was standing on the verandah, looking out across his courtyard and garden. There was no moon, and the only light came from lanterns within the house, so Syed Omar did not see Syed Yassin until he was very close. Syed Omar was surprised when he saw the man who had cheated him walking up the path towards him, but his surprise turned to alarm when he saw the murderous look in Syed Yassin's eyes, and the kris in his hand. He ran back into the house, and fled by a back door that lead out into an alley. He was grateful that his uncle was visiting a friend at Kampong Glam, and hoped that he would not return any time soon. He circled round the edge of the river until he reached the residency, breathless and highly agitated.

Meanwhile, Syed Yassin ran through the house, brandishing his kris, calling on Syed Omar to come out and face him. He threatened the servants, and demanded to know the whereabouts of their master, but they only cowed in fear or ran away from him, their eyes fixed in horror on his dancing kris. Syed Yassin searched all the rooms of the house, but there was no sign of Syed Omar. In anger and frustration, he ran out of the house to search the garden.

26

Ronnie and Colonel Farquhar were at the residency discussing Ronnie's tax assessment when Syed Omar was brought before them and reported the attempted assault. Colonel Farquhar spoke to him in Malay, and advised him to calm himself. Farquhar could not tell who had assaulted him, since Syed Omar was so distressed that he was making little sense.

He said that Syed Yassin had attacked him, but the man was locked in jail, so he must be mistaken about that. But it was clear that an assault had taken place at Syed Omar's house, so Farquhar determined to go there right away.

Farquhar told Syed Omar not to worry, and to stay at the residency where he would be safe until things were sorted out. He sent one of his guards to summon Captain Davis from the military cantonment, to meet him with a company of sepoys at the home of Syed Omar. Colonel Farquhar snatched up his walking stick, and he and Ronnie set off at a brisk pace towards the house of Syed Omar, carrying two lighted torches. On the way they met Munshi Abdullah, who was walking ahead of them. Farquhar asked him where he was going.

'I go to the house of Mr John Morgan, Tuan Farquhar, to teach him some more words of Malay. He is a good student.'

'I would advise against it, Abdullah,' Farquhar replied. 'We have a man running amok close by. Better to stay with us in the meantime.' Abdullah nodded his agreement and followed Farquhar and Ronnie toward Syed Omar's house.

* * *

Mehmood was standing in the darkness at the outer gate when he heard the commotion. He turned round to see Syed Yassin running out of the house, and went forward to meet him. But why was he running? By the time Mehmood saw the kris in the gloom of the garden it was too late. Syed Yassin drove the blade up through his throat and into the back of his brain. The gloom of the garden suddenly exploded in a flash of brilliant light, then faded to the darkness of death, as the blood gushed from his throat and he fell backwards to the ground.

Syed Yassin dragged his body behind a sago hedge, and looked around to make sure nobody had seen him. Just when he thought he was safe, he suddenly noticed Colonel Farquhar and two others coming towards him, their torches spreading a pool of light before them. He ran back to the house to hide.

Captain Davis arrived with six sepoys and met Farquhar and Ronnie as they approached the outer gate. Farquhar ordered them to follow him and search the house for an intruder armed with a kris, who had threatened the life of Syed Omar. They passed by the body of Mehmood bin Nadir, but they did not notice it hidden in the bushes. They searched the house, but there was no one to be found, not even the servants, who had all fled in fear. They reassembled in the courtyard, while the colonel considered what to do next. He was about to order Captain Davis to send for more soldiers and conduct a general search of the town, when his eyes lit upon the balei, and the mangosteen trees surrounding it, which were closely bunched together. I wonder, Farquhar thought to himself. He walked across and began prodding the trees with his stick.

'Watch out, Colonel!' Ronnie cried out, seeing a sudden movement in the bushes. But it was too late–Syed Yassin leapt out and drove his kris into Farquhar's chest. Farquhar staggered back, the blood spreading fast over his white linen shirt. Munshi Abdullah rushed forward and caught him before he fell, as his cane dropped from his hand. Ronnie stepped in front of the colonel and fought with Syed Yassin for possession of the kris. Ronnie managed to wrestle it from his grasp, but not before Syed Yassin had sliced open his left hand. Then Ronnie drew his dirk from his belt with his right hand, and slashed it across Syed Yassin's face, slicing open his mouth and right cheek, and causing him to stumble backwards. As he did so, the sepoys rushed forward on Captain Davis's command and stabbed Syed Yassin with their bayonets, in his groin, in his stomach, in his chest and in his eyes. They continued to stab long after the life had gone out of him, until ordered to cease by Captain Davis.

Ronnie bound up his left hand with his handkerchief and helped Abdullah carry Colonel Farquhar across the street to the house of Alexander Guthrie, who sent his servants to alert Dr Montgomerie, Mr Bernard and Sir Stamford Raffles. Captain Davis ordered one of the sepoys to return to the cantonment to bring up more men and three cannon, which he ordered directed towards the temenggong's compound. Davis was concerned that the attack was the work of one of his Malay followers, perhaps as a prelude to a general uprising, as did a good many of the European and Chinese merchants who had gathered outside Syed Omar's house to see what was going on—for the temenggong was known to be unhappy about having been ordered to move himself and his followers out to Telok Blangah. Shortly afterwards the sepoys arrived, many only half-dressed, but all armed with muskets and bayonets. The cannon were directed towards the temenggong's compound as ordered.

At that moment Raffles arrived in his carriage. As he descended, John Morgan came up to him and said:

'It's a Malay uprising, Raffles, we're sure of it. The colonel's badly wounded, and probably won't last the night. We have to do something about this quickly. We need to attack them before they attack us—and blast that damned temenggong into his Mohammedan hell.'

'We will keep a cool head before we do anything, Mr Morgan,' Raffles replied in a calm voice, 'but first I must see the colonel.' He questioned Captain Davis briefly, and told him to have his men stand ready for any action, but warned him not to fire into the temenggong's compound until he had got to the bottom of the matter. Then he strode across the road to Guthrie's house. Dr Montgomerie was already there, treating the colonel's wound.

'It looks much worse than it probably is, Sir Stamford,' he said, 'but I don't want to take any chances. The colonel's lost a fair bit of blood, but I'm hoping it's only a flesh wound ... I don't think any vital organs are damaged. But he needs to rest up until we are sure he is out of the woods. Thank God the man did not strike his heart ... he came very close.'

'Thank God indeed,' said Raffles, looking visibly relieved. 'How are you, Colonel?'

'Och, I'm fine, Raffles,' Farquhar said, sitting up. 'Never saw the bugger coming. I suppose he's dead by now.'

'As a doornail,' replied Raffles. 'I'm glad to see you're taking this in your stride, Colonel, but you must rest. And I had better go back and find out what's going on, before things get out of hand.'

'On ye go, Raffles,' Farquhar nodded to him. 'I'll be fine. And so will Ronnie. Dr Montgomerie will see to us.'

When he returned to Syed Omar's house, Raffles came across Mr Bernard, who was standing over the body of Mehmood bin Nadir, which had recently been discovered. Bernard identified the body for Raffles, and told him how he had released Syed Yassin from jail, and sent him with Mehmood bin Nadir to Syed Omar's house, so that he could beg his forgiveness and ask for more time to repay his loan.

'It seemed like a good idea at the time,' he said lamely, looking down with sadness at Mehmood's crumpled body.

'Did you not search the man in jail?' Raffles demanded.

'I'm afraid we did not, Sir Stamford.' Bernard replied. 'There didn't seem any need, since he was a debtor and not a dangerous criminal.'

Raffles gave him a withering look, then raised his hand and knocked Bernard's hat off his head.

'If the colonel dies, Bernard, I'll see you hang for it!'

Then he entered the garden and walked up to the balei, and stood over the body of Syed Yassin. He ordered Captain Davis to disperse the crowd peacefully and then have the sepoys return to the cantonment, bringing with them the cannon that had been directed on the temenggong's compound. Raffles explained that he had discovered the reason for the attack, and there was no danger of an uprising. He arranged for Major Farquhar to spend the night at Alexander Guthrie's house, before returning to the residency the next day. He then gave Captain Davis orders to send one of his men to find a blacksmith, and the man returned fifteen minutes later with a Chinese blacksmith and two coolies. Raffles instructed the blacksmith to make an iron cage about the size of a man, and to have it ready by seven the next morning. He picked up a stick and drew out a design in the earth to show the blacksmith exactly what he wanted.

The next day Raffles gave orders that Syed Yassin's body be paraded through the streets in a buffalo cart, and the gong beaten to announce what he had done. His body was then placed in the iron cage that Raffles had ordered made, and hung from a mast at Tanjong Malang, near Telok Ayer point, where it remained rotting in the sun for the next two weeks. Raffles announced that such would be the fate of anyone who ran amok in Singapore. Their body would be given to the winds.

* * *

Mehmood bin Nadir's brother and cousins carried his body home, where preparations were made for his funeral. They washed his body, and wrapped it in a white muslin cloth. That night incense was lit around the body of Mehmood bin Nadir, as family and friends came to pray over him.

'We have come from God and unto him we shall return,' they recited.

The following morning Ronnie arrived to pay his respects, and handed over some money that had been donated by Colonel Farquhar, Mr Bernard, and Syed Omar to help support the family of Mehmood bin Nadir.

His brother and cousins carried Mehmood on their shoulders to the graveyard. Prayers were said and the open grave was sprinkled with perfume. Then the body of Mehmood bin Nadir was laid in the grave on his right side, with his eyes facing towards Mecca. After the grave was sealed, the Fatiha for the deceased was recited.

That evening the son mourned his father. Adil bin Mehmood was going to work for his uncle on the river, but he made a solemn promise to the Prophet that when he was old enough he would be a policeman like his father.

* * * *

Colonel Farquhar paid a visit to Raffles at his bungalow on Bukit Larangan, now known as Government House. His chest was still bandaged from his wound, but he had made a speedy recovery. Raffles inquired after his health, and Farquhar thanked him for his concern. Then he came straight to the point.

'I really must protest, Sir Stamford,' he said. 'You do no good by displaying his body in that cage. Yassin deserved to die, but he didna deserve to be treated like a dog. You cause great offense to the Malays, who consider him a holy man.'

'Holy man, indeed,' Raffles scoffed. 'What you need to

understand is that these people need to be led back to civilization, and taught to respect the principles of justice and humanity. Why, they were once monarchs of a great empire ... think of the Srivijaya Empire[lii] and the ancient rajahs of Singapura. But they have been corrupted by this false Mohammedan religion, which has drained their minds and spirits, and spawned nothing but idleness, despotism and piracy ... they have been ruined by this damned robber religion!'

'I dinna care too much for the sultan and temenggong at times,' Farquhar retorted, 'but you would do well to remember that they are the rightful rulers of the settlement we occupy in the name of the Company and the British Government. Seems to me sometimes that we're the robbers and nae them.'

'You don't understand these people, Farquhar,' Raffles responded angrily, 'and I'd advise you to drop that insolent tone.'

'I understand them well enough,' said Farquhar, slowly, 'and I'd advise you to release Syed Yassin's body before we have an uprising on our hands. The Arabs will hate you as much as the Malays. Good morning to you, Sir Stamford.'

Raffles thought to himself that he had had just about enough from Colonel Farquhar. The man was impossible, and he had no vision. But later in the day he issued a proclamation allowing that Yassin's body could be removed for washing and burial. He cited as his reason the sultan's request for a pardon from the King of England, but warned that the same fate would befall any other man that ran amok in the town. The following day a party of Malays came to claim his body, which was buried at Tanjong Pagar. Andrew Farquhar, the colonel's son, who supervised the removal of the body, would never forget the look of pure hatred on their faces.

lii Malay maritime empire that dominated South-east Asia from the eighth to the twelfth century.

27

In early April, Raffles held a meeting at his bungalow, during which he set forth his proposal for the creation of a college that would reinvigorate the cultural heritage of the region. This had long been his dream, and as he explained to his assembled audience, the goal of the college would be to educate the 'higher orders' of the native populations, principally the Malays and the Chinese; to instruct Company servants in the native languages, in order to further communication and understanding; and to gather together for posterity records of the literature, customs and laws of the region.

Later that month the first meeting of the trustees of the Singapore Institution was held, with Mr John Maxwell as honorary secretary, and A. L. Johnston and Co as honorary treasurer. A subscription of seventeen and a half thousand dollars was raised from the merchants, Company officers and clergy present. Raffles pledged two thousand dollars for himself and four thousand dollars for the East India Company; the sultan, temenggong, Colonel Farquhar, and Reverends Moore, Milton and Thompson pledged one thousand dollars each. Lieutenant Jackson presented a plan for the institution, which was to be built on a plot of land that Raffles had selected by the beach bordering the eastern bank of the Bras Basah stream. The plan was approved, and the sum of fifteen thousand dollars was voted towards the construction of the building.

* * *

Farquhar went with the temenggong to inspect the land that had been assigned to him at Telok Blangah, and had brought his children to see the kelongs that had been erected at Telok Ayer point. Previously the local Malays and orang laut had caught their fish by spearing them, but the Malaccan Malays who had come down with Farquhar had taught them how to fish with a hook and line, which dramatically increased their catch and left them with a surplus to sell in the town and to the ships in the harbour. One year after the settlement had been founded, a Malacca Malay named Haji Mata-mata had set up rows of kelongs along the beach, large fish-traps built upon rows of stakes that stretched out into the water, with a plank walkway leading to the traps. As the tide rose and fell, the fish that had swum into the traps suddenly found themselves suspended in the netted cages, and were collected by the local fishermen; this new method of fishing increased their catch even more dramatically. Farquhar and his daughters followed the fishermen down to the traps, the girls squealing in delight as they tried to grasp the slippery silver fish in their hands and drop them into the fishermen's baskets.

'But what is there here for us, Colonel Farquhar?' the temenggong asked. 'The fishing is good, I grant you, but the land is all mangrove swamp and quite useless for rice, and the gambier and pepper farmers are moving inland. How are we to make a living for our people?'

Farquhar knew perfectly well how Abdul Rahman would make his living, in addition to the allowances due him from the government—by selling information to the local pirates, and taking his share of the profits. But he made no reference to this. 'I know it disna seem much to you at the moment, Abdul,' he granted, 'but this land of yours will be very valuable some day soon. That piece of water before you is probably the best deep-water anchorage for ships around here. I came across it a few months after we arrived, and had Captain Ross do a survey. I suggested to Raffles that we ought to use this new harbour to relocate the commercial town, but he wouldn't have any o' it. I tried again the following year, but by then it was too late. All the merchants had their godowns along the river, with all the ships congregating at the river mouth. But that canna last for very long—it's getting fair crowded as it is already. One o' these days they're going to have to move their wharfs and anchorage out here, because they canna go east with the sandbank and the mud. So someday soon this land of yours will be worth a pretty penny, mark my words.'

'Well, then, Colonel Farquhar,' Abdul Rahman replied, with what Farquhar swore was a twinkle in his eye, 'until that day I will remain content to live on my allowance and the bounty of the seas.'

Aye, thought Farquhar to himself, I know very well what kind of bounty you're thinking of, but he said nothing. He bowed farewell to the temenggong and returned with his daughters to town.

* * *

By the end of April, Raffles had had enough. Trouble had been brewing for some time, but the last straw was when Farquhar accused Captain Flint of violating the principles of free trade by enforcing an effective monopoly on the lighter trade, and had the audacity to attend an official meeting with Raffles dressed in a native sarong. He informed Colonel Farquhar that he was relieved of his official duties both as resident and military commandant, duties that Raffles would himself assume until a new resident was appointed.

The merchants protested vigorously, but Raffles informed them that the matter had already been settled. He had written to the governor-general some time ago declaring Colonel Farquhar unfit for service, and requesting that a new resident be appointed as soon as was convenient. He was simply taking over from Colonel Farquhar in the interim, to ensure that his plans for the settlement were properly implemented before he returned to Bencoolen. Colonel Farquhar immediately sent off a letter of appeal to the governor-general, requesting that he be reinstated as resident, but he moved out of the residency to his private home on Beach Road.

With Farquhar out of the way, Raffles issued a series of regulations governing the administration of justice in the settlement, which were based upon the principles of English law—according to which every person was equal before the law—but with due consideration to the 'usage and habits' of the native peoples, so long as these were not contrary to reason, justice or humanity.

One of the habits that Raffles deemed contrary to reason, justice and humanity was the slave trade. He issued a proclamation prohibiting the sale of slaves in Singapore, and declared that nobody who had come to Singapore after January 1819 could be considered a slave. But as John Morgan wryly remarked, Raffles' prohibition against slave traders was like his prohibition against individuals profiting from prostitution: it simply removed them from public view.

Raffles also issued new regulations governing debt-bondage and work tickets. The claim of a debt-creditor was limited to five years, and the cost of a work-ticket was fixed at twenty dollars, with both types of contract to be registered in the presence of a magistrate. Unfortunately, there was no government office charged with the enforcement of such regulations, so coolies remained bonded to their employers for years beyond their contracts, if the coolie did not expire before his contract did.

Another habit that Raffles deemed contrary to reason, justice and humanity was gambling and cock fighting, beloved by the Chinese, Malays and Bugis, habits that he condemned as 'disgraceful and repugnant to the British character and government'. Both activities were banned. Those found engaging in such activities were to be publicly flogged, and those in charge of them were to be fined and have their property confiscated. Raffles ordered Mr Bernard to close down the gambling dens and cockpits, and abolished the tax-farms for gambling that Farquhar had introduced against his explicit wishes. When a gambling den was raided, those who had lost money were allowed to petition the court for the return of their losses. Few did, although Chan Hian Chuan, a Teochew trader from Penang who owned a small house and shop on Telok Ayer Street, successfully prosecuted Tan Che Sang for the five hundred dollars he had lost in a game of dice. Tan Che Sang paid without demur.

Raffles also banned fireworks, on the grounds that they represented a fire hazard, and specifically prohibited their use in and around the keramat on Bukit Larangan, which he declared a disturbance of the peace (including his own, since his bungalow was located nearby). He prohibited the public carrying of weapons, except for officers of the army and police force, but since the police peons only carried bamboo canes, the regulation was rarely enforced. Raffles also tried to have Farquhar's son-in-law, Francis Bernard, removed as chief of police, but backed down when the merchants and magistrates expressed their unanimous confidence in him.

Raffles abolished the tax-farms for opium and arrack, but did not ban the sale of opium or arrack itself. Instead, he imposed stiff taxes upon their sale.

28

And so it came about. John Crawfurd [19] was the new Resident of Singapore, appointed by the Governor-General of India.

Crawfurd arrived in Singapore on the twenty-seventh of May, where he was received with a guard of honour and a fifteen–gun salute. 'Welcome tae Singapore, John.' Colonel Farquhar shook the hand of his old friend and countryman. 'I'm afraid Sir Stamford couldna come down to meet you, on account of his headache, but I'm sure he's already filled ye in on your duties and his expectations.'

'Good to see you again, William,' Crawfurd replied, returning the handshake. 'And you're right about Raffles—I've a set o' instructions as lang's my arm.'[liii*]

'Well then, why don't ye come back to my place, and I can gie you my side of the story before he blackens my name forever.'

'Be my pleasure, William,' Crawfurd replied. 'I don't officially take up my position until the eighth of June, the day Raffles departs for Bencoolen. Although nae doubt I'll hear from him before then.'

* * *

Chan Hian Chuan slept soundly, without care or worry, his money chest safely locked at the foot of his bed. A slave from Sarawak stood guard outside his window, a former pirate who had been captured and sold by a rival fleet—he had cruel scars on his face and body that proved he had been in many fights. In the room beyond,

---

liii Reference to a line in the poem 'To a Haggis' by Robert Burns:
Weel are ye wordy (worthy) o' a grace / As lang's my arm.

two Chinese servants slept on mats outside Chan's bedroom door.

Lee Yip Lee hid in the shadows behind a chilli bush at the edge of the courtyard—it provided just enough cover for a man of his size. He signalled to the tiger soldier who crouched at the side of the house, and the man opened a bag to release a black cobra, which hissed and reared its head in its unfamiliar surroundings. The slave, distracted as he was meant to be, turned towards it, sword drawn, and Yip Lee rushed up behind him. He split the man's skull with one great sweep of his axe, and caught his body before it fell. The black cobra slithered off into the darkness. Yip Lee laid the body gently on the ground, then, lifting the matting from the window, he climbed silently into Chan Hian Chuan's bedroom.

The merchant still slept soundly, and Yip Lee crept across to where he lay. He raised his axe again, and brought it down across the merchant's throat. Bright red blood sprayed from his severed jugular and splashed across the bed and Yip Lee's chest. Chan Hian Chuan did not cry out, but gurgled as he gasped his dying breaths. Yip Lee struck three more times, until Chan's head was completely severed from his body.

When he was done, Yip Lee went over to the merchant's money chest, smashed the lock with his axe, and taking out a small sack from under his shirt, proceeded to fill it with silver dollars. He counted out five hundred dollars, then one hundred dollars more. Then he lifted Chan Hian Chuan's head from the bed and placed it in the money chest. He closed the lid over the dead man's eyes.

As he handed the bag of silver out to the waiting tiger soldier, the two Chinese servants entered the room. They stared in horror at the scene before them, their eyes moving from the headless body on the bloody bed to the axe in Yip Lee's hand. Yip Lee pulled his shirt over his right shoulder,[liv] challenging them to fight, but they stood as still as statues, their eyes staring wide and wild in their sockets. Yip

---

liv Secret society sign of challenge to a fight.

Lee turned and climbed out the window, and slipped into the night with the tiger soldier following close behind.

The next day Mr Bernard took down descriptions of the murderer from the two Chinese servants. He thought their descriptions narrowed down the number of potential suspects to about two thirds of the Chinese population in Singapore. And he knew it was futile to search for the man, for he knew the servants would never testify in court. The next day the servants disappeared, and were never again seen in the settlement.

A few days later the White Fan, the officer of the Ghee Hin charged with enforcing society discipline, visited the home of Tan Che Sang and handed over the bag of silver. It contained five hundred dollars, plus twenty per cent interest, the repayment of Chan's gambling debt.

29

Raffles was now engaged with his preparations to leave for
Bencoolen. He entrusted the packing and cataloguing of his
accumulated manuscripts, prints, and collection of flora and fauna
to Munshi Abdullah, who had served as his informal scribe and
secretary for the past year. Three days before he left Singapore,
Raffles laid the foundation stone for the Singapore Institution,
at a ceremony attended by Sultan Hussein, the temenggong, the
merchants, and representatives of the Chinese, Arab, Parsi, Tamil,
Armenian, Bugis and Javanese communities. Raffles buried a gold
sovereign under the foundation stone, and a detachment of the 23rd
Bengal Native Infantry fired a salute. Raffles formally designated
the new college as the Singapore Institution, dedicated to 'the
cultivation of Chinese and Malay literature, and for the moral and
intellectual improvement of the archipelago.'

Raffles and Sophia boarded the *Hero of Malown* for Bencoolen
on the eight of June, with their nephew Charles Flint, whom they
were taking back to England, to save him from the fate that had
befallen Raffles' own children. Raffles had persuaded Captain Flint
and Mary Anne that this would be for the best; he would arrange
for Charles's schooling, and show him the sights of London and
the delights of the English countryside. A few days before Raffles
left, Crawfurd presented him with a silver tube containing an
address from the leaders of the merchant community. They thanked
him for his unwearied zeal and vigilance, to which they owed the
'foundation and maintenance of a settlement unparalleled for the
liberality of the principles on which it has been established', and

expressed their sincere respect and esteem. In his response, Raffles assured them that 'Singapore will long and always remain a free port, and that no taxes on trade or industry will be established to check its future rise and prosperity.' He thanked them for the kind expression of their personal regard for himself and Lady Sophia.

Just before they departed, Munshi Abdullah came on board to bid farewell to the man whom he had come to love as a father. Abdullah and Raffles shook hands, and Raffles said to him, 'If it is to be, I shall see you again.' Lady Sophia gave Abdullah some money for his children in Malacca, and there were tears in his dark eyes when he left and boarded the sampan that waited to take him back to shore, through the small fleet of native craft that had come to wave farewell. In his diary that night, Abdullah wrote, 'Were I to die and live again, such a man I could never meet again, my love of him is so great.'

As Raffles watched the river-mouth recede in the distance, he gazed out over the red-tiled roofs of the town and the flag-post on Bukit Larangan, and remembered the day nearly three and a half years before when he had stepped down into the longboat with Farquhar and Simpson on their visit to the temenggong. How much had changed in such a short space of time! He knew he had finally achieved what he had always dreamed of—the establishment of a free British trading factory in the Eastern Archipelago, and he was proud of his achievement. But he also knew that he would never see Singapore again, and it brought great sadness to his heart.

Ronnie and Sarah watched him go. Ronnie did not know what to think of the man. He respected him for his vision and energy, and was grateful for the opportunity that Raffles had given him the day he had invited Ronnie to join him and Colonel Farquhar in the longboat. But he found it hard to forgive Raffles' treatment of Farquhar, and his failure to acknowledge the vital role Farquhar had played in establishing the settlement. Without Farquhar in charge during Raffles' three-year absence, the Malacca merchants might never have come down to Singapore. He found it particularly offensive that Raffles was now taking credit for the reclamation of the west bank after refusing to allow Farquhar to do the same thing, simply for want of funding. Raffles had done the right thing, but he found the man a bit of a prig, although not half the prig as his brother-in-law Captain Flint. As for Sarah, she had never warmed to Raffles, although she had counted Sophia as her friend.

* * *

John Crawfurd took over as resident and immediately began to implement Raffles' injunction to curtail government expenses—something that Raffles himself had singularly failed to do. This enabled Crawfurd to eliminate what he took to be unnecessary charges, such as anchorage and port clearing fees.

This did not go down well with Raffles' brother-in-law Captain Flint, who profited from these fees. But worse was to come for Captain Flint. Crawford eliminated Flint's monopoly control of lighterage, and opened up the port services of wooding, watering, ballast and repair to free enterprise—to the great delight of the Indian lightermen, who quickly reestablished control of the river traffic. Flint protested vigorously, but he had met his match in John Crawfurd. Crawfurd also abolished Flint's position as magistrate for shipping, since there were no longer any disputes over anchorage fees to adjudicate, and evicted him from Raffles' bungalow on Bukit Larangan.[20] Raffles had given the bungalow to the Flints as a parting gift on his departure, but Crawfurd commandeered it as his official residency.

Crawfurd discontinued Raffles' system of merchant magistrates, when they tried to enforce Raffles' regulation mandating the public flogging of gamblers and confiscation of their property. He wrote to Calcutta requesting a Charter of Justice for Singapore, to replace Raffles' blatantly illegal system. In the meantime Crawfurd dealt with the more serious cases himself, and assigned minor cases to a court of requests run by his assistant George Bonham. Crawfurd also rescinded Raffles' ban on gambling and cock fighting, causing Raffles a near fit of apoplexy when he heard about it. Crawfurd thought the ban impractical, since he held it well nigh impossible to stamp out gambling and cock fighting among the Chinese, Malays, and Bugis, so ingrained were these practices in their ways of living. In any case, he thought they brought them harmless pleasure and provided some welcome relief from the rigours of their working lives. He legalized public gambling, and licensed ten gaming houses in the town and a cockpit at Kampong Bugis. He reintroduced the tax-farms on opium and arrack that Raffles had eliminated, and introduced new ones for pawn broking and the sale of gunpowder.

Just over a month after Raffles departed, a Company ship arrived from Madras carrying eighty convicts, many of whom were convicted murderers, dacoits[lv] and thugees.[lvi] One week later another ship arrived, bearing one hundred and twenty convicts from Bengal. Crawfurd put them to work constructing roads and reclaiming the remaining marshlands, into which they deposited the rubbish from the town, along with earth and stone from nearby hillocks. They were housed in temporary huts on the eastern side of the Bras Basah stream, a few hundred yards north of the foundations of the Singapore Institution. There were no guards, since no provision had been made for them, and Bernard had only two dozen peons to maintain order in the whole settlement. Every month he sent his sergeant to conduct a roll call, to ensure that all the convicts remained in the settlement, and to document deaths

---

lv Members of bands of gang robbers.
lvi Members of bands of professional assassins, devoted to the goddess Kali, who befriended travellers before murdering and robbing them.

through accident, disease and violence—which turned out to be rare among the convicts. It was still rarer that any ran away. The dacoits and thugees had journeyed across the kala pani, the black water, and they were defiled and denied their caste. To them this was worse than death. They were condemned to a jeta junaza, a living tomb. They were subdued shadows of their former selves, who laboured like men in a dark private stupor of pain and anguish.

PART THREE

THE DUEL

1823-1824

1

John Morgan went to visit Father Docherty, an Irish priest who was staying at a boarding house on Hill Street. He introduced himself as a merchant and magistrate, and Father Docherty invited him into his room.

'Father Docherty,' he said, 'I've come to ask you a favour. I believe you can read and write the Siamese language.'

'That I can, Mr Morgan. I've got translations of the Bible, which I'm going to deliver on my next visit, and a printing press with their letters. Can I print something for you.'

'Well, not exactly, but I would like you to translate a letter for me into Siamese.' He drew a sheet of paper from his inside coat pocket. 'But I must first ask you to swear not to divulge its contents.'

'My, my,' replied Father Docherty, with a crooked grin. 'Now I'm asking myself what could be in such a letter?'

'Oh, nothing very exciting,' said Morgan, 'just a list of the cargo.'

'You can put your trust in me, Mr Morgan,' Father Docherty replied. 'I'll do it tonight, in return for a small donation to my mission. Shall we say ten dollars?'

'Done,' said Morgan, who normally haggled over money but not in this instance. 'I'll see you tomorrow, then, Father Docherty,' he said, before he took his leave.

Father Docherty sat down to translate the letter John Morgan had given him. As he transcribed its contents, he frowned and scratched his head vigorously. And this man a magistrate, he thought to himself. When he was done, he poured himself a whisky from a bottle he kept hidden in his case of Siamese bibles, and let out a low whistle. 'Holy Mother of Jesus,' he said to the empty room.

The next day Father Docherty handed over the letter to John Morgan without comment, and thanked him for his ten-dollar donation to his mission. Then he left his room and went into town.

* * *

Ronnie Simpson met John Morgan the following day as he walked along Boat Quay.

'Good tae see you, Mr Morgan,' Ronnie said, walking towards the other man. 'I've been meaning to hae a word wi' you. I still havna been paid for that shipment o' nails I delivered to you. Going on six weeks it is now, if I'm nae mistaken.'

Morgan did not reply. He grabbed Ronnie by his shirt and brought his knee up sharply into his groin.

'You fucking highland scum! Don't you dare talk to me like that,' he screamed, as he punched Ronnie sharply on the side of the head.

Ronnie fell down on his knees to the packed earth. His head spun and his groin was racked with stabbing pains, but he struggled quickly to his feet before Morgan could strike another blow, and raised his fists ready for the fight. But as he stepped forward, he was stopped in his tracks by a silver cane that was thrust across his chest like an iron bar. At the same time he noticed that a large Negro was holding Morgan's arms.

Ronnie turned towards the man with the cane. He was about his own age, with long grey hair and cold blue eyes. He looked a bit of a dandy, with his black frockcoat and magenta waistcoat, and his silver watch and chain. In an easy Southern drawl, he told them both to cease and desist.

'What business is it of yours,' snarled Ronnie, looking the man straight in his cold blue eyes.

'I make it my business, sir,' he replied. 'I intend to keep Mr Morgan ship shape and Bristol fashion, as you fellows say. My name is Harry Purser, at your service.'

But Ronnie's blood was up. He snatched the end of the cane, and pulled it from Purser's grasp. Then he swung it in an arc and brought it down hard across the man's left cheek. Purser staggered back, but did not fall, and his eyes flashed like cold steel.

'Keep out of my business,' Ronnie said, flinging the cane to the ground.

'It is my business now,' Purser replied in a measured tone, as he bent down to retrieve his cane. Then in a flash he drew a concealed blade from inside the silver cane, and pressed it to Ronnie's throat. 'I demand satisfaction,' he whispered aloud, like the hissing of a snake. 'Name your weapons. The Negro will be my second.'

'Pistols,' replied Ronnie, without hesitation or thought. 'I'll meet you tomorrow night at seven. Take the road out past Bukit Selegie, and follow the path into the jungle. In about fifteen minutes you'll come across a clearing. Captain Pearl will be my second.'

'Agreed. I'll meet you there, at seven sharp. Make your peace with your God before you come.' He bowed, and then motioned his companion to release John Morgan.

Morgan adjusted his coat and turned to Ronnie with a nasty smile. 'A big mistake' he said. 'Purser's killed about a dozen men in duels, and a dozen more on the side. You're a dead man, Simpson.'

* * *

The next morning Ronnie went out to his ship, the *Highland Lassie*, to supervise the unloading of a cargo of rice and sago. He intended to spend the day in as ordinary a way as possible, so as not to dwell on his evening assignation. He would work the morning, and spend the afternoon with Sarah and his father. It was too late for practice or prayer—what he needed was a calm spirit and a steady hand. He cursed Morgan for starting the fight and getting him into this mess, but the thing was done and there was nothing he could do about it. He wondered whether Morgan had been trying to scare him when he told him that Purser had already killed a dozen men in duels, but when he remembered the cold blue eyes of the man he was to fight he did not doubt it.

Suddenly he heard one of the deck hands calling out a warning. He looked around but saw nothing, but then he noticed that the man was pointing upwards. Too late he saw the heavy rope that had come loose from the foresail, as it came snaking down towards him. It missed his body, but one end of it slammed into his right hand, which had been resting lightly on the starboard rail. He winced as the burning pain shot through his hand. He immediately went below deck and plunged his hand into a bucket of water, and then wrapped it in a bundle of wet rags. He called for the longboat, and was taken ashore, where he went to his house.

When Sarah saw him, she gave a short gasp of horror at his bandaged hand.

'It's your right hand,' she exclaimed, 'you can't fight a duel with that man tonight.' She began to unwrap the bandage carefully to take a look at his hand, and told him she would ask one of the boys to fetch Dr Montgomerie.'

'You know I can and will,' he replied, in a tone that she knew meant that he could not be persuaded otherwise. These Scots were as stubborn as mules at times, although she had no doubt he would consider it a matter of honour.

Ronnie told her there was no need to send for Dr Montgomerie. 'I've had worse afore,' he said, 'and the bones are nae broken. I just need tae to keep the swelling down until tonight.'

'God, I wish I was back in Ardersier just now,' he joked. 'I could stick it in the Moray Firth and it would be down in no time. Cold as ice a' year round.'

Sarah looked at his hand. It was turning black and blue from bruising, and was beginning to swell, although Ronnie could still move his fingers.

'I know the best thing for this,' she said. 'Camphor, but we're out of it. You stay here and rest. Keep these bandages wet, and I'll be back as soon as I can. I'm going across to the Chinese apothecary.'

Ronnie's father came in. 'Whit's up,' he said, as he saw his son sitting in the chair with his bandaged hand. 'Oh my God!' he exclaimed, when he recognized the implication of what had happened.

'You stay here with him, John,' Sarah said, 'I'll be back within the hour.'

'Where's she off to?' John Simpson asked his son.

'Gone for some camphor, I believe,' he replied.

'Best thing for it,' his father agreed, 'but why no send one o' the boys?'

But Sarah was already gone.

* * *

Sarah managed to catch a dhoni[lvii] that had just deposited a passenger on her side of the river, and which took her back across to Boat Quay. She asked the ferryman to drop her off at Alexander Johnston's jetty, and after she had paid him his one doit[lviii] fare, she ran straight into Johnston's office. She begged him for the loan of a horse or pony, which he readily granted, although he was somewhat taken aback by her urgency. He told her there were two mares stabled in his yard, and that she was welcome to take her pick.

---

lvii Wooden ferry boat.
lviii Cent.

Sarah rode off towards Telok Ayer Road and past the new fish market, then turned north towards Pearl's Hill. She urged the horse up the winding road to Captain Pearl's house, praying he would still be at home.

He spied her coming up the hill, and went out onto the verandah to greet her.

'Is anything wrong?' he cried out. 'Is Ronnie all right? I thought the thing was not until tonight.'

'He's all right,' she replied, 'but he's hurt his hand. I came to talk to you about it.'

She dismounted, and Captain Pearl told one of his servants to look after her horse.

'Please come in,' he said, 'and tell me what I can do to help. Would you like some lemon water?'

She accepted, and they went into his house. Then she told him her plan. At first he was shocked and refused to cooperate, but she eventually persuaded him.

As Sarah prepared to leave, and waited for her mount to be brought up, she suddenly turned to him and said, 'Do you have a bottle of camphor I could borrow, Captain Pearl? It would save me some time.'

Pearl raised his finger and nodded his head, then stepped briskly back into the house and reemerged with a shiny glass jar with a Chinese inscription upon it. Finding Sarah already mounted, he handed it up to her.

'I keep a stock of the stuff. Best thing for my aching bones. I'll see you at five, then, Mrs Simpson,' he said.

'Thank you, Captain Pearl. At five,' she replied.

2

When Sarah got back to the house she worked the camphor into Ronnie's hand. It was now black and blue all over, and although it was not so swollen as to prevent the movement of his fingers, she knew they must be stiff and painful to bend. Ronnie also knew they were, but said nothing.

'Please, darling,' she begged him, 'please change your mind. There's no shame in telling the man that you've had an accident. I'm sure any gentleman would be willing to postpone.'

'I dinna think he's a gentleman,' Ronnie replied, 'and I'm not going to gie him the satisfaction of turning me down. We'll meet tonight. Enough on it, my love.'

She sat with him most of the afternoon, bathing his hand and gently working the camphor into his hand and fingers. She kissed his hand before she went off with his father to clean and test the pistols—the same pistols they had fired on their first outing together.

At five o' clock, Captain Pearl arrived and was admitted to the house. 'I have the horses ready,' he said, 'What happened to your hand, Ronnie?'

'You're early, James,' Ronnie replied, 'but very welcome. Thank you for agreeing to do this for me. Ship's rope fell on it, but I can still move my fingers. Let me just change my shirt and freshen myself up afore we go.'

He walked to the bedroom that he and Sarah shared. Sarah followed him in, and so did Captain Pearl. He wondered about that as he pulled off his shirt, but it was too late. Before he could say anything Pearl dropped a sack over his shoulders and pushed him hard down onto the bed. He was so completely surprised that they had him pinned down and his arms and legs bound before he could resist. They sat him on a chair and tied him to it, leaving his hands free to prevent further swelling, but with a gag in his mouth to prevent him from cursing them all to high heaven and deepest hell. He stared at them in anger and amazement. His father came into the room, but did nothing. In fact he did not look in the least surprised.

'John's going to stay with you until it is over,' Sarah said, and kissed him hard on his open lips.

'I'm going to take your place,' she explained. 'Forgive me, but your hand is no good and you know I'm a better shot.'

Ronnie shook his head violently, and struggled desperately with the ropes, but to no avail. Captain Pearl and Sarah left, and his father turned his head away to avoid his son's accusing eyes. While Captain Pearl waited outside with the horses and the pistols, Sarah changed into a suit of Ronnie's clothes: white shirt and a black coat and britches. She was grateful that they were about the same size and build, except for...but it was a big shirt. She picked up his captain's tricorn and a roll of bandages and pins, and joined Captain Pearl outside.

They rode out the road to Bukit Selegie, and stopped at the edge of the jungle. Sarah took off the tricorn, and wrapped the bandages around her head, leaving only her eyes, nostrils and mouth exposed. She put the tricorn back on, and then got Captain Pearl to wrap another bandage around her right hand, but loose enough to keep her fingers free.

'It might just work,' Pearl mused. 'The light is growing faint, and it will be dark soon. But are you sure you want to go ahead with this?' When she assured him that she did, Pearl said, 'You're a very brave woman, Sarah Simpson. Your husband must be very proud of you.'

'Proud is the last thing he is at the moment, Captain Pearl,' she said. 'Let's get on with it.' Then they rode off into the jungle, with Captain Pearl in the lead. When they entered the clearing, they saw Purser and the Negro on the opposite side. Purser was in his shirtsleeves, checking his own weapon; his coat, waistcoat and watch and chain were neatly folded on a log beside him. The Negro carried a shotgun, both barrels leveled towards them.

They dismounted and tethered the horses. Sarah removed the pistols and began to prime the one she considered the better balanced, while Captain Pearl walked across to Purser and the Negro and showed his empty hands. Purser nodded to the Negro, who raised the shotgun and slung the barrels over his shoulder.

'Good evening, Captain Pearl,' said Purser in a conversational tone. 'I trust all is well with your party.'

'And to you, Mr Purser,' Pearl replied. 'Mr Simpson has had an accident. He was struck on the head and the hand by a falling rope, but he will not be deterred. You could of course grant a postponement, or you could forget the matter altogether. I'm sure it did not merit this dangerous meeting.'

'We heard about his hand, but not about his head,' Purser replied. 'But if he is not deterred, then neither am I. On your count of ten, then, when you're ready, Captain. I must say, though, that your fellow looks like some phantom from the grave. A good job I'm not of a nervous disposition.'

A phantom from the grave. So she does, Pearl thought to himself as he returned to where Sarah stood ... but it suits our purpose well enough.

Sarah was ready. She thought for a moment about the absurdity of his choice of this place as the dueling ground, the place where she had first kissed him. But perhaps he had hoped it would bring him luck. She hoped it would bring her luck, as she began to walk out to the centre of the clearing, her pistol by her side, and Purser came out to meet her.

Beads of sweat began to form on her neck, but only on account of the humid air. Her hand was steady and she was not afraid. She was not going to let this man kill her husband.

Suddenly she heard the drumming of hooves, getting closer and closer. The Negro lowered his shotgun, and Purser cocked his pistol. Sarah cocked her own, and Captain Pearl drew his own pistol from beneath his coat.

Their guns all pointed at the approaching riders. Pearl saw them first, and called to the others. 'Hold your fire! It's Ronnie Simpson and his father.'

'What's this? A trick?' cried Purser. 'Then who's that villain with the bandages? Damn you all and your cheating ways.'

'His wife,' replied Pearl, as Sarah removed her tricorn and the bandages around her head. Her brown curls fell over her shoulders.

'My, my,' said Purser, with a sneer, as Ronnie reigned in his horse. 'Well here's a pretty picture. A man sends his wife to fight for him—some poor excuse of a man.'

'I did nothing of the kind, Purser,' Ronnie replied, dismounting. 'But I'll spare you the story.' He handed the reins to his father, who had ridden up behind him.

'I'm sorry tae the both o' ye,' John Simpson said, in a tortured voice, to Sarah and Captain Pearl. 'I let his gag loose to gie him a drink o' water, and he cursed me and called me a' the names o' the devil. He said he wid never forgive me if I let Sarah die, and that he'd kill the both o' us if I did. I've got a strong constitution, but he was worse than a crowd o' harpies. I dinna think auld Odysseus himself could have bided it, and that's the truth.'

'A touching scene,' said Purser, as Ronnie embraced Sarah. 'But which one of you do I kill tonight?'

'I love you for what you did,' Ronnie said and kissed her quickly. 'But I canna let you take my place.' He eased the pistol from her hand. She saw him flinch as he took it in his. But she did not resist or try to argue with him. She knew her chance was gone.

Purser continued to taunt him. 'I don't mind killing your dear wife,' he said, 'but I'd much prefer to kill you, Simpson. That would make her a very eligible widow, very eligible indeed! But it grows dark, and we must get on. I must say, all you fellows being here is really quite irregular, but I'm willing to tolerate it for the satisfaction of my honour. But if anyone makes a false move the Negro will blast you to hell.'

'Let's get to it then,' said Ronnie, and went forward to meet him. They stood back to back in the centre of the clearing, as the sun sunk behind the tall palms and the golden gloom began to descend.

'Goodbye, Mr Simpson,' said Purser, as Captain Pearl began the count, and they began to pace.

'One, two, three, four, five ...'

'Good riddance, Mr Purser,' Ronnie replied.

'Six, seven, eight, nine, ten,' Pearl finished, and they turned and faced each other, pistols raised.

Ronnie fired first, but the pain in his swollen fingers caused his hand to flinch—only by a fraction, but enough that his shot flew harmlessly by the side of Purser's head.

Purser's pistol was now pointed directly at his brow. Ronnie looked death in the face—in the blue ice of Purser's eyes, and the cruel smile on his lips. He wanted to turn to look at Sarah one last time, but he could not—it would look like an act of cowardice. Damn him, but the man was taking his time ... he was savouring the moment. Then he saw his finger close over the trigger, and heard the sharp crack of the pistol. And then he thought he heard a second shot, as the ball whistled past his right ear.

3

He was alive. He blinked his eyes and looked around him quickly. There had been two shots, and now he saw what had happened. Someone had shot the Negro, now spreadeagled on the ground, just before Purser had fired, and the sudden distraction had spoiled his aim. He turned and saw Captain Davis marching into the clearing, musket in hand, followed by a squad of sepoys, their muskets leveled at the duelists. Mr Bernard and a party of police peons came close behind.

'Stand where you are, gentleman, and lay your pistols down,' Captain Davis commanded. As the two men did so, Mr Bernard came forward and arrested Purser. Sarah ran to Ronnie and wrapped her arms around him, as the relief flooded through her body.

'We've just arrested your partner, Mr Morgan,' Bernard said to Purser. 'He's cooling his heels in the jail. We found three thousand muskets, ten cannon and two hundred bags of saltpeter on board his brig, all bound for Siam, and enough to start a major war. We know you had a hand in this, and I want to know where you got those guns. I'll wager many came from the pirates that ply their bloody trade on the seas around these parts.'

'Excuse me, sir, but how do I know where they came from?' Purser replied. 'I buy them where I can, and sell them where I can, and don't ask any questions. You surely don't intend to charge me for selling these guns—this is a free port, the grand emporium of the eastern seas, if I recall.'

'That is true enough, but I could charge you with dueling, which is a capital crime,' Bernard replied.

'Then we'll hang together, Simpson,' Purser laughed, turning towards Ronnie. 'But we know you won't,' he continued, turning back to Bernard. 'Very bad for business, especially Mr Simpson's.'

'You're right, I won't,' said Bernard. 'But you have two choices, Purser. You'll be on Captain Murray's schooner leaving for Brunei on the evening tide, or we'll send you to the King of Siam on Morgan's empty brig, and you can explain to him why he is not getting the arms he paid for. I hear the king knows tortures that would make a grand inquisitor flinch.'

'You leave me no choice, then,' Purser replied, opening his hands in a gesture of resignation. 'I have some business with His Highness the Sultan of Brunei that I have been meaning to attend to. I'll leave on your ship tonight, if you will allow me to retrieve my coat and vest, sir.'

'Very well, and you may do so,' Bernard responded. Purser went over to the tree stump where he had placed his clothing, and dressed as calmly and carefully as if he were dressing for dinner.

'Lead on, then, MacDuff,' he said, as the peons came to take him away. He paused as he passed by Ronnie and Sarah. 'I have unfinished business with you, Simpson. We will meet again one day.' His eyes flashed, and he drew his finger across his throat.

'As sure as I breathe, Purser,' Ronnie replied, and then walked back with Sarah to where Captain Pearl was waiting with his father.

* * *

'But how did you know we were here?' John Simpson asked when Mr Bernard and Captain Davis approached them.

'We didn't,' Bernard replied. 'We were following Purser. Father Docherty translated a letter for Morgan that listed the munitions, and he reported it to me. We arrested Morgan this afternoon, and he told us it was Purser that sold him the arms. I have no doubt he bought them from pirates or gunrunners, but there's little we can do about it. It's not actually a crime, although such transactions do require government approval, which was never requested. We had two peons keep an eye on Purser and the Negro; they followed them into the jungle, and one of them came back to alert us. We knew they were armed, so I brought along Captain Davis and his soldiers. They don't give us guns for this job, although I've got an old French cavalry pistol for my own use. When we came upon you, the Negro turned his shotgun on us, and Captain Davis shot him between the eyes. An excellent shot, I must say.'

'And I'm very grateful to you, Captain Davis,' Ronnie said. 'Spoiled the man's aim and saved my life. I was a' ready tae meet my Maker.'

'But this was a foolish thing to do, Mr Simpson,' Bernard responded. 'You could have got yourself arrested for dueling—or worse, you could have got yourself killed. And what is Mrs Simpson doing here, dressed in your clothes?'

They told him, and he shook his head in wonder.

'Well, I suppose I'm going to have to turn a blind eye on this. We can't go hanging a woman, especially with so few women around.'

Then he turned serious. 'Take your wife and father home,' he said to Ronnie. 'If you ever come across this Purser again, let me know and I'll deal with him. Leave your pistols, now, for I'm confiscating them.' And, he thought to himself, they might come in handy one day. 'Now leave, all of you.'

They mounted their horses, and rode back into town. As they said goodbye to Captain Pearl and thanked him, he let out a great sigh.

'What's wrong, Captain Pearl,' Ronnie asked him.

'Well, that was an exciting adventure, I must say, and I'm glad you both came out of it alive. But it set me wondering, where on earth am I going to find a wife willing to fight a duel for me?'

They all laughed, and wished each other goodnight.

Later than evening, Ronnie and Sarah made love with a passion that left them breathless in each other's arms. They had both wondered if they would see the night and each other again, and their love blazed with their sheer joy of being alive.

4

A few days later Mr Bernard went to see Father Docherty, who was preparing to leave for Siam.

'Thanks again for your help, Father Docherty,' he said. 'I hate to trouble you, but one thing's been bothering me these last few days, been sort of rolling around in my mind.'

'What troubles you, Mr Bernard?' Father Docherty replied. 'You can speak freely here, it will not go beyond these walls.'

Mr Bernard looked uncomfortable, and shifted his weight from one foot to the other restlessly. 'Well, that's just the thing of it,' he said, finally. 'I thought priests were bound by their oath of confidence. Morgan told me that you swore not to divulge the contents of his letter, but you straightway reported them to me.'

'Ah, yes now,' the priest sighed. 'Although my oath to Mr Morgan was not bound by the seal of the confessional, 'tis true it was a great sin to break my word. But I had no choice. I could not go letting him send all those arms to those heathens, quite enough to start a war. Or at least not until we have a chance to convert them to the ways of our Lord. I have prayed for forgiveness, and have written to the bishop asking for absolution. You could pray for me too, if you felt like it, or you could make a small donation to our mission.'

Mr Bernard gave a wry smile, and handed over the ten dollars that Father Docherty suggested would be appropriate.

* * *

Bernard went to visit Crawfurd at the residency. He explained all that had happened, and apologized for not having notified him sooner, but events had moved too fast. When Bernard told him about the duel, Crawfurd exploded in anger, and slammed his fist upon his desk, scattering his papers over the floor. But he quickly recovered his composure, and carefully considered the situation before responding to his Chief of Police's report.

'You did the right thing, Bernard,' he said at last. 'We'll leave the Simpsons alone, but warn them that I won't tolerate this kind of behaviour again. Let's go and see Morgan.'

When they arrived at the jail, Morgan was sitting dejectedly on a plank bench, his head in his hands. Whatever happened, he knew he was finished as a merchant in Singapore. He made to speak, but Crawfurd silenced him.

'Listen to me, John Morgan,' he began. 'You have been nothing but trouble since you arrived in this settlement, and I'm inclined to send you back to Calcutta for prosecution. But I'll be frank—you never know how these things turn out. They might find you guilty, or they might not. I have legal right to confiscate your arms, which I will do, since you did not seek my permission for their sale. I also have the authority to exile you from the settlement, and put you on the next ship out. But I'll make a deal with you, if you are willing to accept my conditions. You may ship some of the muskets to the Siamese, whose trade we want to maintain and encourage. You can cite restrictions from Calcutta to explain why you cannot supply the rest of the shipment, and refund any money paid to you for it. I will do my best to have the Company or other merchants find respectable buyers to purchase the rest of your merchandise, although I can offer you no guarantees. In return you will swear that you will never to do such a thing again, and cease your arrogant and violent behaviour. Well, sir, what is your answer?'

'Can I take some time to think about it,' Morgan said in

response.

'No, Mr Morgan, you cannot,' Crawford replied curtly.

'Then I accept,' Morgan replied. 'I promise you will have no more trouble from me.'

'Grand,' said Crawfurd. 'I'm glad to hear it and hope you mean it—you can show good faith by stopping the nonsense with your morning canon. Mr Bernard, you may release this man.'

Morgan did mean it and did keep his word. He despised Crawfurd as much as he despised Farquhar and Raffles, but he was making such huge profits from his trade with Siam and throughout the archipelago that he did not intend to jeopardize his position again. The next morning only the official gun on Government Hill signalled the beginning of the working day.

5

Musa bin Hassan lived in the kampong that had sprouted on the plain between the temenggong's former compound and the sepoy cantonment. Most of the Malay families living there had come down from Malacca at Tuan Farquhar's request. Musa's father was a boat builder, an occupation very much in demand in the early years of the settlement. The boy, who had just turned ten, was learning the trade, and seemed to have a special gift for carpentry and design. A gift from God, his father said.

Tomorrow was the day of his bersunat.[lix] His hair had been trimmed, and he was dressed in baju and kain samping—a long sleeved shirt and short sarong made of gleaming red silk with gold and silver threads. He sat upon the pelamin couch that had been specially made for the occasion, and laid out on the verandah of his father's house, where he greeted the invited guests before joining them in the ceremonial feast. When the guests left that evening, Musa's father presented them with a bunga telor,[lx] a dyed red egg pierced with a stick and crowned with paper flowers.

As he lay in his bed after the feast, Musa was filled with fear. He was not afraid of the pain of circumcision, but of the shame he would feel if the cockerel made no response to his penis. It would mean that he would be impotent and unable to pleasure his wife when he became old enough to marry. One of the older boys, Abdullah bin Ahmad, had teased him one day, when as young children they had been swimming naked in the sea. When

---

lix Circumcision.
lx Flower-egg.

they had rested on the beach, Abdullah had taunted him about his small penis, and warned him that it meant he would never be able to satisfy a woman or sire children. Musa had fought Abdullah to demonstrate his manhood, but he had lost, and all the other boys had laughed at him. But tomorrow would be the real test, and he dreaded it, for he had already seen the girl he wanted to marry. She was Rashidah, the daughter of Ali bin Osman. She walked with the lightness of a young deer through the kampong, and she had smiled at him some days as he passed by her house.

Early next morning, just before sunrise, Musa bathed himself and waited for the mudim to arrive. When he did, the mudim bathed the boy again with water from a bowl that the family had left out for him, along with a small bale of white cloth, the stem of a banana tree, a sireh-box containing betel nut, a live cockerel, and three dollars in payment for his services. Then the mudim led Musa to the top step of the stairway to his father's house, and made him sit astride the bamboo tree stem. The mudim laid out the boy's penis carefully on the stem, and then stretched out his foreskin. Musa tensed in anticipation of the pain. But it all happened in a flash—the knife suddenly appeared in the mudim's hand, and the mudim sliced off the end of his foreskin. It was painful, but not as much as he had anticipated. But now came the dreaded moment. The mudim snatched up the cockerel, and pressed the birds's head toward his penis. The cockerel screeched so loud he was sure that everyone in the kampong must have heard it, including Abdullah! It puffed out the feathers around its neck, a sure sign of his sexual potency! The mudim dressed his wound with the white cloth, but Musa no longer noticed the pain, and paid no mind to it when the mudim returned each of the next three days to check on his progress. He was full of his own manhood. And when Rashidah walked by him a few days later, he was sure she smiled a special smile.

Raffles, Sophia and their nephew Charles Flint arrived back in Bencoolen in July. They were dismayed to learn that the first ship available to take them home, the Indiaman *Fame*, would not arrive until January the following year. Sophia gave birth to their fifth child, a daughter named Flora, in September. Almost immediately she went down with a fever, and was treated with leeches and heavy doses of laudanum. She recovered, but over the next few months more of Raffles' staff and friends died from dysentery and cholera. Then baby Flora was carried off in December, and joined their three other children in the European cemetery. Raffles and Sophia felt their spirits broken. They were desperate to leave, to get away from the morgue that was Bencoolen, before the disease took their nephew Charles. Raffles' headaches become more intense, and came at shorter intervals. He wondered if he would make it home alive.

* * *

Colonel Farquhar, who had stayed on as a private resident after Raffles had taken over from him in May, departed in late December. At a farewell dinner hosted by the principal European merchants, they presented Farquhar with a set of silver plate, whose value was estimated at three thousand rupees. The Chinese merchants presented him with a silver epergne, crafted by London silversmiths.

On the day of Farquhar's departure, the troops formed an honour guard from his house to the waterfront. Most of the European and Chinese merchants, and the Malay, Bugis, Indian, Arab and Javanese communities, followed him down to the river mouth, and it was hours before all the presentations and speeches were made. Farquhar, who loved the native peoples, was deeply moved. As Munshi Abdullah wrote in his diary, the scene on the waterfront was like a 'father among his children, till all were weeping; he wept also.' They had respected Sir Stamford Raffles, but they loved Tuan Farquhar.

As the longboat took Farquhar and his wife and children out to their ship in the harbour, it was followed by hundreds of native craft decorated with flags and streamers, whose occupants waved, sang, played their instruments, fired their guns and set off firecrackers. As Farquhar boarded the *Alexander*, they called out to him: 'Salamat! Salamat! Sail with a fair wind! Long life that you may return to us again!'

Ronnie was sorry to see him go. The colonel had been a good friend, and Ronnie knew that he would not return.[21]

6

1824

Naraina Pillai thanked Arjun Nath for his five years of service, and for one last time tried to persuade him to stay. They had both come down from Penang with Raffles the year the settlement was founded, and when Naraina had set up the first brick-kilns in Singapore, Arjun had worked for him. Naraina had been so impressed with his brick-making skills and ability to manage the other workers that he had put Arjun in charge of half of his kilns, as his business expanded with the growth of the town and the demand for solid brick structures.

Arjun had done quite well for himself, having managed to save a decent amount of money and built himself a small but comfortable brick house. But he did not wish to spend the rest of his life as a brickmaker. There were two things in life that he desired with a passion: cattle and a wife. The first desire he had already managed to satisfy. He had purchased a small dairy herd from an Arab merchant who had arranged for their shipment from Penang. It had cost him dearly but he had been willing to pay the price: it had been his dream to be a dairy farmer since he was a young boy, when he had first seen the cattle herds in the open pastures on Prince of Wales Island.[lxi] But a wife was another matter altogether. Where on earth was he going to get a good Hindu bride in Singapore, or any kind of bride in Singapore?

lxi Name given to Penang Island when it was first settled by the East India Company in 1786. Later joined with Wellesley Province to form the new settlement of Penang.

After he had said his farewells to Naraina Pillai, and thanked him for his support, Arjun visited the Hindu temple on South Bridge Road, which ran through the Chinese part of the town. It was a small wood and attap structure with an inner sanctorum dedicated to the goddess Sri Mariamman.[22] Arjun made an offering of rice and green gam[lxii] bean to the mother goddess, and humbly asked for her help in finding him a wife. As he walked home afterwards, he wondered how even a goddess could help him find a wife in this lonely place.

Then that night as he lay asleep on his cot he had the strangest dream. He was walking along a path. He could not tell where, because everything was engulfed in a thick white mist. All of a sudden he came upon a tiger standing directly in his path. He stopped dead in his tracks and stared at the tiger, stricken with fear. He wished he had brought some weapon with him, but he was naked save for the loose dhoti he wore around his waist. The tiger stared back at him, making no movement or sound. In the yellow eyes and bared fangs of the great cat he saw a vision of his own death—a sudden roaring, tearing, bleeding death—but he held his ground, and the tiger's eyes in his own. He stood frozen to the spot, waiting for the animal to pounce. He knew there was no point in trying to run, for he knew this much about tigers—they preferred to take their victims from behind.

Then as he waited the mist cleared from the path, and he saw her standing straight and tall behind the tiger, her long black hair hanging down almost to her waist, her breasts pressing full and proud through her cotton shift. Her face was beautiful beyond words, with high cheekbones, full lips, a long slender nose, her eyes dark and deep as the night. He looked into them and saw, not his own death, but his own future life, his happiness and his children. He was wondering on this when he suddenly noticed the letters

lxii Green soybean.

emblazoned on her forehead. D–o–o–m–g–a. Murder!

He heard a goat bleating urgently nearby, but before he could turn his head, the scene before him dissolved into darkness and silence. Arjun woke from his dream, drenched in sweat, and trembling in fear and wonder. What did it mean? A few weeks later he found out.

*　*　*

Arjun was walking back home from Telok Ayer market. He had thought about his dream, and had gone to the Sri Mariamman temple to seek guidance, but it remained as much a mystery to him as before. Then as he approached the well that served the market, he saw her, standing tall before him, a water pitcher poised gracefully on her head. She stood still as a statue, like the figure in his dream. And there was the word, D-o-o-m-g-a, written on her forehead. Murder! What did it mean?

Arjun slowed to a stop, and stood staring at her. She was clad in a long red cotton robe, that hung suspended from her breasts, and she looked directly at him, her dark eyes imploring him...To do what? She did not move, and did not utter a sound, but she was trying to speak to him with her eyes.

He inched forward, very carefully and cautiously, until he passed by the edge of the well. The tiger stood straight in front of him—teeth bared, its yellow eyes full of evil—as if it had been waiting there for him all the long time. Arjun cursed himself for not having brought any weapon. He had been warned in his dream, but had never thought to take precautions against a real tiger. Now it was too late. What had been ordained had come to pass. The tiger would kill him, in front of this beautiful and graceful woman he had come to love, if only in his dreams. The tiger growled softly, as if savouring the moment. Arjun looked away from its hateful, cruel eyes, and looked back into hers, as he prepared for death, no longer in a dream.

The goat bleated, softly at first, but then with increasing frenzy. She had smelt the tiger, and could not escape—she was tethered securely to a post at the edge of the road. The tiger turned around and bounded towards her, tearing out her throat with a stroke of its mighty paw. The tiger bent over the lifeless body and took the goat between its teeth. Then it ripped the animal from its tether and padded off into the narrow alleys of the Chinese town.

Arjun went to the woman, who was trembling violently. He took the water jug from her, and placed it upon the ground, then led her towards the well, where he made her sit upon the makeshift bench that ran around it, and brought her some water. He told her that everything was all right, and that he would take care of her from now on. She gave him a puzzled look, and then he told her about his dream. As he spoke, she put her hand to her mouth, and her eyes opened wide. She had the most beautiful brown eyes he had ever seen, deep and dark and penetrating the depths of his being. She told him that she had dreamt of him also, and of the tiger and the bleating goat, and then they knew that they were meant for each other.

She was a convict, a murderess who had been transported from Calcutta some months before. She had been married to a man whom she had greatly admired when they had first met. He was handsome and clever, and a minor landowner who was greatly respected in her home village. Her parents had assured her that they had made a good marriage for her, and she had looked forward to a good life. But her husband was a cruel man with a twisted passion, who beat her regularly, but most often during intercourse. He seemed to find it necessary in order to perform his duty as a husband, although he appeared to derive no pleasure from it, and nor had she. She had put up with his behaviour for the sake of her parents and her own children. Their son had died when he was very young, after a black cobra had bitten him, but their daughter had grown up to become a beautiful young women, and had become a great source of comfort and pride to her.

Then one day she had come in from the garden to find her husband forcing himself on their daughter. He held her by her long black hair on her knees before him, and was trying to force the girl to take his swollen member in her mouth. She had been harvesting red chillies in the garden, and when she saw what was happening she went straight up to him and rubbed them into both of his eyes. Her husband screamed in rage, and in his rage he kicked their daughter hard in the chest, hurling her with great force against the edge of the iron stove, where she split her skull and spilled her young brains across the earthen floor. Then he came for her, his outstretched hands reaching for her neck. She stepped away from him and snatched up a heavy chopping knife, which she drove into the side of his neck. The blow struck an artery, and the red blood sprayed across the room and over her body. He had stumbled forward and fallen to the ground, but she had not stopped—she kept on chopping, chopping, chopping, until he was a bloody pulp upon the floor, and her arm was too weak to strike another blow.

They had found her there, in a great pool of congealing blood, sitting with her dead daughter in her arms, tears rolling down her cheeks. She had shed her tears for her daughter, but not for her husband. She was glad that he was dead, and she was glad she had killed him. She was merely the instrument of his evil karma. She had been quickly tried and found guilty of murder, and they had branded her crime on her forehead. But the authorities had commuted her death sentence to transportation, because of their reluctance to execute a woman. She had been sent to Singapore with a shipment of other convicts some months before. There had been only one other woman with them, and she had died of fever on the voyage. She expected the worst, but had not cared whether she lived or died for she knew her life was over.

Yet the authorities had treated her well enough. The convicts were given a great deal of freedom, and within a week she had been placed as a servant with a wealthy Chinese shopkeeper, who also owned fruit and vegetable stalls in the market. He treated her like any regular servant, no better and no worse. She was free to leave his premises in the course of her duties, and allowed to sleep in the hut at the back of his shop at night. So here she was, a murderess serving out her sentence in Singapore. She told him she did not imagine he would still believe that they were meant for each other, now that he had heard her story. But Arjun assured her that he did. He told her that he wanted to marry her and have children by her. He had not the slightest doubt about that. She smiled broadly when he said this, and wondered at how quickly a life could change. She told him her name, Chandi, which means moonlight.

Arjun spent days negotiating her release into his custody. There was no problem with the authorities, since Naraina Pillai spoke for him, but the Chinese shopkeeper held out for as much compensation as he could get. He tried the limits of Arjun's patience, so he succeeded in securing far more than Arjun had expected to pay. Ho Liang Chiang could tell that Arjun wanted this woman very badly, so he had negotiated hard. But Arjun did not mind. He had solved the mystery of his dream, and he had discovered the mystery of love.

* * *

The Anglo-Dutch Treaty signed in London in March 1824 finally removed all doubts about the future of Singapore. The Dutch ceded Malacca to the British, formally withdrew all their objections to the occupation of Singapore, and recognized the Malayan Peninsula as a British sphere of influence. In return the British ceded Bencoolen to the Dutch, and recognized Dutch authority in all the territories south of the Strait of Singapore.

By this time Singapore was well established as a thriving commercial centre, whose trade greatly surpassed that of Malacca and Penang combined. In the first official census taken that year, the population numbered nearly eleven thousand. The Malays were still the largest community, with four thousand, five hundred and eighty, with the Chinese a close second, with three thousand, three hundred; the Bugis were the third largest, with one thousand, nine hundred and twenty five. There were seven hundred and fifty Indians, seventy-four Europeans, sixteen Armenians and fifteen Arabs.

Crawfurd oversaw the improvement of the town streets and the laying out of new ones, including the new Commercial Square, where the merchant godowns and shops on Boat Quay backed up from the western side. The new resident also supervised the erection of street signs with English names, and introduced street lighting to the town in the form of coconut-lamps.

Crawfurd received a letter from the Governor General questioning Raffles' commitment of four thousand dollars of Company money to the Singapore Institution. Crawfurd admired Raffles' noble educational goals, but thought his idea of an institute of higher education hopelessly idealistic and premature. Farquhar did request financial support for a more modest use for the Singapore Institution, to introduce a form of primary education that would be of immediate practical benefit, by training the native population in the basic linguistic and mathematical skills that would be in high demand in the expanding economy. Yet his request was also refused. The Singapore Institution was built as planned, but to little avail. When three Chinese workers fell to their deaths from the scaffolding while the final sections of the roof were being secured, it was considered a bad omen. The building was not used for either primary or higher education, and stood as an empty shell for many years afterwards.

7

The sultan's istana at Kampong Glam lay silent under the carpet of silver stars. Grey clouds flitted across the moon, which cast a spectral light over the grey walls of the palace. It was just after two in the morning. The only sounds to be heard were the whirr of crickets and the croaking of frogs, and the occasional bird screeching by the river. The mosque stood in dark shadow behind the istana.

Everyone seemed to be asleep. There had been a banquet that night, in honour of Sultan Hussein's birthday, and it had been a night of great debauchery. The sultan himself had passed out early in the evening, as he did most evenings, but by now most of the men had joined him. Even the palace guards seemed to have succumbed, for they were nowhere to be seen. Siti looked out over the empty hall, then slipped across it as fast as she could, her bare feet slapping softly on the tiled floor. She reached the main door ... and found it was not locked! She pulled it open as quietly as she could, terrified that the sound might waken someone, and the ghostly moonlight flooded in. She made a sign to the other girls, who raced across the hall and followed her out the door—all twenty-seven concubines from the royal harem.

They made their way along the beach, past the Arab Quarter, the European town, the Singapore Institution, and the great banyan tree that stood at the mouth of the Bras Basah stream, until they reached the lights of the coconut lamps by the river. They met a Malay peon on night duty, who thought he was dreaming as he saw them emerging from the darkness. He took them to the house of Mr Bernard, who opened the door bearing a lantern and a pistol.

Bernard was as amazed as the peon had been, but brought them all into his house. They sat on the floor of his parlour, taking up just about every inch of space, while Siti told their story.

They had fled the sultan's palace, she said, because of his cruelty. He had beaten them with canes and cudgels, placed burning pitch upon their breasts and privates, and hung them naked from the walls. She offered to show him the evidence, but Bernard told her to wait until he reported the matter to the resident. She began to describe the horror of sex under the mounds of fat that made up the sultan's body, and the grotesque acts he required of them, but Mr Bernard, his face flushed bright red, told her there was no need to go into such detail at present. Siti begged him not to return them to the sultan, who would send men out looking for them in the morning.

Bernard assured them he would not, and told them they could sleep on his floor until the morning. He then went out and arranged for four peons to stand guard around his house. When he returned, he checked that the girls were all sleeping peacefully. Then he tiptoed up the stairs to his bedroom. As he climbed into bed, he said to his wife:

'Funny to think we have a harem of native women in our parlour.'

'Try not to think about it, Francis,' she replied.

* * *

The next morning Bernard requested that Crawfurd meet him at his house, on a matter of some urgency. When Crawfurd arrived he was appalled when Siti told him about their treatment. At first he did not believe her, but needed no further convincing when one of the girls stripped off her clothes and showed him her scars and burns.

Crawfurd was furious, angrier that Bernard had ever seen him.

He told his Chief of Police he had a good mind to call out the police and the 23rd Bengal Infantry and march right out to the istana and arrest the sultan, and drag him back in chains. Yet Crawfurd knew he had no legal authority to arrest the sultan, so for the moment he contented himself by arranging for the girls to be quartered in Mr Innes's godown, which had recently been completed but was not yet stocked with trading goods. He arranged for a police guard to be placed on them day and night, and instructed Dr Montgomerie to check on their general health. He ordered proper sleeping mats and pillows to be provided for them at his own expense, and allowed them to take turns bathing in the facilities at the old residency that Farquhar had used, and which was now due for demolition. And he steadfastly refused the sultan's demands that his property be returned to him.

'But what are we going to do with them, Mr Bernard?' Crawfurd wondered aloud once the girls were settled in the godown. That, however, turned out to be no problem at all. In a town bereft of single women, the news spread like wildfire, and there was no end of offers to settle the girls. Some were taken into the homes of European, Chinese and Arab traders to work as servants, while others ended up as wives or concubines in the homes of the Peranakan Chinese. Three agreed to go with Tan Hong Chuan, who offered them food, board and a small cash payment in return for caring for his vegetable gardens beyond the marshlands bordering the Rochor River. Siti was one of the three who agreed to go with him, and she thought it was the closest thing to freedom she had ever known.

The following year, Francis Bernard left the police force and founded the *Singapore Chronicle*, the first newspaper in Singapore. One of the first stories he reported was the completion of the new road that Crawfurd had ordered Lieutenant Jackson to lay out from the town to the Bugis kampong at Kampong Glam, which passed directly through the istana compound, to the great displeasure of Sultan Hussein.

* * * *

When Bencoolen was returned to the Dutch according to the terms of the Treaty of London, one hundred and twenty Bengal and eighty Madras convicts were transported from Bencoolen to Singapore. More huts were erected beside the Bras Basah stream to house them, and Lieutenant Chester of the 23rd Bengal Native Infantry was appointed superintendent of convicts. Provision was made from the tax revenues for the appointment of an overseer, an Indian doctor, and a writer, and one peon for every twenty-five convicts.

Crawfurd wrote to Calcutta requesting permission to make a new agreement with Sultan Hussein and Temenggong Abdul Rahman, one that would eliminate their lingering power and authority. When the Company authorized his request, Crawfurd persuaded both men to sign a new Treaty of Friendship and Alliance—after holding back their monthly allowances for three months to encourage their cooperation. Sultan Hussein and Temenggong Abdul Rahman agreed to cede to the East India Company permanent title to the island of Singapore and the neighbouring islands for ten miles around, in return for which they received cash payments and increased pensions. They and their relatives and descendants were entitled to live in the areas allotted to them by the Company, but they were prohibited from interfering with the administration of the settlement in any way, and from entering into negotiations with neighbouring states without the Company's permission. Crawfurd also offered them generous additional cash payments—twenty thousand dollars to the sultan and fifteen thousand to the temenggong—to leave the island, but to his surprise and disappointment both declined to do so. Crawfurd despised both men, but could not rid himself of them.

At the end of August, Crawfurd sailed around the island to take formal possession of Singapore in the name of the Company. The trip was uneventful, as he drifted by acres of virgin jungle, the only signs of habitation being a few woodcutters' huts on Pulau Ubin, some abandoned fishing huts now swallowed up by jungle, and some houseboats of the few remaining orang laut. When they returned to the bustle of the river-mouth, Munshi Abdullah, who had accompanied Crawfurd on his circumnavigation of the island, wrote in his journal:

> I am astonished to see how markedly the world is changing. A new world is being created, an old one destroyed. The very jungle becomes a settled district, while elsewhere a settlement reverts to jungle. These things show us how the world and its pleasures are but transitory experiences, like something borrowed which has to be returned whenever the owner comes to demand it.

8

Raffles, Lady Sophia and their nephew, Charles Flint, left Bencoolen in April, and arrived back in England on the twenty-fourth of August, after a frightening passage round the Cape of Good Hope. They stayed with Sophia's parents in Cheltenham, where they were reunited with their daughter Ella, now three years old.

In November they rented a small house in Piccadilly, where Raffles prepared a long memorial to the Court of Directors of the East India Company, petitioning them for compensation for expenses incurred during the foundation of Singapore, and requesting a pension appropriate to his years of service to the Company. In July the following year, Raffles bought a house and farm acreage at High Wood, near the country village of Hendon. But that year passed with no word from the Court of Directors.

Finally, in April the following year, Raffles received a thick package marked 'Private and Confidential'. It contained two letters. The first was from the Court of Directors. They commended Raffles for the role he had played in the administration of Java and Bencoolen, and in the foundation of Singapore. But they strongly disapproved of his excessive expenditures, objecting in particular to his profligate use of Company funds for public works in Singapore, before agreement had been reached with the Dutch about the future of the settlement. Having willfully ignored their direction on countless occasions, he could not expect to be rewarded with a pension.

The other letter was from the accountant general of the Company, which disallowed many of the expenses Raffles had claimed for his administration of Java, Bencoolen, and Singapore, and presented him with a demand for the twenty-two thousand pounds he owed to the Company.

* * *

Raffles woke with a start. He could hear shouting in the distance, and the alarm bell ringing. He dragged himself out of bed, and rushed over to the window. Dear God! The place was on fire! The Chinese town glowed orange and red in the distance, and the flames had managed to spread across the river by way of Presentment Bridge, which was now collapsing into the dark waters of the river. The government buildings on the east bank were ablaze, and the fire was spreading along the east beach at an alarming rate. Raffles pulled on his pants and boots, pausing only to tuck in his nightgown and grab his coat, before he rushed out of the bungalow and made his way down Government Hill as fast as his legs could carry him.

He ignored the cries of the servants as he raced down the hill, his eyes set on the blaze like an animal fixed by the stare of a cobra. He ran faster and faster, tripping over thickets and careering into small trees. The sepoy cantonment was ablaze, and the soldiers were fleeing the smoking barracks. He must get there before it was too late. Then his foot caught on the exposed root of a tree, which snapped his ankle like a dried chicken bone. He stumbled in his pain, and pitched forward. As he floated through the air, time seemed to stand still. Then a searing silver light flashed in his head, and the darkness swallowed him up.

* * *

Lady Sophia found him at five o'clock in the morning, sprawled at the foot of the stairs. One of the servants had come to tell her that although the master's door was open, he was not in his room, and she had gone to look for him. Sir Stamford Raffles died on the fifth of July 1826, the day before his forty-fifth birthday. The physician who carried out the autopsy recorded that he died of a stroke caused by an abscess on his brain.[23]

9

Musa bin Hassan was broken-hearted. Rashidah, the daughter of Ali bin Osman, had been promised in marriage to Abdullah bin Ahmad, when she reached the age of womanhood. Musa knew there was nothing he could do about it; if it was the will of God, he had to submit to it with gladness, despite the pain in his heart. It was not surprising. Rashidah was the most beautiful young girl in the kampong, and Abdullah came from a noble family. It was well known that Abdullah and his father served the temenggong in his secret relations with the pirates who operated in the waters around Singapore, and were much favoured for their service. Abdul Rahman had already given his blessing to the marriage, and had promised gifts to the bride's family.

Musa wiped away his tears as he polished the wood on the sleek black prahu that he and his father were building for Lim Guan Chye, whose trading house would compete in the boat races that Tuan Crawfurd had announced he would hold at the end of the Christian year. He loved his work, but not as much as he loved Rashidah.

* * *

Ebenezer Oates peered out into the darkness of the night, and for the hundredth time cursed his luck. No matter how clouded the sky, or blackened by storm, there were always guards keeping a watchful eye on the gates and walls of the stockade. Many a night he had decided to chance it all on a wild run, but he always saw the men who would stop him—as they had stopped the Malays who had made a run for it, and who had been most cruelly tortured as an example to the others.

Many a day as he had pulled his oar for the pirates, he had thought about trying to break free from his rattan halter and swim to safety, and many a day he had hoped for the sight of a man-of-war that would come to his aid and bring swift justice to his captors. But he had always thought twice about it, for although he had seen many men make a desperate attempt to escape, he had never seen a single man escape with his life. And he had never seen a man-of-war come close to the pirate fleet.

Some might think me a coward, he thought to himself, for not even making an attempt. But Ebenezer Oates had promised himself one thing. He was not going to risk failure. He was going to wait until he could make certain of his freedom, so that one day he could lead his own kind back to take revenge on the men who had murdered Captain Ramsey and his son.

PART FOUR

THE RECKONING

1832-1836

1

1832

Ronnie and Sarah walked down to the small jetty that ran out from the beach in front of their house. Their son Duncan, six years old, ran on ahead; their daughter Annie, four years old, struggled to keep up. She tripped over a piece of driftwood and sprawled in the sand, but her cousin Lizzie helped her up and the two girls hurried off in pursuit of Duncan. As he watched Duncan running ahead, Ronnie remembered with a tinge of sadness his first son Malcolm, who had died of a fever at age two. He was buried in the Christian cemetery behind Government Hill. He would have been running with the others today—all children seemed to have a natural love of the sea.

It was a Saturday in late September, and they were waiting for the longboat from Ronnie's *Highland Lassie*, which was anchored in the roads, while the lighters offloaded its cargo of cottons and opium. He had promised the children that he would take them to see the Bugis fleet, which had arrived a week before at Sandy Point, close by the Bugis Village and Kampong Glam.

Ronnie and Sarah waited with Sarah's sister Rosemarie and her husband John Hancock, a Company writer, who were down visiting from Penang.

'Are ye still firm in your decision, John,' Ronnie asked his brother-in-law, 'or are ye still thinking it over?'

'As firm as we were last night, Ronnie. We talked it over again before we went to bed, but not for long. It seems clear to us that Singapore has a much more promising future than Penang, and we would love to move. That is, if your generous offer still stands.'

'Of course it does,' Ronnie assured him, 'we can aye do wi' a good man tae help us wi' our books.'

The previous evening over dinner, John Hancock had told them that they expected to be returning to England soon, since he had been told that the Governor was planning a new round of administrative economies. When Sarah became visibly upset at the thought of her sister leaving, Ronnie had suggested that John could join their company in Singapore if he did not want to return to England, and his father and Sarah had enthusiastically endorsed his suggestion.

John and Rosemarie agreed that they did not want to leave, and also that they would much prefer to live in Singapore than Penang. So they had accepted Ronnie's offer with warm gratitude. John had said he would give his notice to the Company as soon as they returned to Penang at the end of the month. Given the pressure from Calcutta to reduce expenditures, he was sure it would be readily accepted—he might even be able to reduce the normally required notice period. Either way, they would sell up their home and come down to Singapore as soon as they could manage.

'So it's decided then,' Ronnie had said, when he proposed a toast to their future health and happiness in Singapore. 'Ye can stay wi' us until ye get your own place—we certainly hae plenty room.'

Ronnie looked through his telescope and saw that Willie Fraser was waving from the distance; the longboat was weaving towards them through the maze of native craft and square-riggers. He handed his telescope to his son, who loved to peer through it, and soon trained it on the ships anchored in the roads.

'Look, father!' he cried, 'an East Indiaman coming in past St. John's Island.'

'So it is,' Ronnie replied. Even at this distance, there was no mistaking the distinctive black hull and yellow gun-ports. 'See any pirates?' he joked.

'I suppose I do, although it's hard to tell unless they are actually pirating, father.'

That's true enough, thought Ronnie—it was half the battle.

As they waited on the beach, Ronnie looked back and admired his new house on Beach Road. He and his father had done very well over the past twelve years, and had made a small fortune through their trade with India and China. They bought birds' nests and sharks' fins from the local traders, and transported them to Canton, where they picked up tea and silk; they brought woolens and iron from England, and opium—their most lucrative commodity—from India, which they sold in Singapore and Canton. They had a large godown on Boat Quay that backed onto Commercial Square. They had lived above the godown in the early years, but had since moved into the Palladian mansion that shimmered in the bright sunlight behind them.

The house was white with dark green shutters, with a red tile roof that projected outwards to form deep eaves, providing shelter from the sun, and homes for the families of swallows and swifts that flitted across the sky as the sun set in the early evening. The house was fronted on Beach Road by moulded classical columns, and its tall doors and windows opened on to a wide green verandah that ran all the way round the house, about six feet above the ground. The lower part of the building was partly hidden by the lush green shrubbery that ran around it and into the garden beyond. A large portico covered the carriageway and a flight of stairs led up to the main hallway. Ronnie, who had been born in a mean cottage in Ardersier, could hardly believe he owned such a house, and his Presbyterian upbringing made him feel a little guilty about it. Sarah had no such misgivings, although she thought the house was a little pretentious. Old John Simpson thought it was just grand.

Like many of the mansions along Beach Road, Ronnie's

house was the work of George Coleman, the Irish architect who had worked with Raffles' Town Planning Committee. Since then Coleman had made his distinctive mark on the architectural landscape of Singapore.[24]

Coleman had been appointed superintendent of public works, overseer of convict labor, and land surveyor in 1830. He had continued with land reclamation, employing convicts to carry the street sweepings and rubbish from the town to the higher reaches of the Singapore River, and to the mangrove swamps that bordered the Rochor River. Last year he had employed over two hundred convicts to drain twenty-eight acres of land and to lay down roads in and around Kampong Glam, and already about a fifth of the area was taken up by good upper-roomed houses. Coleman also employed the convicts to cut timber and make bricks, and to labour in the quarries at Pulau Ubin, using the stone they cut in the construction of private houses and public buildings. Coleman formed a good relationship with the convicts who worked for him. He was fluent in Hindustani, Tamil and Malay, and treated his workforce like ordinary craftsmen and labourers rather than convicts. In consequence, he got far more useful work out of them than most other superintendents of convicts in other Eastern ports and cities.

Coleman had built most of the mansions along Beach Road, which came to be known as Yi Shap Kan,[lxiii] including Ronnie's own home. There was one feature of their house that Ronnie and Sarah loved more than anything else. The brick walls had a stucco finish, and were plastered with white Madras Chunam, which was a mixture of shell lime beaten with egg whites and course sugar into a thick paste, and then blended with water in which the husks of coconuts had been soaked. The walls of their house had been plastered with the Chunam, and then polished to a smooth and

lxiii Twenty Houses Road.

glossy finish with round stones. This finish was a distinctive feature of many of Coleman's buildings—it was more durable than ordinary plaster in the tropical climate, and much cheaper to produce. Ronnie had paid extra to have the whole house dusted with soapstone, and the result was quite spectacular. The walls shimmered in the sunlight of the day, and sparkled in the moonlight like a fairy castle. It was a magical effect, and a far cry from the dark stone castles of Ronnie's native Scotland.

Ronnie wished Coleman had done something with the Singapore Institution, that doubtful monument to Raffles' vision for the education of the native peoples and Company servants. The money had run out before it was completed, and the building now lay in ruins at the head of the Bas Basah Stream—an eyesore that was one of the first sights to greet visitors arriving in Singapore.

Fraser arrived with the longboat and they went out on to the jetty to board. As they were rowed towards the Bugis fleet, Ronnie kept an eye on the children, who seemed intent on tumbling out of the boat at the first opportunity.

'Quite a sight, isn't it,' said Fraser, as they drew close.

'A bit like a floating Covent Garden,' Sarah replied. 'Let's go see what they've got.'

There were about two hundred square-sailed Bugis padewakang anchored at the mouth of the Rochor River, with a crew of about thirty men on each. They had come from the Celebes, and from Bali and South Borneo. Their two-masted craft were like small schooners, with an attap–roofed structure in the centre or rear, which looked like a small house, and in which they displayed their merchandise. They brought coffee, sarongs, sandalwood, tortoiseshell, ebony, shark fins, birds' nests, rattan, beeswax, tin, gold dust, and a host of other products from the archipelago. The smell of coffee and spices filled the air as they toured the great floating market.

'Dragon's blood, Daddy!' shouted Duncan in excitement.

'Where do the dragon's live?'

'In your imagination only, I'm afraid,' Ronnie replied. 'It's just the Malay name for tree resin.'

The Bugis sailors were dark-skinned and fearsome to behold, for they were all heavily armed, but they went peaceably about their trade, as did their countrymen who had settled on the eastern shore of the mouth of the Rochor River. Sarah and Rosemarie haggled for exquisitely embroidered sarongs, while Ronnie bought coffee for himself, and shark's fins, bird's nests, and tortoiseshell for the company, which he arranged to be transported to their godown. He also bought a magnificent red, white and green parrot for Duncan, after his son had pointed out that the bird had the same colours as his house.

They all had great fun bargaining with the Bugis traders, offering insultingly low amounts to match their grossly inflated prices, until they agreed upon a more reasonable price somewhere in between. Sarah had become a master of the art over the years, but Ronnie hated it—it went against his straight-talking Highland grain. But he enjoyed the excursion with his family, and settled back contentedly in the longboat as they prepared to return home. He turned his telescope to scan the shoreline, and frowned at what he saw.

Despite Raffles' prohibition of slavery, and despite the reaffirmation of his policy by later residents, it was quite clear that the Bugis were still selling slaves. They could be seen negotiating with Chinese and Arab merchants, who led off the unfortunate men, women and children that were placed in their custody. Of course it was no longer *called* slave trading, rather bonded or indentured labour, but it amounted to much the same thing.

The same was true of the Malay pirates, who could also be seen openly displaying their spoils upon the beach, and buying and selling arms. There had been continuous trouble from them over the past ten years, but again little had been done. Chinese and European and native trading vessels were regularly attacked on their passage to Singapore, and eight years ago pirates had attacked the Dutch schooner *Anna* as she left Singapore for Batavia, in full view of the lookout at Fort Fullerton at the western mouth of the river, and the men at the signaling station on St. John's island. The pirates had come on board disguised as pilgrims returning from Mecca, and had attacked the crew in the roads.

Farquhar had sent out an armed merchantman in the early days, and a few years ago a gunboat had been sent out fitted with native rigging, but neither had made much of an impression. No one seemed willing to do what was necessary, which was to punish the pirates in their own coin, as the Americans had done the previous year. Malay pirates had slaughtered the officers and crew of the American brig the *Friendship*, while she had been loading a cargo of pepper at Kuala Batu, on the west coast of Sumatra—they had come aboard disguised as villagers offering to help load the cargo. Although the local chiefs had denied any knowledge of their action, the US frigate *Potomac* had returned and burned the town to the ground, leaving three hundred souls dead. Why the hell could the great British Navy not do the same? They had seen the French and Spanish off at Trafalgar, and the local pirates ought to be child's play compared to the carnage of that day.

Yet with the reduced administrative service and the legal quagmire over the past eight years, [25] Ronnie knew that nobody was going to do anything about it anytime soon.

Despite these problems, the commercial base of Singapore had expanded as dramatically as Ronnie had hoped and believed it would. He had just heard from Kenneth Murchison, the resident councillor, that the population now exceeded sixteen thousand, and he knew that the tonnage passing through the port had long surpassed that of Penang, Malacca and the establishments of the

Dutch East Indies. Ah well, he thought to himself, there were always naysayers who claimed that the bubble was about to burst—but he thought that few would be found in the godowns on Boat Quay, in the busy shop houses beyond, in the brick and lime kilns to the east and west, in the market gardens and paddy fields beyond Bukit Selegie, or on the gambier and pepper plantations in the interior of the island.

Ronnie looked around for any sign of his nemesis, Mr Harry Purser, gunrunner and duelist. He had not come across him these last ten years, although he had heard reports of him from captains returning from ports in the archipelago, and from China and Siam. He had once heard that Purser had been staying at John Francis's Billiard Room and Refreshment Hall in Commercial Square, but there had been no sign of the man when he visited and questioned John Francis about him. There was no one registered in his name, which did not really surprise him. The only man who loosely fitted his description had long black hair, and had already left. Ronnie knew that he would get no help from the law, for the man who had sworn to kill him had committed no crime that would be recognized in a Singapore court of law. So it was between them if they ever met.

* * *

As Ronnie looked towards the shore, Musa bin Hassan looked out towards the Bugis fleet. He had walked along the beach to view the sleek padewakang, whose craftsmanship he greatly admired. He was about to leave when he noticed Abdullah bin Ahmad standing with a group of heavily armed men, laughing and joking together, and lounging against the hulls of the craft that were beached upon the sand. He had no doubt that they were pirates, or that Abdullah worked for Daing Ibrahim, the son of the Abdul Rahman, the former Temenggong of Singapore,[26] who had taken over as leader of his father's remaining followers at Telok Blangah.

Musa had never married. He had felt duty bound to do so, but found he could not muster the strength of will to do so after Abdullah had married Rashidah binti Ali. He and his father argued about it often, and at one point his father threatened to throw him out of his house if he did not marry. But he did not do so for three reasons. He could see how much Musa loved the girl, and knew his pleas and threats were useless to persuade him. He had two other sons whose wives had blessed him with two grandsons and three granddaughters, with whom he was well pleased. And he could not afford to lose his youngest son, for Musa was by far and away the most skilled boat builder he had even known. All his sons worked in their father's boatyard, but Musa's craft was beyond compare. So Musa's father had resigned himself to the situation; he supposed it was the will of God, and God be praised for the gift He had bestowed upon his son.

Musa did not envy Abdullah, for all his wealth and position. He had married Rashidah, but she had borne him no children. Abdullah had blamed the failure on her barrenness, but everyone knew that the fault really lay with him, for his second and third wives had both remained childless. Abdullah knew this also, at least deep in his heart, and it made him a bitter man; but he continued to blame them for it, and refused their regular requests to adopt a child, or to grant them a divorce. He no longer cared for any of them, but wanted to punish them by keeping them in his power.

Musa knew that Abdullah would never divorce Rashidah, because Abdullah had gone out of his way to tell him. Musa thought he kept her merely to spite him, even though he spited himself into the bargain, for it brought Abdullah no pleasure—only a resentful heart. Musa's own heart still burned for Rashidah. The light-footed young girl had now grown to a beautiful young woman, although she was rarely seen in public, and then always covered from the sight of men. When Musa imagined what his life would have been like if it had been written in the Book Of Life that he was to marry her, he experienced great happiness and great sadness. But it was the way of the world that God in his wisdom had ordained, and God be praised for his wisdom and mercy.

2

In the middle of the year, George Armstrong opened an Exchange Room, Reading and News Room, and Circulating Library in Commercial Square. It was originally intended for the use of captains and supercargoes,[lxiv] but it soon became a popular place for merchants and citizens to congregate, to read the newspapers and discuss the topics of the day, and it quickly became the unofficial general meeting place.

Aside from the vicissitudes of import and export figures, commodity prices and exchange rates, complaints about pirate attacks, the state of disrepair of Presentment Bridge and the regular flooding of South Bridge Road, one of the hot topics of conversation during that year was the tiger attacks. A tiger had attacked two Malays at Tanjong Pagar, and George Armstrong had reported spotting a tiger that had run across his path while he and his wife were out on a drive on the road to Telok Blangah. But most of the attacks were upon workers on the gambier and pepper plantations in the jungle interior of the island.

The Chinese had continued to develop their early investments in pepper and gambier, fuelled by the development of the British dyeing and tanning industries. The two crops were grown together, since the waste from gambier production served as a fertilizer for pepper. The most successful planter was Seah Eu Chin, known as the King of Gambier, who had made a huge personal fortune when

---

lxiv An officer on a merchant ship in charge of managing the purchase and sale of its cargo.

he planted a huge acreage of gambier and pepper, just before the price of the crops rose internationally. Although the gambier and pepper plantations brought a fair return on investment, they had certain disadvantages.

The pepper quickly exhausted the soil, and large supplies of wood were required to provide fuel for the vats in which the gambier leaves were boiled, before they were pressed to extract their juices, and then dried into a concentrated paste. The Chinese planters left a trail of devastation in the jungle as they kept moving their plantations further and further inland, and the wasteland they left behind was quickly overgrown with course lalang grass. And as they moved further and further inland, they encroached more and more on the jungle ranges of the tigers, who snatched away increasing numbers of labourers, until it was said that they took at least one Chinese coolie for every day of the year.

Nobody had reported having seen a tiger in the early years following the foundation of the settlement, and some speculated that they must have swam across the narrow strait between Johor and Singapore, since they were common on the Malayan Peninsula. Others maintained that they had been on the island for a long time, but had been content to remain deep in the interior where there were plenty of deer and pig. It was only when the expanding pepper and gambier plantations had begun to encroach on their hunting grounds that they had begun to come into contact with humans, especially when the coolies bent over the gambier and pepper plants presented such an easy opportunity.

* * *

The China trade was brisk and continued to grow. Eighteen junks came down on the northeast monsoon in February, including two from Shanghai, up from ten the previous year. Signor Masoni staged the first public entertainment for Europeans when he played a violin concert. The officers of the 29th Madras Infantry allowed their band to play once a week in the middle of the Padang, when the chain enclosure was taken down to allow carriages to be driven in.

Later in the year the Malaccan merchant Chua Chong Long gave a great dinner for the most prominent residents of the settlement, on the occasion of his forty-fourth birthday. Already a rich man before he had left Malacca to set up business in the new settlement ran by Tuan Farquhar, he had multiplied his fortune by becoming the majority owner of the opium farms, which had proved to be extremely lucrative. He lived in Commercial Square, and was fond of hosting lavish parties to celebrate his good fortune.

Tan Hong Chuan was pleased to be considered one of the prominent residents, when he found himself invited to the dinner along with such distinguished persons as Tan Che Sang, Seah Eu Chin, Alexander Johnston, Alexander Guthrie, John and Ronnie Simpson, Graham McKenzie and George Coleman. He had done very well for himself since he had arrived in Singapore twelve years before. His fruit and vegetable business had expanded rapidly, especially with the help of Siti and her sisters from the sultan's compound. He now had extensive vegetable plots and paddy fields beyond the town, and a coconut plantation at Tanjong Katong. Hong Chuan had managed to pay off his original loan to the Ghee Hin, and with the profits from his fruit and vegetable business he had set himself up as a ship's chandler, selling sails, spars and provisions to the ships in the harbour; he had done a roaring trade as the tonnage passing through Singapore increased year after year. He also served as a comprador for some of the European and Chinese merchants, especially in their dealings with the local Malays, whose language he spoke fluently.

He had done so well that he built himself a fine house at Telok Ayer, and had married Tong Swan Neo, the first daughter of Tong

Tek Kee, an established Malaccan merchant. His wife was very plain and not very intelligent; her whole life seemed to revolve around her pet dogs. However, she had given him a son, Tan Eng Guan, and he was very grateful to her for that reason alone. He had made Siti his first concubine, on her condition that she could have her sisters from the harem as her maidservants.

Siti knew how to please a man, including ways that his first wife would never have dreamed of, but she also had excellent business sense. It was Siti who had advised Hong Chuan to extend his fruit and vegetable business, and she who had advised him to cultivate coconut, durian and pineapple rather than nutmeg, coffee, and cotton, which were favoured by the other merchants. She said they were much better suited to the soil and climate of Singapore. And it was Siti who was always telling him to buy land—as much land as he could possibly afford.

Thus it was with a great sense of pride in his own achievement and status that he attended Chua Chong Long's dinner. Toasts were drunk to the health of Mr Ibbetson the resident, who could not attend because he was visiting Penang, and to the memory of Sir Stamford Raffles.

Chua Chong Long made a long speech in which he praised the Duke of Wellington, the hero of Waterloo and the recent prime minister of Great Britain, and proposed a toast in his name. As he raised his glass to toast the duke, Hong Chuan felt himself at the heart of the thriving settlement that was Singapore, and looked forward to a future of continued prosperity. As they all did.

3

The hideout of the Illanun pirates Si Rahman and Sri Hussein lay in a wide tributary of the Rimau River in Eastern Sumatra. One day, when they were visiting Sultan Tating, who ruled over the land that included their stronghold, Sri Hussein fell in love with one of his slave girls, whose name was Ningsih. She was a beauty with piercing black eyes and flashing white teeth, with a voluptuous body that drove Sri Hussein mad with desire. When she smiled her sensual smile he felt that his body was on fire, and he determined that he must have her for his own.

He made a generous offer to buy her from the sultan, but the sultan refused. Then he went before the sultan and made a personal appeal to him, but again the sultan refused. He agreed that Ningsih was a great beauty, which was why he wanted to keep her as his own. She brought great credit to the island of Lombok, from which she had been taken by another group of pirates, the sultan said with a smile. He told Sri Hussein to forget about her, and to find another like her in the slave markets of Pulau Nias, from which the girl had been bought.

Sri Hussein was now twenty-six years old, and cut a dashing figure. He was about five foot ten, with long flowing brown hair and a muscular body, hardened by his years at sea and pirating. He still had a beautiful smile, with a touch of femininity, which women found alluring, including the sultan's slave girl. One night Sri Hussein sent a message to Ningsih asking her to meet him outside the sultan's compound. When she appeared, the two lovers embraced, and Sri Hussein led Ningsih deep into the jungle, where he had prepared a secret hiding place. For the next few days they lived on the food of love, and Sri Hussein and Ningsih swore each other eternal love. Sri Hussein knew he could never let her go, and would rather die than give her up.

Their secret hiding place did not remain secret for long, and soon a party of elders came to summon Sri Hussein to appear before the sultan's council, which would deliberate on his crime of stealing the sultan's property. Sri Hussein took the girl back to the pirate camp, where he placed her in the charge of one of his captains, while he went with his brother to appear before the sultan and his council. The sultan's audience hall was a large bamboo structure set inside his compound, raised above ground and entered by a flight of plank steps. The sultan sat on a teak throne flanked by his council of ministers; his people sat around the walls of the chamber and outside in the courtyard. Sri Hussein and Si Rahman knew no fear. They arrived at the sultan's compound without any guard, and marched up the steps to the audience chamber decked out in their silver breastplates and red feathers, looking more like royalty than the sultan himself. When they stood before the sultan they held their heads high, and their hands were on the handles of their poisoned krisses. If there were any signs of treachery they would kill the sultan where he sat.

Sri Hussein made his case before Sultan Tating and his council. He told them that he meant no disrespect to the sultan, whom he honoured as a father, but that he loved the girl and could not live without her—he truly believed that they had been put on the earth to be together. He reminded the sultan that he had offered to buy Ningsih from him, and repeated his offer, begging the sultan to reconsider now that he knew how strongly he felt about the girl. Sri Hussein said that he was willing to do anything to appease him, save for giving up the girl—for that was something he could never do.

Sri Hussein and Si Rahman stood like stone statues while the sultan and his council deliberated. The sultan and his council knew they had to be careful and diplomatic, for the pirates commanded a powerful force, and brought much wealth to the river and the sultan's treasury. Yet Sri Hussein had insulted the sultan by stealing his slave girl, and that could not be ignored—he would have to pay dearly for his crime. Abdul Haqq, the sultan's chief minister, delivered the verdict of the sultan and his council. Sri Hussein would be allowed to keep the girl Ningsih and would enjoy the protection of the law from the sultan's righteous anger, if he presented Sultan Tating with the sum of twenty thousand silver dollars by one year from that day.

This was a huge sum of money, and far more than Sri Hussein had originally offered the sultan. But Sri Hussein agreed to the judgment, and he and his brother left the compound. All they needed were some rich merchantmen and the matter would be settled.

4

When they returned from their visit to the Bugis fleet, the Simpsons and the Hancocks changed into evening dress, and prepared to enter the carriage that would take them to the dinner party at the home of Dr Jose d'Almeida,[27] which was the last of the line of twenty sparkling white mansions than ran eastwards along the beach towards Kampong Glam.

Jose d'Almeida and his wife Rosalia were famous for the large dinner parties that they regularly held, and their home was one of the centres of Singapore's social life. The d'Almeidas and their many children were talented musicians, and most of their dinner parties were preceded by accomplished renderings of Mozart, Brahms, and their favourite Portuguese composer Juan Crisostomo de Arriaga, who had died tragically six years earlier at the age of nineteen. When Signor Masoni had played the first violin concert in Singapore, he had played in the d'Almeida's sitting room, and it had been a night to remember.

John Simpson came out to join them in the carriage. Sarah though he looked very dashing in his black frockcoat and britches, with his silver buckles and silver hair. The children clambered into the carriage behind them to say goodbye and goodnight to their parents, since they would be long in their beds by the time they all returned—the d'Almeida's parties *always* went on late into the night.

'Goodnight mama! Goodnight papa! Goodnight Grandpapa John! Grandpapa John was the name the children had taken to calling their grandfather.

Mrs Stables, the spinster that John Simpson had brought out from Ardersier to look after the children, hurried them back into the house, and Ronnie signalled to the Indian syce to drive on. He though it ridiculous to take a carriage for a journey that would last all of five minutes, but his father had insisted that they must do so to keep up appearances. With such indulgence, he thought it small wonder that he was a little tight in his neatly pressed white trousers and waistcoat, and black coat. It would be good to be back at sea next week, he thought; he was taking a cargo of opium up to Canton, and would go on to Manila to bring back a shipment of sandalwood. A few weeks before the mast would soon get him back in trim again. He would miss Sarah and the children, but he was looking forward to having John and Rosemarie and young Lizzie come and stay with them after he returned. It would be a full house, but they had plenty of room to spare—Coleman did not build small! And God knows they could do with a good accountant. He looked across at Sarah, who smiled back at him. She wore a blue silk evening gown, with a string of pearls from the Sulu islands. She looked as beautiful as the day he had met her, and they were both still very much in love.

The d'Almeidas greeted them at the door, where the men were invited to exchange their black coats for white dinner jackets, which they had conveniently brought themselves, knowing the custom. The party began with a musical concert, followed by the usual twelve-course dinner with wine, beer and champagne.

When he judged they were suitably full of good cheer, Reverend Darrock, the residency Chaplain, appealed to John and Ronnie Simpson and Alexander Johnston for a contribution to the building fund for the new church.

'I'm afraid the old Mission Chapel will no longer suffice. Plank and attap was good enough in the old days, but we need a more substantial structure of brick and mortar. I don't know if you've heard, but Mr Bonham has granted the Armenians a piece of land between the Botanical Gardens and Hill Street, and Mr Coleman has been appointed architect and engineer for the new church. Is that not right Mr Coleman?'

George Coleman, who was sitting between Sarah and Ronnie, nodded his assent, and told them he was looking forward to working on it.

'But how did they manage to raise money for a church?' John Simpson asked Reverend Darrock. 'There canna be more than twa dozen o' them in the town.'

'Thirty-five, I believe, at the last count. But they've been here since day one— Aristarchus Moses came the year the settlement was founded. Been in business in the archipelago—and India—for years, and like the Peranakans, they brought their families with them. Tight-knit little community, and fiercely proud of the fact that Armenia was the first country to adopt Christianity as its official religion, at the beginning of the fourth century, I believe. They built a temporary Gregorian chapel a few years ago, and they now have a resident priest, the Reverend Gregory Johannes, a very good fellow. The ten leading families donated the initial money from their businesses—which are thriving, I can tell you—and they've raised money from the Armenian communities in India, Java and the Malayan peninsula.

Now given their history, I don't begrudge Mr Coleman building them the first proper Christian church in Singapore. But I would say to you gentlemen that we want the next one to serve the larger Protestant community, so I'm asking if you would be so kind as to pledge something to our building fund. We hope to raise enough funds so we can contract with Mr Coleman to have him build our own church—for a finer architect you won't find in this town.'

'Agreed,' said Alexander Johnston, although he had not personally contracted with Coleman to build himself a fine mansion along the beach like the other merchants, preferring to live above his godown on Boat Quay. 'You can count me in for five hundred dollars, and five hundred more if you need it.'

John and Ronnie Simpson agreed to contribute five hundred dollars, as did Dr Montgomerie and George Coleman, even though he was Irish and Catholic.

After dinner, while the small orchestra was being set up and the ballroom prepared for dancing, Sarah returned from the powder room to find Ronnie standing talking with some of the Malacca merchants, and sharing an opium pipe with Chua Chong Long.

'Do you really think you should be doing that?' she exclaimed. 'I don't want you to end up like those poor souls in Chinatown.'

'Oh, I dinna think there's ony danger o' that,' said Dr Montgomerie, who had come to join the small party. 'He's a sensible laddie. There's no more harm from a few puffs on an opium pipe than from a cigar and a good malt whisky at the end of the day. Both take the stiffness out o' the bones, and are a grand all round tonic.'

'The rule is everything in moderation,' Dr Montgomerie concluded, taking another large whisky from the tray offered by the Malay servant.

'Well, let's just test that theory, then,' said Sarah, with a grin. 'They've just announced the first dance is the Gay Gordons. On the floor, Captain!'

As Ronnie went to join Sarah on the dance floor, Dr Montgomerie went out to the verandah, with Alexander Johnston and Naraina Pillai following close behind. Dr Montgomerie looked out over the dark ocean, and listened to the low surf rolling in the distance. A light breeze drifted from the water and cooled his brow.

'That's probably it,' he wondered aloud, as Johnston and Pillai joined him on the verandah.

'What's probably it?' they responded together, laughing.

'Well, you know, I've been wondering why we've not been bothered with malaria and other tropical fevers, despite the noxious vapors from the marshlands behind us, and the poisonous miasmas from the river. There's not been a single case of malaria among the Europeans since the settlement was founded. Really quite remarkable, when you compare it to the charnel houses of Bencoolen and Batavia. It must be this grand breeze that comes up from the sea. Not whit ye would get from the Firth of Forth, of course, but it must be enough to dispel the vapors.'

'It probably also explains the outbreaks of fever among the Malays at Telok Blangah,' Montgomerie continued. 'They're landlocked behind Pulau Brani and Pulau Blakang Mati, and don't get the benefit of the sea breezes; and they get stagnant vapors off the mangrove swamps.'

'Sounds plausible enough,' Johnson replied, 'and the Lord preserve us from epidemics. But don't you have your own plantation out there? How do you manage to protect yourself?'

'Oh, that's easy,' Montgomerie replied. 'I'm a great pipe smoker, I am, and there's nothing better than tobacco smoke to combat foul air. But I pity the poor Malays with their betel nuts—they offer no protection at all.'

'Just stay away from the opium,' said Naraina Pillai. 'Whatever you said to young Mr Simpson, it has ruined the lives of many of my countrymen, and it is an evil thing.'

'Perhaps you are right,' said Johnston thoughtfully. 'But you and I know that opium is what makes this settlement pay.' The other two men nodded their silent agreement.

* * *

Later that year the Chinese merchants, disgusted with the constant pirate attacks upon their shipping, and frustrated by the failure of the British administration to do anything about it, equipped four large junks with guns and well-armed thirty-man crews. The merchants offered a bounty of two hundred dollars for every pirate vessel they attacked and destroyed, and compensation to the family of any crewmember that was killed in their service.

The brave little fleet set out and attacked some of the smaller pirate vessels that waited to ambush native craft just outside of the harbour. They sank one ship and drove off another, killing many pirates with only the loss of two of their own. Their action shamed the government into equipping two gunboats manned by Malays, which patrolled the waters around Singapore, but made no contact with any pirates. The merchants continued to press the government for concerted action, many complaining that they were unable to purchase opium on credit from Calcutta merchants because of the danger of pirate attacks.

5

1833

The *Mary Ellen* departed Singapore harbour on the early tide, bound for Penang. She passed through the Strait of Singapore into the Strait of Malacca, and made good progress north. As she rounded Pangkor Island on the second day, the first mate, Jack Fleming, spotted a fore-and-aft rigged schooner drifting from the northwest. He called up to the foretop man on the masthead.

'Hey, John Ware, do you see thon ship ahead—she looks like she's drifting.'

'That I do,' Ware responded. 'She's a queer-looking sort of thing, with her fore sail flapping in the wind.' He hailed the deck to report on the vessel, which rolled in the gentle swell.

The captain, Tom Harkness, a former navy officer now trading out of Singapore, peered through his telescope. He scanned the deck and rigging, but could not see a living soul. Then he noticed with a start the motto on the bow of the ship.

'It's the *Rose of Dublin*, John Grover's rig,' he exclaimed. 'But she has no command!'

All eyes now turned toward the drifting vessel. The officers looked through their glasses, while the crew strained their eyes against the sun, which shone in a white haze through the clouded sky. Although the noonday sun beat down on his balding head, Captain Harkness felt as if a cold dark shadow had passed over him, and he shivered involuntarily. He ordered the first mate to lower the ship's boat and take a party of men and marines to overhaul the *Rose of Dublin*.

'And arm the men, Fleming' he called out to him. 'There may be danger still.'

One of the older deck hands voiced what many feared.

'I'll tell you what it is, mates,' he hissed, 'it's pirates. I'll bet any man a week's grog to a tot that they've all been murdered and thrown overboard. The seas around here are crawling with Illanun and Balanini trash, and there's no point in chasing them—ye might as well look for a needle in a haystack.'

'Well, let's find out what it is, shall we,' said Fleming, as he pressed the men into the boat, and ordered Mr Devlin to take the rudder. Devlin was a Connemara man, nearly six feet tall and broad chested, with a thick black beard. He was afraid of no man, and was a good man to have by your side in a fight; but like all sailors, he was superstitious. He crossed himself as he sat down in the boat, and stared at the drifting schooner. The oars dashed in the water and the ocean spray splashed in their faces, but nobody spoke as they made their way towards the drifting *Rose of Dublin*.

They were about halfway there when Devlin bent over to the first mate and spoke his mind.

'I tell you what, Mr Fleming, I don't like to go on board her. I've heard many a terrifying tale o' those ships that sail around themselves with no crew, just waiting to tempt poor Jacks likes us. Like the Flying Dutchman, or Mos Moses who spent five years with old tough britches. True as the salt in the sea.'

'Well, I've heard of the Flying Dutchman, but that's no ghost ship, Devlin, it's the *Rose of Dublin,*' Fleming responded, with some exasperation, 'And I've never heard of Mos Moses.'

'Never heard of Mos Moses, Mr Fleming, but it's the most miraculous tale to be told. Three days out of Newfoundland, with a full crew, bound for the whaling waters. Captain Moses sick in his cabin, dosed with grog and laudanum. He wakes up and calls for the bosun, but no one replies. He goes up on deck, but there's not a soul to be found, with the ship driving before the wind, and the sky as black as night. He searches the cabins, the galley, the stores, but no sign of any man below. Dumfounded, Mos returns to the deck with a ship's lantern, and sees a tall shape at the helm. And Mary, Jesus and Holy Paul if it isn't the devil himself steering the ship, with his great tail slapping on the deck! And bless me, if he didn't drive poor Mos Moses round the seven seas for seven years, afore abandoning the ship off Gibraltar rock.'

'Get a grip, Devlin,' said Fleming, who could see that the boat crew was clearly agitated by the sailor's tale. He scanned the deck of the *Rose of Dublin*, as if to establish there was no evil presence on board. Then all of a sudden a great black Irish wolfhound appeared on the ship's gangway, with its paws laid over the netting, its tongue hanging out red as blood in the sunlight. Devlin's yell told him that he had seen it too. The crew turned to see what was happening, and let out a collective gasp when they saw the great black dog. They immediately stopped rowing, and the longboat bobbed idly in the water as they stared in horror at the dreadful apparition.

Fleming himself was shaken by the dog's sudden appearance on the deserted ship, but quickly recovered his composure.

'It's just a dog,' he told the men, but he cursed inwardly, since he knew that a black dog figured in many sailors' tales as an agent or incarnation of the devil. 'Carry on toward her.'

Nobody moved. The men were frozen to their positions at the oars.

'But sir,' Devlin began.

'Shut it,' said Fleming, before turning to the men in the boat. 'Move yourselves, now, or I'll report you to the captain, and you'll feel the nip of his lash,' he commanded, and brought a boat hook down with a crash on the edge of the craft to distract their attention from the dog. 'Bring us alongside, Devlin,' he roared.

Reluctantly the crew began rowing again, with many an anxious turn of their heads towards the ghost ship, riding high in the water before them. The black dog stared back at them from the gangway, then disappeared as suddenly as it had come.

They were now alongside the *Rose of Dublin*, and preparing to board her. Fleming looked back at Devlin, and saw that the man was shaking violently.

'I tell ye, Mr Fleming,' he stammered, 'a man has no business wi' a ghost ship, and any God-fearing man ought to fear the consequences o' boarding a brig that is devil commanded. I'm a brave man sir, and I served with Collingwood, God bless his memory. I was on the *Royal Sovereign* when we took the *Santa Ana* on the twenty-first of October, God bless the day, but it's sheer bloody madness to tempt auld Nick.'

Fleming had had enough of ghost ships and auld Nick. He drew his pistol and placed it against Devlin's head.

'Damn my soul, you mad Irishman. I'll put a bullet in your brain and send you down to Davy Jones if you don't get up on this ship right now. Davy Jones or devil dog!'

He cocked the pistol.

Devlin rose from his seat with a great sigh, and wished aloud that he would rather be back fighting the Frenchies than bein' a party to an infernal ghost chase. He drew his cutlass and began to climb up the rigging single-handed.

'Let's go and see what's in her then,' said Fleming, and led the rest of the men on board.

When they reached the deck, there was no sign of the dog or the devil, or any of the crew of the *Rose of Dublin*. The deck was strewn with straw and canvas, as if many of the overturned chests scattered there had been emptied in great haste. A huge bale of red silk, which had obviously been ransacked, blew back and forth in the breeze across the quarterdeck. For a few moments they all stood in the eerie silence, with only the sound of the waves slapping on the ship's hull, and the creaking of her bulkheads. Then one of the marines pointed to the dark footprints on deck.

'Blood it is for sure, sir,' he exclaimed. 'This ship's been boarded by pirates, and all the crew murdered.'

'It may be as you say, Lieutenant Brown,' said Fleming, 'but let's be sure. Morgan, take the hands and search the deck. Lieutenant, take your marines and follow me and Devlin down to search the cabins. Arms at the ready!'

They had to clear the remains of some opened bales from the stairway, but soon they stood before the door to the captain's cabin. Devlin was no longer trembling, but his face was graveyard grey behind his great beard. Fleming stepped forward and rapped upon the door with the butt of his pistol, but no sound came from within. As he did so, he almost stumbled, for he suddenly realized the floorboards were wet and sticky beneath his booted feet. A dreadful premonition assailed him as he gripped his pistol and turned the handle of the door. It opened easily upon a sight of pure horror.

There were eight people in the room, six men and two women. They sat on chairs around the captain's table, as if preparing to eat dinner. The men's throats were cut from ear to ear, and their heads lolled with the swell of the sea, exposing their gaping wounds. The women, a mother and daughter, had been strangled, and the ropes that had been used now hung from their necks like hideous scarves. Their bulging eyeballs and swollen black tongues gave them a hellish appearance, like figures from some medieval painting of the underworld. All the bodies were horribly mutilated, and the pirates had cut the hair from the heads of the women, along with parts of their scalps. Fleming retched at the stench of blood and the corruption of death, and stumbled backwards into the stairwell. He sat down on the bottom step, his senses reeling. Great black flies hummed in the humid air and clamored over the corpses, which were already beginning to putrify.

Despite their horrific appearance, Fleming knew who the women were. They were Rosemarie and Lizzie Hancock, the wife and daughter of John Hancock, a Company servant in Penang, who now sat with his throat cut at the end of the table. He knew that Rosemarie Hancock was the sister of Sarah Simpson, the wife of one of the Scottish merchants in Singapore, Ronnie Simpson, whom Fleming knew well; he had once served on one of his ships. What a tragedy for the family, he thought to himself. He also knew the captain of the *Rose of Dublin*, with whom he had shared many a friendly cup. The captain now sat at the head of the table, his white shirt stained through and through with his own black blood.

Devlin, who had held back in the shadows, now proceeded cautiously into the cabin, plainly afraid but also driven by his morbid fascination with the dreadful scene. Fleming followed him back in. He saw that the floor was slick with the blood from the mutilated bodies around the table, and that the pirates had ransacked the cabin. Every cupboard and drawer had been torn open, and their contents strewn on the blood-dark floor.

While clearly shocked, Devlin now seemed to be taking the ghastly scene in his stride. He was no stranger to death, and he began going round the table untying the bodies. Fleming did the same from the other side. The bodies of the men slumped forward in their chairs when they were released, but the table prevented them from falling to the ground.

Proceeding from different directions, the two men arrived together beside the two women. Fleming removed the ropes with which they had been strangled, while Devlin untied their bodies. Yet unlike the men, they did not pitch forward, but continued to sit bolt upright in their chairs, their eyes staring wide in their sockets. Yet this was not what caused both men to stand silently beside them, overcome with sadness and pity. For they saw that the mother and daughter's hands were tightly intertwined. Whether this was their last act of courage and comfort, or a cruel trick played by the pirates, they could not tell. But they were overcome with emotion by the pathos of the scene.

They were dragged from their reverie by the sound of musketry below decks. Both men rushed toward the cabin door, their pistols cocked. As Fleming reached the stairwell, a great black shape rushed by him and bounded up the stairs. He was about to fire, when he realized it was the dog they had seen earlier at the side of the ship. Lieutenant Brown, who came forward out of the shadows, quickly confirmed this.

'Only the dog, Mr Fleming. Must have been hiding in the for'ard cabin. It looks like pirates all right. Every man jack on board is dead and mutilated. They're long gone I'd say, by the state of the bodies...at least a day.'

Fleming nodded his head in agreement, and told Lieutenant Brown to get his men back on deck. He turned to Devlin, who now stood in the doorway, looking a grisly sight. In his rush to locate the cause of the musketry, Devlin had slipped and fallen on the floor of the cabin. His white cotton shirt and pants were dark red with sticky blood, which he was futilely trying to wipe clean with a rag. Fleming suddenly felt sorry for the man, and put his hand on his shoulder.

'Get yourself up too, Devlin,' he said, 'and see if you can organize some sailcloth for these bodies. And send some men back to inform Captain Harkness what has happened here.'

Devlin climbed back up the cabin stairs. Just before he reached the deck, he turned back and apologized to the first mate:

'I'm sorry about my foolishness afore, sir' he said. 'But one thing's for sure, the devil's been here ... he's been here for sure, sir.'

'For sure, Mr Devlin,' Fleming replied, and followed him up.

The *Mary Ellen* hove to shortly after, and Captain Harkness came on board. He ordered the decks and cabins washed with vinegar, the rubbish cleared away, and the bodies brought on deck, where they were bound in sailcloth sewn into makeshift shrouds. Captain Harkness led the funeral service, after which the bodies were consigned to the deep. As Fleming organized a skeleton crew to take the *Rose of Dublin* back to Penang, he asked one of the men what had happened to Devlin.

'We gave 'im a cup o' grog to calm his nerves,' said the sailor. 'He was sat down by the mizzen mast when yon black dog comes right up to him and licks his hand, all a whimpering like. Turns out the marines put a bullet in its shoulder, which Devlin got the surgeon to remove. He gave the dog some hard tack, and now they're the best o' friends. Calls it Mos Moses—a daft name for a dog, and I don't know why.'

'I think I do,' said Fleming, as he prepared to return to the *Mary Ellen.*

6

It was early morning when they brought her the news. Ronnie was at sea, and Sarah was alone in the house with Mrs Stables and the servants. Grandpapa John had taken the children to Reverend Darrah's Singapore School on Hill Street. Alexander Johnston was the first to hear the news, which was common enough, since his pier and godown was the first on the river mouth, and Johnston was always alert to the latest shipping intelligence. He dropped everything and rode out to the Simpson mansion. He told Sarah only of their deaths, and not the horror of their mutilation.

She did not scream or faint or curse or tear her hair. She blanched and put her hand to her mouth when he told her the news, but regained her composure quickly. She thanked Alexander Johnston for the courtesy of coming to tell her personally; she would not have cared to hear the news from a messenger or servant. Johnston offered his condolences, and his services if she thought there was anything he could do for her while Ronnie was away. Then he took his leave, saying he would try to get word to her husband as soon as possible. There was a free-trader bound for Canton that might be able to catch him before he left for Manila.

Sarah walked up the stairs to her bedroom like a somnambulant, purposeful but scarcely conscious of her own movements. She closed the door behind her and locked it, and went over to the windows to draw the drapes. But then she changed her mind. She went out and stood on the verandah overlooking the garden and the ocean beyond. Black storm clouds rolled over the horizon, and the thunder rumbled in the distance. As she stood gazing out over the ocean like a woman in a waking dream, the sky grew blacker and blacker until it seemed as if night had fallen in the middle of the day—as if the whole wide world awaited the end of days. The wind rushed through the palms and frangipani, sweeping back and forth across the garden and the balcony, and raising a white spray across the dark waters. The wind felt cool and fresh on her face, and whipped her loose hair behind her head.

A large egret, stunningly white against the jet-black sky, flew across the garden and headed out to sea. Her thoughts swooped and dived with the flight of the egret, racing ahead and beyond her control. She remembered family days in England as a child, of afternoons on the riverbank with her sister, of Sundays in church and Christmases and birthdays at home.

She remembered the day of her sister's wedding in Penang, and her own in Singapore when Rosemarie and John had come down to join the celebrations. She remembered Annie playing with Lizzie the last time they had visited in Singapore. She thought of the last time she had seen them, when they had said goodbye on the dock. She thought of her plans for when they returned. She felt the emptiness and the pain in her heart. She saw the blood on the deck and their dead faces in the deep of the ocean. Lightning crackled along the wrought iron rails of the verandah, casting up little daggers of blue light that pierced the darkness.

Then the rain came down suddenly like a great waterfall, straight and flat and torrential. She stood still in the darkness as the wind drove the rain against her face and body. It soaked her clothes and hair, and washed like a fast-moving stream around her ankles. It washed away the tears that streamed down her face as she grieved for her sister and her family.

When Grandpapa John returned home and heard the news, he sat outside her door, listening to the rain hammer on the roof and shutters. He did not bother her, for he thought it best to give her time to herself. He sat in the gloom reflecting on the tragedy of young lives taken in their prime. He would gladly have given his own life if it could have saved theirs, but all he could do was to sit helplessly and share his daughter-in-law's sorrow. She had a strong heart, he knew, and she would survive it. But he felt for her. He remembered when he had first heard of his own brother's death, struck down with the smallpox at the age of eighteen, and newly engaged to a bonnie lassie from Inverness.

A few hours later she unlocked the door and he went in to her. She embraced him, and he could tell immediately that her resolute spirit had accepted the fact of the matter. She grieved as deep as any other, but her thoughts were now focused on taking her revenge upon the pirates, about whom she had joked so many years before.

When Ronnie returned three weeks later, she was still stunned by the news, but her mind was clear and made up.

'We must find them,' she said in a voice that was both calm and chilling. 'We must find them and kill them.'

* * *

Ronnie went to see Kenneth Murchison, the resident councillor. Murchison was sympathetic and said that he would communicate his concern to Governor Ibbetson in Penang, but Ronnie was sure that nothing would be done, despite the uproar among the residents of Singapore, Malacca and Penang over the brutal murders.

Sarah also went to see him, but received less sympathy. Kenneth Murchison could not believe the foul language she used to describe his failure to protect innocent lives. Then Ronnie went to his merchant friends, in the hope of a raising a private fleet to hunt down the pirates, like the small fleet that had been raised earlier by the Chinese merchants. The merchants were sympathetic, but pointed out that it was one thing driving off some of the more brazen Malay prahus that stood off like vultures at the far edges of the harbour, but quite another matter to hunt down the Illanun fleet that many believed had been responsible for the attack on the *Rose of Dublin*. For one thing, they had no idea where to find them, and they could search aimlessly for weeks or even months without much chance of a sighting.

'And I think the Company will finally do something,' George Armstrong told Ronnie when he came to see him. 'I spoke to Deputy Resident Bonham the other day, and he said they were sending some ships out from Calcutta. I also think we're likely to have Bonham as resident soon, and he may be more sympathetic.'

Ronnie was doubtful, and Sarah was mad with frustration and anger. She also went to see Deputy Resident Bonham, who briskly showed her the door when the air turned blue and Bonham's cheeks turned red.

'If they don't do anything soon,' Sarah told her husband, 'I want you to arm as many ships as you can and we'll go in search of them ourselves.'

Ronnie thought about how much such an expedition might cost. It might go on for months or years, and it might ruin them. But he knew she would never rest until she found her sister's murderers, so he prepared himself for it. He also did not like her use of the pronoun 'we,' but he said nothing, because he also knew that nothing would dissuade her from joining such an expedition.

7

Musa bin Hassan put his finishing touches to the long black prahu.
He had worked on the boat for months, sometimes late into the night
by torchlight, and now it was almost ready. He walked round it with
a file and polished stone, removing even the smallest imperfections
from the sleek black surface. Although in many respects this boat
was just like the other boats that he and his father crafted to service
the crews of the merchantmen in the roads, he had taken special
care with this one, which he planned to enter in the races that were
to be held on the day the Christians marked as their New Year.

There would be races between the European yachts, the
Chinese dragon boats, and the longboats that ferried the crews
from the merchantmen to town. Musa and his father had seen
their business grow over the years, as the Malay boat builders had
cornered the market in providing fast prahus to ferry the crews
from the merchant ships and junks to the river mouth, as the Indian
lightermen had cornered the market for cargo in their tambangs.
And like the European merchants in their yachts, the Malays loved
to race their craft against the Chinese and European crews in their
ship's boats. Almost every day there were informal races held along
the coast, and the Malay boats usually beat all comers.

Musa loved this new boat, which he had created with his own
hands, and wondered at his own blasphemous thought: God must
have felt like this when he created the world. Or at least this must
be the way a woman felt when she gave birth to a child. The prahu
was about twenty foot long and four foot wide, her lines straight
and true. He would take it out tomorrow, but he already knew that

it would speed over the water like a great black bird.

He heard a movement at the back of the boathouse. He thought that he had heard someone come in earlier, but had been too busy working on the boat to pay much notice. He turned and was surprised to see Abdullah, who had been standing in the shadows watching him. Abdullah marvelled at the workmanship, and the fine lines of the sleek black hull. He wanted to own that black prahu—he wanted to own it very badly. He wanted to run it in the races and win.

'A fine piece of workmanship, Musa,' he said. 'You have a rare gift, God be praised. I have been looking for such a boat, which I would like to enter in the races against the infidels. I am willing to make you a generous offer for it, far more than you could ever hope to gain from racing or selling the craft.'

Abdullah told Musa how much he was willing to pay, and Musa wondered at the amount. But Musa was not for a moment tempted, for nothing would persuade him to part with this boat; it was his special creation, and was part of his very being. He thanked Abdullah for his generosity, but regretted that he could not accept his offer.

Abdullah was used to getting his own way, even if he had to pay for it. Musa's refusal only made him want the black prahu even more, and he increased his offer. But Musa was not interested in his money, and he would not be moved.

'With all that money you could easily buy yourself another boat. Why, you could even buy yourself a wife,' Abdullah sneered, suddenly losing his control. 'Why don't you think of that?'

Musa did think of that, although not in the way that Abdullah intended.

He stood silent for a moment, and then gave Abdullah his answer. 'Here is what I am willing to do,' he said. 'I will race this boat, and I will win my race. I will not sell it to you, but after I win the race I will wager this boat against your money in a cockfight. You may have first choice of the animals, and we will let them decide. But I have one condition. You must first divorce Rashidah. You do not love her, and you have no children by her. That is my last word.'

Abdullah raised his eyebrow and a thin smile spread over his face. 'I will think on it, and I will wait and see if you do win your race. Then I will give you my answer. Good night, Musa bin Hassan. May the blessings of the Prophet go with you.'

'And with you,' Musa replied, as he watched him leave.

* * *

For months nothing happened, and the Simpsons had no news of any kind of the Illanun pirates, or of the willingness of Calcutta to help them deal with the menace. But finally Ronnie and Sarah had a stroke of luck. One morning they received a note from Alexander Johnston urging them to meet him at his home on Boat Quay. Unlike most of his European and Chinese colleagues, Johnston still lived above his godown at the mouth of the river. When they were ushered into his front room, Johnston approached them with a thin smile on his face.

'My good friends, I have some information that I know you will want me to share with you. Please sit down.'

They did so, and Johnston told them about an old sailor whom the crew of a Dutch man-of-war had picked up, after they had sunk an Illanun war prahu that had been damaged and become detached from the main pirate fleet.

The sailor had been the first mate on the *Fair Maid of London*, which had been attacked and burned by Illanun pirates, led by Si Rahman and his half brother Sri Hussein. They had killed Captain Ramsey and his son Adam, and had taken the first mate and some of the crew prisoner. Since then the man had served twelve years in the pirate galleys. They had treated him well enough, apparently, all things considered. He had even received a share of their plunder, and had taken a Bugis slave girl as his wife. But he had sworn an oath that he would make his escape whenever a safe opportunity arose, and would have his revenge upon the men who had killed his captain, and dropped his poor young son to the bottom of the ocean at the end of a ship's anchor.

'But where is he?' Ronnie and Sarah said together.

'He's staying with me at the moment, in one of my spare rooms. Only my people know he is here, and none of them know his story. I think it best if we keep it that way at the moment. Too much information about ships and their crews gets out of Singapore as it is, and I don't want this man's news to reach the wrong ears.'

Johnston got up quickly and left the room. He returned a few moments later with a short but very tough looking old sailor clad in faded blue overalls; he was brown as a dark nut, and his arms rippled with hard muscles from his years at the oar.

'Mr and Mrs Simpson, I'd like you to meet Mr Oates, former first mate of the *Fair Maid of London*.'

'Pleased to make your acquaintance,' said Oates, who motioned them to sit down as they began to rise to greet him. 'I'm very sorry to hear of your loss, Mrs Simpson.'

Before Ronnie or Sarah could say anything, he continued: 'I've got many stories to tell about them brothers, and maybe you'll want to hear some of them, and maybe you won't. But I can tell you two things you will want to know. The men who killed Captain Ramsey and his son Adam were the same as killed your sister, and her husband and daughter. I was there the day they took the *Rose of Dublin*, although I did not go on board and see it with my own eyes. But Si Rahman boasted about it afterwards. He said that a holy man had told him he would attain immortality if he killed a white woman. He came back carrying locks of their hair, which he now wears round his neck like a talisman. He's a twisted bastard, beggin' your pardon, ma'am.'

Sarah began to cry, in huge gulping sobs. Ronnie put his arm around her.

'You said there were two things we would want to know,' said Ronnie, quietly. 'What was the second?'

'I know where they are,' Oates replied. 'I've been holding the map in my memory since they captured me, just waiting for the day.'

'Thank you, Mr Oates,' said Sarah, in a voice that had turned from sobbing to steel.

8

1834

It was New Year's Day, according to the Christian calendar, and the occasion of the first official regatta, although informal boat races had been held for years between merchants, ship crews and the local communities.

Eager spectators lined the Esplanade, Europeans with picnic hampers and Peranakan Chinese with servants bearing three-tiered baskets of delicacies suspended at the ends of wooden poles. Chinese and Indian hawkers plied their trade among the others, and Malay fruit sellers offered mangosteens and pineapple slices. Everyone used whatever device they had at hand to shade themselves from the fierce rays of the sun, which blazed high in the cloudless blue sky— parasols, paper umbrellas, wide brimmed hats and shady trees.

George Bonham, recently promoted to resident councillor, started the races with his pistol and awarded the prizes from an elevated stage, where he sat with the Company officers and local dignitaries. The first race was between the Chinese dragon boats; the second between the Bugis palari with their curved sterns and keels. All ranks, classes, and nationalities placed their bets, even though gaming had been officially banned once again—except during the fifteen days of Chinese New Year, because the authorities mistakenly believed that it formed an essential part of the Chinese religious celebrations. In the race between the five European yachts, the *Waterwitch* led the *Maggie Lauder*, *Shamrock*, *Hawk's Hill* and *Jenny Dang the Weaver*, but as she passed the halfway mark, she lost her topmast, and the *Shamrock* seized the advantage and overtook her to win the race.

The last race of the day was between the longboats that served the merchantmen; between the ships' own boats and the native craft that brought the officers and men to the mouth of the river. As the gun went off, the sleek black prahu piloted by Musa bin Hassan sped ahead, the light hull slicing through the water like a razor sharp blade. The sleek black craft led for the entire four-mile course, and crossed the finishing line a hundred yards ahead of the nearest competitor. As they passed the final flag, Musa dived from the boat and swam ashore, where he collected his prize money from Mr Bonham. He swam back to the boat with his bag of silver dollars held high above his head, to the loud cheers of his Malay supporters.

Everyone enjoyed the spectacle, with the exception of Abdullah bin Ahmad, who stood gloomily beneath the great banyan tree by the Bras Basah stream, while his followers continued to cheer the victory of Musa bin Hassan. When he returned to his home that night, Abdullah assembled his family and servants.

He asked his first wife Rashidah binti Ali to step forward, and divorced her by reciting 'Talaq' [lxv] three times as she stood before him, in accord with Sharia law. He avowed that he bore her no ill will, and would continue to support her until she found herself another husband. He knew that would not be for long, and he knew who that would be, but he did not say.

Later that evening, he sent a messenger to Musa bin Hassan, arranging to meet him at the cockfight at Kampong Glam in three days' time. He would have that black prahu. He lusted after it the way that other men lusted after women.

* * *

_____
lxv 'I divorce you.'

It was early evening, and the sun was setting over the kampong, casting golden shadows between the coconut trees and the stilted wooden houses. Evening prayers were over, and the families gathered in the common area between their houses. Some sat on attap mats, others reclined on the sand or flattened lalang grass, but all left the place of honour in the centre to the storyteller.

As the sun set and the golden gloom deepened all around, Musa bin Hassan took his place beside his family, as coconut lamps were lit and hung from the trees and the verandahs of the houses. The children danced in and out of the crowd, but came to sit with their parents when the storyteller entered the circle, for the storyteller told tales of ghosts and demons: black-winged female pontianaks who disemboweled pregnant women with their talons, and drank the blood of unsuspecting young men, to whom they appeared as dark beauties; of penanggalans that swept through cemeteries and mortuaries, dangling their bloody entrails from their disembodied heads, and feasting on the hearts of the newly dead; and terrible and deadly creatures of the sea and sky. Beyond the coconut trees, the low waves lapped gently along the seashore.

The storyteller was a wizened old man as skinny as a beggar, but with bright black eyes and a deep voice that was like the rolling of thunder before a storm. After asking for the blessings of God, he began with an old tragedy, the story of Radin Mas.

He told how in the days of Temenggong Abdul Rahman, Radin Mas had lived with her father in a cottage in Telok Blangah. Although they lived a quiet life, everyone knew them, for Radin Mas had a special beauty, with golden eyes that enchanted everyone who looked upon her. The old men said that she must be especially beloved of God, and the young men could not sleep at night for thinking of her.

One day her father saved the village by helping to repulse a pirate attack, and was brought before the temenggong, who recognized he was no ordinary man. Pangeran Adipati Agung admitted that he was a fugitive from the kingdom of Java. He was brother to one of the rajahs, who disapproved of his laison with a beautiful slave girl named Chahaya. They had married in secret, and had been blessed by the birth of their golden-eyed daughter Radin Mas. But when the rajah found out, he had executed Chahaya, and Pangeran Adipati had fled with his daughter to Singapore.

Abdul Rahman was greatly moved by Pangeran Adipati's story, and impressed by his royal heritage. To show his gratitude for his route of the pirates, the temenggong offered Pangeran Adipati the hand of his daughter Princess Kera in marriage, which Pangeran Adipati accepted. In due course Princes Kera gave birth to a baby boy, Tunka Chik, which should have brought her great joy, but she grew jealous of the way that Pangeran Adipati looked at his daughter Radin Mas, and came to believe that he loved her more than his wife and infant son. Tengku Bagus, who was Princess Kera's nephew, fed her jealousy. Together they hatched a plot that would rid Princes Kara of Radin Mas and let Tengku Bagus take her as his bride.

Princess Kara prepared an evening meal for Pangeran Adipati and his daughter Radin Mas, which was drugged. Tengku Bagus and his servants carried Pangeran Adipati away in a cart, and hid him at the bottom of a well some miles west of the village. When Radin Mas awoke, Princess Kera told her that if she ever wanted to see her father alive again she must marry Tengku Bagus and go to live with him in Sarawak, far away from Singapore. Radin Mas demanded proof that her father was still alive before she would consent to the marriage, but when they brought a letter written in her father's hand she consented to the marriage.

On the morning of her wedding day, Radin Mas looked out of her window towards the sea, where a great storm was gathering in the dark clouds. She wondered if she would ever see her father again, even though Princess Kara had promised her she would. But as she turned and made her way back to the centre of the room, she heard her father's voice, and saw him standing in the doorway. Pangeran Adipati rushed forward and embraced his daughter. He told Radin Mas he had been rescued by a fisherman, who had heard him praying to the Prophet.

But their joy at reunion was shattered when Tengku Bagus suddenly appeared in the doorway, with Princess Kera beside him. Tengku Bagus drew his kris, and rushed towards Pangeran Adipati, who turned to make a grab for Tengku Bagus's arm to deflect the weapon. But Radin Mas suddenly stepped out in front to protect him, and the thrust that Tengku Bagus had aimed at Pangeran Adipati drove into her chest. She crumpled before him with a soft moan.

As Tengku Bagus stood stunned by what he had done, Pangeran Adipati struck him on the head with his bare fist, and knocked him unconscious to the ground. Princess Kara backed slowly out of the room, then turned around and ran along the beach until she came to a fishing kelong, at whose end a small boat was moored.

The storm welled up with frightening intensity. The sky turned black as night, black as the caves of hell, as if the very forces of nature were responding to the evil that had been done. The thunder roared and the lightning crackled in the air like an angry jinn, casting sudden silver shadows across the room where Radin Mas lay dying.

Princess Kara was halfway down the kelong when the bolt of lightning struck her. The spear of silver fire scorched her body black and pitched her into the sea, but she was dead before she hit the water. As she sank beneath the waves, Radin Mas sighed her last breath.

As the news of Radin Mas's death spread throughout the village, the men and women and children crept bowed and barefooted into the house of Pangeran Adipati, to pay their last respects to his beautiful daughter. They sat in humble silence around the body of Radin Mas, their tears falling like rain when they saw that the golden light had gone out of her eyes. They buried Radin Mas in a small keramat in a grove at the foot of the hill behind the village. The villagers remembered with great fondness the golden-eyed beauty that had lived among them, and in time they named their village after her. On the temenggong's orders, Tengku Bagus was executed with his own kris.

As the storyteller completed his tale, the audience sat in hushed silence. A storm was brewing out at sea, and silver lightning flashed across the dark waters. Some of the younger members appeared anxious, as if they feared to see the ghost of Princess Kera rise up from the sea. Then they broke into spontaneous applause, urging him to tell them another story.

During the pause, Musa looked around at the eager faces in the lamplight, and gave a sudden gasp of delight as he saw a figure pass through the shadows and enter the house of Ali bin Osman. Although her head and face were covered, he knew it was Rashidah—she still walked like a deer through the forest. So Abdullah had kept his end of the bargain! Tomorrow he would ask his grand-uncle to visit her family to initiate a marriage proposal.

The storyteller continued with the tale of the great crab that causes the tide to ebb and flow.

When he returned home, Musa received a request from Abdullah to meet him at the cockfight at Kampong Glam in three days time.

9

Ronnie began to assemble a small fleet, without fuss or public display. It was impossible to hide their intentions from the pirates, who where known to visit the island, or their Malay informants. But he did not expect them to be surprised or alarmed, since they were only doing what the Chinese merchants had done in previous years, save for the fact that this time they were doing it together.

Moreover, those hidden eyes did not know where they were going, or—more to the point— did not know that *they* knew where they were going. Mr Oates had been kept in the back bedroom of Johnston's godown, with a plentiful supply of roast beef, malt whisky and the novels of Sir Walter Scott. He did not mind being kept under wraps, although he was itching to lead them to the pirate lair.

Ronnie provided three ships of his own, armed with broadside cannon and swivel guns fore and aft, and equipped the crews with muskets, cutlasses, and axes. It cost him dearly, but he had no choice, and no disinclination either—he was as anxious as his wife to see their relations revenged. And he had an additional incentive. Oates had told him that Purser was frequently to be seen at the pirate stronghold, no doubt negotiating deals for arms and opium. Oates had, in fact, offered the man money to help him escape, but had been coldly denied. So he had a chance of killing more than one bird with a single stone.

The European merchants provided four ships, and the Chinese merchants, eager to inflict some real punishment on the men who had plagued their businesses for years, provided five others. The

European merchants had been reluctant at first, but changed their minds when Ronnie told those he trusted that he knew the location of the pirates' hideout, so that the expedition would not be a wild goose chase. As Ronnie watched the heavily armed crews being assembled on board the Chinese junks, he wondered aloud to Andrew Hay, one of the contributing European merchants, whether some of them might be tiger soldiers from the secret societies.

'I suspect many of them are, but I don't much care. It's going to be the pirate throats they're going to cut, not ours. Personally I would not care if Bonham armed the convicts and sent them out with the promise of a bounty on each pirate head—especially those murdering dacoits and thugees.'

'Not a bad idea,' said Ronnie, 'but he's never going to agree to it.'

Nevertheless, when Ronnie went to see the acting resident councillor, Mr Church, he agreed to let Captain Congalton accompany them on the Company schooner the *Zephyr*, along with a squad of marines, commanded by Lieutenant William James. Congalton had just returned from a fierce action against fifteen pirates prahus at Point Romania, and was preparing to return to Malacca, but Church was sure he would be ready and eager to leave at the drop of hat.

'A right little Nelson is Captain Samuel Congalton,' he said. 'A small man, and not much to look at, but very direct and honest, and always ready for a scrap.' Church also had some good news for Ronnie to convey to the other merchants. The Company had finally paid attention to their petitions, and had informed him that later in the year they would to send out HMS *Wolf*, a heavily armed sloop, to help clear the seas, along with the Company Steamer *Diana*.

'But I'm afraid this is all going to come at a price,' Church advised him, with a sigh that anticipated the likely reception of this news. 'The Company is planning to impose a new port tax to pay for it.'

'That winna go down well,' Ronnie replied. 'But between you and me, I'd pay the de'il to help me hunt down thae murdering bastards.'

* * *

Musa met Abdullah in the clearing at the edge of the jungle which had been set up for the cockfight.

A ring had been created from planks and rattan, and the lallang grass had been cut away to form a sandy arena. A large crowd gathered in the clearing as the sun began to set behind the high trees, and coconut lamps were lit around the edges of the clearing. There were local and Malaccan Malays, Bugis and Javanese, and sailors from the ships in the harbour, who were always eager for a sporting opportunity. Musa spotted Abdullah in the crowd and went forward and gently touched him on the shoulder.

'I have come as arranged. I thank you for keeping your part of the bargain.'

'Easily done,' said Abdullah, turning to face him. 'I hope you will keep yours. I will wager a fair price for your black prahu, and you will wager the prahu. Since you have got what you wanted, I hope you will do me the courtesy of letting me choose my bird.'

'If you so wish,' replied Musa. 'Yet I have been thinking it over. As you say, I have got what I wanted. My grand-uncle has visited with Rashidah's parents, and they have consented to our marriage proposal. The date and the dowry have been set.'

Of course, thought Abdullah to himself. Nobody else would want that barren woman.

'But in my happiness,' Musa continued, 'I have seen that my own passion for that prahu was a shameful thing, borne of pride. Now I am to marry Rashidah, my only true love, God be praised,

I see the pettiness of my own obsession with the boat. When all is said and done it is only a piece of wood.'

'But not to me!' Abdullah almost spat in reply. 'What do you mean by this! Are you going back on your bargain!'

'Of course not,' Musa replied. 'I only meant to say that if you still want to buy the prahu, I will happily sell it to you for a fair price. I can always build another, perhaps not so true and fair, but one that will serve its purpose well enough.'

'Bah!' Abdullah exclaimed, giving Musa a look of high disdain. 'Do you want to deny me the pleasure of winning it for myself in a fair contest? Or are you afraid of the shame you will suffer if you lose?'

'Neither,' said Musa, looking surprised. 'I was hoping you would be pleased that I am willing to sell it to you. And you may lose yourself, you know.'

'Oh no, you will not deny me the pleasure of winning so easily!' Abdullah replied. 'Are you still willing to let me choose my bird?'

'If that is what you wish,' said Musa, tiring of the exchange. 'I will sell it to you for two hundred dollars, or you can wager that amount, whatever you wish.'

'You insult me with your offer and your wager!' Abdullah retorted. 'I will wager one thousand dollars for the boat, so you must wager the same, your prahu and eight hundred dollars more.'

'That is not what I said,' said Musa softly, but realized he had been trapped. He could not put the value of the prahu any higher than what he had already committed to, and he was too proud to refuse the bet, even though he knew he would find it difficult to pay the dowry for Rashidah if he lost.

'So be it,' Musa replied, 'please choose your bird, Abdullah.'

They stepped forward to view the two birds that were being displayed for the next fight. Both were black gamecocks with their combs and wattles cut. One of the birds, slightly larger and stouter than the other, had a bright red head plumage; the other, smaller and scraggier, had an orange plumage with white-tipped feathers. The larger bird was scarred in places, and had bald patches in its coat: it was obviously a survivor of previous fights.

To Musa's surprise Abdullah chose the smaller bird. Then they committed their bets, along with the others. By now the darkness had fallen all around, and the coconut lamps cast a ghostly flickering light over the ring, as the breeders brought their cocks forward, and held them facing each other. Each bird had steel spurs tied to its legs with leather straps, like ancient gladiators at martial games. The crowd was hushed, eagerly anticipating the beginning of the match.

The umpire placed a coconut with a pierced hole in a bucket of water; when it sunk the first round would be completed.

Immediately they were released, the cocks flew at each other in a wild mass of clawing spurs and tearing feathers. For the first three rounds the birds were evenly matched—both were blooded, but neither gained an advantage.

However, by the fourth round, the larger bird seemed to tire quickly. Abdullah smiled quietly to himself. He had paid the trainer to poison the red-plumed cock, and had privately arranged to place an additional bet on the smaller orange-plumed bird. In a sudden movement the orange-plumed bird tore out the left eye of the red-plumed bird, and just as the coconut was about to sink, plunged one its steel spurs into the right lung of its failing rival. During the short interval, as the trainers tended to their wounded birds, Musa watched with dismay as his bird gasped for air, its blood bubbling from the wound, and prayed to God that it might survive at least until the fifth round.

The umpire replaced the drained coconut in the bucket, signaling the beginning of the fifth round. Musa's bird staggered forward, close to death, the poison burning in its stomach, its breath gasping and bubbling from its punctured lung. The bird's left eye dangled from its empty socket, and swung around its head like some obscene decoration. Abdullah's bird leapt in for the kill, and Musa despaired. But the poison burning in the older bird's stomach drove it to a killing madness, as it peered out through the bloody haze of its one remaining eye, and summoning its last reserve of strength, it leapt into the air and drove its spurs down into the chest of its tormentor. The force of the attack drove the other bird onto its back, and the old warrior stood triumphant for a few seconds, its head held high in the air and its spurs embedded in its opponent's chest. Then it toppled over and died, its dangling eye now buried and sightless in the bloody sand. But its right spur had pierced the heart of the smaller bird, which did not rise again. The umpire declared that Musa's bird was the winner, and those who had bet upon it roared their approval.

Abdullah was beside himself with rage. He had lost Rashidah, the coveted prahu, and now one thousand dollars, not to mention his side bet and the money he had paid the trainer to poison the victorious bird. But he graciously acknowledged his loss before the company, and agreed to pay Musa the amount he now owed him. Both men left after the first match. As he returned home, Musa thanked God for his benevolence, and thought about the gifts he could now purchase for Rashidah and her family, and what a splendid wedding feast he could now provide!

As he returned home, Abdullah's thoughts were much darker, as he cursed Musa, the cock trainer and his ill fortune. He would find a way to make Musa pay, and deny him the fruits of his victories. Just when he thought his happiness was complete, Musa would taste the cold steel of the assassin's knife, and know before he died who had denied him his happiness on earth.

Musa and Rashidah were married shortly afterwards, and within the year Rashidah gave birth to a beautiful baby boy, which they called E'jaaz, meaning 'miracle'. They and their families were overjoyed, but Abdullah was beside himself with jealousy and anger. How could God bless Musa with a son by a wife who had borne him no children, he thought to himself, never for a moment thinking that the fault could be his own. He decided that now was the time to take his revenge, and he would have done so right way had he not been summoned by Daing Ibrahim, the son of the late temenggong, who sent him on a secret mission to Sumatra.

10

Ronnie argued, begged and pleaded with her, but she would not be moved. He told her there was great danger, how much of a worry and distraction her presence would be to him, and asked her to consider what would happen to the children if she did not return—if they both did not return.

'You know well enough what would happen.' she replied, stonily. 'Grandpapa John and Mrs Stables would look after them and their future interests, and I would rest easy in my grave in the knowledge of it. But nothing is going to happen to you or I,' she said, suddenly kissing him softly. 'Si Rahman and Sri Hussein are the ones who should be afraid, for they are about to answer to their masters in Hell.'

Oftentimes, and especially with the children, she could be a tender and loving woman, but at other times, he knew, she could be as strong and determined as any Navy captain. Nothing would keep her from her revenge.

They took Mr Oates on board the *Zephyr* at the last minute, and the captains and their lieutenants assembled in her main cabin before setting sail. Ronnie, whom all agreed should lead the expedition, told them they were heading for the southeast coast of Sumatra. The pirate base was on a river about thirty miles south of Bangka Island, where they would assemble in four days to prepare for the attack. The European captains were none too happy about having a woman on the expedition, but they knew well enough why she was there, and held their tongues. One of the Chinese junks sprung a leak two days out and had to turn back to Singapore, but the other twelve ships made it to the rendezvous without mishap, and the captains reassembled in the cabin of the *Zephyr*.

Mr Oates informed them that the pirate stockade was located on a large tributary of the river about a mile inland. He said it was unlikely that they would be able to take the pirates by surprise, since they had lookouts at the mouth of the river, but if they made good speed they ought to be able to block the entrance and prevent them from escaping to the open sea. Ronnie told them that he would bring Mr Oates aboard the *Highland Lassie*, and that he would lead them in. When they reached the river, the force would divide, leaving six ships to cover the mouth of the river, while the rest of the fleet would sail upriver to the pirate stockade—Oates had assured them that the water was deep enough on the lower reaches. The *Highland Lassie* and *Zephyr* would go in first and bombard the stockade and the pirate prahus, providing cover for the other ships to send in their landing parties in their longboats.

They arrived at the river mouth in the early hours of the following evening, just as the sun was setting. They were immediately met with cannon fire from the high hills at the mouth of the river, which they returned in kind. Ronnie ordered the ships to anchor out of range across the mouth of the river, and to prepare to attack at dawn. A watch was established, but few slept in their bunks and hammocks. Gongs sounded from upriver throughout the night, which told them that the pirates were preparing to fight. Ronnie and Sarah stood on the deck of the *Highland Lassie*, looking up at the stars, shining hard like diamonds in the deep darkness of the night. She had agreed to stay on board, and provide covering fire as they landed the men at the mouth of the tributary. She was a crack shot, and this was where she would be most useful. But he doubted she would stay on board — she was just as likely to join the general attack when it got under way. What kind of woman had he married?

He knew well enough, and he had no regrets. But he hoped the Good Lord would watch over her tomorrow — that he would watch over them all.

They set out as dawn broke blood red across the mouth of the river and rode in with the morning tide, which carried them up river at speed. Musket balls thudded into the deck from the jungle on the north side of the river, but most of the cannon fire went high, although one lucky ball smashed the top of the mizzenmast on the *Highland Lassie*. Then as they turned into the tributary, they saw the pirate stockade about five hundred yards ahead on the right bank, and the pirate prahus bunched together just beyond the stockade.

But as they entered the tributary, Ronnie saw the look of surprise and dismay on Oates's face.

'What's wrong, man!' he cried out to him.

'Not enough! Not nearly enough boats!' Oates exclaimed, his face turning ashen. 'There should be many more! The main fleet must be out at sea. Good God man, we've been betrayed! It must be a trap—they must be coming up behind our ships at the mouth of the river.'

Ronnie cursed, and Sarah looked at him in alarm.

'Well, trap or no trap, there's nae turning back,' Ronnie said to them. 'We're here to fight them, and fight them we will.' But he did send a longboat back to the ships at the river mouth to warn them of a possible trap.

As they drew alongside the stockade, Ronnie ordered his ship's guns to fire, and they raked the walls of the stockade. The pirates responded with cannon and musket fire, as the *Zephyr* came up and brought her own guns to bear. Ronnie sent in two heavily armed companies in longboats with buckets of tar and pitch to set fire to the pirate craft. Within a few minutes flames and smoke were rising from the burning pirate prahus, providing some cover for the marines, sailors and secret society men who were now landing on the riverbank.

Lieutenant James ordered his marines to fix bayonets, and let them in a direct assault on the stockade, whose gate had been badly damaged by the cannonade. Parts of the stockade were already on fire, and a dark plume of smoke rose from within. The marines were closely followed by the less disciplined but more fearsome groups of sailors and society men, who carried muskets, pistols, cutlasses, axes, spears, and long knives, as well as some cruel looking weapons of their own device.

Lieutenant James was within a few feet of the gate when he took a musket ball in his left shoulder, but he carried on regardless. A group of sailors had brought up a battering ram, which they used to smash through the damaged gate, and within a few minutes they had broken into the compound. Captain Congalton was hard on their heels, a little ahead of Ronnie, who had led his own men ashore.

Congalton was a small man, but broad shouldered and wiry-muscled, and he charged into the pirates like a madman, cutting, hacking, and gouging with a cutlass in one hand and an axe in the other, all the time calling them by all the names that God had given men to curse their enemies. Ronnie managed to avoid a spear thrust to his stomach and cut his man to the ground, but was suddenly bowled over by a blow from a cudgel. He spun over on the ground and managed to drive his cutlass into his attacker's groin, the point scraping the man's pelvic bone as he fell screaming to the ground.

Ronnie struggled to his feet. Through the smoke and flames he could see that the pirates were in retreat. The rear gate of the stockade had been flung open, and many were fleeing into the jungle. Then he cursed as he saw Sarah running ahead, a pistol in each hand, heading towards an outbuilding at the back of the stockade.

Then he saw why. Purser was standing in the doorway, securing a knapsack, which he then flung across his shoulder, before heading off into the jungle. Ronnie set out in pursuit, but watched in horror as Sarah headed him off, and then stopped to aim her pistol. But before she could do so, Purser raced towards her and struck her down with a blow to her head from his cane. Then he continued his flight into the safety of the jungle.

When Ronnie reached her he was relieved to find that she was shaken but unharmed.

'I'm all right,' she said to him. 'He put me out for a moment, and I've got a thumping head … but I'll be fine. You must get him, before he escapes. I'll be safe with these two gentlemen,' she assured him, indicating the two marines who had also come to her assistance.

Ronnie squeezed her hand, and after pressing the two marines to stay with her, set off in pursuit of Purser. By now the pirates were scattering in all directions into the jungle, which would make it well nigh impossible to hunt them down. But Ronnie focused on the figure in the black frockcoat who ran down a narrow footpath and disappeared into the depths of the jungle. He tightened his grip on his cutlass and raced after him.

Soon he was deep in the jungle, and the sounds of the battle at the stockade began to recede. He had no doubt they were the victors, and that they had killed many of the pirates. But there had been no sign of the two brothers, and they might yet find themselves in a trap, if Si Rahman and Sri Hussein were waiting out at sea with the rest of their fleet. He wondered whether he ought to go back, and whether he might not be needed to help them fight their way out of a trap. He was now deep in the jungle. He might not be able to find Purser, and he might easily run into a group of pirates or hostile local Malays at any time.

He looked around him. The early morning sunlight filtered through the high branches of the trees, shooting shafts of white light into the green gloom of the jungle floor. A troop of monkeys shrieked above him, leaping from branch to branch in the treetops overhead. He decided to go on a little further. The pathway ahead seemed to be opening into a small clearing, and he could hear the sound of running water.

As he broke through the jungle cover, Ronnie saw him, taking his rest on a tree stump at the far edge of the stream that ran through the clearing. The knapsack was at his feet, and he was picking idly at the ground with his walking stick. He looked up at Ronnie, and gave him a cold smile when he approached, cutlass in hand.

'We meet again at last, Mr Simpson,' he said in a clear and calm voice, which betrayed no sign of breathlessness from his escape through the jungle. 'I'm sorry I was denied the pleasure for so long. I suppose that fellow Oates led you here—I'm sure I saw him in one of your boats. A most ungrateful fellow, I must say. Si Rahman saved his life, even gave him a share of the plunder and let him take a pretty wife. And this is his gratitude?'

Purser shook his head in mock wonder.

'However, I'm afraid you've missed Si Rahman and Sri Hussein, dear fellow. They left a few days ago, and won't be back for weeks, but I don't suppose you can stay around that long, can you? Because when they do come back, they'll still be around, you know,' he said, raising his hands and arms outwards to indicate the pirates they both knew to be hiding in the jungle around them.

'I do feel sorry for your poor wife, cheated of her revenge, and she such a plucky young thing. They were the men who killed her sister and the rest of her family, you know, in case you had any doubts about it. Si Rahman boasts of it all the time, and says their deaths have made him invincible. All the time, all the time, very tedious it is.'

'So I suppose you'll have to be satisfied with my good self. I'm sure you think I'm partly to blame, running guns and other weapons to the pirates, and bringing them intelligence about the richest prizes. Well, you're probably right. But believe me, I do regret what happened to your sister-in-law and her family, since none of them had a sporting chance. It's one of the unfortunate costs of doing business with these bloodthirsty fellows. And speaking of business, we have some unfinished business of our own.'

Purser rose, and walked slowly to the centre of a small circle of low grass at the edge of the clearing. Ronnie followed him. Both men took off their jackets and dropped them on the ground beside them.

'But you have no weapon,' Ronnie said suddenly.

'Not true,' said Purser. 'I regret having left my pistols back at the stockade, but all I need for you is this.'

He drew out a long steel rapier from the head of his walking stick, and Ronnie suddenly remembered it from the day years before on Boat Quay, when he had felt it against his throat. The cold blue steel flashed in the sunlight, as Purser sliced the air in front of him with practiced strokes, the narrow blade whistling sharply in the still morning air.

'I shall have your heart on the point of this before we part,' he said, with a thin smile, as he adopted a fencer's pose. 'Whenever you're ready, Mr Simpson.'

Ronnie was in no mood for talk, and simply said: 'I mean to kill you, Purser, so let's get on with it.' Then he ran at him very fast, sweeping his cutlass down towards Purser's neck. But Purser easily parried the blow, and the next, and what Ronnie had thought was a clever feint followed by a quick lunge to his chest.

'Oh no, this really will not do!' said Purser, laughing and taunting him. 'Did your father never teach you how to fence, sir? This is very amateur, all cut and thrust, just like a pirate! You need to control your emotions, you know, and learn to fight with your head and not with your heart. Skill helps too, of course, but I'm afraid you don't seem to have very much of that.'

Ronnie understood the sense of the words, but it made no difference. His blood was up, and he renewed his attack with increased ferocity, driving Purser backwards by the sheer force of his onslaught. The clash of steel rang out across the clearing, sending the birds in the neighbouring trees rushing into the air. But he could not get behind the man's defenses, no matter how hard he pressed his attack. It was obvious that Purser was a master swordsman, who was toying with him, and he knew the man would kill him if he did not finish it quickly. He was tiring fast, and sooner or later he would let his own guard down. He circled his opponent, trying to catch his breath, and then put all his strength into a powerful swing that he brought down over Purser's head. He yearned to sink the blade into his cold cruel eyes.

But Purser was fast, much faster than Ronnie. He deflected the blow, and with a deft flick of his wrist, he caught the handle of Ronnie's cutlass and swept it around on his own blade, sending it spinning off into the trees. And now Purser's blade was once again at his throat, pricking his skin—a thin trickle of blood ran off its point and ran down his neck.

'Enough,' he said, with a thin smile. 'You are becoming a bit of a bore. I'm sure your pretty wife would have given me better sport.'

Purser stood back a little, to prepare for the final thrust, and waved the point of the rapier across Ronnie's chest, like a master noting the killing positions to a student.

'Say goodbye to your dear wife, and make your peace with your God,' he said, and he was no longer smiling.

Ronnie said nothing in reply, but as the point of the blade drifted by his left shoulder, he rushed forward onto it, grasping Purser's right arm with both hands as he drove himself forward onto the blade. The pain sliced through his body like a hot knife, but it seemed to add new strength to his free arm. With a sudden look of surprise and fear Purser realized what he was doing, but it was too late. Ronnie drew his dirk from his belt and drove it up to its hilt into Purser's neck, severing his jugular vein. As the blood gushed over his right hand, he grasped Purser by his shirt collar and slowly lowered him to the ground, easing himself off the rapier blade, and grunting in pain as he did so. Ronnie withdrew his dirk and washed the blade in the stream. He tore a strip from his shirt and made a makeshift bandage for his own wound. Then he went over and retrieved his jacket and the knapsack that Purser had been carrying; it was full of gold, silver and jewellery.

He knelt down beside the dying man. Purser's breath was very faint, and bubbled through the blood in his throat. He tried to speak, but could not.

'I'll be awa then,' Ronnie said, 'and ye'll be awa tae hell. As ye said about business, sometimes it has its costs. Now ye can pay them.'

He left him to die in the clearing, and made his way back though the jungle to the pirate stockade.

* * *

When he returned, the fight was already over. After the initial attack, most of the pirates had fled into the jungle. They had not pursued them, for fear of an ambush, and being caught in a trap—although so far there was no sign of the pirate fleet returning.

'You're the only one crazy enough to go after them,' said Congalton, as he welcomed Ronnie back to safety. 'Although I understand from your good wife you had some personal business with one of them.'

'That we did,' Ronnie replied, with his good arm around Sarah, 'from a long time ago. I killed him back there in the jungle, but we seem to have missed Si Rahman and Sri Hussein. Purser said they left a few days ago, and won't be back for weeks. So I don't think we need to fear a trap, although we ought to keep a sharp lookout.'

'So we've failed then,' said Sarah. 'The killers remain free.'

'I'm afraid so,' he replied, 'But we will get them in the end, I promise you.'

'I wouldn't say we have failed, exactly,' said Congalton, in a businesslike fashion. 'We've missed the leaders and the main fleet, to be sure, but we've dealt them a heavy blow nonetheless. We've destroyed part of the fleet, and taken a huge amount of treasure: gold and silver bullion, jewellery, and enough opium to send half a dozen merchantmen to Canton. If nothing else, it should more than pay for this little expedition and help us finance the next.'

'So you'll stick with us until we hunt them down?' Sarah asked him.

'Be my pleasure, ma'am, for so long as I'm assigned to the straits. And we'll have the *Wolfe* and *Diana* to help us soon. But I'd be very grateful if you'd stay on board ship the next time, Mrs Simpson, as I thought we had agreed. It's most unnerving having a woman running around a battlefield.'

'Especially when it's your wife,' said Ronnie, with a grin. 'But you're going to have to tie her up the next time, if ye want to keep her back, for she'll no listen to me.'

Congalton was about to opine that a husband ought to be able to control his own wife, but was silenced by Sarah, whose look made it clear she would not be controlled.

'You can jest all you like, the both of you,' she said. 'But I will be there on the day that we kill them.'

They loaded the treasure on board the ships, along with the dead and wounded. Their losses had been light, with only two dead marines and one dead Chinese—sailor or secret society member they could not tell. Their bodies were buried at sea, to prevent desecration of their graves by the returning pirates. The bodies of the dead pirates were left to rot where they lay, as was their practice with their own victims. As the ships were turned before making their way back to the mouth of the river, a party of men from the *Highland Lassie* set fire to the remains of the stockade and the huts and sheds that surrounded it. A tall plume of black smoke rose over the jungle and drifted high into the sky, like a giant black jinn dancing over the souls of the dead.

From a high hilltop, Abdullah looked down on the scene of devastation. He had been preparing to return to Singapore, but had been trapped by the attacking ships. Like most of the other pirates, he had fled into the jungle when the attackers had broken down the main gate of the stockade. He dreaded bringing the news of this disaster to his master, but hoped that he could reach home before the pirates returned to their base. For the rage of Daing Ibrahim would be like that of a whimpering kitten before the roaring tiger rage of Si Rahman and Sri Hussein.

11

Sri Hussein was the first to return to their base in Sumatra. Si Rahman had split the pirate fleet, taking the bulk in pursuit of a Portuguese merchantmen rumoured to be transporting a shipment of silver to Manila, while allowing Sri Hussein to leave with the remainder, so that he would return in time to keep his appointed meeting with the sultan and his council. Si Rahman hoped to join his brother in time, but it was more important that Sri Hussein appear before the sultan, since he had made the pledge on behalf of his woman.

When Sri Hussein returned to their base he was shocked to discover the damage that had been inflicted by the Singapore expedition, and greatly alarmed by the loss of bullion and treasure from the storehouses. With the spoils from their latest voyage, he had thought he would have more than enough to satisfy the sultan's demand, but now he realized he would have a good deal less. If his brother returned in time, he might still be able to make up the difference, if the plunder from the Portuguese merchantman was as good as they anticipated. But would he return in time? Sri Hussein knew he could not postpone his meeting with the sultan and his council, and in any case postponement meant danger. The Singapore raiders might return at any time, and he might lose Ningsih for good.

The day of Sri Hussein's appearance before the sultan and his council drew near, but still his brother did not come. Sri Hussein spent the last few days with Ningsih in their secret place in the jungle, and then went alone to the sultan's audience chamber to plead his case. Sri Hussein told Sultan Tating and his council that he had accumulated the amount that had been pledged, but that most of it had been lost when the forces of the infidel had attacked their camp. He assured them that he had brought all that he had gained from his latest voyage, which he now had his men lay before them, and requested more time to accumulate the remainder of the promised sum. He told them that his brother Si Rahman would return soon, and would be able to contribute a substantial amount, perhaps enough to satisfy the sultan's original demand.

Sultan Tating sat stone faced while Sri Hussein explained his failure. Then he and his council debated the matter for over an hour, while Sri Hussein remained kneeling in supplication before them. Finally, Chief Minister Abdul Haqq delivered the verdict:

'Sri Hussein, you have failed to honour your pledge, and we demand that you surrender your kris to demonstrate your good faith toward his Highness Sultan Tating. Then we will inform you of our judgment.'

Sri Hussein was stunned. His kris was the most precious thing he owned. His uncle, who had been a famous pirate, had given it to him, and his uncle had received it from his own father. The blade had been crafted a long time ago by a pandai keris, a master craftsman and magician, who only began work on the blade after weeks of fasting and prayer, in order to drive away the evil spirits. Like those who had gone before him, Sri Hussein had made offerings to the marbled black blade, so that he might become one with the spirit of the kris. The handle was inlaid with gold and silver and precious jewels, and the long wavy blade had tasted the blood of many men, and not a few women and children. Yet he knew he must comply or lose Ningsih. His own small squadron was weakened by their recent action, and the sultan's armed guards, who lined the walls of the audience chamber, heavily outnumbered his own men.

Yet still he hesitated. He could not bear to part with this marvelous weapon, which had sent so many unbelieving souls to hell. Then he thought of Ningsih, and his passion overcame his prudence. He slowly removed the weapon from his belt, and laid his sacred blade upon the pile of treasure that he had presented to the sultan. As he rose to his feet, tears formed in his eyes, and blinded him to Abdul Haqq's signal. He was suddenly seized by the sultan's men and forced down on his knees again. They raised his arms behind him, making escape impossible. Then one of the sultan's men drew Sri Hussein's kris from its jewelled scabbard, and drove the long black wavy blade down through his shoulder blade and into his heart. He died immediately, with a vision of Ningsih before his eyes.

When the sultan's men descended on the pirate camp, they found that the captains had already learned of the execution of Sri Hussein, and had escaped with their boats and crews. The only person who remained in the camp was Ningsih, whom they had abandoned because of the ill fortune she had brought them. Ningsih was taken before the sultan and strangled at his feet.

* * *

Thomas McMicking went to his bed early. He thought he had a touch of fever, so he had a couple of stiff whiskies, closed the shutters to block out the moonlight, and climbed in under his mosquito net, hoping to sleep it off. His bungalow was at Duxton, on the western outskirts of town, on the verge of Dr Montgomerie's nutmeg plantation; the far wall of his garden backed onto the jungle. Suddenly he heard the loud slapping of feet on the verandah, as a horde of Chinese men knocked down his door and rushed into his bedroom, armed with knives, axes and sticks. Others clambered through the window, and quickly surrounded his bed. McMicking was unarmed, and practically naked except for his underwear; his new flintlock revolver lay on the top drawer of his dressing table behind the crowd of men. All he could do was to try to make a break for it, but as he drew aside the mosquito net and made to rise from his bed, they flung him to the ground and kicked and beat him with their sticks until he was unconscious. Then they ransacked his home, smashing open chests and cupboards, and bundled their contents into canvas bags they had brought with them. They left before McMicking regained consciousness. He had two English friends visiting him, who to their shame had hidden in the garden when the gang of Chinese burglars had broken in, but who now attended to him as best they could. One brought him water to drink and to clean his wounds, while the other went off to inform the police.

About an hour later a police sergeant arrived, accompanied by five peons. The sergeant was Adil bin Mehmood. Sergeant Adil was the son of Mehmood bin Nadir, who had been a peon in the service of Francis Bernard, and who had been murdered at the hands of Syed Yassin.

After his father had died, Adil had worked on his uncle's tongkang on the Singapore River for many years. He felt he it owed it to him; his uncle had married his widowed mother and looked after him as a child. But when he turned eighteen, Adil told his uncle that he had applied for and been accepted into the police force. His uncle was disappointed, although Adil knew there were plenty of eager young men willing to take his place in the tongkang; his uncle did a good business up and down the river. But his uncle could not understand why Adil wanted to join the police force; the pay of a peon was only half of what he paid him for lightering. Adil could not fully explain why, except for the promise he had made to the Prophet on his father's death, and his own sense of justice. He wanted to play his part, however small, in maintaining the precarious order of the world. He had done well in the police force, and had been quickly promoted for his bravery and intelligence.

Adil questioned Mr McMicking, who had regained consciousness. He had been badly beaten, and was covered in cuts and bruises, but did not seem to be seriously injured. McMicking said he remembered the scene vividly—it would live in his dreams until the day he died—but he did not recognize any of the men, and did not think he would be able to identify any of them if they were captured. It had all happened so quickly, and he had only got a fleeting glimpse of them in the darkness before they had thrown him to the ground and beaten him. His two English friends rather sheepishly admitted that they had not seen anything either.

Sergeant Adil explained to Mr McMicking that there was a large Chinese gang who had a secret hiding place deep in the jungle, and who ventured out at night in groups of about thirty or forty to rob godowns or commit burglaries in private houses. There had been various incidents recently, including a double burglary of the house on Java Road belonging to Hajjah Fatima, which had been burned to the ground on the second occasion. Hajjah Fatima was the daughter of a wealthy Malay family from Malacca who had married a Bugis Prince who traded in Singapore. When he had died young, Hajjah Fatima took over his business and greatly expanded his trading fleet, and had made a considerable fortune. Fortunately she had been visiting relatives in Malacca when the house had been robbed and burned, and when she returned she was so glad to have survived the attack and arson that she designated the land as the site for a future mosque.[lxvi]

Sergeant Adil told McMicking that the resident councillor was preparing a proclamation to warn citizens to protect themselves. He said the gang in the jungle had nothing to do with the Chinese

_____

lxvi Which came to be named after her. The Hajjah Fatimah Mosque was built in 1846.

societies, but were unemployed coolies and men who had broken their contracts of indenture.

'Well, from now on I'm going to sleep with my revolver, and buy myself a bloody great elephant gun,' snorted Mr McMicking, spitting out some bloody mucus into his handkerchief. 'Bloody Chinese,' he snorted again.

Sergeant Adil suggested that Mr McMicking should spend the next few days in hospital or with one of his friends, while his servants cleaned up the mess.

'Well I suppose I could stay with Dr Montgomerie, a friend and a sawbones to boot,' McMicking replied. 'There's no need to worry about leaving this place, since they've taken everything they could carry.'

When Sergeant Adil questioned the servants, he discovered that the Chinese gardener was missing, although he had no idea whether the man was involved with the burglary or whether he had simply run off and hidden in the jungle out of fear. But when the man did not return the following morning or the next few days, Adil suspected he had probably had played some role.

Two weeks later the gang struck again. This time they attacked the home of Sarawan Soundara Rajahn, who lived with his fellow Bengalis in a kampong at Kandang Kerbau, on the northern edge of town beyond Government Hill. But the Bengalis had heard about the recent burglaries, including the attack on Mr McMicking's home. They kept loaded muskets in their houses, and fired at the robbers when the kampong dogs alerted them to intruders during the night. Sarawan discharged his musket into the chest of the first gang member to approach his home, and his neighbours fired their own muskets or threw spears at the surprised attackers, who fled back into the jungle leaving three men dead and one man wounded. When Adil arrived on the scene with his peons, he asked to see the wounded man, whom he intended to question. But the man had been beaten to a senseless pulp, and he died the next morning in the hospital.

After consulting with the Bengalis, Adil had a feeling that the gang might return the following evening. They might come back for whatever it was they believed the Bengalis had that was worth stealing, or out of revenge for their losses they had suffered. So he suggested to his supervisor that it might be a good idea to put a watch on the area at night. His supervisor agreed, and that night Sergeant Adil and a body of armed peons hid in the jungle surrounding the Bengali kampong at Kandang Kerbau. He also warned the Bengalis about the possibility of another attack, and they immediately set about arming themselves with muskets and pistols, either their own or those they bought or borrowed from friends. As the sun set behind the tall trees, Sergeant Adil and his men settled down for the night. He told them to keep as quiet as possible, for fear of waking the dogs and alerting the gang. They spent a couple of miserable hours waiting in the jungle darkness, while the mosquitoes bit them mercilessly, and reptiles slithered across the jungle floor. They were far enough back in the jungle to remain unseen from the kampong, but close enough to keep it in clear sight in the moonlight.

Just before midnight, Adil saw a man emerge from the shadows of the trees to his left, with a pistol in each hand, and a knife in the belt of his ragged trousers. Another man armed with an axe followed him, and then the whole gang crept out into the open area between the houses. Adil smiled to himself. He had them surrounded, and the Bengalis, whom he had instructed to wait his signal, would have a clear line of fire. One thing puzzled him, however. The men were in the clearing, but the dogs had not roused themselves. Then he realized they must have been poisoned. So he led his men out of the jungle, and as he they approached the kampong he called out and commanded the robbers to lay down their weapons. For a moment the robbers stood frozen in the moonlight, like actors on a stage waiting directions. Then their leader turned and fired one of his pistols at the closest peon, who tumbled forward with a lead ball in his brain, before pandemonium broke out.

Other gang members fired off their weapons, and another of the peons went down. But their fire was met with a fusillade of musketry from the Bengalis, and pistol fire from Adil and his men, who charged into the crowd of robbers in the clearing. They were soon joined by the Bengalis and their neighbours, who were armed with knives, axes, parangs, clubs and in some cases nothing more than sharply pointed stones. For a few minutes they fought hand to hand and were evenly matched, but gradually more and more of the gang members abandoned the fight and fled back into the jungle, pursued by the jubilant Bengalis and their neighbours, including a Javanese family who had already suffered at the hands of the robbers.

Adil made straight for the leader, who aimed his other pistol directly at him. But the pistol jammed, and Adil bore down on him, hoping he could cut the man down with his parang before the other could draw his knife from his belt. Adil raised his blade to strike, but then had to bring it down upon another gang member who tried to fell him with an axe. He buried his blade in the man's shoulder, but left himself open to attack by the leader, who had now drawn his knife. Adil released his grip from the parang and grasped the leader's right hand with both of his own, but the force of his attack knocked Adil off balance, and they fell together to the ground. Before he could recover, the gang leader was kneeling over him, driving the knife down towards his chest. Adil still held the man's hand tightly in his grasp, but he was winded by the fall, and felt his strength ebbing away as the blade came closer and closer to his chest, and he saw the gleam of victory in the leader's dark eyes.

Does it end now? Adil thought to himself. Do I die now, in the same manner as my father? He made a silent prayer, but prepared for death even as he struggled for his life—perhaps the same story was written in the Book of Life. But then the leader made a mistake. He tried to raise himself to put more pressure on his knife arm, and as he did so Adil kneed him in the groin and twisted his body to the side. As the gang leader tried to break his fall, he loosened his grasp on the knife, which Adil managed to knock from his hand.

The gang leader leapt up and made to retrieve his knife, but suddenly realized that most of his men were either dead or wounded or had fled back into the jungle, and decided instead to make a run for it himself. As the gang leader turned to escape, Adil snatched up his knife and slashed it across his leg tendons, and the man screamed and stumbled to the ground. He tried to crawl away into the jungle, but the peons quickly pinned him down and tied him up, along with a number of other gang members they had captured.

They questioned the men and demanded that they reveal the location of their jungle hideout on penalty of severe punishment, but they responded with stony silence.

Three months later the gang leader and his men were tried for murder and robbery. They were found guilty and expected to be sentenced to hang, but the judge commuted their sentence to transportation to Bombay. The gang leader, whose name was Ho Chock Meng, told the judge that he would rather be hung than transported. Most judges would have been happy to oblige him, but this one decided that justice was not best served by satisfying the prisoner's preference. That night Ho Chock Meng hung himself in his jail cell.

Adil was promoted to captain for his action, and was proud of his modest achievement. But he never managed to discover the location of the gang's hideout, either by questioning the prisoners or by sending out parties to explore the jungle. While the gang roamed free, the townspeople wondered whether it was really formed by unemployed coolies and indenture breakers, or by men who had come to Singapore with the express purpose of committing robberies. They never found out. The robberies continued for a few more months, until the young hothead who had taken over as leader made the mistake of attacking a rich Hokkien merchant in his mansion in the hills of Twa Tang Leng.[lxvii]

One of the robbers was wounded in the attack and captured. Lee Yip Lee cut off his ears and his nose, and then cut out his eyes. He shaved the man's skin from his body until he screamed out the location of the hideout. Then at dusk Lee Yip Lee led a troop of tiger soldiers into the jungle, where they massacred every last member of the gang, and left their bodies to the tigers and wild pigs.

---

lxvii Meaning 'great east hill peaks', later known as Tanglin.

12

1836

A strange wailing sound drifted down from the upper rooms of the Court House, which alarmed the Chinese coolies working on High Street, who thought it sounded like the howling of a hungry ghost. Yet it was only Sergeant Andrew Gordon of the 29th Madras Infantry warming up his bagpipes for the first St. Andrew's Ball, which was to be held that evening.

The guests began to arrive in their gharries and carriages in the early evening, as the sun was setting over the town, bathing the white stucco of John Maxwell's old mansion in a golden light. Many of the ladies, including some of the Nonyas,[lxviii] sported tartan sashes, and a number of the men, including John and Ronnie Simpson, wore kilts. Sergeant Gordon piped them in with 'Scotland the Brave', 'Highland Laddie' and 'All the Blue Bonnets are Over the Border'. Dr Montgomerie and Mr William Napier had hosted the first St. Andrews dinner the previous evening, with Messrs. Spottiswoode, Lorrain and Carnie serving as Stewards.

The St. Andrews Ball also began with a dinner, served as a buffet. There were the usual 'substantials', soup and fish, Bengal mutton, Chinese capons,[lxix] Kedah fowls and Sangora ducks, Yorkshire hams and Malay ubi keledek,[lxx] curry and rice, sambals,[lxxi] Bombay ducks, turtle eggs and omelettes, with macaroni puddings

---

lxviii Conventional name for female Peranakan women.
lxix Roosters castrated to improve quality of their meat.
lxx Sweet potatoes.
lxxi Chilli-based sauces.

and custard for desert; plus all the varieties of tropical fruits laid out on silver platters on the polished rosewood tables. There were also some 'unusuals', Mrs Duncan had managed to conjure up two large haggises, although she had found it devilishly hard to get her hands on two sheep stomachs from Penang, and had made up a mess of carrots and turnips mashed together as an accompaniment. The Chinese chef had taken care to include the favourite dish of Tan Che Sang, which was puppy ragou. The American Consul, Joseph Balestier, could not decide which of these was the most revolting, a difficult decision made more difficult by his refusal to partake of either. The food was washed down with copious amounts of beer, wine, champagne, arrack and even more copious amounts of whisky.

Over dinner, Reverend Darroch thanked the Scottish merchants for their contribution to the building fund for the new Protestant church:

'We already have sufficient funds to proceed with our plans for the new building—the committee laid the foundation stone last week—and we have been fortunate to engage the services of Mr Coleman. The church will be built facing the esplanade, on ground that Syed Omar generously donated to the Christian community some years ago, for just such a purpose. He is a very generous man, as you are all generous men. In fact I have to confess to you here and now that the largest sum raised for the church was from the Scottish merchants of this community.'

'A toast!' cried John Simpson. 'Tae a' o' us!' And the Scottish merchants raised and drained their glasses.

Reverend Darroch smiled and said:

'You will understand the new church will be of Episcopalian denomination, but given your generous contribution, the church committee has agreed that it should be called St Andrew's Church, after the patron saint of Scotland.'

'I'll drink to that!' exclaimed John Simpson again. 'A toast to Saint Andrews Kirk!' And they all drank to that.

'One thing surprised me though,' Reverend Darroch continued. 'Generous as you all were, your contributions were individually matched by three of the Armenian merchants.'

'Not so surprising,' replied Alexander Johnson. 'Some of us also contributed to the fund for the Armenian Church. We merchants have to support each other, and provide work for the talented Mr Coleman. And I must say that he has excelled himself with the Armenian Church, which is a masterpiece of Doric design adapted to the tropics, maximizing shade and ventilation. One of the most ornate and best-finished pieces of architecture that this gentleman can boast of, was how I believe our new *Singapore Free Press* [28] described it. You really should visit it if you get the chance, and hope that Mr Coleman does as well with St Andrews church.'

'Thank you for these kind words, Alex,' said George Coleman. 'The design was based upon the mother church of St Gregory in Northern Armenia, as described to me by the elders. I'm planning another Doric structure for St Andrews Church, with shading porticoes enclosing the carriage road, and finished in Madras Chunam of course.'

'Speaking of the new paper,' John Simpson interjected, addressing his question to its new editor, the law agent William Napier, 'why did ye ca' it the *Free Press*.'

'Simple really,' Napier replied. 'We did it to celebrate the repeal of the Gagging Act, which subjected all newspapers to government censorship. The old *Chronicle* had to be approved by the resident councillor before it went to press.'

'Interesting article you had in your paper last week about preserving the tallest trees on a sugar cane estate, to protect the soil from the sun and attract the moisture from the clouds. I'll certainly bear it in mind on my estate,' said Joseph Balestier, the American consul. Balestier had recently planted a thousand acres of sugarcane on the plain on the northern fringes of Serangoon Road, which led from the town to Serangoon Harbour on the northeast of the island. 'Don't you agree, Dr Montgomerie?'

'I'm not sure about that,' Montgomerie replied, 'but in any case it's too late now. I leveled the field before I planted mine.'

'Quite an operation he has out there,' Montgomerie continued, when Balestier left to answer the call of nature. 'He has elephants to draw his ploughs, and a series of canals to transport his cane from the fields to his stream-driven mill, and then from the mill to the river. Done very well for himself, has our American consul.'

'Well he deserves it,' Alexander Johnston responded. 'When President Jackson appointed him consul to Riau in thirty-three, Joseph managed to get his appointment transferred to Singapore by convincing the administration that this was where the future lay. He worked very hard to get the restriction on American shipping lifted—a daft hangover from the war of 1812—and now of course he profits handsomely from it. He's the agent for most American shipping in Singapore, and his company services most of their ships.'

'Weel, we canna begrudge him that,' agreed John Simpson, 'and he told me his people came frae Ayrshire, so we can count him as an honourary Scot. Along wi' oor guid Celtic friend Mr Coleman.'

They all raised their glasses once again to George Coleman and the returning Joseph Balestier. Then there was the call to the dancing.

'But how on earth will you be able to dance?' said Balestier in amazement. 'I can hardly stand straight on my feet with all this food and drink!'

But dance they did, and with a passion that rivaled the Samoan islanders, at least according to one English sea captain who had spent some years trading with them. The Malaccan band had been practicing for weeks under Mr Napier's tutelage, and managed what John Simpson thought were passably fair renditions of 'The Dashing White Sergeant', 'The Duke of Perth', 'The Eightsome Reel', the 'Gay Gordons', 'Strip the Willow', 'John Peel', 'The Braes Of Breadalbane', and 'The Montgomeries' Rant'.

Tan Che Seng, who normally stood stone-faced in his black silk robe, his arms folded inside his sleeves, rocked with laughter as he watched the men in skirts leaping into the air and spinning round the ballroom, his eyes wide with amazement. Mrs James Guthrie tried to persuade him to dance with her—to no avail—but a tall Bengali lady married to a Parsee managed to get Tan Hong Chuan to take the floor. The pair leapt round the room with the wild abandon of highland loons and lassies, while the other dancers did their best to avoid Tan Hong Chuan's long back queue, which whipped and whistled through the air as he spun around on his black slippers.

After two hours, even the most energetic were on the point of exhaustion, and were glad when the band took their break. During the interval waiters served mince pies and shortbread, and more whisky. Sergeant Gordon played a haunting lament on his pipes, 'The Black Isle', and Alexander Johnston sang 'My Love is Like a Red, Red Rose', accompanied by Sarah on the piano. Then the lights were dimmed and a hushed silence fell over the crowd, as a young Chinese merchant called Hoo Ah Kay, who had come from Guangzhou province in China to work in his father's shop on Boat Quay, gave an eloquent and chilling rendering of one of the speeches from *Macbeth*, Shakespeare's 'Scottish' play:

> Come, seeling night,
> Scarf up the tender eye of pitiful day;
> And with thy bloody and invisible hand
> Cancel and tear to pieces that great bond
> Which keeps me pale! Light thickens; and the crow
> Makes wing to the rooky wood:

Good things of day begin to droop and drowse;
While night's black agents to their preys do rouse.
Thou marvel'st at my words: but hold thee still;
Things bad begun make strong themselves by ill.
So, prithee, go with me …

His English was excellent, even if it did lack a Caledonian accent.

Impressive as Hoo Ah Kay's performance was, the star turn of the evening was performed by Captain William Scott, the harbour master and Post Master, who was known to everyone for his hospitality and generosity of spirit. He was forty-nine years old, his brown face lined and weather beaten from his years before the mast. He had long white hair and a heavy beard, but his bright blue eyes sparkled like a young gallant as he recited *Young Lochinvar*, the poem by Sir Walter Scott:

O young Lochinvar is come out of the west,
Through all the wide Border his steed was the best;
And save his good broadsword, he weapons had none,
He rode all unarm'd, and he rode all alone.
So faithful in love, and so dauntless in war,
There never was knight like the young Lochinvar …

By the time he finished the poem he had all the ladies in a swoon:

One touch to her hand and one word in her ear,
When they reach'd the hall-door, and the charger stood near;
So light to the croupe the fair lady he swung,
So light to the saddle before her he sprung!
'She is won! we are gone, over bank, bush, and scaur;

They'll have fleet steeds that follow,' quoth young Lochinvar.
There was mounting 'mong Grſmes of the Netherby clan;
Forsters, Fenwicks, and Musgraves, they rode and they ran:
There was racing and chasing, on Cannobie Lee,
But the lost bride of Netherby ne'er did they see.
So daring in love, and so dauntless in war,
Have ye e'er heard of gallant like young Lochinvar?

'Hurrah, hurrah,' they all roared when he was done. 'A toast to Captain Scott!'

And then the band struck up again and they returned to the dancing. As the night wore on and the whisky continued to flow freely, the ball lost all semblance of structure and sobriety. The men and women flung themselves around and leapt through the air in a wild frenzy, driven by the Malaccan band who seemed to have got caught up in their passion, and who increased their pace as the night roared on, and the whisky continued to flow.

'My God!' exclaimed George Coleman, who was Irish and no stranger to drunken jigs. 'You'd think they were captured by the Fairie Queen, and made to dance to the end of their days! I've never seen anything like it!'

Mr Thyson, a Dutch visitor to the town, was not amused, and remarked to his Scottish hosts:

'Is this how you spend your time, eating, drinking and dancing?'

'We dae, and ain't it grand!' replied John Simpson, with much enthusiasm. 'We dae some work as weel,' he added, as an afterthought.

It was after midnight when the ball ended. The band had given up an hour before, but James Guthrie and Sergeant Duncan had brought out their fiddles and continued the festivities with a series of highland reels, but by now they had given up as well.

As the revellers made their way to their gharries and carriages, none too steadily, Sarah went up to Captain Scott and told him how much she had enjoyed his poem.

'I bet you were a young Lochinvar in your day,' she teased him.

'And ever will be,' he replied with a twinkle in his eye.

'Why don't you and your young Lochinvar come and visit me next Sunday afternoon?' he suggested. 'We could have tea, or we could have something stronger! And bring your father if he wants to come along. Take the road from Dhoby Ghaut,[lxxii] behind Government Hill, where the Indian washermen beat their clothes, and follow it out towards the eastern hills, which the Chinese call Twa Tang Leng, and you'll find my cottage about halfway down on the right. Hurricane Cottage. It's got a pretty garden that I think you'll like.'

Ronnie and Sarah agreed to visit Captain Scott the following Sunday. They both liked him very much.

'Where is your father?' Sarah suddenly asked Ronnie, after they had said goodnight to Captain Scott.

'I'm sure he's still asleep under the table wi' a bottle of whisky in his arms, which is where I last saw him. But I'd best go fetch him I suppose!'

---

lxxii 'Washing place' in Hindi. So called because it was an open space (gaut) where Indian washermen (dhobis) did their laundry.

13

In early December Lim Guan Chye came to visit Mr Bonham, the resident councillor. As Guan Chye entered the office, Bonham rose to greet him warmly, and asked him to take a seat.

Lim Guan Chye thanked the resident councillor kindly, but said he would prefer to stand. And stand he did, looking very uncomfortable as he rubbed his hands together and shuffled his feet.

'So what can I do for you, Lim Guan Chye, and how can I be of service to you and your merchant colleagues?' Bonham said amiably.

Lim Guan Chye stood in silence for a few more moments. He was clearly uneasy and embarrassed. Eventually he spoke in a low voice, but in clear English.

'There is a rumour going about,' he began, 'that I think you should know about. It concerns St. Andrews Church. Have you heard of it?'

'The only rumour I've heard is that they will use Madras Chunam, and shine it up as bright as any cathedral,' Bonham replied. 'And I'm sure Mr Coleman will do an excellent job as usual.'

Lim Guan Chye wiped his brow, but not because of the heat.

'It is rather more serious than that, I'm afraid,' Guan Chye said. 'The rumour I have heard is that the government requires the blood of thirty-six men to consecrate the Christian Church. I have also heard it said that nine heads have already been taken, and that the police and convict thugees hunt the town at night for more. I am afraid that many of my people are deeply suspicious and resentful of the government on account of this rumour, as are many of the

Klings and Malays.'

'But who believes in such nonsense?' Bonham replied, trying to make light of it. 'Surely you don't, Guan Chye?'

'I believe in many things,' Lim Guan Chye replied. 'I believe in the spirits of my ancestors, in hungry ghosts who descend to earth on the fifteenth day of the seventh lunar month, and in the demons who torment the wicked in hell. Yet I know enough about Christianity to know that the consecration of a church does not require a blood sacrifice. Only a financial one,' he added with a chuckle. 'But many of my countrymen are not well educated in the ways of Westerners, whom they treat with awe and suspicion—especially the hordes of illiterate sinkeh that pour into Singapore every year. And as for the Klings and Malays, they believe all sorts of stories about blood sacrifice and demons of the night.'

'Well, I can see that this rumour, however ill-founded it may be, could do unnecessary harm to the reputation of the government,' Bonham replied. 'Thank you for warning me about this, Guan Chye. I'll have proclamations issued tomorrow in all our languages, categorically denying the rumour.'

'Thank you,' Guan Chye replied. 'I would also encourage you to hasten the consecration of the church, once it is completed.'

'Don't worry about that,' Bonham replied. 'I'm sure the faithful will want that as much as those who fear for their heads! Good day to you, Guan Chye.' And I thought the Irish were superstitious, he wondered to himself, as Lim Guan Chye left his office.

* * *

Sarah took up Captain Scott's invitation to visit him on the following Sunday afternoon, with her husband and her father-in-law. They rode by carriage to Dhoby Ghaut, and took the road that led out towards the western hills, past the Chinese orchards and market gardens that lined the edges of the road. They passed through a beautiful canopy of overhanging trees, through which the sunlight filtered green and bright, framed by rows of frangipani and traveller's palms, which made it seem as if they were riding through some great natural cathedral. Just over a mile down the road they came across another road that crossed at right angles, and turned off to the right as they had been instructed. On the corner, set a little back from the road, and fronting a large orchard, was a wooden framed house with an attap roof, surrounded by a low rattan fence and a wooden gate, which was carved with the inscription 'Hurricane Cottage'. They knew they had come to the right place. They sent the syce back with the carriage, and asked him to return later in the afternoon, in time for them to return home before it grew dark.

They walked through the gate and up the path, but there was no sign of Captain Scott, although the door to the cottage was open.

'Hullo! Hullo, Captain Scott!' Sarah called out as they approached the door.

Then all of a sudden his head appeared above a row of cocoa plants he had been tending a short distance from the cottage.

'Ahoy there maties!' he cried out. 'I'm glad ye could come. I'll be down in twa ticks o' a sheepie's tail.'

He walked over to them through the most beautiful garden she had ever seen. It was a wonderland of fruit and spices, a blaze of marvelous colour and fragrant aromas. There was purple cocoa, peach nutmeg and crimson cloves, sea cotton, arrowroot, set amid a wide canopy of betel nut, durian, mangosteen and rambutan trees. Captain Scott was wearing a white cotton shirt with bell-bottomed sailor pants, and a gigantic straw hat, which he swept off his head before he bowed and took Sarah's hand.

His long white hair was tied back with a black ribbon, and

his bright blue eyes sparkled with the vigor of a sixteen year old, although he had just passed his fiftieth year.

'Thank you for coming, Mrs Simpson,' he said to Sarah, as he kissed her hand. Then he greeted the two men heartily, with vigorous handshakes and slaps on their shoulders. Sarah said it was her pleasure, and that it would also be her pleasure if they could call each other by their first names, to which Captain Scott, whose first name was William—but Willie to his friends, he said—readily agreed.

'Would you like some refreshments, or would ye like to see the garden first?' he asked.

They all agreed that they would like to see the garden first, so he gave them a tour of the carefully laid out rows of fruit and spice trees, and the pathways that wound through shaded canopies of bamboo. Garden was hardly the word to describe it. Although it was laid out as neatly as any garden, and although the bushes and shrubs around the cottage gave it the appearance of a garden, it was really a large plantation that stretched out for about a quarter of a mile beyond the cottage.

'I've got some Chinese laddies to help me with the rest o' it,' he explained, 'but I like tae look after the area around the house myself. But come on in and I'll get ye all something tae drink. You need tae keep yourselves well watered in this place, just like the flowers,' he joked.

They spent a pleasant afternoon in Captain Scott's company. They learned that he was the cousin of Sir Walter Scott and that he and John Simpson shared a love of chess and a good malt. When the syce drew up outside the cottage to take them home, Captain Scott walked them to his gate.

'Easy to find your way back,' he said. 'Just head back down Orchard Road the way you came.'

'Is that what it's called?' asked Sarah, as she climbed into their carriage.

'I dinna ken,' Captain Scott replied. 'But that's what I call it, wi' them Chinese orchards all around.'

'Sounds good to me,' said Ronnie, climbing in to join his wife. 'That's what we'll call it in future. And we'll call this one Scott's Road, after our new friend.'

And they became the best of friends in the months that followed. Captain Scott was a regular guest at the Simpsons' home, and old John Simpson spent many a Sunday afternoon with Captain Scott at Hurricane Cottage, where they played chess and exchanged stories of the sea and Napoleon's war. John Simpson usually arrived home a little the worse for wear—that is, on those evenings when he did arrive home—and he only very rarely beat his friend at chess.

* * *

In early April, Tan Che Sang, the Malacca merchant who had stood surety for some of the early credit advanced to his countrymen in Tuan Farquhar's time, died in his sleep among his money chests, at the age of seventy-three. He had built up a great fortune, but had also lost a good deal of it through gambling.

When his funeral was held on the thirteenth of April, over ten thousand townspeople, mainly Chinese, but also many Europeans and Company officials, lined the route as the procession wound its way through Commercial Square towards the Hokkien burial ground west of the Chinese town. A long black cloth covered the great black lacquered coffin, which was supported by twenty men in black uniforms. A Buddhist priest headed the procession, accompanied by a lantern bearer. A small band followed, clashing cymbals and beating drums. The mourners walked behind the coffin, the men in black, the women in white.

Sang had become a respected citizen and leader of the Hokkien community, although he was also rumoured to be one of the leaders of the Ghee Hin kongsi. He liked to boast, if merely in jest, that he only had to give the word and the Hokkien community would rise up and drive the Europeans from the settlement. Whether true or not, it was fortunately never in his interest to do so. When the procession reached the cemetery, a large crowd gathered around the open grave, where copious amounts of imitation paper money were deposited before the coffin was laid to rest. In death, as in life, Tan Che Sang slept with his money.

* * *

George Coleman did eventually do something about the Raffles Institution, and much more besides. Early in the year, Alexander Guthrie had convened and chaired a meeting at which it was agreed to rescind Raffles' original scheme for an institution devoted to the higher education of the sons of the Malay nobility, and instead focus upon elementary education in reading, writing and arithmetic. Those present at the meeting had also agreed to raise funds for the completion of the institution, and to use the money that had been already raised for a statue of Sir Stamford Raffles, which had never been completed. Coleman had been contracted to repair and refurbish the original building in a manner that would allow for its ready expansion to meet the increasing educational needs of the community, and he began work on the building in June. When it was completed the following June, the boys from the Reverend Darrah's Singapore School Society, who attended elementary classes in English, Tamil, Malay and Chinese in a house at the top of High Street, were transferred to the Singapore Institution. One of the upper rooms of the new building was designated as the library and museum, and donations of books and natural specimens were solicited from the community.

That same month Coleman completed St. Andrews Church, a Doric building surrounded by wide porticoes that enclosed carriage rows, with a stucco finish plastered with sparkling Madras Chunam. It was an elegant building, but it had no spire, which led some to complain that it looked more like a town hall than a church. Although of Episcopalian denomination, it was called St. Andrews Church because the Scottish merchants raised the bulk of the funding.

Due west of St. Andrew's Church was the house Coleman had built for his Dutch-Javanese mistress, Nyai Takoye Manuk, and her daughter, Meda Elizabeth, resplendent with Ionic pillars and porticoes. Next to it, Coleman had built his own home, a two-storey piazza with a Georgian interior, which, like all of his best work, was dedicated to the maximization of ventilation and shade.

Using convict labour, Coleman had surfaced North and South Bridge Roads, and reclaimed much of the swampland northeast of the Singapore River and beyond the European town and Kampong Glam. He transformed the Telok Ayer Market from a dilapidated timber and attap building to an orthogonal cast iron structure with ornamental columns at its entrance.

14

Ronnie finished a game of fives with Charlie Singer, a bookkeeper for Armstrong, Crane and Company, at the new court that had been built beside the courthouse. This was largely due to the efforts of Dr Montgomerie, who praised the game as the best form of early morning exercise in a tropical climate, and who had managed to raise the money by persistently nagging merchants like Ronnie.

Yet Ronnie had to admit that he enjoyed the game, which was simplicity itself. Two players (or two sets of two players in the doubles version) batted a small leather ball with their bare hands against the far wall of the rectangular court, the goal being to return the ball to the wall above the white penalty line before it bounced more than once; when the receiver failed to do so, the other player (or pair of players) was awarded a point. The game was over when one player (or pair of players) attained fifteen points.

Ronnie and Charlie had played three games; he had won the first, Charlie the second, and he the close third, which was a source of some satisfaction since Charlie was a good many years younger than himself. Ronnie thought it an excellent form of exercise, since it involved a great deal of effort running from one side of the court to the other, and from the front to the back, but he wondered about Montgomerie's claim that it was especially suited for a tropical climate. Sometimes as he ran back and forth in the humid air he felt like he was running through treacle, as if the heavy air in the court slowed his every movement. But he felt invigorated after his victory and a good scrub and ladling in the washroom, and thought it a good tonic for a day at his desk in the office. He and Charlie hired a Tamil boatman to take them across the river, and they went their separate ways when he set them down on Boat Quay.

After a few hours at the offices of Simpson and Co. in Commercial Square, Ronnie took himself across to the Exchange Room to read the newspapers and pick up what news there was from the other merchants. The talk was all about the recent slump in business. The previous year the East India Company had lost its monopoly on the China trade, and the last of the Company Indiamen, with their distinctive black hulls and yellow gun ports, had gone home. The merchants had confidently assumed that the free or 'country' traders would pick up their business and continue to use Singapore as an exchange-mart, unloading goods from Europe and India, and reloading with goods bound for China. But many of the free traders were making longer voyages to maximize their profits, and were using the Dutch controlled Strait of Sunda rather than the Strait of Malacca, bypassing Singapore altogether. The volume of imports and exports that passed though the port had dropped from sixteen million to twelve million tons. On top of this Calcutta was threatening to impose a port tax, which would strip Singapore of its distinctive status as a free port, and would further stifle trade.

Ronnie sat down in a comfortable chair in the corner and picked up a copy of the *Calcutta Journal*. James Guthrie came over and sat down beside him. 'They're all doom and gloom, Ronnie, but I'm sure things will pick up as the market grows, as it surely must,' he said.

'I hope you're right,' Ronnie replied. 'I'm finding it hard going these days myself.'

Ronnie and Guthrie were in the corner by themselves, and Guthrie leant over and half-whispered to him: 'I've been thinking about your business with the pirates, and the problems they cause us. I've also been talking with Bonham, who wants something done about it. He came up with an idea that might interest you. It means attributing rather base motives to our local Malay leadership, and it might involve some danger to your good self. But it might just work.'

'Tell me more,' Ronnie said, his interest pricked.

'I don't know if you know, but His Highness Sultan Hussein passed away recently in Malacca, and Bonham's not likely to recognize his son Ali as the new sultan. The boy is only fifteen and all he's inherited is his father's debts to the Chettiars. Now, Daing Ibrahim, the temenggong's son, has been doing quite a decent job of leading his people at Telok Blangah since his father's death, and...'

'But he's almost one o' them himself!' Ronnie interrupted. 'We all know how the pirates get to find out about cargoes and schedules, from that...'

'Keep your voice down, man,' Guthrie snapped at him, as some of the other merchants in the room turned their heads towards them. 'I don't want everyone to know about this, and I especially don't want Daing Ibrahim to know about this!'

'I'm sorry,' Ronnie replied, dropping his voice so that only Guthrie could hear him, 'but he's in the thick of it if anyone is.'

I'm sure he is,' replied Guthrie, 'but that's exactly what gives us our opportunity. I've got a pretty good feeling he wants to be recognized as temenggong, perhaps even as sultan. We could help him, or we could make life very difficult for him, and we could make him understand that. So I think we could get him to help us with the pirates, and with your man in particular. Of course he'll never admit that he has connections with them—he's a wily fox just like his father—but he might be persuaded to use these connections to help us for a change. Certainly worth a try, Ronnie.'

'Agreed, James,' Ronnie replied. 'So let's gie it a try.'

* * *

The slump in trade was also affecting Tan Hong Chuan, although with Siti's help and advice, he had weathered the economic downturn better than most. While his ship's chandlery business suffered as a result of the reduction of shipping in the harbour, his fruit and spice plantations continued to thrive, except for those devoted to nutmeg, coffee and cocoa, which did not seem well suited to the soil and climate. On the positive side, the increase in land values had slowed, which made it a good time to buy—he had sold some of his unproductive plantations and used the money to purchase some choice lots in the Chinese town.

So he was not unduly worried by the slump in trade. He was puzzled by one thing, however. He had noticed that of late there seemed to be fewer dishes for the evening meal, with less meat and fish, and only rarely the special dishes he loved, such as shark's fin and bird nest soup. He had asked his wife about this, to which she had angrily responded that he ate too much, and that she was only concerned about his health; she did not want him to leave her a widow and their son without the guidance of a father. But her vehement response had seemed disproportionate to her avowed concerns about his health and their son's welfare, and as the portions got smaller and smaller he got increasingly annoyed. He had enough to worry about, he thought to himself, and needed a good meal at night to sustain him.

He asked Siti what she thought was going on. At first she looked away, and seemed reluctant to discuss the matter. But when he pressed her she eventually told him that Song Neo had been playing cherki and chap ji kee[lxxiii] with the other Nonya wives, and had got herself quite deep in debt. She had pawned some of her jewellery to cover her losses, but this had not been enough, so she was now trimming the household budget to stay ahead of her creditors.

Hong Chuan was furious when he heard this news, and asked

lxxiii Chinese lottery game.

Siti why she had not warned him about his wife's behaviour before. Siti replied that as his concubine it was not her place to criticize or to make accusations against his first wife.

'That will change, and right away, I assure you,' Hong Chuan replied. 'I will make you my second wife, as reward for all you have done for me, for which I am truly grateful. I had intended to do this in any case, and should have done it sooner. But as my second wife, I will expect you to keep an eye on Song Neo, and warn me if anything like this happens again.'

Siti thanked Hong Chuan and told him she would be honoured to be his second wife, and would do her duty as second wife to protect the interests of the family.

'How much does she owe?' Hong Chuan asked.

'I'm not sure exactly, but I believe around three or four thousand dollars.'

Hong Chuan sucked in his breath and stood for a moment clenching his fists in anger. Then he ordered one of his servants to summon his wife for a meeting in his study, and to accept no excuses. He also instructed Siti to attend the meeting.

'What is it you wish to see me about?' Song Neo asked reproachfully, when she entered his study. 'And why is she here?' she continued, indicating Siti with a curt nod of her head.

Hong Chuan told her in a calm and controlled voice that he had learned about her gambling debts. He also told her that he had asked Siti to become his second wife, and that she was going to keep an eye on her behaviour in future. When Song Neo began to protest, Hong Chuan demanded to know the extent of her debts, and his anger returned when she told him she owed a little over five thousand dollars. She promised Hong Chuan she would pay the money back, and would sell the rest of her jewellery if she needed to do so, but Hong Chuan told he to be silent.

'Song Neo, my first wife, I will forgive you this one time. I will pay off your debts and redeem whatever jewellery you have pawned, so we can rebuild our life together again, for the sake of our son and the honour of our family. In return, I demand that you make a pledge to our ancestors never to gamble again, and never again bring the dishonour of debt upon this house.'

'I will do as you wish, husband,' Song Neo replied. 'I am deeply sorry for what I have done. I was weak, but you have made me strong, and I promise you it will not happen again. But you will surely not deny me the company of my friends or the freedom to go out. I think I would rather die than be imprisoned in this house every day.'

'You are free to come and go as you wish, my first wife. I accept your promise, and will trust you to remain in charge of the household. But I will also expect to see more of a banquet when I return in the evening.'

Song Neo bowed in respect, and thanked her husband, although her cheeks blushed red from shame and embarrassment.

'But I also promise you another thing,' Hong Chuan continued, in a stern voice. 'If you disobey me, I will not give you a second chance. I will divorce you and disown you. I will place an advertisement in the paper that I am no longer responsible for you or your debts, and you will be put out on the streets to join the other paupers. That I promise you, and I will have Siti watch over you, and report to me at once if you break your promise to me. That is all.'

Song Neo bowed in acknowledgement of Hong Chuan's command, but as she rose to leave, Siti could see her cheeks were flushed with anger.

Siti immediately recognized how the situation could be worked to her advantage. She knew she had only to aid and encourage Song Neo in her addiction to games of chance, and she could displace her as Hong Chuan's first wife. But Siti could not do such a thing. Although she had little affection for Mrs Tan, who treated her with lofty disdain, she was her husband's first wife and the mother of his beloved son, and she knew she owed it to Hong Chuan to do her best by him—he who had given her a life of freedom and happiness. And she felt genuinely sorry for Song Neo. Hong Chuan paid her only perfunctory attention, in the hope of a second son, but she knew there was little affection between them, and that he generally took his pleasure with Siti, both in her body and her company.

She had seen those advertisements in the newspaper in which men disowned their wives and their debts, and had seen the abandoned women in the dark alleys of Cross Street, where the lowest form of prostitutes plied their trade. She shuddered at the thought, and hoped in her heart that everything would work out all right.

15

A few days later Ronnie and James Guthrie met with Resident Councillor Bonham. He encouraged them to approach Daing Ibrahim, and told them he had already done so himself. A few days later, Ronnie and James Guthrie led a small delegation of European and Chinese merchants to visit Daing Ibrahim at his bungalow at Telok Blangah. They included Ronnie's father, John Simpson, Alexander Johnston, George Armstrong, Graham Mackenzie, Chua Chong Long, Seah Eu Chin and Hoo Ah Kay.

Daing Ibrahim was short of stature, but muscular in frame. He had dark intelligent eyes, a dominant forehead, and sensual lips that seemed to shiver between a smile and a sneer. He wore a baju shirt and a kain sarong, made of fine blue silk interwoven with gold and silver threads, and a silk serban[lxxiv] upon his head. Daing Ibrahim offered them refreshments, and listened patiently to them as they made their case.

After the merchants had finished speaking, Daing Ibrahim told them that he very much regretted that they had wasted their valuable time coming to visit him, although he was flattered that they would think him such a powerful man as to have any influence over the pirates. He complained that the pirates preyed upon his own people as much as they did upon the merchants, and had once attacked them within sight of his lodge. Yet although he insisted he had nothing to do with the pirates, Daing Ibrahim said that he would make inquiries and find out what he could for them.

But this was not enough to satisfy the merchants.

---

lxxiv Turban.

'We trust that ye will, Daing Ibrahim,' said Ronnie, 'and we're no accusing ye of being a pirate yourself. But there is one thing ye can do that would demonstrate your good will and concern for the security of *our* people. Ye can let it be known, and to the pirates Si Rahman and Sri Hussein in particular, that my ships will be transporting a large consignment of opium to Canton in four week's time. We will put in at Pulau Gaya on the way, and then head north to Canton. If we meet them at sea, we shall know on whose side you stand.'

'But even if I could do such a thing,' Daing Ibrahim protested, 'you are asking me to put your life in danger, Captain Simpson. These men show no mercy, even to Europeans.'

'Or women and children,' said Ronnie, his voice gone suddenly cold. 'We know that, and we mean to put an end to them. Will ye help us?'

'As I told you,' Daing Ibrahim replied, 'I have no power in these matters. But I assure you that I will do my best to find out what I can and will quietly spread the word about your shipment. But you alone must accept the consequences. God go with you,' he said, as he made his farewell and wished them all success in their businesses.

As they left Daing Ibrahim's bungalow, James Guthrie turned to Ronnie and whispered: 'We've got him. He sees the future, and he knows which side his bread is buttered on.'

Yet they had scarcely reached the foot of the steps of Daing Ibrahim's bungalow when his servant summoned the two men back to the audience chamber. Daing Ibrahim stood waiting for them in the middle of the room. He looked the two men up and down, and for a long time seemed to be deciding whether he should talk to them or not. But then he addressed them in a serious tone. 'I know you two men are the leaders of your delegation, so I wished to speak to you in private. I understand and sympathize with Captain Simpson's concern in this matter, but I want you both to understand my own position. You think of us as pirates and yourselves as merchants, but it was you who made us so.'

Ibrahim motioned both men to sit. But they indicated they preferred to stand. 'As you wish. Now, we are not an aggressive or warlike race, and we much prefer the path of peace and prosperity. Generations ago my people were traders like yourselves, as indeed was the Prophet himself in his early days, and we exchanged our goods and produce with others of our race throughout the archipelago. We had to pay homage to the Majapahit Empire and the local sultans, but they left us to pursue our own business in peace. When the Chinamen came down on the northeast monsoon, they would buy our spices, rattans, camphor, shark's fins and pearls. But then the Europeans came—the Spanish, the Portuguese, the Dutch and later the British—who created their factories, their monopolies, and interfered with our governments to suit their own selfish ends.'

'When we cultivated cloves and nutmeg to make our living, you would destroy them to inflate the price, or prevent others of your breed from profiting by them,' Daing Ibrahim exclaimed, his voice rising in barely controlled anger. 'All trade in spices had to go to the European company, on pain of death. We were forbidden to export a great many articles, whose trade you Europeans kept to yourselves, even though my people had traded them for generations—pepper, tin, copper, silk, cotton yarn and cloth, gold, arrack, guns, gunpowder—and many, many more. Only vessels with a European pass were allowed to trade, and these passes restricted the guns, shot and powder a ship could carry, to ensure our inferiority to your men-of-war. So what choice did we have? My people are proud and free, and we are never freer than when we sail the open seas. When you took everything we had, you left us no choice but to take back from you by force what you had stolen from us.'

'Wait up, Daing Ibrahim,' said Guthrie. 'I grant there's some truth to what you say, and that there's been some bad dealing in the past. But you must surely admit that your family and your followers have been fairly treated by Sir Stamford Raffles and those who succeeded him. We're a free port, and you've been free to trade with whom you like without interference or taxation.'

'Well, Mr Guthrie,' Daing Ibrahim replied, with a thin smile that was not really a smile, 'do you really think your governor would allow us to produce our own opium and sell it directly to the Chinese?'

But before Guthrie could answer, Daing Ibrahim held up his hand to stop him. 'Do not concern yourself on this matter, Mr Guthrie, for I would not profit from such an evil trade. It is bad enough that many of my people destroy their lives with arrack, while others sell it to the sailors, but opium takes a man's soul and leaves him an empty shell until he dies. It surprises me that the Honorable Company and the Great John Bull talk of their high principles but take their profit from such a trade. There is also some truth in what you say, that my late father and I have been treated fairly by the civil authorities. But you cannot expect my people to give up their pirate ways overnight when this is how they have survived for generations. Old habits die hard, as you say, and a leopard does not change its spots. But know that I have heeded what you have said, and once again bid you good day. And may God go with you.'

With that, Daing Ibrahim bowed, then turned and left them.

Ronnie and Guthrie looked at each other but said nothing. There seemed nothing left to say.

When they were clear of Daing Ibrahim's compound, James Guthrie smashed his fist into his hand and exclaimed: 'We've got him, Ronnie! We've definitely got him.'

Daing Ibrahim watched them go. Let them think they have persuaded me, he thought. It will do no harm. He had already decided to cooperate with Resident Councillor Bonham.[29]

Although successive residents from Crawfurd to Ibbetson had treated him with disdain, Daing Ibrahim was on better terms with Resident Councillor Bonham, with whom he had already cooperated in cases involving piracy. At Bonham's request, he had used the inherited authority of his father to persuade the Bendahara Tun Ali of Pahang to surrender some slaves captured from a Cochin junk, who had been sold to the Bendahara by Johor pirates. He had also advised Bonham of the location of a pirate stronghold on Pulau Galang in the Riau Archipelago. Bonham had dispatched a squadron headed by Captain Henry Chads of HMS *Andromache*, a Company gunboat that had recently been sent out from India to suppress piracy and to institute a system of passes for identifying legitimate traders. Chads had destroyed the pirate stronghold at Galang, and had attacked any suspicious vessels he had come across on his return from Riau to Singapore.

While some of his subjects and followers saw this as an act of betrayal, others had recognized that he was their best hope of protection against both the pirates and the aggressive searches of the British ships. Daing Ibrahim had seen the power of the *Andromache*'s guns, and he knew it was only a matter of time before his pirate brethren would be driven from the seas. So he had decided to throw his lot in with the British, since this seemed to best serve both his own interests and those of his people, at least at this moment in time. Although no formal commitment had been made, Bonham had indicated to him that his cooperation against the pirates might eventually be rewarded by his official recognition as temenggong. Daing Ibrahim trusted George Bonham, whom he considered to be an honourable man. But he knew he must make his own destiny, for he knew that the British might easily discard him if they had no further use of him, or if they thought they could advance their own interests better by supporting the claims of the late sultan's son Tengku Ali when he came of age.

* * *

George Bonham thought that Daing Ibrahim was an illiterate degenerate, and would have preferred to leave him to live in squalor with his followers at Telok Blangah. Yet he had little choice but to court his support in dealing with the pirate problem. After a loud and boisterous public meeting at which the merchants had protested the actions of the pirates, and then written to the governor-general and the King-in-Council warning of the threat to British trade in the East, the Indian Government had responded with a scheme that proposed that expeditions to suppress the pirates be financed by a small port duty.

The response of the Singapore merchants to this threat to their laissez-faire trade was loud outrage, and with the support of the London mercantile community led by John Crawfurd, the former resident, they managed to get the proposal quashed. So Bonham was in a bind. The merchants, upon whom the economic prosperity and future of the settlement depended, demanded action against the pirates, and were liable to take their business elsewhere if they did not get it. But they were also adamant that they would not pay for it. So Bonham had to look to Daing Ibrahim for help.

16

Two weeks later, Ronnie received a message asking him to meet with Daing Ibrahim in the offices of Guthrie and Clark. When he arrived, Daing Ibrahim and James Guthrie were standing talking in Guthrie's office. When Ronnie entered, Daing Ibrahim greeted him and recounted the death of the pirate Sri Hussein.

'But you must beware, Mr Simpson,' he cautioned. 'For I have heard that his brother Si Rahman is raging in his grief and anger, and has sworn to kill you. And I have heard that he knows about your shipment of opium.'

'Thank you, Daing Ibrahim,' Ronnie replied. 'I am grateful to you, and I know that I speak for the other merchants and the governor when I say that your aid in this matter is greatly appreciated and will not be forgotten.' James Guthrie seconded his sentiment.

Ronnie went straight home and told Sarah the news. She just nodded her head, and said she would come with him. She ignored his protests, but she feared for him. She could not bear to lose him.

There was danger, but this time they would have more government support. Along with his own ships and two Chinese junks, three Company ships would join him. These were the heavily armed sloops HMS *Wolf*, commanded by Captain Edward Stanley, and HMS *Andromache*, commanded by Captain Henry Chads, and the Company's steamer HMS *Diana*, commanded by Captain Samuel Congalton, who had led the *Zephyr* in Ronnie's earlier attack on the pirate stronghold. Ronnie went aboard HMS *Wolf* to meet with the three captains. As they stood together on the deck, they watched the *Diana* chugging along beside them, her paddles thrashing the water and her chimneystack belching black smoke.

Ronnie looked doubtful.

'Is she seaworthy, Congalton?' he asked.

'Well she made it out from Glasgow, but I have to admit she had a few problems since I picked her up in Calcutta. But we have a first-class engineer—a fellow who can work magic with the steam engines—and we've had no trouble since we passed Pulau Rupat. I'll admit she's not a pretty site aside these sleek Navy sloops, but she has two advantages over them. She has a shallow draft, which means she can travel further upstream in pursuit of pirates, and best of all, she does not depend on the wind.'

'So long as she disna break down,' said Ronnie, who was not impressed.

'Well, if anyone can get the *Diana* to demonstrate her mettle, it's Captain Congalton here,' Captain Stanley offered in support of his colleague.

'Well, maybe he can scare them away with a' that thrashing water and belching smoke,' Ronnie mused, as he watched the ugly steamer make its way across the bay.

* * *

Although only a few weeks had passed, it seemed that Tan Song Neo had already mended her ways. She still visited her Nonya friends, and continued to play cherki and chap ji kee with them, but she did not appear to be losing any more money. There were plenty of dishes on the table for the evening meal, including the delicacies that Hong Chuan loved and, as Siti carefully noted, Song Neo seemed to have retained all her jewellery. Indeed she appeared to have purchased some new pieces, including a jewel-encrusted kebaya[lxxv] with an ornate gold belt. Tan Hong Chuan was grateful

---

lxxv Blouse-dress.

and very much relieved to hear this news.

* * *

Ronnie was on his way from the offices of Simpson and Co. on Boat Quay to meet Graham Mackenzie for tiffin. They were going to discuss the sale of some land out at Bukit Timah that Mackenzie had offered him. Like many of the other merchants, Ronnie fancied himself as a gentleman farmer, and was thinking of starting a nutmeg plantation. Nutmeg seemed to be all the rage these days.

He looked around at the bustle along the quay. Indian lightermen were loading and unloading all along its length. Coolies were struggling under bags of rice, spices, and sago, while heavier items were being transported to and fro on bullock carts. Ronnie loved all the activity—it made him feel alive just to be in the thick of it.

He saw the man as he passed the godown of Spottiswoode and Connolly. He was a Chinese man in his thirties, of medium height but very muscular. He wore a white cotton shirt and baggy black trousers, which flapped around his legs as he ran directly towards him. The man had pulled out the axe almost the moment he had begun running, and now drew back his arm to throw it. It was a small weapon, but deadly looking. The man's black queue flew behind him, and his eyes were the eyes of a man intent on killing. Ronnie had seen that look many times before, and in that instant wondered if he would ever see it again. For in the fleeting moment it took him to draw out his pistol, he knew he was too late, for he knew he could never fire it in time to stop the throw. Ronnie thought he recognized him—in fact he felt sure of it—but he could not tell from where.

He ducked his head down instinctively, and the axe flew by him, well clear of his head. He heard the dull thud as it sank into the chest of the tall Malay who stood behind him, and now dropped to the ground by his side. As Ronnie turned, he saw the long black kris slip from the man's grasp. The axe had stuck the assassin deep in his chest, and the man was already dead when Ronnie bent down to investigate his condition. The man was dark-skinned, with long black hair and swirling images of snakes and tigers tattooed on his arms and chest. Ronnie looked up to see Lee Yip Lee slip into an alleyway and disappear into the darkness. He made no effort to pursue him. Then Ronnie remembered where he had seen the man—he had been on one of the Chinese junks on the expedition to the pirate stronghold on Sumatra. The man was on his side, and had saved his life.

After he had given the details of the attack to the police peon who arrived on the scene, he went on to join Graham Mackenzie for tiffin.

'Sorry I'm late, Graham,' he said, 'but I was almost killed by a Malay on the quay. Some Chinese fellow saved my skin, although for the life of me I don't know why.'

'I'm sure it's the work of one of our Chinese partners in this affair,' said Mackenzie. 'They've probably got some of their society men watching out for you.'

'But at least we can be sure of one thing,' he continued, 'Daing Ibrahim has got the word out on you. How does it feel to be the bait?'

'I dinna mind,' said Ronnie, 'although I'll need to keep a closer lookout than I have. I'll be glad to get the thing over with at last.'

* * * *

Siti heard the commotion downstairs and came down to see what was the matter. The servants were crowded round the door to Song Neo's bedroom, but were afraid to go in. She pressed by them and the Malay houseboy who had found her, lying on her bed in a pool of blood. Song Neo had cut her wrists with a miniature silver kris, a gift from Tan Hong Chuan's parents. She lay white as an alabaster statue upon the bed, her empty brown eyes staring at the ceiling, her thin lips drawn tightly in a frozen smile. All the blood seemed to have drained from her body, and seeped down from the bed onto the delicately shaded floral tiles at Siti's feet.

Siti quickly took charge. She ordered the servants to send Tan Eng Guan and his tutor into town, to inform Tan Hong Chuan, and then the undertaker and the Coroner, Mr Bell. There would have to be an inquest, and it would be an embarrassment to the family. Yet it would be much worse if they tried to cover it up and the news leaked out, as she knew it would—such news burned on the tongues of servants like hot chillies.

But what had happened? When she found and read the suicide letter that Song Neo had left, she understood why. Song Neo said that she had tried so very hard not to shame her husband and her son by her behaviour, but that she had been slowly drawn into deeper and deeper debt as a result of her gambling, like her good friend the Bibik Chwee. The old lady had done much worse, and had incurred such a huge debt that her own had seemed to pale by comparison. But eventually Song Neo had realized that she was in too deep, and that her creditors would soon come knocking on her husband's door demanding repayment. So she had done the only honourable thing and taken her own life. She hoped that her husband, her son, and Yan Luo, the king of hell, would take pity on her tortured soul.

But how had she managed to run up such debts, when she had maintained a more than adequate table, had managed to keep her jewellery, and had even purchased some new pieces? When Tan Hong Chuan returned home they discovered the reason why. Song Neo had somehow managed to make a copy of the key to his safe, and had removed most of the bullion that he had stored there, replacing the silver dollars and gold bars with copper coins and bricks covered with silver and gold-coloured paper.

This alone amounted to a loss of many thousands of dollars, but far worse, some of the deeds to Hong Chuan's properties were missing. They assumed that Song Neo had mortgaged these to unscrupulous merchants or shopkeepers in order to support her gambling habit, and they wondered to themselves just how much debt she had incurred beyond the immediate losses from her theft. It could cripple his business, and drive them onto the street—the self same fate that Tan Hong Chuan had threatened his wife with.

* * *

It was worse than they thought. It was far worse than they could have imagined. They had lost nearly ten thousand dollars in cash and bullion, and twice that much on the notes owed on the land deeds. After discrete inquiries, Tan Hong Chuan managed to redeem most of the notes, although he had to sell some of his plantations and land to do so. Siti persuaded him to sell off the less productive nutmeg, cocoa and cotton plantations, and to save those planted with pineapple and coconut.

But then real disaster struck. A Hokkien merchant, Kong Ong Tuan, held the remaining land mortgages. He had got into serious financial trouble himself, but had absconded and fled back to Canton before his creditors could have him arrested. He had used Hong Chuan's land deeds to pretend that they were partners, and exploiting the respect in which Tan Hong Chuan was held by many of the European and Chinese merchants, he had managed to procure a great many goods on credit.

Tan Hong Chuan had never formed any sort of business partnership with Kong Ong Tuan, and published a statement in the *Singapore Free Press* to that effect, but it was too late. George

McKenzie, who had accepted Kong Ong Tuan's claim when he was shown the land deeds, sued Hong Chuan for his losses. Unlike European partnerships, which were recorded in legal documents in the home country, Chinese partnerships were based upon family or informal social ties, and nothing was committed to paper. In consequence, it was George McKenzie's word against Hong Chuan's, so the legal case was based upon any documentary evidence that counted one way or the other.

Unfortunately the land deeds to Hong Chuan's properties found in Kong Ong Tuan's abandoned and empty godown counted heavily against Hong Chuan. The magistrates found in favour of George McKenzie, and ordered Hong Chuan to compensate him and pay his court costs. Many of the merchants thought the decision was unfair given the circumstances, but there was no way round the law. Even George McKenzie felt sorry for Hong Chuan, but business was business, and he was fighting for survival like everyone else in a difficult market.

Hong Chuan was forced to sell off all his land and remaining plantations, save for one pineapple plantation out towards Bukit Timah. He was also obliged to sell his fine house at Telok Ayer, and to move with Siti and his son into the room above his godown on Boat Quay, where he had managed to retain his chandlery business. That he was able to do so was largely due to the generosity and public-spiritedness of the merchant community, both European and Chinese. Merchants such as Ronnie Simpson gave him longer terms of credit in return for preferential service for their vessels, and Lim Guan Chye arranged a temporary loan that was raised from contributions by the merchant community, many of who were sympathetic to Hong Chuan's case—including George McKenzie, but only on condition that his contribution remain anonymous.

17

Towards the end of June the small flotilla left Singapore harbour and headed out through the Strait of Singapore and into the South China Sea. Ronnie led them in the *Highland Lassie*. He was the only merchant to sail with them, although he had the financial support of the merchant community, and many of the European and Chinese sea captains who had suffered at the hands of the pirates had volunteered crews and supplies.

He had three heavily armed European merchantmen, supplemented by a detachment of marines, and two Chinese junks, which he knew were reinforced by tiger soldiers from the secret societies. The Company's ships — the *Wolf*, the *Andromache*, and the *Diana* — followed behind within signaling distance. Ronnie was also accompanied by Mr Oates, who said he wanted to see the matter to its final conclusion, and over his hopeless objections, by Sarah, who had brought along her new Baker rifle.

'You'd better get him with your first few shots,' he said, 'for they're devilish things to reload. The debris quickly clogs up the barrel, and ye soon lose the advantage of the rifling. Watch it disna blow up in your face—for it's such a bonny face.'

'Don't you worry,' Sarah replied. 'I've been practicing, and I won't be wasting shots on the riff-raff. I'll leave them to you.'

'Daing Ibrahim told me that Si Rahman believes that killing a white woman has made him invincible,' Ronnie told her, turning serious.

'Well in that case, perhaps I should have brought my silver bullets,' she replied with a grim smile. 'But I aim to prove him wrong.'

One week later they arrived off Pulau Gaya, where they took on water and cargoes of bird's nests and tortoiseshell, taking care to let the Malay carriers see the chests of opium that were stored on board the ships. As they lay at anchor that night, a sleek black prahu raced north ahead of them.

Two days out of Pulau Gaya, they came across the *Griffin*, a marooned British schooner that had struck some hidden rocks. She was close to the point of sinking, despite the desperate efforts of her crew at the pumps. The cargo of rice was lost, since the salt water had reached it, but they took the captain and crew aboard their ships, along with the passengers: two Chinese merchants and the Reverend William Macpherson of the London Missionary Society, his wife, Annie, and their eight-year-old daughter, Jenny.

As he helped them store their trunks below deck, Ronnie warned the reverend about the secret purpose of their mission.

'Out o' the frying pan into the fire,' Macpherson growled, stroking his long white beard, as he grinned back at Ronnie. 'But there's aye room for the Lord's work, whatever mysterious ways he chooses. Annie and Jenny can help out below decks, and I can give ye a hand above,' he said, as he removed a great double-bore shotgun from his trunk, along with a belt of cartridges.

'There's no need for you to get involved in our fight,' said Ronnie, 'although I'm grateful for your offer.'

'There's every need,' Macpherson replied, no longer grinning, 'to send these murderous bastards tae hell.'

Ronnie raised his hands in the air. 'As ye wish, Reverend.'

* * *

Two days passed, and they made good progress north, but with no sight of the pirates. Then on the dawn of the third day, just as the wind began to drop, they spied a large fleet of armed prahu bearing down upon them from the northeast. Ronnie managed to signal the Company ships so they had time to come forward, but he knew that the pirates with their oar-driven craft would have them at a disadvantage now that the wind had dropped. Yet they had their secret weapon, the paddle steamer *Diana*, whose maneuvers did not depend upon the wind. Ronnie just hoped it would maintain its head of steam. It had lost power twice already on the trip out, and had had to resort to sail.

As the pirate prahus approached, their lines of dark oars beating the surface of the water like the wings of giant birds, Ronnie asked his Malay helmsmen if he thought they were Illanun pirates. The man said that he was certain that they were, and that he was also certain that the famous pirate Si Rahman led them. Ronnie did not bother to ask him why he was so certain about that. He had the man taken below and kept under watch, as he prepared his ships for battle.

They had agreed upon the basic strategy beforehand. They would try to take out the Illanun gunners with musket and rifle fire when they came in close, and then rake their decks with round shot and grape; they had assembled cannon balls and bags of iron shards on deck in preparation. They had hoped to be able to ram the leading boats, but that was out of the question now that they were becalmed, although every ship was ready to make sail if the wind picked up. And the *Diana* was waiting for her moment of best advantage.

The Reverend Macpherson gave his wife a pistol and told her to take their daughter below deck. He embraced them, and told his wife 'You ken what to do if things get hot.' She nodded politely, as if she were receiving instructions on where to place the hymn books. Then Macpherson took up position beside Ronnie and Sarah on the foredeck, his shotgun cocked and ready.

As the Illanun fleet surrounded them, the leading prahu, which was much larger than the rest, armed with long black canon and swivel guns, and decked out with bright flags and feathers, came into hailing range. On the central platform stood a tall dark man with long black hair, clad in scarlet robes and a silver breastplate, with bright red feathers dancing in his headdress. They all knew who he was, Si Rahman, the leader of the Illanun pirates who had killed Sarah's sister and her family, and the unfortunate Captain Ramsey and his son Adam, along with countless others. They could see the magic charm that hung from his breastplate, a twisted length of human hair that he turned between the fingers of his left hand. In his right hand he held a huge Tampilan sword, decorated with bright red feathers around its scabbard.

He hailed the *Highland Lassie*, and called out that he had come to trade his spices for some tobacco, and meant them no harm. He requested permission for some of his party to come aboard.

'I have him in my sights,' said Macpherson, 'but I'll give you the honour, Mrs Simpson.'

'So do I,' Sarah responded. 'I don't much care who kills him, so long as he dies.'

Ronnie gave Mr Oates the honour of responding to Si Rahman's request.

'Permission denied,' Oates called out in a load clear voice. 'We have not come to trade but to kill you Si Rahman.'

The moment he said this, Sarah and the Reverend Macpherson fired together, and Ronnie signalled for the fight to begin. Musketry, round shot and grape poured into the Illanun craft, which instantly returned their fire. They had obviously been prepared and waiting for their own signal, which they had received from Si Rahman, who now stood waving his sword in the air and directing the attack.

'Fuck it,' said Macpherson, 'we missed the bastard.'

Sarah said nothing, and was already reloading. She wondered whether she should have brought the silver bullets. Don't be so stupid! she chided herself. He's just a man and can die like any other.

The battle raged for half an hour, with neither side gaining an advantage. The defenders managed to inflict heavy casualties on the Illanun craft, and prevented the pirates from boarding. They also managed to sink a few prahus, but others waiting in the rear quickly took their places. They also took their own casualties, including Mr Oates, who caught a musket-ball in his chest, and died in Ronnie's arms.

'Make sure you kill him,' were his last words.

When the fight was at its height, Sarah caught a movement behind her from the corner of her eye. She turned to discover to her horror that Jenny was up on deck, with musket balls and poisoned darts flying all around.

Sarah ran back and grabbed her arm. 'You must go back down below, Jenny,' she cried out above the din of battle. 'It's far too dangerous up here.'

'Mama needs your help down below,' the girl replied briskly, ignoring the carnage around her. 'Some of the sailors were using torches to find the gunpowder, and they started a fire. Mama says we need to remove the gunpowder, and put out the fire.'

Sarah nodded her head quickly, and followed Jenny down into the hold, where she was amazed to find Mrs Macpherson giving instructions to the crew, and carrying barrels of gunpowder away from the flames.

'Help me with these barrels, Mrs Simpson,' she called out. 'The men can take care of the fire.'

By the time they had carried the barrels to safety, the sailors had managed to put out the fire, and the danger was averted. Sarah insisted that Mrs Macpherson keep Jennie below, despite the girl's obvious desire to see what was going on above.

'You're a brave girl, Jenny,' she said, as she prepared to return to the fight, 'and so is your mother. But you've done enough. Take a rest, and maybe a drop of brandy—you both deserve it.'

When Sarah returned to the foredeck, the Illanun fleet had pulled back, but they all knew it was only to regroup and prepare a fresh assault. There was scarcely a breath of wind, and it was only early morning, so the pirates knew they had plenty of time.

Then the Diana fired up her engines and seized the moment. She steamed out and alongside the pirate prahus, her paddles churning the water and her chimney belching black smoke like some demon out of hell. Or so it seemed to the pirates, who were completely taken by surprise, since they had never seen a ship moving without wind or oars. The Diana's guns poured shot and grape into the pirate decks as she drew level with them, carving bloody swathes though the ranks of their warriors. She did one sweep from her starboard mounted guns, and then turned around and swept the pirate decks again from her port side. Her guns were now too hot to continue firing, but she had not yet completed her surprise assault upon the enemy. For she returned for a second double sweep, this time venting the hot steam from her hoses directly onto the pirate decks, burning boiling flesh from bones and melting eyes from their sockets.

The pirates were thrown into total disarray, and the carnage was terrible to behold, as bleeding and scalded bodies littered the water around them. But the pirates were not finished—not by a long shot.

'They're as angry as hornets whose hive has been attacked,' said Lieutenant Hyde, in charge of the marines on the *Highland Lassie*. 'And that's when they're most dangerous. They'll be coming in for the kill this time, and they won't stop until they kill us or we kill them.'

'Bring your marines forward,' said Ronnie, 'and direct your fire on that mad dog Si Rahman. He's managed to survive all our efforts to kill him so far, and his followers believe he is invincible. If we can kill him and dispel that myth we might be able to break them up. I want all guns firing at Si Rahman when he comes in again.'

They did not have to wait long. The oars rose and fell as the slave masters drove the war prahus forward once again. Drums rolled and gongs crashed, and the warriors clashed their swords and spears against their shields as they roared out their curses and war cries. As the pirates came in close once again, they poured a hail of musket fire and poisoned darts and arrows into the merchantmen, and fired round-shot into their sides close to the water line. One lucky shot took out one of the *Highland Lassie*'s guns, spraying the gunners in a bloody wave across the lower deck. As Si Rahman's prahu approached them once more, he tore off his breastplate in a raging gesture of defiance, baring his chest to them and raising his great Tampilan sword in one hand, his talisman of female hair grasped in the other.

'Fire on him,' screamed Sarah, as she and Macpherson and the marines emptied their weapons on him.

But when the smoke cleared, Si Rahman still stood there unharmed, urging his men forward. A great roar went up from the pirates, as they followed the man whom they thought was protected by special magic.

'They're under our guns now,' shouted Lieutenant Hyde, 'and it looks like all our ships.' The pirates were closing in for the kill, and preparing to board.

'I've had enough o' this sharn,' said Ronnie in a low voice. 'Hyde, Macpherson, bring some men and follow me.'

He ran down to the twelve-pounder on the starboard deck, under which the pirates were closing.

'Is it loaded?' he yelled to the gun crew.

'Aye, sir,' the head gunner replied, 'but they're in too close now!'

'Stuff some wadding down the barrel to hold the shot, and prepare to fire,' Ronnie cried to him. 'You others—help me raise this gun!'

The head gunner used a ramrod to push some wadding down into the gun barrel to keep the shot from falling out, while the others grabbed some spars from the deck, and raised the gun carriage so that the barrel pointed down into the Illanun war craft, directly at Si Rahman.

'Now let's see who's invincible!' he yelled, and taking the taper from the head gunner, fired off the twelve-pounder. The recoil blasted them and the gun back across the deck. They struggled to their feet and ran back to look over the side. When the smoke cleared the war prahu of Si Rahman was gone—there were only blasted strips of timber drifting upon the bloody water to mark the spot where Si Rahman had gone to join his brother.

Now the men on the *Highland Lassie* let out a great cheer, a roar of victory that was heard and caught up by the other ships. The pirates fought on, but the tide of battle had turned against them, and the spirit seemed to go out of their fight as the news of the death of Si Rahman spread throughout the pirate fleet. As the pirates' prahus began to turn around and flee, the first mate came running up to Ronnie and pointed up at the main mast, where the short sails were cracking in the rising wind.

'Make sail,' shouted Ronnie, 'and let's hae after them!'

The *Highland Lassie* and the other merchant ships were slow to get under sail and pursue the enemy. Their crews were tired, and they had borne the brunt of the forward battle. But the *Wolf* and the *Andromache* remained fresh, and their crews had trained for just this opportunity. The men-of-war raced after the pirate prahus, and fired withering broadsides from port and starboard as they drove through the scattered pirate fleet, and rammed any boats that they caught in their way. The *Diana*, now under both steam and sail, sped among the scattering prahus and raked their decks with grape, inflicting heavy casualties. Of the hundred or so prahus that had attacked them, about fifty were sunk, and many of the others were set on fire or badly damaged. By midday, the battle was over, as the remains of the pirate fleet fled in different directions, and the Company ships returned to join the merchantmen. Those who had survived prayed to their God or their ancestors, and attended to their dead and wounded. Reverend Macpherson delivered a short sermon of thanksgiving aboard the *Highland Lassie*, and conducted the service that committed the dead men to the deep.

Afterwards Captains Stanley, Chads and Congalton came on board the *Highland Lassie* to congratulate Ronnie.

'Well done, Mr Simpson,' said Captain Chads. 'We've taught them a lesson they won't forget in a hurry. We've not seen the last of these pirates, but I think today marks the beginning of the end for them. We will hunt them down again as we hunted them down today, until we have rid these waters of their vile breed.'

Captain Congalton stepped forward. 'I thought you might want this, sir,' he said. 'One of the lads found it in the water, and said he saw Si Rahman waving it around.'

He handed Ronnie the length of twisted hair. Ronnie turned to Sarah, who took it from his hand, and burst into tears.

'It is done, my love,' he said, putting his arms around her. 'It is done.'

'It is done,' she whispered, and buried her head in his chest.

18

Abdullah bin Ahmad was concerned. He had not heard from Daing Ibrahim for weeks, and had not been paid for his last mission. He had heard of the death of Si Rahman at the hands of the Singapore expedition, but it was not his fault that his message had laid the trap—he had merely been the messenger. He waited a few more weeks, and then went to see Daing Ibrahim at Telok Blangah. When Abdullah arrived at Daing Ibrahim's bungalow, he sent one of his servants to announce his presence. When the servant returned, he looked perplexed and afraid.

'Please master,' he said, 'please do not blame me for what I have to report. I do not understand. Daing Ibrahim said that he does not know Abdullah bin Ahmad, and has no business with him. He wishes you to leave immediately.'

Abdullah struck the man a vicious blow across the face with the back of his hand. 'You stupid, lying dog,' he yelled at his servant. 'There is obviously some mistake. Go back and tell him that it is Abdullah bin Ahmad that has come, Abdullah bin Ahmad who has done so much business with him in the past.'

The servant went back to report what Abdullah had said. When he returned, he was accompanied by one of Daing Ibrahim's servants, a small man with a bald head, who addressed Abdullah in a tone that he found officious and offensive:

'Abdullah bin Ahmad, my master has asked me to come and say to you that he does not know you and has never done business with you. You are to quit his residence, and never return, on pain of death.'

Abdullah was dumbstruck, but he understood the import of what had been said. Daing Ibrahim had sold out to the Singapore merchants, and had no further need of his services after his betrayal of Si Rahman. He knew the danger he faced if he tried to demand the compensation he was due for that action. As Abdullah turned to leave, the servant fixed him with his small beady eyes. 'A final word of warning, Abdullah bin Ahmad. Do not speak of this to anyone, or be assured that you will regret that you ever lived, and beg God for the release of death.'

The advisor smiled at him. It was an ugly, evil, deadly smile.

* * *

Abdullah stood in front of his writing desk. He was dressed in a dark green baju shirt and kain sarong, edged with gold thread, and he wore a black velvet songkok cap upon his head. He lifted the sheathed kris from his desk, and positioned it inside his waistband. He took up the parang in his left hand, and the pistol, which he had primed and cocked, in his right. He swayed slightly on his feet, and took a deep breath to clear his head. He had not tasted food or drink for days, and he felt light headed. He turned around and looked out through the doorway of his house to the sun-washed street beyond. The world around him seemed to glow with a bright fire, and his eyes seemed to burn in his skull. He walked across the room and out the door onto the wide balcony. His servant came forward and bowed before him.

'Master,' he began, but did not finish, for Abdullah placed the pistol against his forehead and fired, spraying the man's brains across the steps in front of him. Flinging the pistol aside and transferring the parang to his right hand, he stepped over the body and down onto the street. He cut down an Indian dhobi who crossed his path carrying a bundle of laundry, and drawing his kris with his left hand, stabbed the man through the heart. The cry of 'Amok! Amok! Run Amok!' went up from those who had seen what had passed, and alerted those who had not. An elderly Chinese hawker turned and tried to run from him, but Abdullah sliced at his leg tendons with the parang, and then cut the man down with a vicious blow to his neck. He came across two Malay children, mere toddlers, standing laughing at their reflections in a large puddle of water, and sliced off their heads. The puddle of water turned into a puddle of blood. Their grandmother, who had watched with horror from the steps of her own house, ran at Abdullah with a stick, but Abdullah stabbed her in the eye with his kris, and smashed in her face with the butt of his parang.

Now his anger and his hatred consumed him, and the world turned red before his eyes. He cut down an Arab merchant in a flowing white robe. The old man displayed no fear, but fixed him with his black eyes as Abdullah brought the blade down upon his turbaned head. Abdullah sank the blade in so deep that he could not withdraw it as the man slumped to the ground, and had to release it to defend himself against an Indian peon who came at him with a wooden baton. The peon managed to land a blow against the side of Abdullah's head, but it hardly seemed to affect him, except for a loud echo that rang in his ears, like the roaring of the sea in a storm. It only served to stoke his fury, which now reached a crescendo in his burning brain. He stabbed the peon in the throat with his kris, and the man fell dead at his feet.

Then as Abdullah bent down to retrieve his parang, he saw her in the dim distance, hastening off to his left with her infant in her arms. It was Rashidah, and he marked her for death. When he had begun, he had not cared who he killed—he had only wanted to kill. But now he had seen her, he would take his revenge. He had earlier planned to kill her husband, Musa bin Hassan, but now he realized he could inflict greater punishment by taking the life of his wife and child. He ran after her, his songkok tumbling from his head, his now bloody sarong flapping around him. He cut down a young boy carrying a songbird in a cage, and a beggar who stood with his mouth open in wonder as Abdullah drove his kris into the back of his skull. He leapt over the beggar's body and was gaining fast on Rashidah, when she tripped and pitched forward on the ground, landing heavily on her shoulder in an attempt to protect the infant. But to no avail. The child struck his head upon a rock, dashing his brains upon the dusty road without even a murmur.

Now Abdullah stood over her, his heart pounding in his breast and the anguished and angry cries of the crowd ringing in his ears. The world around him blazed in a fierce red light, shed by the raging fire that burned deep into his soul, and he screamed in rage at all who had beaten and betrayed him. He bent down and grabbed Rashidah by her hair, and raised his bloody kris for the killing blow. But then the blazing light before his eyes was suddenly extinguished, and his consciousness fled from his brain. The Bugis captain, who had struck him on the head with his club, pulled Abdullah from Rashidah's body. He helped the terrified mother to her feet, and mourned with her the death of her child. Musa, who had come to investigate when he heard the commotion and cries of 'Amok', stood aghast for a moment when he saw his dead son, and the trail of blood and bodies that led from Abdullah's house to where he stood. For a moment he wondered at the evil of men, and the great mystery of their existence. Then he went to comfort his wife, whom God had preserved.

A constable and three peons arrived on the scene, and carried the unconscious Abdullah away in a bullock cart they commandeered for the purpose. They had to fight off the relatives of the victims and the crowd that had gathered around them, who wished to render immediate justice with their own krisses on the body of Abdullah bin Ahmad. They would very likely have done so if police reinforcements had not arrived soon afterwards, and taken him away to the safety of the jail, where armed guards were placed outside his cell.

Abdullah was tried a week later, but the outcome was a foregone conclusion. After the witnesses were brought forth, and the case heard, the judge delivered a lecture to the packed courthouse on the subject of the murderous practice of running amok, which he attributed to forms of pride, rage and fanaticism unique to Mohammedans, though he reminded the court that they were no worse than men of any other religion who committed crimes against innocent women and children. Then he passed sentence upon Abdullah.

> The sentence of this court is that you, Abdullah bin Ahmad,
> be remanded to the place from thence you came, and that in
> the morning of Wednesday next you be drawn from thence
> on a hurdle to the place of execution, and there hanged
> by the neck until you are dead. Your body will then be
> handed to the surgeon for dissection, and your mangled
> limbs, instead of being restored to your family and friends
> for decent internment, will be cast into the sea, thrown into
> a ditch, or scattered on the earth at the discretion of the
> Magistrate. And may God Almighty have mercy on your
> miserable soul.

Abdullah said nothing. He thought nothing and felt nothing. He was already dead to the world when was hung the following Wednesday from Presentment Bridge. His remains were given to a relative of the Chinese hawker who had been Abdullah's third victim, who fed them to his pigs.

Captain Scott went to visit Musa bin Hassan to offer his condolences to him and his wife. He knew Musa well, having purchased two skiffs from his father's yard for his use as harbour master, and had been greatly impressed by the young man's workmanship. But he was shocked to find that Musa and his wife did not seem to be badly affected by their loss, but went about their business as if nothing untoward had happened to them. Captain Scott told Musa that he must be a very strong-hearted man to cope as well as he did in the face of such a tragic loss. Musa looked at him in surprise, and then explained to Captain Scott that in their eyes there had been no tragedy, for he and his wife knew that God welcomed young children into Heaven. God had ordained when their son would die, as he would ordain whether or not they were blessed with another child. And blessed they were, for the following year Rashidah was delivered of twin boys.

* * *

Tan Hong Chuan had worked his way up from a humble hawker to a prosperous businessman, and had nearly lost it all again. But he had been determined to make his way back up the ladder, and with the help of his friends and his now first wife Siti, he was well on his way to doing so.

He had let his manager go and now ran the chandlery business himself, taking full advantage of the improvement in trade. Siti managed his pineapple plantation, and doubled its profits in the first year. In the early days she had helped to sell the produce, arriving in town at six in the morning bearing the freshly cut pineapples on baskets suspended from a shoulder pole. What sort of wife was she, he thought too himself? He wished he had given her control of his business earlier on—they would have been millionaires by now! But Hong Chuan was a man to learn from his mistakes, so when his business began to prosper again and he had paid off all his loans, he put Siti in charge of the development of all his fruit plantations.

She made him a rich man again on her own behalf. Then, as if to quell those gossipy Nonya women who complained that her first duty to her husband was to produce a son, Siti promptly produced a healthy boy who yelped his way into the world on the first day of the Chinese New Year of the Dog.

* * *

Arjun Nath made an offering to the goddess Sri Mariamman, and thanked her for her blessings. His wife had borne him a son, his cattle herd was thriving, and he was doing good business with European merchants and Indian lightermen. He was grateful for his good fortune, but he had heard the reports about the tigers, and hoped that he would never again in his life have to face one.

Lee Yip Lee had risen in the ranks of the Ghee Hin and become a tiger general. Now he was in a position to order his tiger soldiers to do his killing for him, but most of the time he did not. He still drew his strength from draining the life from an enemy.

Ibrahim bin Aman had been promoted to the rank of captain, and was proud of his contribution to the peace of the settlement. He wished that his father were still alive so that he could share in his pride, but Ibrahim vowed that he would honour his memory by bringing justice to those who robbed and murdered, including the cruel servants of the Ghee Hin.

* * *

Ronnie stood talking to Alexander Johnston in front of his godown at the mouth of the river. They had just come from a meeting at which the European merchants had dispatched a letter to the governor protesting levy charges contemplated by the Indian Government.

'I'm confident they'll back down on this again,' said Johnston.

'Our present prosperity depends on our continuing status as a free port.'

'I hope you're right about that, Alex,' Ronnie replied, 'but I dinna trust those politicals to do anything right.'

'Still, you have to admit,' he continued after a pause, 'we're nae doing so bad at the moment.'

'I can't argue with that, Ronnie, not at all bad at the moment,' Johnston replied, as their eyes wandered down the length of the river and out to sea.

All was bustle and clamour the length and breadth of Boat Quay, as lighters and sampans unloaded their cargoes at the merchant godowns, and took on new cargoes that they carried out to the forest of shipping in the Singapore roads—European and American square-riggers, Chinese Junks, Malay and Bugis prahus, and Cochin-China Topes. The British Flag flew high above on Government Hill, but many of the Malays avowed they could still hear the ghosts of the past whispering on the monsoon winds as they wound around Forbidden Hill.

Endnotes

1 The East India Company, known colloquially as the Honorable Company or John Company, was founded in the late sixteenth century by a group of merchant adventurers, and had been granted a Royal Charter by Queen Elizabeth I in 1599. These merchants had sought to make their fortunes by acquiring precious spices from the East Indies, such as nutmegs, which were commonly used as a preservative in brines and marinades; pepper, which was employed to improve the flavour of stewed meat (and to hide its smell when it turned bad); and cloves, which were valued for their medicinal as well as their culinary properties.

The sale of these spices brought huge profits to those captains willing to risk the passage round Cape Horn and across the Indian Ocean. On Pulo Run, one of the tiny Bata Islands at the eastern tip of the Malay Archipelago, where the Company's ships anchored in 1603, ten pounds of nutmeg could be purchased for less than half a penny; back in Europe, the same amount could be sold for over one and a half pounds sterling—a fabulous profit of nearly 32,000 per cent! Over the years the Company established factories around the world as depots where their goods could be unloaded and exchanged. The officers—or factors—in charge of these depots found that their trade frequently developed into land acquisition, which in turn led them into inevitable wars with local populations and competing trading powers such as France, Portugal and Holland. In this fashion the East India Company and its paid armies came to dominate and control most of the sub-continent of India, administered by a governor-general in Calcutta, which was itself a new city that had been created as an administrative centre for the Company.

2 Sir Thomas Stamford Bingley Raffles was born aboard the West India-man *Ann* on July 6, 1781, off the coast of Port Morant, Jamaica. His father was engaged in the lucrative slave trade, but drank and gambled his money away. Raffles managed to secure a position as a clerk in the offices of the East India Company in Leadenhall Street a few years before his father died, when he became the only source of support for his mother and four sisters.

For eight years Raffles worked to master the intricacies of the Company's operations and bureaucracy, in the hope of one day being able to make his fortune in India, which was now the centre of the Company's trade. His diligence earned him promotion and a modest increase in salary. Then he met and fell in love with Olivia Marianne Fancourt, a widow recently returned from Madras, and the daughter of an Irish father who had disgraced his family by marrying a Russian Circassian Muslim while serving in India. Raffles had begged William Ramsay, the First Secretary of the East India Company, to secure him a position in India so that he could afford to marry. Ramsay could not do so, but had offered him a position as assistant secretary to the Governor of Penang Island, on the Malayan Peninsula. Raffles had accepted the position, and he and Olivia had married soon afterwards. On the six-month voyage out, Raffles learned the Malay language with the help of some Malay sailors on board.

Raffles quickly established his reputation as an able administrator, earning him promotion to the rank of Chief Secretary to the Governor. Raffles took part in the invasion of Java in 1811, led by Lord Minto, then Governor-General of India. For his services he was appointed Lieutenant-General of Java, where he tried to institute a wide range of reforms inspired by his enlightenment ideals and progressive economic theories. He was recalled from his position in 1818 after being accused of financial mismanagement and corruption, although he was later cleared of the latter charge.

3 The dispute over the succession to the Riau-Lingga-Johore Sultanate had arisen because although Sultan Mahmud Shah had designated his eldest son Tengku Long as his rightful heir, tradition demanded that the Sultan's heir be present at his death, but Tengku Long had been in Penang attending his marriage ceremony at the time. Seeing his opportunity, the powerful Bugis prince Muda Rajah Ja'afar of Riau had pressed the claim of the younger brother Abdul Rahman, who had been present at his father's death. Muda Rajah Ja'afar had failed to install Abdul Rahman as Sultan, because Mahmud Shah's widow Engku Putri Hamidah, who supported her eldest son, refused to give up the royal regalia, but Muda Rajah Ja'afar had declared Abdul Rahman Regent, and in his name had banished Tengku Long from the Royal Court.

4 Major William Farquhar was born in Aberdeen, Scotland on February 26, 1774, and joined the East India Company as a cadet in 1790. He became an ensign in the Madras Engineers the following year, and served in the Mysore War with Lord Cornwallis, who was then Governor-General of India. In 1795 Farquhar served as chief engineer in the expeditionary force that took over Malacca from the Dutch. Aside from a number of temporary assignments, after which he was promoted to Captain, he spent the next twenty years in Malacca, serving as Commandant and Resident from 1803 to 1818, for the period of British occupation during the Napoleonic wars.

During the British invasion of Java in 1811, Farquhar served as chief coordinator of guides and intelligence. For his services he was promoted to the rank of major and offered the Residency of Yogyakarta in south-west Java, but he turned it down in order to return to Malacca. He was married to Nonio Clement, a French-Malay beauty who gave him six children.

While he was still the British Resident in Malacca, Major Farquhar had gone to Lingga to negotiate with Muda Rajah Ja'afar, and had secured his permission to explore the potential of the Riau islands for a British factory. However, Muda Rajah Ja'afar had also intrigued with the Dutch, who in return for acknowledging Abdul Rahman as the legitimate heir had secured exclusive rights to set up factories throughout the Johor-Riau-Lingga Sultanate. They had nullified Farquhar's agreement by sending in their own Resident and troops to Riau, and laid claim to all the islands of the Johor-Riau-Lingga group, including the island of Singapore.

5 From the Temenggong, Singapore16th Rabia-us-sani, 1234 (February, 1819)

To Tuan Muda, Riau

I have to acquaint you with the proceedings of the English, that is to say, Mr RAFFLES and the Rajah of Malacca, who came to Singapore. I was simply forced to submit to this proceeding, of which I had no notice or knowledge. When Mr RAFFLES came, I was simply told that he intended to settle in Singapore, and I had no power to prevent him. Thereupon he landed his men and stores and proceeded to build a blockhouse. Of course I could say nothing. While this was going on, Tengku Long arrived in Singapore, having been alarmed by the news there were a number of ships there, and having come for the purpose of fetching his son, Tengku Besar. On his arrival in Singapore, Tengku Long went to see Raffles, whereupon the latter laid hold of him and forcibly made him rajah, with the title of Sultan Hussein. He also presented him with a sealed letter of appointment, and used so much insistence that Sultan Hussein could offer no opposition to what he did.

From Tengku Long16th Rabia-us-sani, 1234 (February, 1819)

To Tuan Muda, Riau

I have to inform you that Abang Johor came to me one night in the middle of the night and announced that there were a great many ships at Singapore, and that numerous soldiers and quantities of stores were being landed. I was a good deal surprised by this news, and not a little anxious and uneasy on account of my son who was there. Without taking thought of what I was doing, I set off that very same night. I completely lost my head and never thought of letting you know of my departure. When I reached Singapore, I went to see Mr RAFFLES, who immediately laid hold of me and would not let me go again, but insisted on making me a rajah with the title of Sultan. There was nothing else for me to do and I had to comply with what he proposed, but I pointed out that I was under the Dutch company. Thereupon he gave me a sealed document of appointment. These things I make known to you, and I ask for your pardon and forgiveness, for it is in you I trust, for I regard you as my father in this world and the next, and I have in no wise acted against you or abandoned you.

Further, RAFFLES has directed me to bring to Singapore the women and children of my family, and I am now ordering Rajah Shaban to take them together with any property of mine.

6 Strictly speaking what I have called the eastern shore of the river is actually the northern shore, since the Singapore river curves westward at its mouth. I have called it the eastern shore because it is the side of the river that adjoins and was originally part of what was called the east beach. See map on page 6, Beach Road facing east beach. [Map: John Crawfurd, *Journal of an Embassy to the courts of Siam and Cochin-China* (London, 1928).]

7 During the fifteenth century the Malaccan Sultanate had paid tribute to the Chinese Emperor. When the great Admiral Zheng had visited Malacca, he had presented the Chinese Princess Hang Li Po as a gift to the Sultan of Malacca. Her royal companions and ladies formed the basis of the original Peranakan community in Malacca, and similar communities developed in Penang, Riau, Sumatra and Java—wherever, in fact, Chinese merchants had commerce with Malay peoples. The Chinese men married Malay women, in the absence of suitable Chinese brides. The female children of their unions were not allowed to marry Malay men, and became available as brides for future generations of Chinese men. The male Peranakans were called Babas and the women Nonyas. By the beginning of the nineteenth century, there were about three thousand Peranakans living in Malacca.

8 In the end it was not canon or troops that saved Singapore from armed intervention by the Dutch, but Colonel Bannerman's vehement condemnation of Raffles' action in his reply to Baron van der Capellen's official protest. Bannerman assured Capellen that the Governor-General and the Court of Directors would repudiate Raffles' occupation of Singapore and installation of Tengku Long as Sultan, and that Raffles would be ordered to quit Singapore and recalled to London. When he received Bannerman's assurances, Baron van der Capellen decided that military action was unnecessary as well as expensive, and was content to write an official letter of protest to the Marquis of Hastings. He reminded the Marquis that with the return of Malacca to the Dutch, the islands of the

Johor-Riau-Lingga group—which included Singapore—had automatically become Dutch, so that Raffles' occupation was unlawful as well as prejudicial to relations between Britain and Holland.

9 In later years the flower, which botanists called a vegetable monster, came to be known as *Rafflesia arnoldi*.

10 After leaving school, John Morgan had been apprenticed as a clerk to James McDougall, an Edinburgh lawyer. When McDougall complained about a minor error in Morgan's accounting, a matter of two and a half pennies, Morgan was enraged and flung his inkwell at the man. He stormed out of the office and returned to his lodgings, where he tossed his law books out the window. He then packed his bags and took the evening stagecoach to London.

A few days later he joined the crew of an East Indiaman bound for China, intending to work his way up through the merchant marine to become master of his own vessel. But he hated the drudgery of life at sea, and jumped ship at Batavia, where he set up a small shop, trading with the native craft and Dutch merchant ships. His business prospered, despite the Dutch commercial restrictions and his own reputation for shady dealings, from which he derived the bulk of his profits. When he heard that the East India Company had established a new settlement in Singapore, he decided that he would make his fortune there. He sold up his business and took the next ship out.

11 Abdullah bin Abdul Kadir was born in Malacca in 1796, the fifth and only surviving child of Sheikh Abdul Kadir, a Muslim of Arab-Indian descent. His father worked him hard at his language and religious studies, but Abdullah was an eager learner, and became an accomplished scholar by the age of thirteen. He translated Arabic texts into Malay and Hindustani, and wrote letters and petitions for local merchants. The Muslim soldiers of the Indian garrison at Malacca called him 'Munshi', or teacher of language, and he became known to all as Munshi Abdullah, or simply Munshi. He taught Malay to the East India Company officers in Malacca, where Tuan Farquhar befriended him, and introduced Abdullah to Sir Stamford Raffles, when Raffles was convalescing there. Raffles employed Abdullah as an interpreter in his communications with the neighbouring rajahs, and as a scribe to aid him in the transcription of Malay laws and literature.

A few years later Abdullah, a strict Muslim, attended Bible classes for local children taught by Reverend Milne of the London Missionary Society, in order to improve his English. Reverend Milne in turn asked Abdullah to teach him Malay, and Munshi was happy to oblige. He worked on a Malay translation of the Gospels for Reverend Milne and Reverend Claudius Henry Thomsen, a German missionary with whom he became friends. Six months after the new settlement was founded, Abdullah travelled to Singapore, where he had bought a house, and became a teacher of Malay to the soldiers, missionaries and merchants.

Abdullah had intended to bring his wife and family down to Singapore, but he had graciously acceded to their wish to remain in Malacca, after their friends and relations there had begged them not to leave. Abdullah sold his house to John Hay, and never took Tuan Farquhar and Tuan Raffles' advice to buy land, even though he had the money and the opportunity. As he described his state of mind at the time in his later memoirs, the *Hikayat Abdullah*:

> At that time I was like a person frightened out of his sleep—when it rained hard, I took no notice to catch some water—now I trust with full confidence in the Lord, that directs the rain to fall, giving to each his share, and not a whit more nor less than is right, and I offer up a thousand of praises to Him, as I have received my portion before and now.
>
> For, by my desires and covetousness, I would wish for what is more than right. On that account I was as one asleep during a heavy shower, and only when it had stopped falling did I awake to set about gaining that which is right.

But he had no regrets, for as he also recorded, quoting the Malay proverb, 'Realize your mistake in time and you may gain something, realize it too late and you gain nothing.'

12 William Flint was born in Clackmannanshire in Scotland in 1791. He joined the Royal Navy as a boy and rose through the ranks to become captain of HMS *Teignmouth*.

13 The kongsi brotherhoods were associations whose origins could be traced back to the Hung brotherhood, the Triad of Heaven, Earth and Man, which had been formed in southern China to oppose the Qing Dynasty after the Bannermen armies of the Manchu overthrew the Ming Dynasty in 1644. According to legend, the monk Ti Xi founded a brotherhood known as the Tiandihui, or Heaven and Earth Society, in the town of Gaoxi in Fukien province, on the banks of the Nine Dragon River. Ti Xi and his followers met in a temple to the Goddess of Mercy known as the Red Flower Pavilion, where they vowed to overthrow the Qing and restore the Ming, and swore a blood oath of everlasting brotherhood. Although the rebellion failed, the surviving members spread out across southeastern China and formed local lodges of what became known as the Hung or Three Unities Society in the provinces of Fukien, Guangdong, Zhejiang, Guangxi, Jiangxi, Hunan, Yunan, Hupei, Sichuan and Jiangsu.

In southern China, these brotherhoods or associations were known as huis or tongs. They generally functioned as mutual aid societies for different family, clan and dialect groups, as well as providing funds and manpower to support peasant rebellions against the Manchu. They were rooted in traditional village life, which was itself organized into largely independent enclaves based upon family, clan or dialect group. They provided members with loans, shared resources such as oxen, and contributed to the celebration of births and marriages, and the proper mourning of the deceased. Their members were generally poor, lower class males.

In Singapore and other settlements in the Nanyang, they were known as kongsis, and likewise functioned as mutual aid societies for their members. The kongsis provided security, jobs and loans for sinkeh or 'new arrivals': they looked after them if they we sick, and buried them if they died. They protected members who ran foul of the law, providing money for their defense, bribing officials, and threatening witnesses. In return, members were expected to support and fight for the interests of the kongsi, which in Singapore extended to extortion, prostitution, coolie brokering, robbery, kidnapping and murder. Members were sworn to absolute secrecy and loyalty to the kongsi. Betrayal meant death.

The Ghee Hin kongsi was the earliest and most powerful secret society founded in Singapore, although it was later challenged by rival societies such as the Ghee Hok, the Kwan Teck and the Choo Soo Khong. Many of its original members were Hokkien from Fukien and Guangdong provinces, from which most of its leaders were drawn, but it also included members from other dialect groups, such as Cantonese and Hainanese. Many of the owners of the pepper and gambier plantations were members of the Ghee Hin, as were many of those who controlled the coolie trade.

14 Alexander Laurie Johnston was born in 1780 in Dumfriesshire in Scotland to a middle-class family. He joined the merchant marine of the East India Company, where he rose to the rank of Chief Mate. He then quit the merchant marine, and bought and captained his own vessel, trading in India, China and the Eastern Archipelago. When he heard of the establishment of the free port of Singapore, he decided to retire as a free trader and set up his own company in the settlement. Johnston brought with him a shipload of trade goods, which he landed in Singapore, and then sold his ship to his First Mate. Johnston absolutely refused Colonel Farquhar's offer of land along the east beach, which he declared to be quite unsuitable for landing goods, because of the high surf during the northeastern monsoon and the long sandbar offshore.

15 Alexander Guthrie was born in 1819, the son of a crofter from Brechin in Angus. He left home to work for Thomas Talbot Harrington & Co. in

Cape Town. When he had heard about the establishment of Singapore, he applied for and received an indenture from the East India Company, which gave him permission to live and trade in the new settlement. The company he formed in Singapore in 1821 survives to this day as Guthrie Group Limited.

16 Eventually the stone was broken up, although a portion of the original is now on display in the National Museum of Singapore.

17 Shortly after Captain Methven returned to Calcutta, he went out riding, and was thrown from his horse. He died of his injuries a few hours later.

18 The first magistrates were A. L. Johnston, John Argyle Maxwell, David S. Napier, John Morgan, John Purvis, Alexander Guthrie, Graham Mackenzie, Dr William Montgomerie, Charles Scott, John Morgan, Christopher Rideout Read and Andrew Hay.

19 John Crawfurd was born on August 13, 1783, on the Isle of Islay, the southernmost of the inner Hebridean islands on the west coast of Scotland. He completed his medical degree at the University of Edinburgh and joined the East India Company as a surgeon in 1803. After serving as a military surgeon in India, he transferred to Penang in 1808 as civil surgeon. Like Raffles and Farquhar, Crawfurd served with Lord Minto during the military invasion of Java in 1811, and stayed on as Resident at the Court of Yogyakarta after Major Farquhar turned down the position in order to return to Malacca. Crawfurd's quick mastery of the Javanese language and culture, which he developed through his personal friendship with the Javanese aristocracy and literati, had made him an invaluable servant in Raffles' administration, although the two men quarrelled over the question of land reform.

20 Captain Flint stayed on in Singapore as harbour master for a number of years, and built himself a new house on Bukit Selegie, where he grew spices. He renamed the hill Mount Sophia, in honour of Raffles' second wife and his daughter Mary Sophia Anne, who was born at the end of the year. He maintained his life of luxury but grew deeper and deeper in debt until he died in 1828. His house, furniture and land were sold to cover his debts, but the hill retained its name.

21 When Colonel Farquhar arrived back in London he petitioned the Court of Directors, complaining of his ill-treatment by Raffles and requesting that he be reinstated as Resident at Singapore. In due course the Court issued a proclamation that restored Farquhar's reputation, and elevated him to the rank of Lieutenant Colonel, but they declined to re-

instate him as Resident at Singapore. Farquhar spent the rest of his life in retirement in Perth in his native Scotland, where he died in 1838 at the age of 69.

22 The temple was built on land that Naraina Pillai had donated for the purpose.

23 Raffles' funeral took place a week later, with only family and close friends in attendance. The vicar of Hendon, the Reverend Theodore Williams, refused to conduct the service, and also denied Lady Sophia's request for a memorial tablet to be placed inside the church, because he was bitter over Raffles' support for William Wilberforce's emancipation legislation. Williams had shares in the sugar plantations of the West Indies, which depended upon slave labour. A vicar from another parish, the Reverend J. Roseden, conducted the service, and Raffles' coffin was laid in the vault of the church, without any visible record of his internment. (A memorial statue was erected in Westminster Abbey in 1914).

Six months later Lady Sophia wrote to the Court of Directors, informing them that she could raise only ten thousand pounds toward the debt they claimed that Sir Stamford Raffles owed to the Company. The Court agreed to accept that amount in final settlement of the Company's claims against the estate of Sir Stamford Raffles. She stayed on at Highwood, and her *Memoir on the Life and Public Services of Sir Thomas Stamford Raffles* was published in 1830 to critical acclaim. She died in 1858 at the age of seventy-two. Ella, their last surviving child, died tragically in 1840, at the age of nineteen, on the night before her wedding.

24 Coleman had recently reconstructed Raffles' original wooden bungalow in brick and tile with a neo-classical motif, so that it now looked more like an official residence. He had also designed the house of John Argyle Maxwell at No.1 High Street, a graceful building with Doric pilasters and columns, and elegant loggias and porticoes. Unfortunately for Maxwell, who came to Singapore in 1822 to establish a branch office of G. Maclaine & Co. of Batavia, he never got the chance to live in it. Farquhar had allocated Maxwell a plot of land for his house at the foot of High Street, adjacent to the original residency. But after Coleman had completed the house, Raffles rescinded Farquhar's land allocation, and Crawfurd upheld his judgment, so Maxwell had been forced to lease the house to the government, who used it as the Courthouse. After many additions and alterations, the building became the first home of the National Parliament of Singapore when it became an independent republic in 1965.

25 John Crawfurd retired as Resident at Singapore in August, 1826, and returned to London, where he continued to champion the cause of British

commerce in Singapore.

When he departed, the East India Company united Singapore with Penang and Malacca to form the Presidency of the Straits Settlements. Penang became the official seat of the new Governor Robert Fullerton, with Resident Councillors appointed to each of the three settlements. In the early years the military and civilian administration had been expanded, but when the Straits Settlements began to accumulate a large fiscal deficit, both had been drastically reduced. The Charter of Justice that Crawfurd had requested had been granted in 1926, but it proved useless for Singapore, since the Court Recorder refused to come down from Penang. Governor Fullerton had closed the courts in 1830, ruling that nobody had the authority to administer them. They had only reopened that year, when Robert Ibbetson had become Governor.

26 Temenggong Abdul Rahman had died in 1825, the year before Raffles, and his body was interred in a royal tomb at Telok Blangah.

27 While serving as surgeon on a Portuguese man-of-war, Jose d'Almeida had stopped off in Singapore in 1819. He had been so impressed by its position and prospects that he had a left some money with Francis Bernard to secure a plot of land on the east beach and build a house for him. When Dr D'Almeida returned with his family from Macao six years later, he purchased a shop in Commercial Square, where he set up a clinic and dispensary. A few months later, a Portuguese vessel bound for Macao and a Spanish vessel bound for Manila were held up in the roads by the northeast monsoon. They asked Jose d'Almeida to help them dispose of some of their cargo, which he did so successfully that he decided to set up his own import-export business, José d'Almeida and Sons, which concentrated on trade with Portugal and China.

28 The first edition of *The Singapore Free Press and Mercantile Adviser* was published in October 1835. William Scott Lorrain, the senior partner in Lorrain, Sandilands and Co., had purchased the *Singapore Chronicle* in September, which he had edited with the help of Edward Boustead. But within the month the paper had been bought out by James Fairlie Carnegie of Penang, who announced that he intended to turn it into a general publication for distribution throughout the Straits Settlements. In response, William Napier, the first law agent in Singapore, in partnership with William Scott Lorrain, Edward Boustead and George Coleman, founded the *Singapore Free Press* as a publication devoted to the interests of Singapore. William Napier edited the paper until he retired to Scotland in 1846.

The *Singapore Free Press* started as a weekly paper, published every Thursday. It was four pages long, and included news reports, articles, and letters; the last page contained shipping reports and commodity prices.

29 After his father Temenggong Abdul Rahman had died in 1825, the future had not looked good for Daing Ibrahim. The leadership of the Telok Blangah community had fallen to him, but he was only fifteen years old, too young to inherit the title of Temenggong; his older brother, who was old enough, was hopelessly insane, and had to be kept under restraint. Daing Ibrahim continued to draw the pension that had been assured to the Temenggong's descendants by the Treaty of 1824, but that same treaty had forfeited the Temenggong's sovereignty over the island, except for the land assigned to him at Telok Blangah. Daing Ibrahim also knew that what had been given by the East India Company could also be taken away, treaty or no treaty. He knew that the governor-general in Calcutta had denied pensions to those descendants of Indian princes who did not cooperate with the Company, and they could easily do the same with his. The *Singapore Free Press* had in fact already suggested this course of action in retaliation for his alleged connections with the pirates that operated in the region.

These alleged connections were true, but he had little choice in the matter. His Company pension was barely sufficient to support his family and followers, and he had no other source of income than his connection with the pirates. Moreover, his ability to protect his own people was dependent on his cooperation with them, for unless he could protect his own people, there was no way he could gain the respect of the sea-going peoples and be accepted as their Temenggong. And in this matter he had faced a constant and persistent threat from Sultan Hussein and his son Tengku Yahya Petra, who had been intent on establishing their power at his expense. Many of his father's followers had gone over to Sultan Hussein, and others had left for Riau or Lingga.

Daing Ibrahim was fortunate that an expedition that Tengku Yahya Petra had led to establish control over the tin mines that had been opened in the Carimon Islands had ended in a humiliating defeat at the hands of the Riau Malays and the Dutch, and that support for Sultan Hussein and his son had fallen away as a result—a process that accelerated with the Sultan's increasing dissolution and indebtedness. Sultan Hussein eventually left Singapore for Malacca in 1834, where he had died the following year. He had designated his younger son Tengku Ali as his successor, but the boy was only ten years old and did not represent a present threat.

Chasing the Dragon

John D. Greenwood

Chasing the Dragon (Singapore Saga, Vol 2) continues to vividly portray the lives of the early pioneers of Singapore as the port city develops in the 1840s and 1850s. Duncan Simpson comes to manhood when he joins James Brooke, the White Rajah of Sarawak, on his expeditions against the piratical Borneo Dayaks. An Indian cattleman turns to tiger hunting when his herd is decimated by disease, a wife is haunted by the ghost of her abandoned child, and secret society gangs murder Christian farmers in the interior of the island. As troops ships of the British Expeditionary Force assemble in Singapore in readiness for the first Opium War, Hong Xiuquan has a dream that will launch the Taiping Rebellion in China, which will take the lives of twenty million and powerfully impact the fortunes of the new citizens of Singapore.